CRIMINAL JUSTICE THROUGH SCIENCE FICTION

Makeup on the other side of bars.

CRIMINAL JUSTICE

Through

SCIENCE FICTION

Edited by Joseph D. Olander
and Martin Harry Greenberg

New Viewpoints
A Division of Franklin Watts
New York / London / 1977

To Steven, Terri, and Lisa,
and to Kari and Katie

New Viewpoints
A Division of Franklin Watts
730 Fifth Avenue
New York, New York 10019

Library of Congress Cataloging in Publication Data

Criminal justice through science fiction.

   Bibliography: p.
   CONTENTS: Introduction—Culture, community, and
crime: Koontz, D. R. The undercity. Porges, A.
Guilty as charged. McComas, J. F. Shock treatment.—
[etc.]
   1. Science fiction, American. 2. Science fiction,
English. 3. Criminal justice, Administration of—
Fiction. I. Olander, Joseph D. II. Greenberg, Martin
Harry.
PZ1.C8687   [PS648.S3]   823′.0876   77–8557
ISBN 0–531–05392–X
ISBN 0–531–05602–3 pbk.

Acknowledgments

Ext Wilson Tucker: Time X

— Zoo 2000

Personal Acknowledgments

The editors would like to thank Sally Greenberg and Cookie Olander for putting up with the alternative universes of their husbands and to express appreciation to Cookie for her typing of the manuscript. A note of sincere gratitude is also in order for Will Davison, senior editor at New Viewpoints, for his patience and helpful suggestions.

Contents

Teenage Jail
Long Run
Eagles

Jail of his Mind
The Best of Circlet
Press

Introduction

Although science fiction as a literary genre is a product of the twentieth century, its roots and traditions go back as far as *The Republic* of Plato. Many writers throughout history have used imaginary situations as literary devices and as vehicles for social and political criticism.

The knowledge explosion, which took place during the latter half of the nineteenth century, and the rise of science and technology provided the spark for the creation of a new form of literature dealing with these developments. First called scientifiction (the term was coined by Hugo Gernsback), then science fiction, and now increasingly referred to as speculative fiction, this literature has had trouble defining itself and its boundaries. Definitions provided by authors and critics usually stress that science fiction requires "a willing suspension of disbelief" on the part of the reader and focuses on the effects of technology and science on human beings and human civilization.[1]

The most important aspect of science fiction, with implications for educational usage, is its emphasis on consequences. No other form of literature can speak to the consequences of human activity or of social institutions in the way science fiction can, principally because other forms of literature are restricted to the past and the present. Science fiction is free

[1] An excellent discussion of science fiction can be found in Thomas D. Clareson (ed.), *SF: The Other Side of Realism* (Bowling Green, Ohio: Bowling Green University Popular Press, 1971), especially the essay by Judith Merril.

to assert, "If this goes on . . . if you do this . . . then this will be the result."

Science fiction is also useful in looking at our own values, mores, beliefs, and institutions. In the hands of skilled writers, it can vividly portray our society, showing its strengths and weaknesses. Books and movies like *The Manchurian Candidate, Fail Safe,* and *Seven Days in May* are all technically science fiction, although they did not carry a science fiction label and were not marketed as such. Perhaps the best definition of science fiction is the one imposed on the field from outside: if people—including literary critics and book publishers—say that something is science fiction, then science fiction it is. In a sense, there are as many definitions of science fiction as there are writers, readers, and critics of it.

Science fiction became a distinguishable literary genre with the development of specialized magazines, starting with Hugo Gernsback's *Amazing Stories* in 1926. These early stories and novels had two major emphases: adventure and future projections based upon scientific principles. The commercial realities of the day demanded that the stories appeal to young readers, be exciting, and sell; one result was the creation of covers featuring scantily clad girls being menaced by one or more bug-eyed monsters (BEMs). The stereotypes of horror stories and escapism associated with science fiction date from this period.

Although the readership of science fiction consisted mainly of young people, at the same time the literature appealed to professionals and intellectuals, especially to those working in the "hard" sciences. This pattern of readership has continued, with even further rise in the educational level of the average reader.

By the late 1930s, the focus began to shift from a concern with science and scientific devices to an apprehension about the impact of science on society and on individual human beings. The most prominent leader of this movement was John W. Campbell, Jr., who, in his capacity as editor of *Astounding Stories* (later renamed *Astounding Science Fiction* and then *Analog Science Fiction/Science Fact*), attracted talented new writers to the field whose interests ran more heavily in the direction of the social consequences of science and technology than did those of their predecessors.

An important year for the development of science fiction was 1945, the year of the explosion of the first atomic bomb. *Astounding Stories* ran several stories before 1945 that dealt with nuclear fusion. These stories, especially those by Cleve Cartmill and Robert A. Heinlein, were so accurate in their detailing of nuclear fusion that the FBI raided the offices of the magazine, demanding to know who had leaked the secrets of the Manhattan Project. Campbell finally convinced the authorities that the stories flowed from the imagination of the authors and not from any other source.

Science fiction had accurately predicted the development of many other inventions and devices of the war years, including radar. As a result, it began to expand considerably its readership. Two major magazines were launched in the postwar years: *Galaxy* and *The Magazine of Fantasy and Science Fiction.* The latter specialized in quality stories on a variety of topics; it was science fiction's equivalent of a literary "small" magazine. *Galaxy,* under the editorship of H. L. Gold, featured stories that were heavy with social and political satire. During the 1950s social criticism became the dominant characteristic of this magazine, especially—though not exclusively—in the work of the writing team of Frederik Pohl and Cyril M. Kornbluth. *Galaxy* printed also the stories of John Linebarger of Johns Hopkins University, one of the very few social scientists who wrote science fiction. Writing under the name of Cordwainer Smith, Professor Linebarger became a legend in science fiction.

In the early fifties, science fiction enjoyed a boom period with a large number of magazine and book titles published each year. There followed a still unexplained slump in the latter part of that decade and in the early sixties, but science fiction surged again after about 1964, perhaps spurred on by the United States space program.

Science fiction is now being taught and used in hundreds of American colleges, universities, community colleges, and high schools. In short, it has been discovered by the academic community, which spurned it for so long. Science fiction has become respectable; it is no longer necessary to avoid discussing it at cocktail parties or to read it between the covers of a "regular" book. It outsells all other forms of literature in college bookstores and is rapidly losing its specialized status. It is slowly but surely merging with so-called mainstream writing, a development viewed with mixed feelings by its practitioners and readers.

Indeed, many scholars argue that science fiction is *the* literature for the latter half of the twentieth century, because it is the only literary genre that attempts to deal with the impact of science on human civilization and the only writing that presents alternatives to present problems. Whatever the truth of this assertion, science fiction has undeniably become an important part of the lives of students and teachers in a variety of fields of study. It has played—and will continue to play—an important role because its central unifying theme is that change is basic to the human condition.

II

Science fiction is a literature that deals with the consequences of human activity and of social institutions in a way that allows us to contemplate the alternatives to our present world: it allows us to be analytical and critical of our present world through literary devices as traditional as ancient Greek literature; and it postulates change as the central feature of human life. Since criminal justice is an important human activity involving socially significant institutions, is an increasingly serious public policy area in need of continuing analysis and criticism, and is an integral part of our civilization that is undergoing rapid change, the appropriateness of science fiction for the study of criminal justice becomes evident.

In addition, there is a fascinating literary relationship between the detective story and the science fiction story that has implications for the application of science fiction to the study of criminal justice. This relationship began to emerge in the nineteenth century with the appearance of both detective stories and science fiction. Edgar Allan Poe, long considered the father of modern horror stories in the United States, is closely associated with the emergence of both science fiction and detective fiction. This tradition led, in 1945, to the first published anthology of scientific detective fiction in the United States—*The Saint's Choice of Impossible Crime,* edited by Oscar J. Friend (Los Angeles, Bond-Charteris Enterprises). A second major anthology of such stories appeared in 1960, edited and published by Robert C. Peterson and entitled *The Science Fictional Sherlock Holmes* (Colorado). This anthology saw the emergence of contemporary science fiction and fantasy writers like Anthony Boucher, Mack Reynolds, Poul Anderson, and Gordon Dickson. A third anthology, which attempted to bring together the representatives of this kind of fiction, *Space, Time, and Crime,* edited by Miriam Allen de Ford (New York, Warner Paperback Library, 1964), added authors like Frederik Pohl, Avram Davidson, Ron Goulart, Fritz Leiber, and Fredric Brown to the number of science fiction writers interested in crime. Another anthology, which emphasized stories about crimes of the future, appeared in 1969—*Crime Prevention in the Thirtieth Century,* edited by Hans Stefan Santesson (New York, Walker Publishing Company).[2]

Contemporary science fiction magazines, such as *The Magazine of Fantasy and Science Fiction, Analog, Galaxy,* and *Amazing,* regularly feature stories that deal with crime, criminal justice, and the political, social, economic, and cultural situations in which criminal justice operates. Our book brings the reader the best of these stories in order to demonstrate the insights that this literature contains for the study of criminal justice. The reader's imagination is exercised in the development of alternative perspectives on criminal justice— its goals, processes, and outcomes. The stories were selected— and the notes about the stories were written—to emphasize the conceptual richness and the theoretical insights that can be developed about criminal justice from the literature of science fiction.

The relationship between science fiction-detective fiction and criminal justice goes beyond a mere appreciation of the historical or literary interest one may have in the subject. Science fiction and detective fiction highlight the importance of the unknown and of attempts to cope with it. Both the detective and the scientist use what is known to them in an effort to discover the unknown. For the former, the important thing is the solution to a crime; for the latter, it is the building of knowledge. One of the interesting questions that emerges

[2] Sam Moskowitz, *Strange Horizons: The Spectrum of Science Fiction* (New York: Charles Scribner's Sons, 1976), pp. 156–157. For anyone interested in pursuing the relationship between detective fiction and science fiction, this work by Moskowitz is outstanding.

from this perspective is: Do the scientific detectives who appear throughout the pages of detective fiction predate the rise of a class of scientists and social scientists who study crime and criminal justice? This question stimulates another, more important one: What is the state of our knowledge about crime and criminal justice? Finally, we are forced to ask: Can such knowledge help us formulate enlightened public policy in this important area of human activity and concern? If these are significant questions, then science fiction may be a most appropriate literature to be employed in the study of criminal justice. More than anything else, these questions plead with us to be imaginative in the seeking of answers. Let us now turn briefly to some specific reasons for the use of science fiction in the study and teaching of criminal justice.

First, as a literature for speculation, science fiction deals with every subject as a possibility. It does not assume that only one world exists; rather, it postulates a whole range of alternative worlds, any one of which is simply a possibility. Thus *the* future criminal justice system does not exist in science fiction. What does exist are visions of a set of possible future criminal justice systems. This perspective forces us to think about the need to create different futures and not allow "the" future to act upon us. As students and teachers of criminal justice, we must focus on analyzing decisions taken today in terms of their effects upon what is possible tomorrow and what is not. In criminal justice policy-making, we must maintain the view that a decision is a point in time linking the past with a future and that how we decide a particular issue or solve a problem affects whether a future is possible.

Second, far from being escapist literature, science fiction offers us a conceptual laboratory in which we can test our hypotheses about crime, criminal behavior, the effectiveness of criminal justice processes, and the overall worth of criminal justice outcomes. To develop a parallel world of the imagination —to let the intellect fly through relationships that are not possible in traditional research terms—is to give ourselves the opportunity to think differently and experimentally about important variables that affect criminal justice. Alternative conceptions of justice, alternative penal systems, alternative police procedures, alternative punishment methods and philosophies, alternative methods for seeking truth and/or innocence—all of these become part of the inquiry about the "real" world of criminal justice.

Third, science fiction acclimates us to feeling comfortable with change—to deal more effectively with "future shock." Stories that portray judges, police, prison systems, and other actors in the criminal justice system force us to think about the redefinitions that science fiction writers place upon these roles. Indeed, redefinitions of crime and the criminal expand our awareness of the profound impact that time and space have upon our fundamental conceptions of these subjects. Certainly, present-day social pathologies—for example, drug addiction on a wide scale, organized crime, overpopulation, and juvenile delinquency—are accepted today as "normal" problems; but could they have been believable to people living in the middle of the nineteenth century in the United States or elsewhere? For them, these problems would perhaps have appeared science fictional in nature.

Fourth, science fiction is educationally important for criminal justice because it dramatizes the future. For most people, especially for researchers, the future is usually taken as an object for study or thinking. It is easy to point to studies in any major policy area and to demonstrate the existence of data that aim at projecting the future based upon analyzing the trends of today. For example, the supply and quality of food available to humankind in the future is a policy area about which there are many projections, most of which are dire. Yet, if information about dire consequences is not effectively linked to behavioral changes in the present, then the future is not being taken seriously. Research about the effect of cigarette-smoking on health does not seem to have changed society's smoking behavior in any substantial way. When a reader of science fiction finishes a novel or a story about, let us say, overpopulation or being a prisoner in a future criminal justice system, he has experienced that problem through being involved in its dramatization. Reading John Brunner's *The Sheep Look Up*—a novel about a heavily polluted world of the future—would probably have more impact upon an individual's attitudes than reading through impersonal data about environmental pollution. Similarly, "The Public Hating," a story contained in this book, will probably help a student understand more effectively societal expiation as justification for capital punishment than a sociological analysis of the same subject, principally because the student, in part, will experience it.

Finally—but certainly not exclusively—science fiction is insightful for the study of criminal justice because it involves predictions and scenarios about future criminal justice goals, processes, and outcomes. It would be useful to take these predictions and scenarios and to compare them with current trends in criminal justice today and with current research trends in the field. The similarities and/or differences noted in such comparisons would stimulate discussions about the state of the art and of our knowledge in criminal justice and expand the limits of what we currently consider possible methods of inquiry.

There is more involved with science fiction and its possible usefulness for studying criminal justice than a methodological strategy for inquiry. To deal with alternative worlds is also an opportunity to deal with alternative values upon which worlds are constructed; and to deal with alternative values in criminal justice is an opportunity to deal with the fundamental structure of good and evil in society. Perhaps more than in any other area of human endeavor, the study of criminal justice allows us to deal with our collective dreams—and our collective nightmares—and to speculate about the best and the worst capabilities of the human spirit. Science fiction deals with parallel concerns as stories are spun about utopian futures and dystopian futures, the former dealing with our dreams and the latter our nightmares. Superficially disparate subjects and methods of looking at the social world, criminal justice and science fiction, upon closer examination, reveal similar concerns about the fundamental questions of the quality and purpose of life and about the direction of human destiny.

Part I

CULTURE, COMMUNITY, AND CRIME

1 The Undercity

by Dean R. Koontz

Where does crime come from? Some argue that the sources of crime lie in the evil nature of individuals as human beings. Others argue that human beings are essentially good and that, if crime exists, its sources are to be found in the social, economic, and political structures in which they are forced to live. This debate about whether crime is "caused" by individuals or by their environment will exist for a long time. Mixed with these issues is the public's perception of the role of government in the fostering of criminal behavior. For example, some would argue that a major source of crime is official corruption. Others complain that putting restrictions on the abilities of the police to deal with criminals adds to the existence of crime in society.

There may be widespread public and scholarly disagreement about the sources of crime in the United States today, but we can be certain of one thing—the crimes of the past differ from the crimes of the present, and the crimes of the future will differ from the crimes of today. Dean R. Koontz, in "The Undercity," portrays a future in which most of the crimes we know today have become legalized. The story points to the seeming permanence of human needs which will probably always exist and require gratification by illegal means. Wherever there exist demands by substantial segments of society for goods and services that cannot be provided by legitimate private or public groups, alternative—and illegitimate—supply structures will emerge. America's experience with prohibition is a good example. Black markets, gambling, prostitution, and

Lou

Just Another Day
— Paul McCartney

narcotics constitute goods and services for which there is high demand and no legitimate means of supply. It is interesting to speculate whether illegitimate supply structures imply a social benefit because of the possibility of overloading public structures, already burdened with providing legitimate services such as public safety, social welfare, and education, with the responsibility of satisfying illegitimate citizen demands. Decriminalization, often advocated as a method for reducing crime, has the potential for overly taxing governmental units.

But how can we foresee which activities, considered legitimate today, will become crimes of tomorrow and which activities, considered crimes of today, will be "decriminalized" tomorrow? What are our expectations of crime in the future? Will the development of new scientific and technological knowledge require a substantial reclassification of criminal behavior? Will the persistence—and increased severity—of major social problems—for example, food shortage, environmental pollution, and population implosion—also cause us to reexamine the types of behavior we consider to be "criminal"?

Business day

Well, kid, it was a busy day. You might even say it was a harrowing day, and you might be tempted to think that it was somehow out of the ordinary. But you must understand, straight off, that it was perfectly normal as business days go, no better and no worse than ten thousand days before it. And if I live so long, it won't be appreciably different from any of ten thousand days to follow. Remember that. If you want to enter the family business, kid, you have to be able to cope with long strings of days like this one, calendars full of them.

Days before it. *not alone*

Once, when the cities weren't a tenth as large as they are now, when a man might travel and might have business contacts throughout the world, we were called The Underworld, and we were envied and feared. We are still envied and feared, but now we're called The Undercity, because that is the world to us, and more than we can rightly handle anyway. I, for one, would be happy to roll things back, to break down these hundred-story megalopolises and live in a time where we could call ourselves a part of The Underworld, because things were a hell of a lot easier for our type. Just consider . . .

Nearly all forms of gambling were illegal back then. An enterprising

Shelia leading the way through Brother Rice first day!

Busy, harrowing Day!

1,000 Day Template with Entertainment Bundle.

young man could step in, buck the law, and clean up a tidy sum with a minimal financial outlay and with almost no personal risk at all. Cops and judges were on the take; clandestine casinos, street games and storefront betting shops thrived. No longer. They legalized it, and they gave us bank clerks for casino managers, CPA's instead of bouncers. They made gambling respectable—and boring.

Drugs were illegal then, too. Grass, hash, skag, coke, speed . . . God, an enterprising young kid like yourself could make a fortune in a year. But now grass and hash are traded on the open market, and all the harder drugs are available to all the loonies who will sign a health waiver and buy them from the government. Where's the thrill now? Gone. And where's the profit? Gone, too.

Sex. Oh, kid, the money to be made on sex, back then. It was *all* illegal: prostitution, dirty movies, picture postcards, erotic dancing, adultery, you name it! Now the government licenses the brothels, both male and female, and the wife or husband without a lover on the side is considered a throwback. Is this any way to make a buck?

Hell, kid, even murder was illegal in those days, and a man could buy the big trip for wiping someone off the slate. As you know, some folks never can seem to learn the niceties of civilized life—their manners are atrocious, their business methods downright devious, their insults unnecessarily public and demeaning—and these people need to be eliminated from the social sphere. Now we have the code duello, through which a man can settle his grudges and satisfy his honor, all legally. The once-lucrative career as a hired assassin has gone the way of the five-dollar streetwalker.

Now, kid, you have got to hustle all day, every day, if you want to survive in this business. You've got to be resourceful, clever and forward-thinking if you expect to meet the competition. Let me tell you how the day went, because it was a day like all days . . .

I bolted down a breakfast of protein paste and cafa, then met Lew Boldoni on the fifth subbasement level in Wing-L, where only the repair robots go. Boldoni was waiting on the robotwalk beside the beltway, carrying his tool satchel, watching the cartons of perishables move past him.

"On time," he said.

I said, "As usual." Time is money; cliché but true.

We removed the access plate to the beltway workings, went down under the robotwalk. In less than five minutes, we were directly beneath the big belt, barely able to shout above the roar, buffeted by the wind of its continuous passage. Together, we opened one of the hydraulic lines and let the lubricant spew out over the traffic computer terminal, where it was sure to seep through and do some damage. Before a fire could start, we were out of there, up on the sidewalk again, putting the access plate back where it belonged. That done, just as the alarms were beginning to clang, we went in different directions.

We both had other business.

This bit of sabotage wouldn't pay off until much later in the day.

At 9:30 in the morning, right on time, I met a young couple—Gene and Miriam Potemkin—in a public hydroponics park on the eighty-third level, in that neighborhood they call Chelsea. She was twenty-one and a looker, bright and curious and unhappy. He was a year older than she was, but that was the only real difference between them. They sat on a bench by an artificial waterfall, both of them leaning forward as I approached, both with their hands folded in their laps, more like sister and brother than like wife and husband.

"Did you bring it?" he asked.

I removed a sealed envelope from my pocket, popped the seal and let them see the map inside, though I was careful not to let them handle it just then. I said, "And you?"

She lifted a small plastic satchel from the ground beside her and took another sealed envelope from it, reluctantly handed it over.

I opened it, counted the money, nodded, tucked the envelope into my pocket and gave them the map.

"Wait a minute, here!" Mr. Potemkin said. "According to this damn map, we'll be going out through the sewer! You know that's not possible. Sewage is pumped at pressure, and there's no way to survive in the system."

"True enough," I said. "But if you'll look closely at the map, you'll see that the sewage line is encased into a larger pipe, from which repairs can be made to the system. This larger pipe is everywhere twenty feet in diameter, sometimes as much as thirty, and is always enough larger than the sewage pipe itself to give you adequate crawl space."

"I don't know," he said. "It doesn't look easy . . ."

"No way out of the city is easy, for God's sake!" I told him. "Look, Potemkin, the city fathers say that the open land, beyond the cities, is unlivable. It's full of poisoned air, poisoned water, plague, and hostile plant and animal life. That's why the air freight exits are the only ones that are maintained, and that's why they're so carefully supervised. City law forbids anyone to leave the city for fear they'll return bearing one of the plagues from Outside. Now, considering all of this, could you reasonably expect me to provide you with an easy way out?"

"I suppose not."

"And that's damn straight."

Ms. Potemkin said, "It's really not like that Outside, is it? The stories of plagues, poisoned air and water, monsters—all of that's just so much bunk."

"I wouldn't know," I said.

"But you must know!"

"Oh?"

"You've shown us the way out," she said. "You must have seen what's beyond the city."

"I'm afraid not," I said. "I employ engineers, specialists, who work from diagrams and blueprints. None of my people would consider leaving the city; we've got too much going for us here."

"But," she insisted, "by sending us, you're showing your distrust of the old stories about the Outside."

"Not at all," I explained. "Once you've gone, my men will seal off this escape route so you can't come back that way, just in case you might bring a plague with you."

"And you won't sell it again?"

"No. We'll find other ways out. There are millions of them."

They looked at each other, unsure of themselves now.

I said, "Look, you haven't committed the map to memory. If you want, I can take it back and return half of your money."

"No," he said.

She said, "We've made up our minds. We need open land, something more than layer on layer of enclosed streets and corridors."

"Suit yourself," I said. "And good luck."

I shook their hands and got the hell out of there; things to do, things to do . . .

Moving like a maintenance robot on an emergency call, I dropped down to the subbasements again, to the garbage monitoring decks, where I met with the day-shift manager, K. O. Wilson. We shook hands at precisely 10:20, five minutes behind schedule, and we went into the retrieval chamber, where he had the first two hours of discoveries laid out in neat, clean order.

Kid, I don't think I've ever talked about this angle of the family business before, because I'm not that proud of it. It's the cheapest form of scavenging, no matter how lucrative it is. And it *is* lucrative. You see, the main pipes of the garbage shuttle system are monitored electronically and filtered to remove any articles of value that might otherwise be funneled into the main sewage lines and pumped out of the city. I've got K. O. Wilson, of the first shift, and Marty Linnert, of the second shift, on my payroll. They see to it that I have time to look over the day's findings before they're catalogued and sent up to the city's lost-and-found bureau. Before you think too badly of your old man, consider that 20 per cent of the family's gross comes from the garbage operation.

"Six valuable rings, a dozen good watches, what appears to be one folder of a top-quality coin collection, a diamond tiara, and a mess of other junk," Wilson told me, pointing to the good items, which he had set aside for me.

I ignored the watches, took two of the rings, the tiara and the damp folder full of old coins. "Nothing else?"

"A corpse," he said. "That'll interest the cops. I put it on ice until you could get in and check over your stuff first."

"A murder?" I asked.

"Yeah."

Kid, the code duello hasn't solved everything. There are still those who are afraid to fight, who prefer to sneak about and repay their enemies illegally. And there are also those who aren't satisfied with taking economic and emotional revenge from those not eligible for the duels; they insist on blood, and they have it. Eventually, the law has them. We're not involved with people of this sort, but you should know the kind of scum that the city still supports.

I told Wilson, "I'll send a man around after noon to see what else you've got by then."

Ten minutes later, at 10:53, I walked into the offices of Boldoni and Gia Cybernetic Repairs, on the ninety-second floor, Wing-B, where I acted very shocked about the breakdown in the beltway system.

"City Engineer Willis left an urgent message for you," my secretary said. She handed it to me and said, "It's a beltway carrying perishables in the fifth subbasement."

"Is Mr. Boldoni there?" I asked.

"He accompanied the first repair team," she said.

"Call down and tell Willis I'm on my way."

I used the express drop and almost lost my protein paste and cafa —any inconvenience for a good customer, and the city is the best customer that Boldoni and Gia Cybernetic Repairs has on its list.

Willis was waiting for me by the beltway. He's a small man with very black hair and very dark eyes and a way of moving that makes you think of a maintenance robot with a short between his shoulder blades. He scuttled toward me and said, "What a mess!"

"Tell me," I said.

"The main hydraulic line broke over the traffic computer terminal and a fire started in the works."

"That doesn't sound so bad," I said.

He wiped his small face with one large hand and said, "It wouldn't have been if it had stopped there. We've got the fire out already. The only trouble is that the lubricant has run back the lines into the main traffic computer and the damn thing won't shut down. I've got perishables moving up out of the subterranean coolers, and no way to move them or stop them. They're piling up on me fast, Mr. Gia. I have to have this beltway moving inside the hour or the losses are going to be staggering."

"We'll do the job," I assured him.

"I went out on the limb, calling you before you could deliver a quick computerized estimate. But I knew you people were the fastest, and I needed someone who could be here immediately."

"Don't you worry about it," I told him. "Whatever the B & G computer estimates we'll shave by ten per cent to keep your bosses happy."

Willis was ecstatic, thanking me again and again. He didn't understand that the Boldoni and Gia house computer always estimated an additional and quite illegal 15 per cent surprofit, more than negating the 10 per cent discount I'd given him.

While he was still thanking me, Lew Boldoni came up from the access tunnel, smeared with lubricant, looking harried and nervous and exhausted. Lew is an excellent actor, and that is another qualification for success in this business.

"How is it down there?" I asked.

"Bad," Boldoni said.

Willis groaned.

Boldoni said, "But we're winning it."

"How long?" I asked.

"We'll have the beltway moving in an hour, with a jury-rigged system, and then we can take our time with the permanent repairs."

Willis groaned again, differently this time: in happiness.

I said, "Mr. Boldoni has everything in control, Mr. Willis. I'm sure that you'll be in business as usual shortly. Now, if you'll excuse me, I've got some other urgent business to attend to."

I went up in the express elevator, which was worse than coming down, since my stomach seemed to reach the fifty-ninth floor seconds before the rest of me.

I boarded a horizontal beltway and rode twelve miles east, the last six down Y-Wing. At 11:40, ten minutes behind schedule, I entered an office in the Chesterfield District where a nonexistent Mr. Lincoln Pliney supposedly did business. There, I locked the outer door, apologized for my tardiness to the two people waiting in the reception area, then led them into Lincoln Pliney's private office. I locked that door too, went to the desk, checked out my bug-detecting equipment, made sure the room hadn't been tapped, then sat down behind my desk, offered the customers a drink, poured, sat back and introduced myself under a false name.

My visitors were Arthur Coleman, a rather successful industrialist with offices on the hundredth level, and Eileen Romaine, a lovely girl, fifteen years Coleman's junior. We had all come together in order to negotiate a marriage between Coleman and Romaine, an illegal marriage.

"Tell me, Mr. Coleman," I said, "just why you wish to risk the fines and prison sentences involved with this violation of the Equal Rights Act?"

He squirmed a bit and said, "Do you have to put it that way?"

I said, "I believe a customer must know the consequences before he can be fairly expected to enter a deal like this."

"Okay," he said. "Well, I've been married four times under the standard city contract, and all four marriages have terminated in divorce at my instigation. I'm a very unhappy man, sir. I've got this . . . well, perversion that dominates the course of my private life. I need a wife who . . . who is not my equal, who is subservient, who plays a dated role as nothing more than my bedmate and my housekeeper. I want to dominate any marital situation that I enter."

I said, "Conscious male chauvinism is a punishable crime."

"As I'm aware."

"Have you seen a robopsych?" I asked. "Perhaps one of those could cure you of your malady."

"I'm sure it could," he said. "But you see, I don't really want to be cured. I *like* myself the way I am. I *like* the idea of a woman waiting on me and making her own life conditioned to mine."

"And you?" I asked Eileen.

She nodded, an odd light in her eyes, and she said, "I don't like the responsibility of the standard marriage. I want a man who will put me in my place, a man I can look up to, admire, depend on."

I tell you, kid, these antiquated lusts of theirs were distasteful to me. However, I believe in rebels, both good and bad, being a rebel myself, and I was ready to help them. Both had come to me by word-of-mouth referral within the past month. I'd researched the lives of both, built up two thick dossiers, matched them, and called them here for their first and final meeting under my auspices.

"You have both paid me a finder's fee," I told them. "Now, you will have sixty days to get to know each other. At the end of that time, you will either fail to contact me about a finalization of the contract, in which case I'll know you've found each other unsuitable, or you'll come back here and set up an appointment with my robosec. If you find you like each other, it will be a simple matter to arrange an illegal marriage, without the standard city contract."

Coleman wasn't satisfied with that. He said, "Just how will you pull this off, Mr. Pliney?"

"The first step, of course, is to have Eileen certified dead and disposed of. My people will falsify a death report and have it run through the city records. This may sound like an incredible feat to you; it is nevertheless possible. Once Eileen Romaine has ceased to exist, we will create a false persona in the name of Eileen Coleman. She will be identified as your sister; an entire series of life records will be planted in the computers to solidify her false identity. She can, naturally, then come to live with you, without the city records people realizing that there is anything sexual in your cohabitation."

"If you can do it," Coleman said, "you're a genius."

"No, just clever," I said. "And I will do it. In fact, on any date you pick, I'll have a man at your apartment to officiate at a clandestine wedding using the ancient, male chauvinist rituals."

"There will be no psycheprobes, as there are in other marriages?" she asked.

"Of course not," I said. "The city will have no reason to psycheprobe you under the Equal Rights Act because you won't, so far as the city is concerned, be married at all."

At that point, she burst into tears and said, "Mr. Pliney, you are the first person, outside of Arthur here, who's ever understood me."

I set her straight on that, kid, believe me. I said, "Lady, I don't understand you at all, but I sympathize with rebels. You're chucking out total equality and everything a normal human being should desire in return for a life-style that has long been shown to be inadequate. You're risking prison and fines for knowingly circumventing the Equal Rights Act. It's all crazy, but you've a right to be nuts."

"But if you don't understand us, not at all, why are you risking—"

"For the profit, Eileen," I said. "If this is pulled off, Mr. Coleman will owe me a tidy sum." I stood up. "Now, I must see you out. I've many, many things to do yet today."

When I was finally rid of the happy couple, I boarded an entertainment beltway into a restaurant district in Wing-P, and there I had my lunch: a fillet of reconstituted sea bass, a baked potato, strawberries from a hydroponic garden immersed in simulated cream. It was a rich lunch, but one that was easily digested.

A warning kid: Stay away from greasy foods for lunch. In this business, your stomach can be the end of you; it curdles grease and plagues you with murderous heartburn.

By 1:30, I was back on the street. I phoned in to the offices of Boldoni and Gia and learned that the beltway on the fifth subbasement level was rolling again, though Boldoni now estimated permanent repairs as a two- or three-day job. It seemed that one of the B & G workmen had found a second potential break in the hydraulic line just before it was ready to go. He'll get a bonus for that, however he managed it.

At 1:45, I stopped around to see K. O. Wilson again, down at the garbage monitoring decks, picked up the best part of a set of pure silver dinnerware, an antique oil lantern, and a somewhat soiled set of twentieth-century pornographic photographs, which, while no longer titilating to the modern man, are well worth a thousand duo-creds as prime, comic nostalgia. Kid, the strangest damn stuff shows up in the garbage, sometimes so strange you won't believe it. Just remember that there are thirty million people in this damn hive, and that among them they own and accidentally throw out about anything a man could hope to find.

I delivered the dinnerware, lantern and pornography to Petrone, the family fence, and then got my ass on the move. I was twenty minutes behind the day's schedule.

At 2:15, I met a man named Talmadge at a sleazy little drug bar in one of the less pleasant entertainment districts on the forty-sixth level. He was sitting at a table in a dark corner, clasping his water pipe in both hands and staring down at the mouthpiece that appeared to have fallen from his lips to the tabletop.

"Sorry I'm late," I said.

He looked up, dreamy-eyed, smiled at me more than he had to, and said, "That's all right. I'm feeling fine, just fine."

"Good for you," I said. "But are you feeling too fine to go through with this?"

"No, no!" he said. "I've waited much too long already, months and months—even years!"

"Come on, then," I said.

I took him out of the drug bar and helped him board a public beltway that took us quickly away from the entertainment zone and deep into a residential area on the same level.

Leaning close to me, in a stage whisper, as if he enjoyed the role of a conspirator, Talmadge said, "Tell me again how big the apartment is."

I looked around, saw that no one was close to us, and, knowing that he would just grow louder and more boisterous if I refused to speak of it, I said, "Three times as large as regulations permit a single man like you. It has nine rooms and two baths."

"And I don't have to share the baths?"

"Of course not."

He was ecstatic.

Now, kid, this is the racket you'll be starting out in to get some experience in the business, and you should pay especially close attention. Even when your mother was alive, we had a bigger apartment than city regulations permit; now, with your mother gone, it's *much* bigger than allowed. How was this achieved, this lavish suite? Simple. We bought up the small apartments all around this, knocked out walls, refitted and redecorated. Then, through a falsification of land records in the city real estate office, we made it look as if the outsize apartment had always been here, was a fluke in the original designs. Now, although living space is at a premium, and though the city tries to force everyone into relatively similar accommodations, the government repair robots are far too busy to have the time to section up the large apartment, throw up new walls and so forth. Instead, because this sort of thing happens so seldom, the city allows the oversize apartment to exist and merely doubles or triples the tax assessment on whoever lives there. In a city of fifteen million apartments, you can pull a hustle like this at least twice a month, without drawing undue official concern, and you can clean up a very tidy sum from rich folks who need more than the legal living space.

At 2:38, Mr. Talmadge and I arrived at the entrance to his new home, keyed it and went inside. I took him on a grand tour of the place, waited while he checked the Tri-D fake-view in all the rooms, tested the beds, flushed the toilets in both johns, and finally paid me the money yet outstanding on our contract. In return, I gave him his ownership papers, copies of the falsified real estate claims, and his first tax assessment.

At 3:00, half an hour behind schedule, I got out of there.

On my way up to the offices of Boldoni and Gia, in the standard elevator, I had time to catch a news flash on the comscreen, and it was such bad news that it shattered the hell out of my schedule. You heard about it. Ms. and Mr. Potemkin, my first clients of the day, were apprehended in their attempt to sneak out of the city through the sewage service pipes. They accidentally ran into a crew of maintenance robots who gave pursuit. They'd only just then been brought to city police headquarters, but they wouldn't need long to fold up under a stiff interrogation.

I canceled my original destination on the elevator board, punched out the twenty-sixth level and dropped down in agonizingly slow motion, wishing to hell I'd used the express drop.

At 3:11, I rode by the offices of Cargill Marriage Counseling, which was the front I used for selling routes out of the city to people like the Potemkins. The place didn't seem to be under surveillance, so I came back on another beltway, opened up, went inside and set to work. I opened the safe, took out what creds I had bundled there, stuffed half a dozen different maps in my pockets, looked around to be sure I'd not left anything of value behind, then set fire to the place and beat it out of there. I had always used the name Cargill in that racket, and I'd always worn transparent plastic fingertip shields to keep from leaving prints; however, one can never be too careful kid.

At 3:47, I rode back upstairs to the offices of Boldoni and Gia, checked on the beltway repair job with Lew, who had returned to the office. It was going well; the profit would keep Boldoni and Gia in the black; we're always in the black; we see to that.

I sent a man down to seek K. O. Wilson before shifts changed, then dialed the number for Mr. Lincoln Pliney (who is me, you recall), on the fifty-ninth floor in the Chesterfield District. The robosec answered on a cut-in, and I asked for messages.

In a metallic voice, the robosec said, "Mr. Arthur Coleman just stopped in and asked for an appointment, sir."

"Coleman? I just talked to him this morning."

"Yes, sir. But he left a number for you."

I took the number, hung up, dialed Coleman and said hello and identified myself to him.

He said, "Eileen and I want to go through with the deal."

"You've just met each other," I said.

"I know, but I think we're perfect for each other."

I said, "What does Eileen think?"

"The same as I do, of course."

"In one afternoon, you can't learn enough about each other—"

Coleman said, "It's true love."

I said, "Well, it's obviously true *something*."

"We'd like to finalize things tonight."

"Impossible."

"Then we'll go somewhere else."

"To whom?"

"We'll find someone," he said.

I said, "You'll find some incompetent criminal hack who'll botch the falsification of Eileen's death certificate, and in the end you'll have to tell the police about me."

He didn't respond.

"Oh, hell!" I snapped. "Meet me in my Chesterfield District office in half an hour, with Eileen."

I hung up.

I'd intended to see a man who wanted to purchase a falsified Neutral Status Pass to keep him safe from duel challenges. See, kid, there are a lot of people who are healthy enough to have to go armed but who want to avoid having to accept challenges. The government has no sympathy with them and forces them to comply with the system. I'm always ready, however, to give them a paper disability to keep them whole and sane. I sympathize with rebels, like I said. And there's a profit in it, too. Anyway, I had to call the guy who wanted the Neutral Status Pass and postpone our appointment until tomorrow.

Then I ran off to tie the nuptial knots for Coleman and his lady.

You see, now, why I was late getting home. Scare you? I didn't think it would. Tomorrow, you can come along with me, watch me work, pick up some tips about the business. You're fifteen, plenty old enough to learn. I tell you, kid, you're going to be a natural for this business. I wish your mother could have lived to see what kind of daughter she brought into his world.

Well, kid, you better turn in. It's going to be a busy day.

2 Guilty As Charged

by *Arthur Porges*

What is crime? This relatively simple question is the basis for
much heated debate within the field of criminal justice, and
the amount that exists constitutes a major public policy issue
in the United States. But this debate and this issue are not
separate questions, for the amount of crime is partially a
function of how crime is defined. Broad definitions of crime
will generate "more" crime than narrow definitions.

One common way of defining crime is to include all reported
violations of a criminal law. Although this definition is probably
technically correct, it may not cover those violations of norms
that do not classify as criminal law. These violations are usually
referred to as "deviance." Oftentimes people observe violations
of tradition or folkways, classify them as crimes in their own
minds, and demand that the public processes of criminal justice
be brought to bear upon them. In this sense, "crime waves" will
always be with us.

The study of crime and criminal justice tells us about the ways
individuals respond to the society in which they live and the
way society makes a similiar response to them. In addition, the
study of criminal justice may reveal a great deal about
ourselves as human beings. Part of our nature is reflected in
the values which form the basis for a set of rules which
prescribe and proscribe human behavior. It is also reflected
in the systems we use to identify people who break these rules.
Because these identification systems must be formal and public,

they go a long way toward establishing the style and character of a society. Moreover, much is revealed about a society by examining what we do with such rule-breakers after we have identified them. In effect, how we process and treat the individuals we define as deviants in society tells us a great deal about the "normal" foundations of our social life.

In one important way, the existence of crime—or deviance—in society provides a social benefit. It identifies and highlights a set of values which become the essential foundation for cohesion in society. "Deviants" become outlaw groups—the "bad guys"—and "normals" become lawful groups—the "good guys." The study of criminal justice then becomes an examination of the drama that takes place between publicly legitimized good and evil in society.

This drama has an interesting and rich history, for elaborate machinery has been set up in every society to deal with crime. Abstruse and mysterious procedures, complex rituals, ornate trappings and settings—all have been an integral part of the development of criminal justice systems in every culture. Generally, we tend to view these systems in an overall context of progress from "primitive" systems to "advanced" systems. But can a civilization be advanced technologically and yet remain primitive in its identification, treatment, and elimination of "deviants"?

In Arthur Porges's story "Guilty as Charged," time-travelers go to the year 2183 in order to learn about the customs of that future society. They can only see—not hear or be present in—the future. Their time-travel device puts them in a situation where they witness a criminal trial. Much is revealed to them concerning their own expectations about the relationship between the trial and this future society.

His hand on a dial, Manton turned to Kramer, ready with the video-audio tape-recorder.

"All set, Dave?" he asked, a slight hum in his voice.

"Okay," Kramer replied, ostentatiously cool. The tape began to unwind with whispery precision, and Manton faced the screen, now beginning to glow. Shadowy images flitted across it, gradually sharpening to familiar shapes.

It was too bad, Manton felt, that he had been forced to choose a single small region of space-time on which to focus; the restriction was very annoying. But the field equations did indicate an additional range of about forty feet straight ahead, obtainable by varying a particular input factor. And even with all these limitations, the basic calculations had required months of expensive time on one of the fastest electronic brains available.

It had been something of a problem, too, deciding what unique setting should be computed. Manton believed that his conclusion was a logical one. Obviously, there was no point in going too far ahead; the limited view on the screen might seem chaotic—everything new and different, with few ties to his own day. Nor would it be reasonable to look forward a mere fifty years. One couldn't expect really significant changes in so brief a period. About 225 years, he decided, was probably best—not that the machine would hit it on the nose, anyway. And on that basis the months of brain-twisting mathematics, the design of thousands of electronic units, and the hair-splitting calibration of a dozen complex servomechanisms, had all been undertaken and successfully completed.

Gratified as he was, Manton couldn't help feeling a little disappointment. He had focused on the heart of this city in Massachusetts, hoping to capture the image of some busy public place: a scene sure to convey the maximum information about the mores of 2181. It was rather a letdown, then, to find himself viewing what was obviously a mere courtroom. True it was a magnificent, soaring chamber, with countless fascinating innovations of a minor sort, which he planned to study later; but Manton feared that two centuries and a quarter could not have seen any vast changes in English common law, already hallowed by time.

There would be new crimes, no doubt, either political or related to novel, intricate technologies; and a humane, streamlined, efficient courtroom procedure. Certainly, one would look in vain for either a Jeffreys or a Darrow in this enlightened age. The former would not be tolerated; and the latter would not be needed. Yet a court of law would not have changed to the extent, for example, of transportation, communication, or recreation, just to mention a few categories of human activity.

It was with mixed feelings, therefore, that he watched the two-foot-square, glowing screen, less interested at first in the trial itself than in the triumph of his genius, and the people, with their odd clothing, so loose and light, and their vigorous, almost beefy, bodies that radiated health.

There was a huge, illuminated clock calendar just at the border of his field of view; it gave him a glad thrill to see the date: April 14, 2183. He wrenched his eyes away for a brief glance at Kramer. Dave pointed to the calendar and grinned.

"Missed it by only a couple years," he said. "Nice work."

"Lucky," Manton grunted. "Plain lucky." He turned back to the screen.

Just behind the calendar, against the same wall, was a sort of bulletin board, giving data about the case being tried. Manton could read "State vs. Frances Wills," but the next line, which presumably named the charge, was out of focus. And the machine had no leeway laterally. Too bad, but the proceedings themselves ought to clear up that point soon enough. He should be able to tell a murder case from a trial for bigamy, even in pantomime.

Now, as he watched, the accused was seating herself with obvious reluctance in the flowing contours of a witness chair. She had something about her, Manton thought, an air of strange vitality, perhaps. She was not young, about fifty, he guessed, although it occurred to him that anybody who looked only fifty in 2183 was more likely pushing ninety. Even in his day, the visible signs of senescence had been thrust ahead a decade or more within a few years.

The jurors filed in; apparently the court had been in recess. He noted that there were fifteen, and snorted. Fifteen-twelfths more chance (he couldn't help thinking mathematically) for illogical verdicts if this bunch retained anything in common with 1956 juries. Still, they were not a bad looking group, really. Nine men and six women, of middle age mostly, but with three boys and two elderly ladies for balance.

There was the judge. Not much difference in his case. Portly, grave, and seemingly a bear for dignity. No robe. Thank God they'd given up that absurd hangover. Odd; no spectators either. A change for the better; they often put improper pressure on jurymen, just as the papers did. The judge's eyes, Manton noted, redeemed him. They were caverns of melancholy compassion. A jurist who found no perverted pleasure in sentencing social misfits had much to recommend him in Manton's opinion. But then, the cynical thought came, for whom was the compassion? Maybe the judge had ulcers—or were they finally licked after more than two centuries? He doubted it.

It was most unfortunate that he couldn't read lips; understanding this trial was not going to be so easy after all. The prosecuting attorney, a youngish man, with a surprisingly round, good-humored face, was addressing the jury, pointing now and then at the defendant. Although he seemed not unsympathetic to her, she glared at him with alarming malice. She must be, Manton concluded, a vindictive old harridan indeed. You'd think that after so many years the principles of psychiatry would have made such social unfortunates very rare. This one probably owned a fire-trap tenement; she looked the type. No, there wouldn't be tenements in 2183; it must be a more enlightened age than that. A clean courtroom proved something. Public buildings are always cleaned and modernized last. Those even in the biggest cities in his own day: Chicago, New York—why, prison was hardly more depressing than the courtrooms.

Although he knew little enough about law, Manton felt sure that procedures had changed greatly. Witnesses were seated facing the accused, for example. Most of them were restrained, but one woman, with a ravaged, unhappy face, got quite emotional, even waving before the jury a photograph, a wonderful, three-dimensional one, he noted with interest, apparently of a young girl. Later, she tried to attack the prisoner, but guards smoothly intervened. The prosecutor, looking like a chubby, brooding child, helped calm her, but she spat like an angry cat towards the accused, who merely gave her repeated, sidelong glances, half malicious, half contemptuous.

"Whistler's mother," Dave said, pointing at the defendant. "Poisonous old biddy."

Manton pulled his gaze from the bright square, a little annoyed at the comment. He liked to be judicial.

"Lucky you're not on the jury," he said evenly.

The defense attorney, tall and casual, seemed to have very little part in the trial, except for an occasional unemphatic objection. Manton guessed his case had been presented earlier, and that this was the prosecutor's second and last summation. There was an air of fait accompli about the case; it seemed that the defense was merely a routine gesture.

But it was by no means clear just what crime the old woman had committed. Apparently she had offended a number of people, for several of the witnesses showed dislike of a personal nature. There was even a touch of comedy—or so Manton accounted it, although nobody present seemed amused—when one old man, a very shaky and garrulous individual, displayed a photograph of a magnificent prime steer. As a former farm boy, Manton gasped at the meaty perfection of the animal. The old man pointed to the likeness, and shed senile tears; once he shook a trembling fist at the old woman, and the jury looked grave. The foreman slammed his right fist into his left palm, nodding vigorously; one of the old women pursed her lips disapprovingly.

Manton shook his head, running one hand through the rusty hair. He peered at Kramer, who raised one eyebrow comically. What possible connection was there between a steer, for example, and the other picture, that of the young girl? Was this grim old lady a cattle-rustler, and had that old man and the girl owned a prize beef? Manton thought of his own 4-H days and grinned wryly. He'd have been damned annoyed if anybody had stolen his own blue-ribbon steer. Absurd idea, though. If there were one crime most unlikely in her case and considering the date, it was cattle-rustling. As well expect shipwreckers in 1956 Cornwall. And what about that boy with the withered arm? What was his grievance? He had pointed to it repeatedly, contrasting it with his sturdy left arm, and showing, in vivid pantomime, how the atrophy had progressed from fingertips to shoulder.

Ah! Was this it? The old woman was guilty of reckless driving; poor reflexes, no doubt. In some high-speed vehicle of the age, she had crippled the boy, killed the steer—and as for the girl of the picture, she was killed, too. She was the boy's sister; they had been leading the steer down a highway—no, it was all speculation.

And what about the last witness? The gloomy fellow who had shown pictures of a ruined house. The structure lay in a heap as if dynamited; and the man indicated with a kind of melancholy satisfaction, how all the neighboring houses, so similar in their architecture, were unharmed. How did that fit in? Manton gave Kramer a puzzled glance.

"Blows up people's houses, too," Kramer said, shaking his head in reproof. "I told you she wasn't nice."

They were still speculating, when the trial was recessed. Here was a chance to tinker with the input factor and focus ahead a few more feet. Manton felt a glow of pleasure as he saw the foreground fade out, while the courtroom's farthest wall became clear as coated glass to the probing beam.

At the extreme fifty-foot range, just past the courtroom itself, was a chamber he found very intriguing. It was lined with light, hospital-like wall-tile, and housed but a single object: a small, metal hut. The door to this was open; and inside he could see a wheeled table of the sort employed by surgeons, except that the flat top was uncushioned and had eight-inch walls on every edge. There were straps, and yet it could not be for operations; if the person were to lie on, or rather in, that box-like table top, the walls of the metal hut would almost touch him on every side. There was certainly no room for a surgeon at all, and anyway this was not a medical center but a hall of justice.

Manton flashed back to the courtroom, finding that the recess was over. To his surprise, some attendants had wheeled in a great, complex instrument, not unlike the smaller electronic calculators he was so familiar with. But it was not one of those; no question about that. He could read some of the large dials. There was one for blood pressure, another for temperature, and many more marked with terms beyond his comprehension: Rh, Albumin, Ph, Sigma Coefficient, Curie Potential, and Dubos Count. This machine was rolled alongside the witness chair.

Manton stared. It was evident that the device was to be used somehow on the defendant, and that she resented the idea. Only after several husky guards seized her lean wrists, ankles, and shoulders, did the struggling woman submit. Moistened contact plates were fastened to her arms and forehead. Needles were deftly inserted into her leathery skin. She writhed, raving, her lips flecked with foam. The jury shrank from her feral glares. As the burly attendants held her immobile, a specialist flicked various controls on the machine. He manipulated them with bored familiarity; apparently it was an old story to him. Dial needles quivered, and the jury, much concerned, discussed their significance.

Most of these readings meant nothing to Manton, but he did wonder about two of them. The old woman's temperature seemed to be impossibly high: 115 degrees. Even he knew it ought to be near ninety-eight, and that she was well and strong, outwardly, at least, with a fever that should have been fatal. And her pulse, that was only forty, and should have been about seventy. The woman was a freak of nature, if he understood even those few readings.

Whatever the machine indicated, its findings had a decisive effect upon the trial. The defense attorney had been weak enough, and this seemed to finish him. Evidently the old woman's guilt was beyond question, although why sickness was a crime, Manton couldn't imagine.

"That contraption finished her," Kramer muttered, stooping over his camera to adjust the focus. "But just what in hell—?" His voice died away in a querulous mumble.

Certainly the jury had no doubts; their verdict, delivered without leaving the courtroom, took only moments. The judge's pronouncement was equally brief. Now, Manton expected, she would be taken to some cell block beyond the range of the machine, and the courtroom cleared. He leaned forward, almost touching the screen, as the same attendants dragged her not to incarceration, but rather to the mysterious little room he had inspected earlier.

Kramer uttered an impatient sound, and Manton straightened up, aware he was blocking the electronic camera which was recording the trial on tape.

"We'd better shift to the other room," he said. "There's something funny going on."

He refocused in haste, just in time to see the old women, fighting with insensate fury, being strapped to the table, which stood just outside the little hut. Was this some legal, anti-crime treatment? Something to cure the accused's criminal illness?

And now a white-coated man, obviously a doctor, came in, as did the judge and jury foreman, the latter looking particularly queasy. At a nod from the judge, the doctor prepared a hypodermic, and as the helpless woman squirmed and gibbered, made an injection directly into a vein of her arm. In a matter of moments she relaxed, but her eyes still glared hate, and only after a second injection did they close.

Could this be an execution? No, her breast still rose and fell; she was only unconscious. But maybe she would die soon. Manton gulped, tempted to switch off the machine. He had no stomach for such things. Yet a hypodermic of morphine was a great improvement over the gallows or gas chamber. Such a method would be worthy of 2183. That is, assuming there was any excuse for a death penalty, something hardly acceptable even today.

But why were they wheeling the table and its contents into the metal hut? If she were to die, why not in the open? Was it some quirk of 22nd Century psychology?

An attendant shut the door and twirled a locking wheel. The little group drew back. The judge looked meaningfully at the foreman, whose face was dead white. Then the former made a slight, imperious gesture, and one man, moving to the far wall, threw a big knifeswitch.

Manton started as the massive contact points arced in a flash of lacy white. Heart thumping, he saw the spectators wait in silence for thirty seconds. Then, at a nod from the judge, the attendant opened the switch; and the foreman, taking a deep breath, advanced to the metal hut. With a hand that shook violently he turned the wheel; the door swung open, and Manton's stomach snapped itself into a sick knot. He heard Kramer draw in a single hissing breath. There on the table, still smoking, was a heap of dirty gray ashes, almost filling the box-like top.

No misinterpretation was possible. It was a monstrous act. The old woman, murderess perhaps, very likely insane, but a fellow human, had been anesthetized—thank God for so much mercy—and burned to ashes in an electric incinerator. Was this the humanitarian climax of over two hundred years more of civilization?

Kramer was swearing in a monotone, and automatically, without comprehension, Manton followed, with the machine, the execution party's return to the courtroom. It was empty now except for an elderly porter. He was just altering the big bulletin board, and as he shifted it slightly, Manton was able to read the words which had been out of focus during the trial, together with some others added moments before:

> *STATE* vs. *FRANCES WILLS*
> CHARGE: *WITCHCRAFT*
> VERDICT: GUILTY AS CHARGED
> PENALTY: DEATH BY FIRE

Little sheds downstairs
11 Hastings.

3 Shock Treatment

by J. Francis McComas

Death.

What is the worth of an individual in society? When the welfare
of an individual comes into conflict with the welfare of society
as a whole, how is this dilemma resolved? "Shock Treatment"
by J. Francis McComas portrays the creation of a new society
founded on the basis of an extremely enlightened criminal code,
but the killing of an important member of the community forces
radical changes in the law. This is a timely story for reflection
about the apparent backlash in the United States against
leniency toward criminals. Complaints about "coddling
criminals" and about the absence of the death penalty are
heard in public expressions about the state of our criminal
justice system.

It is important to underline the significance of the concept
of the "community's health" in relation to criminal justice. The
needs of the community become the basis for the establishment
of "the rules of the game." One of the most important rules is
that there be sufficient law and order to allow the game to
function and continue to be played. The process of criminal
justice as it relates to the health of the community functions
to create a kind of homeostasis within the community. If society
can be conceived of as a table-of-play based upon a small
number of all-important values, then disturbances entering this
system can be looked upon as diseases which must be regulated
by a mechanism whose purpose is to protect at all costs these
values. Crime functions as a social disease, and the criminal
justice system as the disease regulator.

Thus there is an interdependent relationship between the nature of how a community is put together and the operation of its criminal justice system. One of the challenges facing those who study and work in the criminal justice system is to determine how we can measure the effects of criminal justice outcomes on the community and of social processes on the criminal justice system. We have to ask whether the way we design economic, social, and political institutions adversely affects the sources and incidence of crime. In one sense, the criminal justice system cannot be adequately understood without a thorough examination of the extralegal order in which it exists.

The last witness for the prosecution finished his statement, rose from the witness chair, and walked back to the first row of the spectator section. His footsteps on the rough floor boards were loud in the quiet room. Hugo Blair, Citizens' Counsel, glanced down at his papers, looked briefly at the defense table, then turned to the bench.

"That closes the Citizens' case," he rasped. "I think we have proven beyond any doubt that the defendant, David Tasker, entered the combination store and living quarters of our pharmacist, Leon Jacoby, with intent to steal Jacoby's stock of the drug, dakarine. Jacoby discovered him, tried to reason with the thief, but Tasker stabbed Jacoby several times with a knife. Jacoby was killed instantly. Tasker then broke open a jar of dakarine, took most of the jar's contents, and, we presume, returned to his quarters. He was found there the following morning, wallowing in a dakarine-induced stupor, the blood-stained knife on his person. This horrible crime has removed from the community its only qualified pharmacist. It has . . ."

"Have you any more witnesses, Counselor?" Judge Hrdlicka asked sharply.

"No, sir, I have not . . ."

"You will stand down then, Counselor. I must remind you that the law says Counsel is instructed to present evidence, not comment on it." There was a brief pause, then Blair nodded jerkily and sat down at his table. "You've done very well in our first case, Mr. Blair," Hrdlicka continued easily. "Very well, indeed. Um. I hope your conduct will serve as a model for all future Citizens' Counsels."

Blair's narrow shoulders were hunched and he started down at his table, unmindful of the jury's vigorous nods of approval.

"Now," said Hrdlicka, "we'll hear from the defense. Counselor Giovannetti?"

Lisa Giovannetti arose. She still wore the skirt of her flight lieutenant's uniform but her primly cut blouse was made of recently milled new-world cloth, that dull produce of the plant popularly called the "cotton weed."

"I am faced with a severe problem . . ."

Her voice was almost inaudible.

"You'll have to speak louder, my dear," Hrdlicka said. "Remember, we're all new to this, so there's nothing for you to be embarrassed about."

"I'm sorry . . . I was saying that I have a problem. My—ah—my client has refused to give me any cooperation whatsoever. He just won't talk to me. And I have no witnesses, of course. Frankly, since the defendant won't take the stand—you know he has refused to plead one way or the other . . ." She paused, looked helplessly at the judge, then at Blair.

Dr. Pierre Malory leaned closer to Brandt Cardozo and said softly, "That's the drug, you know." Cardozo nodded, frowning. "Shouldn't really be on trial yet," he muttered.

"Um." Hrdlicka scowled at the defendant. "Refuses to say anything, eh? That does put you in a spot, Miss Giovannetti. Any ideas on the problem?"

"I—under other conditions—back home, that is . . . I suppose I would just throw my client on the mercy of the court. That's the correct phrase? But here—well, we have decided to do things differently. I'm glad . . . I think I will be right to leave everything up to the court—the way the court will operate according to our new penal code. . . ."

"Uh. You're just a little confused, Counselor, but I think I get your meaning. Yes . . ."

"I'm afraid I'm not a very eloquent counsel, Your Honor."

"But a wise one, my dear. Ahem!" Hrdlicka glared at the spectators. "I would remind all present that we are engaged in a very serious business! Um. Since our code makes provision for just such cases, we will accept the fact that Counselor Giovannetti offers no formal defense. Well." The old man leaned back in his chair and pushed his glasses up on his bald forehead. "Ladies and gentlemen of the jury, respected counsel, our penal code has left certain matters to our own discretion. After all, a committee of seven laymen, one steward and six passengers of a space liner, none of them skilled in legal problems, could hardly be expected to foresee every contingency. So it's up to us to establish precedent. Um. Now, our law says every criminal trial must be guided—and in a large sense, *resolved*—by the analyses of the accused by two officials of the court: the court psychiatrist and the state penologist."

He gestured at Brandt Cardozo and Dr. Malory.

"Both of these officials are present, of course. And this court is bound by their recommendations. But it isn't clear just *when* they should offer such recommendations. Now, it seems logical to me that any such, ah, intimate discussions are not in order if an accused person is judged not guilty. Um. That's the way I see it. How about you, Mr. Blair?"

"I certainly do not believe theoretical evidence should be allowed to affect a verdict."

"Miss Giovannetti?"

"Isn't the psychiatric evidence intended to guide the *sentence,* Your Honor? Not the verdict?"

"Right. How about the experts themselves? What do you think, gentlemen?"

Cardozo and Malory glanced at each other and Malory nodded.

"I think Miss Giovannetti has exactly defined our position, sir," said Cardozo. "So we think the order you suggest is the proper one."

"Good." Hrdlicka scratched his nose. Brandt Cardozo was sure the old boy wanted a cigar very badly. "Well. According to USN law, this would be the time for the judge to charge the jury. But this community, marooned on an unknown planet as we are, cannot consider itself one of the United Solar Nations. We have cut out the closing speeches by prosecution and defense attorneys so our judicial procedures won't be cluttered up with tear-jerking rantings about the grand old Solarian flag or the prisoner's dear old mother." The jury chuckled at this. "Further, we have expressly limited the scope of the judge's charge, so no jury will ever be improperly influenced by one man's opinions or— what's more likely—the state of one man's ulcers on one particular day." This time the jury laughed openly. "Or even by one man's attempts at humor," Hrdlicka blandly went on. "Now, much as I'd like to, I can't set any precedent on these lines, for the evidence presents no problems whatsoever. You've heard the testimony of your friends and neighbors, you've listened to the men you yourselves have made your protectors, your police. You've heard the Citizens' Defender say her client has refused to help her set up any kind of defense. Um. So, you'll leave the courtroom now and go and think about all that and reach your verdict. I know you'll do your duty. That's all I have to say."

The jury filed out the small side door, stood around in the afternoon sunshine and had a collective cigarette, filed in, and their foreman solemnly announced that they unanimously found David Tasker guilty of the robbery and murder of Leon Jacoby.

Brandt Cardozo had heard many juries deliver that awful verdict in the courtrooms of several planets. He had never seen anything like this. Now, in this bare room of raw boards that was designed as a Council Hall first and a courtroom second, there wasn't that long sigh shuddering over the audience as all concerned suddenly knew the tension was eased at last and the struggle for a man's life had ended in defeat.

There had been no tension. Eager curiosity, of course, for the spectators felt it was just as much their concern as the judge's, say, to discover how their brand-new laws would work. But there had been nothing to assail their nerves and their emotions, because nothing so tangible as death had been in the offing. Tasker's life or death had never been debated.

Brandt Cardozo glanced over at Tasker. The defendant leered at the jury. Open resentment of his contempt showed on the faces of some.

Hrdlicka muttered a "Thank you, ladies and gentlemen," rustled some papers, cleared his throat, and said, "Um. Well, we're on our own now. Lot of us had some experience with law—know I have with one kind of corporation law or another—so, up to now, we've known what to expect. But now . . . well, when we finally decided we were stuck on this world and had to make our own way, we decided we'd try some new ways of doing things. We're actually going to use one of those new methods right now. And while I'm not a particularly religious man, I say, 'God be with us.' " He looked musingly down at Tasker. The prisoner twiddled his thumbs. "The jury's decided the prisoner's guilty of murder. Only possible verdict, of course. Now, we're going to use our best brains to decide what to do with him . . . all right, I call on Dr. Pierre Malory."

"Well," breathed Malory, "here we go."

He walked over quickly and seated himself in the witness chair.

"Now, Doctor," Hrdlicka said, "I feel you should give your material as testimony. That is, subject to question from bench, counsel, or jury. I said, subject to *question*. Not challenge. Not debate." He flicked a sidelong glance at Hugo Blair. "No cross-examination. Only time we'll bother you is when you're usin' technical terms the rest of us don't follow. Now. Let's have your background. For the record."

"Yes, sir," Malory's voice was quietly purposeful. "I am Pierre

Malory, Doctor of Medicine. I was a passenger on the S. & G. liner, the *Tonia,* when it crashed on this planet. Since I was the only medical man among the survivors, I have served as the community's physician. Six months ago, we adopted a penal code to take care of problems of law and order. That code called for the services of a psychiatrist and, since we had no better trained man, I was elected to the job."

"We've been lucky to have you, Doctor. Now, you have examined the prisoner, David Tasker?"

"I have."

"For how long?"

"Since the day of his arrest, six days ago."

"Know anything about him before that?"

"Not on the ship. He was, I believe, a member of the engine maintenance crew and I, as a passenger, would not come in contact with him. In the year we have been here in the New World, I have had little time to take any note of him. I did treat him once."

"What for, Doctor?"

"Facial contusions. I believe he had been in a fight."

"I see. Well, now, suppose you give us the result of your official observations."

Pierre Malory stretched out his long legs, crossed them, moved his body sideways in his chair.

"It's going to be a difficult job, sir. For three reasons."

"Go ahead. Let's have them."

"First. I am definitely not what I hope my successors will be: a fully qualified specialist in mental disease. You all know I'm just a general practitioner. Second. I haven't had the time or the equipment to make any sort of analysis of the emotions, personality, attitudes of David Tasker. Lord! even if I had all the instruments I could possibly want, plus a complete staff of trained personnel, I couldn't begin an analysis in six days! And thirdly, the prisoner is obviously under the influence of the drug, dakarine."

"Well, Doctor, as to your first two reasons," said Hrdlicka, "we all know how little equipment was salvaged. And we all know how many lives you've saved with it in the past year. We're not worried about your qualifications; this court will take what you say as gospel. There'll be no argument, believe me. But maybe you'd better tell us about this dakarine."

"Dakarine is, briefly, an alkaloid derived from the dakar plant which was discovered on Centauri III. That plant is now grown under government supervision on all Earth-type planets. When used in minute quantities, dakarine has produced marvelous results in the treatment of all types of psychic shock. That is, if it is administered to a patient suffering anything from excessive grief to extreme catatonia, the patient's interest in the world about him is almost immediately restored to normal.

"However, the drug—like so many—has its dangers. It is habit-forming. It produces in its addicts a cheerful conviction that everything the addict wants to do is quite all right. Nothing the addict attempts will ever go wrong—*is* wrong." Malory straightened in his chair, leaned forward. "The prisoner Tasker is obviously still under the influence of the drug. His lack of interest in his predicament is full proof of that. And I don't know how long the effects of the dose he took will last, for the effect of a given quantity of the drug varies with the individual. And I don't know how much dakarine Tasker took or what his personal reaction to it is. I do know that Tasker, being full of dakarine, is a man incapable of any sort of cooperation with a psychiatrist."

Tasker sat impassive under the concerted gaze of the entire room.

"Just how do you mean?" asked Hrdlicka.

"To appraise the mind, we first evaluate the body. Tasker's in wretched physical condition. But his symptoms can be nothing more than those of prolonged use of dakarine. They probably are.

"Now, as to his mind. Naturally, he refused to give me any response to tests. I think I've managed to make a pretty fair guess at his IQ—it's average. About eighty-one Andrews, I should say. Perhaps point eleven Herwig-Dollheim, but that's just a guess. Right now, his personality is, must be, wholly false. He's wholly optimistic, crudely merry —to him everything's a joke, an obscene joke; he's completely self-righteous. He has no approach to problems because for David Tasker *there are no problems.*"

"It seems to me," Blair said coldly, "you don't give us much to go on."

"That is correct, Counselor. I haven't much to go on myself."

The jury glanced uneasily at each other. Hugo Blair tapped his table with a pen.

"Well, Doctor," Hrdlicka said, "what shall we do about it?"

"I don't think we can do anything until Tasker is completely free from the influence of the drug."

Blair jumped to his feet.

"I fail to see your reasoning," he snapped.

Malory was puzzled.

"I don't follow you," he said.

"I submit that, since Tasker was *not* under the influence of any drug when he committed the crime of murder, we have no right to take this business of drug addiction into our present consideration!"

Hrdlicka rapped his desk with his gavel.

"That's ridiculous, Counselor! The law calls for a thorough analysis of the accused; and even a layman like me can see that no analysis is possible if the accused is under the influence of any drug that affects his faculties. And I would like to point out to the entire court that the problem of murder has been settled. We're not concerned with that now, we're concerned with the problem of Tasker. Um. Dr. Malory, I'll take your suggestion for delay under advisement, unless you want me to act on it now?"

Malory hesitated, glanced quickly at Brandt Cardozo. Cardozo looked at Blair, still on his feet, and his mind raced. After a moment he made his decision. Settle it now, he said to himself, and shook his head very slightly.

"I rather think, Your Honor," Malory then said, "that you might hear Mr. Cardozo and then make your decision."

"Very well, Mr. Blair. I see you are still on your feet. Do you wish to address the court?"

"I wish to state that I, both as a citizen of this community and as an officer of this court, consider Dr. Malory's attempts at diagnosis wholly inadequate for the purposes of this trial!"

Hrdlicka opened his mouth, but Malory raised a hand.

"They are inadequate, sir," he said to Blair. His tone was gentle. "Perhaps I should give you my own feeling toward this man. My feeling—the feeling of a man who has practiced medicine for over twenty years—is that David Tasker is essentially a very unhappy person. He's inferior; all drug addicts feel inferior. He's frightened; all belligerent persons are frightened. I hope someday to learn why he's unhappy . . . frightened . . . belligerent. I hope to learn that for my good, for your good, as well as for Tasker's good."

"I think we understand that," grunted Hrdlicka. "Anything further, Doctor?"

"I believe not."

"We'll call Mr. Cardozo . . . if Mr. Blair will yield the floor to him." Scowling, Blair sat down.

"Nice going," Cardozo whispered as he passed Malory on the way to the witness stand.

"Now, Mr. Cardozo," said Hrdlicka, "our penologist. Or warden. We don't have much of a prison for you now, eh? But, as we redevelop the complexities of civilization, I suppose we'll have plenty of them. Um. Now, suppose you tell us just how you follow up Dr. Malory's work."

"Essentially, I investigate any accused as a social, rather than a psychiatric, case. And I try to combine Dr. Malory's findings with the limitations of the situation and set up means for rehabilitation."

"I see. You've an eye to the defendant's future, rather than to his past?"

"That's very well put, Your Honor."

"Well, ladies and gentlemen, for once we have a real expert to help us. Mr. Cardozo was a penologist by profession, associate warden at the maximum-security institution on Pluto. So, while we've been going by-guess-and-by-God so far, now we've got a gentleman who knows what he's talking about."

"Your Honor!" It was Blair again.

"Now what is it, Mr. Blair?"

"I'd like to ask the penologist one question."

"Is it relevant, Mr. Blair?"

"I think it is."

"All right, all right." The old man looked very weary.

Blair bustled up to the stand. Even seated, Brandt Cardozo was a head taller than the little man. "You and I were conversing in the bachelor lounge of the *Tonia* when it crashed," Blair rapped out. "Did you or did you not say to me at that time that you did not believe in prisons?"

Hrdlicka leaned over his desk so suddenly his glasses slid down over his nose again.

"Counselor!" he roared. "A conversation out of the past has nothing to do with this trial! You know that! Now, sit down before I order you to leave the court!"

"Your honor," said Brandt Cardozo, "I've no objection to answering that question . . . if Mr. Blair will let me finish my sentence, this time." He gazed tranquilly at the flushed counsel. "When you interrupted me back on the *Tonia*, sir, I recollect that I was about to say this: I do not approve of prisons as institutions for punishment. I most firmly believe in them as a means toward rehabilitation—if they are so devised."

"That's enough," rumbled Hrdlicka. "Mr. Blair knows the thinking behind our law and what's more, he knows you're a leading exponent of that thinking."

"Yes," sneered Blair, "we all know how bitterly Mr. Cardozo was opposed to capital punishment."

There are your fangs, thought Cardozo, bared at last.

"Sit down, Mr. Blair." Hrdlicka's voice was suddenly quiet.

Blair sat down, a smirk on his gnome's face.

"Now," Hrdlicka sounded his usual rumbling self. "What's your advice to this court, Mr. Cardozo?"

Brandt Cardozo sat relaxed in his chair, a rangy, big-shouldered man with a boyishly cheerful face.

"Sometime, sir," he said, "we'll have a large staff of penal experts. It will be a fairly simple job for the penologist to take the psychiatrist's findings, correlate them with those of his own staff, and be able to make a very accurate recommendation to the court. The penologist can set up a long-range program for the prisoner, defining exactly what is needed in the way of special training or treatment, medical care, minimum security confinement, maximum security . . ."

"Your Honor, I must ask your indulgence once more." Blair rushed on before Hrdlicka could stop him. "Mr. Cardozo, you used the expression 'maximum security.' Are we to presume you admit the need for such an institution?"

"Certainly. I'm afraid we'll need one for Tasker. For a while, at least. Any penologist, or criminologist if you prefer, will admit that we can't rehabilitate certain men and women. In other words, they're incurable. We get to them too late to help. To protect ourselves we must keep these persons locked up. And watch them pretty closely. Of course, we must try to make their confinement useful—useful to them and to society."

"Thank you," said Blair.

"Go on, Mr. Cardozo," said Hrdlicka.

"Your Honor, I can't get any help from Tasker either. I have talked to survivors of the crew about him. Of course, I must regard much of their talk as gossip. They think Tasker's papers were forged; they say he was lazy, a careless worker, a trouble-maker. They think Tasker has a criminal record. I'd say he probably has. At any rate, I'm going to regard him as such until both Dr. Malory and I can accumulate more detailed and accurate information about the man."

"Um. So what do we do with him?"

Brandt Cardozo felt the uneasy gaze of the audience on his back. He looked at the jury. They were frowning, worried.

"Well, sir, here's where we, as a society, meet our first challenge. A well-liked and most useful member of our community has been killed by a man whose worth to us is pretty dubious." Brandt Cardozo straightened his big shoulders. "We have decided we won't take the easy answer to such a problem—we won't shrug off the burden by killing the killer. Let's meet the challenge, then. First of all, hospitalize Tasker, under guard, of course, until Dr. Malory is satisfied Tasker's free of all dakarine effects. Then, let Dr. Malory work on him; I'm confident the doctor can very soon—once the man is his normal self—decide how to order his confinement so Tasker will have every chance for readjustment. There was a method of sentencing the mentally irresponsible in the System; such persons were detained during the pleasure of the court.

"I think you can do the same. Simply order David Tasker to be detained during the pleasure of this court—in the custody of the proper authorities. I would further suggest that you provide for periodic examinations of the prisoner by yourself, assisted by such citizens as you deem necessary—Mr. Blair, Miss Giovannetti—to determine any future disposal of his case. Eventually we can decide whether we can hope for rehabilitation or settle for perpetual confinement."

"Well . . . that makes very good sense to me. You may step down, Mr. Cardozo, and thank you."

Hrdlicka propped his elbows on his desk and rested his chin in his cupped hands. He stared somberly at the crowded room.

"The court's going to follow Mr. Cardozo's program," he rumbled. "But before I make it official, I'd like to say one or two things to all of you, as people of this planet we call the New World. I was on the committee that drew up our civil and criminal codes. I agreed to all the ideas that people like Mr. Cardozo wanted to incorporate into the laws. Voted for them. But I wasn't sure they'd work. I'm an old man and I guess my years have made me cynical. I thought if the pressure was on us, if ever, we'd all take the easy way out. Well, we haven't. I'm glad. Speaks damn well for our future."

He raised his head and dropped his hands flat on the desk.

"If it's agreeable to all concerned, I'll sentence the convicted defendant. Any objections, Miss Giovannetti?"

"Your Honor—I—I'm awfully proud . . . I think this court has done a great thing today . . ."

"Think so, too. D'ye agree, Mr. Blair? Oh . . . I see you've got something to say. Well, go ahead."

Hugo Blair had darted to his feet and stepped a pace away from his chair, so the spectators' view of him would not be blocked by his table.

"Trouble, Brandt," whispered Malory.

"I don't think so. Hrdlicka will handle him."

"Your Honor," rasped Blair, "I am officer of this court."

"So?"

"That means, sir, that I am obliged to speak out when this court fails to serve the interests of the people!"

"Yes, yes. Come to the point!"

Blair turned a little to one side so that, while seeming to face the bench, as was proper, he could still glance out at the spectators. He clasped his hands behind his back and thrust out his big head.

"Mr. Cardozo has beguiled a charitable people into decreeing that there shall be no capital punishment," he cried. "But I must ask you, all of you, what will you have in its stead?" He pointed at the grinning Tasker. "There sits our declared enemy. You have heard him pronounced a drug addict, a habitual criminal. He has already killed one of us. How many more of us will he slaughter whenever he gets bored with our coddling of him?"

"Blair!" roared Hrdlicka. He banged his gavel. "Sit down!" He raised his bulk half out of his chair. "I don't know what you're getting at, but we'll have no ranting by counsel in this court!"

"Ranting, sir? Is it ranting to ask that we stop and observe where the impractical schemes of weak men may lead us?"

"You're in contempt of this court, Counselor. That doesn't mean much—to me. But you're in contempt of the laws of your country and I won't stand for that!"

"Is it contempt to challenge a law that does not protect?"

"Ah, Judge, Your Honor . . ." the foreman of the jury, a sandy-haired, nervous man, raised a thin arm. "I think we have a right to ask Mr. Blair to tell us what he means."

"That's torn it," breathed Malory.

"If that blasted Tasker only realized what was happening to him," groaned Cardozo.

"Very well," growled Hrdlicka. "I'll let you answer the jury, Counselor."

"Thank you, sir." Blair's bow was generally in the jury's direction. "I'll be brief. Mr. Cardozo and Dr. Malory have given us some pretty generalities. Oh, they were sincere. I'm sure of that. But their words were generalities. I, on the other hand, am concerned solely with one, individual matter. The matter of David Tasker—murderer!"

"Mr. Hrdlicka!" Cardozo cried. "I object to that . . ."

"I will correct myself," Blair said smoothly. "Let me say that you are not concerned *solely* with the problem of David Tasker. But I am. For, you see, I wish to live in peace. And safety."

Blair paused, smiled thinly.

"Quiet, boy," murmured the doctor. "Don't argue with him."

"So I will confine myself to the problem of David Tasker," Blair went on. "Now, Mr. Cardozo has said that we should keep him in a sort of perpetual custody. A kindly procedure, but isn't it a bit impractical?" He was speaking directly to the audience now. "I trust that Dr. Malory will agree that he can't spend all his time with one patient. And you'll agree that you, yourself, can't personally guard one lone prisoner day and night, won't you, Mr. Cardozo? After all, we each of us have many different jobs that must be done if this community is to survive. Now, we don't have a prison as yet. Shall we stop all other building—hospital, school, sanitation system—to erect a jail for one worthless man?"

"Are you through?" Hrdlicka asked.

"Just one or two queries more. We have a very small policing force, because most of us are orderly men. So, if we follow the advice of our friends here, we, all of us, men, women—even the few children left to us—must always be on our guard to see that this *enemy* of ours doesn't break free from our weak restraint and, in his mad lust for his filthy drug, kill any of us that get in his way!"

Brandt Cardozo heard a confused muttering behind him. He turned. The spectators moved restlessly, huddling together, whispering. Some were staring at Tasker and their faces weren't pleasant to see. Cardozo arose.

"Your Honor," he said quietly, "I seem to be the principal target of Mr. Blair's wrath. May I remind him that I am acting according to law —the law he himself is sworn to uphold."

"Not necessarily. Mr. Blair doesn't have much regard for law. A matter I'll take up with the Council. Now, Blair, you've done a neat job of stirring us up, so sit down and be quiet."

The muttering among the spectators grew louder.

"There'll be order in this court!" roared Hrdlicka.

He waited.

The muttering did not subside.

The jury foreman coughed.

"Seems to us, the jury, that is," he was embarrassed but stubborn, "there's a lot in what he says. We ain't blaming Mr. Cardozo any— but, well, I guess we don't see how that—the prisoner can be kept locked up so that the rest of us are safe."

"That's our problem!" snapped Cardozo. "We've got to face it! And I, for one, am ready to face it! Your Honor, I wish to go on public record that I assume full responsibility for Tasker's safe custody."

"Very commendable," sneered Blair. "And after Tasker's next killing, you will send us your regrets, Mr. Cardozo?"

Someone in the back of the room stumbled to his feet and cried, "Now, look . . ."

"Silence!" roared Hrdlicka.

For the moment they all obeyed him.

"Now," said the old man, "this is your court and I'm your judge. We're here to carry out your laws. *Your* laws, remember! So let's get on with it. And no more nonsense!"

"Is it nonsense to want to protect ourselves?" cried Blair.

No muttering now, but a loud chorus of agreement.

"Look, Judge," said the foreman of the jury. The hubbub died down. "I don't know how to say it legal, but the jury thinks that, well, Tasker ought to be kicked out. And . . ." he fumbled and the juror next to him plucked his sleeve. They whispered together. "Yeah. And we want it on record that we think so." He sat down.

"But that won't do," purred Hugo Blair. "Really it won't. Suppose we do exile this fellow. Then what? Out in the hills he lurks—mad, hungry—more desperate than ever. We, in our valley, must patrol our homes both day and night. Yet, in the darkness, our few sentries will be easy enough to evade. So, we bar our doors and windows. Children are kept close to home. We huddle together. We are afraid . . . afraid of one man."

And someone in the back of the room yelled, "So kill the son of a bitch!"

Blair smiled.

Hrdlicka rose to his feet and stood, a massive, brooding figure.

"Mr. Blair," he rumbled, "I have mentioned before I am going to report your conduct to the Council. That's all I have to say to you." He looked contemptuously at the jury. "Long ago we decided that we were going to settle down on this planet and live ordered lives. Which means you can't cook up laws on the spur of the moment. You already have laws on your statute books. Those laws provide penalties for this prisoner and I am going to impose them now! David Tasker, stand up!"

Which was a mistake. Brandt Cardozo realized that immediately. The shambling figure of Tasker gave them a focus, a personification for their fear.

Some of them yelled. Hrdlicka beat on his desk with his gavel, but it was no use. Finally, somebody—probably the man who had first cried "Kill!"—started down the aisle. As Brandt Cardozo moved out to block the man, he caught a glimpse of Hugo Blair. Blair was staring at the running man and, to Cardozo's surprise, the little man was no longer smiling.

As the fellow burst among them, Cardozo reached out for him, but the other brushed on by. "Come on!" the man screamed at Blair, "let's get him now."

Blair's eyes bulged under his shaggy brows and he faltered a step backward.

"Guard!" bellowed Hrdlicka. "Arrest that man!"

Lisa Giovannetti stumbled out of her chair. The man tried to avoid her, bumped into her, and knocked her to the floor. The man stopped and looked down at her.

Cardozo saw that Blair was trembling.

"Is this what you wanted, Mr. Blair?" he asked softly.

Lisa Giovannetti tried—not very hard—to get up.

Brandt Cardozo moved swiftly over to the man, grabbed his arm, and swung him around. "Get out of here," Cardozo said clearly but not loudly, "or I'll knock you down."

The other looked at Cardozo, then down at Lisa Giovannetti. He jerked his arm free and stumbled up the aisle. People moved out of his way. Cardozo helped Lisa Giovannetti to her feet.

"Nice going," he whispered, then in normal tones he asked, "Are you hurt?"

"No . . . just awfully scared."

Brandt Cardozo looked up at Hrdlicka. The old man stood, shoulders sagging. He looked very tired.

"Your Honor," Cardozo said, "we all seem to have forgotten ourselves. I respectfully suggest you adjourn this court until we . . ."

"Until we stop acting like silly, hysterical children?" Hrdlicka rasped. "I agree. I'm ashamed. Deeply ashamed. I—never mind, court's adjourned."

There was shuffling of feet, a few started out, but most of them didn't move. They stood, uneasy, watching Hugo Blair.

The little man had recovered his poise.

"I agree with Your Honor that violence will not solve the questions raised by this trial," he said. "But I am sure that an immediate, *public* session of the Council will solve them."

He stalked up the aisle and the people followed him, clustering close, jabbering, nodding their heads. Hrdlicka watched them as the room slowly cleared.

"All right," he said at last. "Guard, take the prisoner back to his cell. By the side door."

"That man is definitely under the influence of some kind of drug," muttered Hrdlicka.

Pierre Malory sighed. Hrdlicka stepped ponderously off his crude platform and joined the little group.

"Well, lads," he smiled without mirth at Cardozo and Malory, "there goes your fancy, progressive penal code. No capital punishment, eh?" He gestured toward Lisa Giovannetti. "One of you had better take this girl home."

"No," she said. "I'm quite all right. Really. I wasn't a bit hurt, you know."

"But you lay there—well, I'll be damned!" He beamed at her.

"She's a smart girl," grinned Cardozo. "Her little act stopped the lynching, Anthony."

"What's going to happen now?" asked the girl.

"Oh," said Hrdlicka, "that little bastard Blair will get what he wants. He'll make his point in Council just like he did today. Better get ready for a full-dress execution, Brandt, my boy."

"What has he got against you, Brandt?" asked Lisa Giovannetti. "He —he was positively venomous toward you."

"It's not me he hates," said Brandt Cardozo. "It's what I stand for."

"But they won't listen to him—they won't kill Tasker!"

"Sure they will," Cardozo nodded. "History bears him out. You see, primitive man couldn't run the risk of keeping his criminals alive . . ."

"But we're not primitive!"

"We've reverted. Under the excuse of necessity, of course. We just haven't got the facilities, you see! Perhaps later, when everything is lovely a few years from now. Ha! We'll never take the first step. There'll always be a Blair around to point out the difficulties . . . *and* the dangers."

They started for the door, walking slowly. Hrdlicka put a hand on Cardozo's shoulder.

"If you live as long as I have, Brandt, you'll just about lose all faith in human beings. They'll cause you nothing but grief." He patted the younger man's shoulder. "Blair . . . wish I knew what makes the little bastard tick."

"Oh," replied Cardozo, "that's simple. I found that out during the debates on our constitution and laws. It's fear. He doesn't like or trust his fellow man, so he's afraid of him . . ."

Anthony Hrdlicka walked slowly down the dim street of the village, headed toward the river. The old man's shoulders were bowed and he puffed jerkily at the cigar clenched between his teeth. One of the planet's two little moons was already high in the sky, shining bravely among constellations uncharted, unknown. Hrdlicka picked his way easily enough along the pebbled path that took over when the street ended.

He passed the towering hulk of the *Tonia*. It was empty now and would stay where it had rammed into the alien soil, a leaning tower of gleaming alloy. As time passed, its former passengers would cut away its metal as they needed it and, unless they found usable ores, one day there would be nothing left of the *Tonia* but a tribal memory.

The path ended at the crude wharf they had built at the river's edge. Hrdlicka walked past a storage shed to the edge of the wharf, sat down and swung his legs over the edge. There he sat, chin in hands, elbows on knees, and stared somberly at the quiet water.

After a while he muttered, "Damn fools!"

The Council had met that afternoon. The old man grinned briefly at the memory of the battle he and Brandt Cardozo had waged before the final vote had beaten them down. Cardozo, he thought, was a damn good man . . . he would have been a great help to Hrdlicka back . . . back in those great days that would never come again. Why, and the old man's eyes lighted up as he remembered, there was that time he'd had the big fight with the government over the ownership of certain mines in Sirius III. He could have used a man like Cardozo in that deal—except Cardozo, the young romantic, would have been on the government's side. Which was all right, too, the USN lads had been a bunch of bright, tough-minded kids. Not like today's hysterical sheep, blatting after Hugo Blair. . . .

He scowled at the gurgling water.

And felt a brief, sharp pain under his left shoulder. Hrdlicka waited and the pain went away. He knew it would come again and again. After all, he was seventy-three. And one day they'd dig another hole in the little cemetery where most of the crew and officers of the *Tonia* now rested and . . . what would he be leaving?

He was a little surprised at himself. That he should be concerned with the brave new laws of a huddle of castaways when he had, well, not broken but certainly evaded the laws of a confederation of sixteen planets! And why should he, Anthony Hrdlicka, be worked up over the coming death of a miserable wretch who was no good to anyone? Hrdlicka's cigar had gone out, but he still puffed at it. With his usual harsh realism he began to examine the situation and himself.

There was a scuffling sound behind him and he turned, alert and wary. This planet had evidenced no intelligent life—yet. A tall figure moved cautiously out of the shadows of the shed. Hrdlicka heard the mutter of a voice and called out, "Who's there?"

The tall shadow moved closer, then spoke. "Is that Hrdlicka?"

"Yes." He squinted, then grinned broadly. "Why, it's Brandt! Welcome to the mourner's bench, lad!"

Brandt Cardozo moved nearer. Hrdlicka saw that he was frowning.

"What are you doing here?" Cardozo said.

"Came down to get away from a bunch of goddam fools. Come on, boy, sit down and have a smoke. You know, we better find some kind of tobacco weed on this place or there's going to be a lot of nervous wrecks soon. I'm down to my last case of cigars myself."

"No. No, thanks." Cardozo walked to the edge of the wharf and looked quickly up and down the river. "Have you seen anyone around here?" he asked.

"No. Why?"

"Ah, never mind." Cardozo paused, then, still not looking at Hrdlicka, said, "You plan to be here much longer? It's—it's getting cool, you know."

Hrdlicka peered up at him.

"What's on your mind, son?" he asked quietly. Cardozo did not answer. Hrdlicka snapped his fingers. "I know! *I'm* the goddam fool! You're worryin' about the execution."

"There'll be no execution."

"Eh? What did you say?"

"I said, there will be no execution!"

Hrdlicka scrunched backward until his feet were on the wharf. Then, with considerable grunting, he hauled himself erect. He stood, hands on hips, staring at Brandt Cardozo. He took the cold cigar from his mouth and tossed it into the river.

"You'd better explain yourself, boy."

Brandt Cardozo still looked out at the river.

"There'll be no execution because I won't stand for it. You might as well know I've got Tasker over there in the shed. I'm taking him down the river on a cotton-weed raft."

"Well . . . I'll be—"

Brandt Cardozo half turned and gazed steadily at the old man.

"There's no use arguing," he said coldly.

"I'm not going to argue. I assume you know what you're doing."

"I do. I know that these people," he jerked a hand back toward the sleeping village, "took a look at their future and made one of the best codes man has ever dreamed up in his nine-thousand-year history. Today, these same people got scared—and the ape scampered back up the tree."

"You know," Hrdlicka grunted, "sometimes I think you make too many speeches."

"Could be." Cardozo took a step toward the shed. "Better get out of here, Anthony. There'll be hell to pay in the morning. And when our Mr. Blair gets his mob organized, you'll be the first one he goes after. I don't want you bothered for my . . . crimes."

"You're really leaving?"

"Certainly. I've got to stick with the poor devil until the drug wears off. And anyway . . ." Brandt Cardozo shrugged and took another step toward the shed.

"In my time," Hrdlicka said, moving with him, "I got a lot of things done. And I got them done by cutting my losses sometimes and starting in all over again."

"Please get going, Anthony. I must be on my way and I don't want to get rough with you."

"Is it that you can't take the idea of—of—well, executing the fellow?"

"Look, my friend!" Cardozo grabbed Hrdlicka by an arm and swung him around. They faced each other. "The first warden of the Pluto house hated executions. Whenever he could, he'd pass the dirty business on to me, as the next in rank. In my time I've supervised the legal killing of some thirty men and two women. Now, leave or stay, whichever you like, but don't interfere."

He stalked over to the shed.

"Come on out, Tasker," Brandt Cardozo said. "And keep it quiet."

Hrdlicka opened his mouth, closed it, and walked away. Tasker slouched out of the shed, bundles in his arms. Brandt Cardozo stood still, listening to the sound of Hrdlicka's feet on the rough planks of the platform. He waited until the sound changed as Hrdlicka reached the pebbled path. Then he walked into the shed and picked up another bundle. When he came out, Tasker stood at the edge of the landing, grinning.

"We'll take the downstream raft," Cardozo said. "Jump aboard and I'll hand the stuff down to you."

Tasker squatted and looked down.

"It's a big jump, pal. Better give me a hand."

"All right, but hurry!"

"No hurry, chum. We got all the time in the world."

Brandt Cardozo stopped, his arm half extended to the condemned man.

"Don't you really know what we're doing?" he asked softly.

"You said we was making a break. You seem to be taking it okay. So what?"

"But don't you know why, really?"

Tasker shrugged.

"You're a queer boy," he said. "One minute you say rush it, the next you stop to do a lot of gabbing. Okay by me. Whatever you want."

"Never mind," Brandt Cardozo said. "Give me your hand."

They clasped hands and Tasker swung his legs out over the bobbing raft. Cardozo braced, Tasker let go with his other hand and landed on the raft. Cardozo let go and saw Tasker sway, then spread his feet wide apart. In a moment Tasker had his balance and stood secure on the wobbly raft.

Brandt Cardozo picked up a bundle. He had gathered together as few essentials as possible, a rough first-aid kit, some food concentrates, a few extra clothes. He himself was armed with a handgun and two knives. Later, when the man was more his normal self, Cardozo planned to give Tasker a knife. He had not looked into the future beyond that.

Cardozo tossed one bundle down, Tasker caught it, dropped it in the center of the raft. Another bundle was passed.

"Lay them carefully, damn it!" Cardozo snapped.

"Okay, okay."

Cardozo had picked up the last bundle when he heard a voice call softly, "Brandt! Oh, Brandt!"

He let go the bundle and drew his gun. A man came toward him across the landing and he saw that it was Pierre Malory. Brandt Cardozo did not lower his gun.

"Take it easy, Malory," he said.

Malory came closer. He was smiling.

"I'm alone, Brandt. I don't plan to start anything, so you can put the gun away."

Brandt Cardozo did not move.

"Hrdlicka came to me," Malory went on in a conversational tone. "When he told me your plan, I thought I'd come along and say good-by." He glanced down at the raft. "Ah, Tasker. How are you feeling?"

"Fine. How else?"

"You won't feel that way much longer, I think. Brandt, I don't believe you know the symptoms of withdrawal. Morbid depression accompanied by extreme fatigue. He won't be much good to you for some time. For just how long, I don't know."

"Please go," Brandt Cardozo said flatly.

"Very well. But I did want to say good-by, Brandt, and wish you luck."

"Psychology, eh!"

"Not at all. It would do you no good. When the thoughtful, contemplative type, like you, finally breaks into violent action, nothing can stop it during the period of such action."

"I'm glad you realize that. Here you go, Tasker."

Gun still in his right hand, he picked up the last bundle and tossed it down to the waiting Tasker. Then he went over to the mooring chain.

"Hell! I forgot this was locked!" He hesitated a moment, fingering the chain, then turned to look at Malory. "I'm going to burn this lock, Pierre. If you try anything, I'll . . ."

"I won't try anything!" Malory sounded exasperated. "Go ahead, burn the lock. But don't get so wound up that you forget your manners. Hrdlicka was hurt that you had no word for him. That tough old man is very fond of you, Brandt."

"He left before I—oh, the devil with it! Tell the old guy cheerio for me, Pierre. You too, guy."

"I will. Mind telling me your plans?"

When Cardozo hesitated, Malory smiled and said, "I'll tell them to Hugo Blair first thing in the morning!"

"I'm sorry. We'll just float down the river as far as we want to, I guess. Then, fish and hunt, live as best we can. I don't think anyone will chase us. It's the cotton season and they'll need the raft. We should learn something about this planet, eh?"

"Let me know when you guys finish your gab," Tasker remarked and sat down on the logs of the raft.

"Shut up, you!" Cardozo barked.

He turned back to Malory. "You don't approve," he challenged.

"It's not that," Malory said thoughtfully. "It's something like watching another doctor treat a patient. His treatment is not what I, myself, would prescribe but, on the other hand, I realize it may work. So, it's not for me to say anything."

"I'm not treating anyone!"

"Oh." Malory thrust his hands in his pockets and gazed down at the planks. "I thought you were," he said after a while.

"What the devil do you mean?"

"I thought you were treating our community. For hysteria."

"To hell with our community! I'm saving a man's life!"

"Hrdlicka was right, then. You know, I'm convinced that old gentleman is *never* wrong. Well, cheerio."

Hands still in his pockets, Pierre Malory turned his back to Cardozo.

"Wait!" Brandt Cardozo cried.

Malory paused, looked over his shoulder.

"You'd better move, Brandt. The night's getting on."

"Tell me what you mean first!"

"It's simple enough. This town's temporarily sick. I'd diagnose its ailment as an acute case of Blair poisoning. Isn't it up to you to give it an antidote?"

"Up to me! I'm finished with that bunch of idiots! You heard them at the Council meeting!"

"I did. There were some extremists, of course."

"Yes, indeed there were! And how about the others. I suppose you approve of them?"

"I don't. Their behavior was abnormal. It was also fairly orderly. And quite legal."

"Legal? My dear doctor, do you consider it legal to sentence a man to death under an *ex post facto* law?"

"You have me there, Brandt. Yet . . . don't forget this is a frontier, and frontier people seldom bother to make the effort our community made today. Legally, Tasker can't die and you and I know it. But a majority of the people have condemned him, so die he must."

"Majority! A bunch of frantic cows mooing after a mad bull!"

"You're shouting, Brandt."

"I—sorry."

Brandt Cardozo drew a deep breath. He looked down at his hands. They were shaking and sweaty. He was surprised to see that he still held his gun. He quickly thrust it into his holster.

"I apologize, Pierre. Thought I'd done all my shouting this afternoon."

A loud snore came up from the raft.

Brandt Cardozo gasped, then ran back and looked over the wharf's edge.

"Christ!" he breathed. "He's asleep! Tasker's gone to sleep, Pierre!"

"Why not? Right now Tasker is incapable of worry."

They were quiet for a moment. The rhythmic snoring sounded over the soft murmur of the river.

"You'd better get going," Malory said. "Somebody just might hear that." He took a step. "Oh. By the way, Brandt. You did leave a message for the Council? Your resignation, that sort of thing?"

"No, I did not!" Brandt Cardozo said defiantly. "I owe them nothing! I'm leaving them—I'm going to save Tasker's life and be damned to them!"

"Very well. I shall make whatever explanations I see fit."

"When? To whom?"

"Tomorrow morning. To Blair, most likely. He'll take over completely, for Hrdlicka and I—as your supporters—will be discredited, of course. And strongly suspected of helping Tasker escape. Ah, well . . . Anthony can handle his problems and I'll try to manage mine."

"You think I'm letting you down," Cardozo muttered.

"My dear fellow, it doesn't matter what I think."

Brandt Cardozo licked his sweaty lips.

"Don't go," he said thickly.

"Why not?"

"I want you to help me get Tasker back to his cell. Will you?"

"Why?"

"I'm not sure . . ."

"It's no good if you're just doing it for Hrdlicka or for me. Or for yourself."

"Well, who the hell else would I do it for?"

Malory gestured briefly.

"For all of us."

"For Tasker, too?"

"I'm sorry—terribly sorry, but Tasker doesn't matter any more. Really he doesn't, Brandt."

"Damn it, Pierre . . . all right, you're my doctor. Help me."

Pierre Malory searched his pockets for a cigarette, found one, and lit it. He smoked slowly as a man does who smokes solely for taste and not for nervous sustenance.

Finally he said, "I honestly can't help you, Brandt. You are the doer now."

"Blast it!" Cardozo strode to the edge and frowned down at the snoring Tasker. "I was doing something. Doing it for Tasker."

"No."

"Eh?"

"You were doing it for none other than Brandt Cardozo! The emotional, embittered Brandt Cardozo."

"Now, look—oh. I see . . ."

"Tasker was Blair's scapegoat. Tasker was Brandt Cardozo's excuse."

"For acting the fool!"

"Not precisely the fool. Put it in reverse. Tasker was your excuse for *not* acting as Brandt Cardozo, the penologist, the responsible servant of the people of the New World."

"I tried that. And lost."

"Well, then, cut your losses."

"The old man said that. I don't know . . . I don't believe in capital punishment, Pierre. It just doesn't do any good. I told the people that. And they listened—until that damned Blair . . ."

"Tell them again."

"A voice crying in the wilderness? Not me."

"That's the voice that won't rephrase its message. Tell the people in another way."

"Another way? What do you mean?"

"I am treating a patient. Sometimes I soothe him. Sometimes I reason with him. And once in a while I bawl the hell out of him! But all the time I am saying the same thing to him. Over and over. In different ways."

Brandt Cardozo stood for a time, looking down at the raft where Tasker lay sprawled on his back. After a while he nodded.

"Ever see an execution, Pierre?" Cardozo's voice was very cold.

"No."

"You will. Now—please help me get Tasker back to his cell."

"Certainly." Malory looked curiously at his friend. "What are you going to do now, Brandt?"

"I'm going to treat my sick community, Dr. Malory. This time, I'm going to try shock treatment . . ."

The four-man procession reached the end of the corridor and stopped. Brandt Cardozo's physical eyes saw the halt and jerked his mind back to the present.

"Open the door," he ordered. "Go on out into the yard."

Tasker's cell had been a small room in the one permanent structure they had yet built, their warehouse. The guard Vanni opened the big door and the four men moved out into the loading yard.

At the far end of the yard stood a bark-covered, newly sawed post about six feet high. Ten feet from it stood five men with flame rifles.

Several yards behind them, in ragged rows, stood some fifty-odd members of the community.

As they marched to the post, Brandt Cardozo checked the silent witnesses. Hrdlicka stood calm in the first row, the sandy-haired jury foreman beside him. Arrayed on either side of those two were members of the jury and at the extreme end away from the post was Lisa Giovannetti.

Cardozo's eyes narrowed. A man slipped furtively into the first row and stood, eager eyes flickering from Tasker to the post and back again. Brandt Cardozo sighed. There was always at least one of those, . . . Always a twisted sadist, savoring another human's terror and death.

Cardozo shrugged. Perhaps even that would help. Make it even worse for the others.

For this was his shock treatment . . . a *public* execution.

When the Council had revoked the law forbidding the death penalty, and instituted capital punishment, it had hastily decreed that all details of an execution should be left to the discretion of the penologist.

So Brandt Cardozo had ordered that all officials of the sentencing court should be present at any execution . . . as well as no less than thirty-five members of the public. He further stipulated that any other adult resident of the community could attend if he or she so desired.

His smile faded.

"Halt!" he barked. Tasker's escort stopped. They were very near the post. Brandt Cardozo strode over to the witnesses. "Where's Citizens' Counsel Blair?" he snapped.

Heads turned. There were a few whispers. Feet shuffled. The whispering grew into an audible murmur.

"I requested all required court officers to be assembled at least twenty minutes before the time for execution," Cardozo rapped out.

"Blair doesn't seem to be present," Hrdlicka murmured.

"Ah." Brandt Cardozo's voice was loud but level. "The Citizens' Counsel apparently wishes to evade the responsibilities of his office. But this execution will not proceed without him!"

He turned toward the firing squad.

"Grover!" he shouted. A rifleman detached himself from the group and ran up to Cardozo.

"Yes, sir?"

"Go at once to Counselor Blair's quarters and bring him here. On the double! You are to use force if necessary."

Grover saluted and ran off. Cardozo stared hard at the witnesses.

"The execution of David Tasker will be delayed for but a few moments," he announced. No one spoke.

Brandt Cardozo walked over to Tasker's group.

Tasker jerked his head up and looked around him.

"Hey!" His voice was uncertain, worried. "What's going on here?"

Malory's eyebrows went up.

"What's going on, I said!"

"You are about to die by shooting for the murder of Leon Jacoby," Cardozo said quietly. "As soon as the Citizens' Counsel arrives, I will read you the death warrant."

"Death warrant!"

Tasker screamed.

Then he struggled violently and, for a moment, broke loose from Vanni's grip. Jerking McCann with him, he staggered toward Brandt Cardozo.

"You said . . ." he screamed. "You said—they wasn't gonna be no choke-seat! No gas!"

Malory moved, but Vanni was before him. The guard regained his grip on Tasker's arm and helped McCann pull the writhing man to a stop.

"Take it easy, fella," Vanni panted. "That's no good."

"Don't kill me!" Tasker babbled. "You said they was no killings—please—I want an appeal—you got no right—it's against the law . . ."

"I told you yesterday that the law had been changed. And made retroactive."

"I was doped. Oh, my God . . ."

"It will be quick and painless," said Brandt Cardozo. "Please try to calm yourself."

"Please, please, please . . ."

Hrdlicka stepped forward from his line.

"Brandt! Can't you do something?"

McCann and Vanni were now wrestling with the screaming Tasker. Despite his handcuffs the condemned man was battling furiously, hunching his shoulders and lunging bull-like in every direction. And all the while he screamed.

"Prisoners sometimes become violently hysterical when death gets this close to them, Your Honor," Cardozo said.

"It's more than that," said Malory. "The dakarine has worn off."

"But can't you do *something?*" asked Hrdlicka. "My God! This—this is dreadful!"

"I don' wanna die!" yelled Tasker. He broke completely free from his guards and flung himself on the ground at Cardozo's feet. "Please," he babbled. "You got no right—I shouldn't have to die—save me! I'll be a nice guy, I'll work hard . . ."

Brandt Cardozo fought hard against pity for the groveling wretch. "Do something!" roared Hrdlicka.

"I was afraid of this," Malory said. "I brought along a sedative. If the penologist permits . . ."

Cardozo felt all eyes upon him. He looked down at Tasker, pretended to think a moment, then nodded. He felt rather than heard a gusty sigh of relief.

The guards hauled Tasker to his feet again and managed to hold him quiet while Dr. Malory administered a hypodermic. Tasker groaned loudly, then went limp. His head bobbled and his knees buckled. His whole body leaned forward a little as the two guards held him upright.

At that moment Blair trotted in, the guard Grover a pace behind him, his rifle aimed at Blair's back.

"What's the meaning of this?" cried the little man. He pranced up to Brandt Cardozo. "I shall report this outrage; this man broke into my room—menaced me with a gun . . ."

"Mr. Blair! Lower your voice! You are in the presence of a man about to die!"

"Uh—" Blair wilted.

"You were required to attend this execution, Mr. Blair!" Cardozo's voice was not loud, but harsh. "Your absence has distressed all concerned. Now, take your place among the witnesses so that we can get this business over with."

"I was indisposed," Blair bridled. "Furthermore, I will not be driven about at gunpoint!" He saw Tasker. "What's he doing? More dramatics?"

"Oh. I should brief you on what has occurred, Mr. Citizens' Counselor. The condemned man was frightened into hysteria and Dr. Malory gave him a sedative. He's unconscious. Doesn't know what's about to happen to him. It doesn't matter, of course."

"But it does!" Blair shrilled. "The condemned must . . ."

A loud, disjointed cry from the witnesses cut him off. Brandt Cardozo raised his hand. The crowd quieted. Hrdlicka very ostentatiously stepped back into line.

"Grover," Cardozo said.

"Yessir?"

"If Counselor Blair does not take his proper place among the witnesses—immediately—you will put him there."

Blair got very pale. He looked at Cardozo, then at the slumped Tasker. From Tasker his gaze flickered to the stark post. His pallor became a little greenish. Then he hurried over to the watching group. Two jurors gave him plenty of room.

"Take your place with the squad, Grover," Cardozo ordered. "All right, Vanni, McCann, let's go."

They walked Tasker over to the post and strapped him to it. He leaned stiffly forward, straps bracing him at his knees, waist and shoulders.

Cardozo stepped in front of him and lifted the death warrant. It had been scribed on a sheet of notepaper by the one battered portable they had salvaged and it wasn't easy to read.

He finished it as rapidly as he could and moved back and to one side.

"The sentence of death will now be carried out," he said loudly. "Ready!"

The squad lifted their rifles.

"Aim.

"Fire."

There was a hiss of blue flame. Tasker's dirty shirt smoked suddenly, his body jerked and he slumped even more.

Cardozo and Malory walked over to the post. The doctor put fingers to Tasker's wrist. After an endless moment he took them away. His face was very white, but his voice was steady.

"I pronounce this man dead," he said.

There was a dull thud behind them. Malory and Cardozo jerked their heads around and saw Hugo Blair lying on the ground, face downward. Malory moved uncertainly.

"It's all right," a juror called out. "He's only fainted."

"The moral of that should be obvious," Cardozo whispered to Malory. Then he turned and addressed the crowd. "The execution of David Tasker has been carried out as prescribed by the law of the New World. You will please leave the place of execution immediately, in a quiet and orderly manner."

They started toward the yardgate, walking fast. One or two stared down at the prostrate Blair. One man suddenly put his hand to his mouth, gazed wildly about him, then ran for the gate.

No one laughed at him.

No one said anything, but Brandt Cardozo saw that none of them stepped near the unconscious Blair as they walked by him.

Part II

THE CRIMINAL JUSTICE PROCESS

4 A Jury Not of Peers

by Pg Wyal

Human beings now judge human beings in the criminal justice process. We know that humans are subject to prejudice, emotion, instability, error, and other similar frailties. Would there be any difference in the quality of judgment if it were done by machines? "A Jury Not of Peers" by Pg Wyal concerns an advanced civilization which has built a "judging machine" to improve the judgment process in the criminal justice system. To have an emotionless machine, incapable of lying or of having feelings, and dedicated only to the search for truth and honesty seems to be an answer to a utopian criminal justice system. It certainly seems to be the answer to achieving "equal justice before the law."

Achieving equal justice before the law implies two radically different approaches. Either everyone in society must be made equal before the law or the machinery of justice must be constructed in order to provide equal responses to persons who are essentially unequal. Certainly, an individual's ability to cope with the criminal justice system varies in terms of racial status, political power, and, most importantly, financial ability.

Judgment about the fate of an individual who enters the criminal justice process by being identified as a criminal comes *after* a series of steps have been completed; for example, arrest, bail, trial, and appeal. One's *ultimate* fate largely depends on the ability to acquire and keep the best available attorneys, to hire competent investigators, and so on. Given these hard realities, the procedures in the machinery of justice have been formulated so as to maximize the probability of equal response to individuals. However, these procedures—because they are rigorous and complex and because they have built-in safeguards —easily foster a situation in which the most privileged are able to "beat the system."

Judgment—especially about behavior and actions that violate the norms and laws of a society—is an integral part of the ethos of a civilization. In earliest times, judgment about the "guilt" of a person considered to have been a violator of society's rules was closely tied to religious ideas and beliefs. Supernatural phenomena were "consulted" for the purpose of determining the fate of individuals. Signs from "gods," sometimes interpreted by shamans and witch doctors, were sought. In some cases, the individual was put through a variety of tests. "Trial by fire" was commonplace. If one was not burned by fire—whether it meant being staked to a pole or walking on hot embers, the procedure varying from culture to culture but the purpose remaining the same—the unharmed individual was exonerated and pronounced "fit" to return to society. In more recent times, particularly during the Middle Ages, "trial by combat" or by "ordeal" was a common method for adjudicating the innocence or guilt of a person.

Determining innocence or guilt, and truth or falsity was a process thought important enough to be taken out of the prerogatives and hands of human beings. An "objective," "outside" source of judgment was continually searched for. Indeed, judgment was considered divinelike. Attempts to refine and perfect judgment occupy much of a civilization's energies. Advances in the development of modern "calculating machines" imply advancements in the judging process. "Computer" judges are not beyond the realm of possibility in our lifetime. What are the costs and benefits of such technology in the improvement of the criminal justice system?

'Neath triple suns on jungle earths, the man ran. The crime was murder, and the fear was great, and he slashed through stinking jungles with the weapon with which he had slayed, smeared with filth and blood, cursing the hand of the fate he could not name. The man was hot and cold and sick and drunk with fatigue, blind with frozen fear and forgotten hate. In an aimless frenzy, he ripped through mud and snarling weeds, sloshed through rivers like tentacles and climbed hills like nests of ants. The man screamed, at nothing; the man cried, for what he had done and what it had done to him. The man ran and ran, going nowhere as fast as he could.

Unseen eyes examined him, unnamed fears pursued him. There had been a bar, and something about a woman, and maybe a quart of bitter tequila (perhaps laced with methyl alcohol), somewhere in a muggy jungle town. In a tin and clapboard quonsit hut, the man had gotten drunk and stumbled into a bloody fight over a company whore. A lieutenant from the trading company had said something about him, a slurred remark concerning mendicants and girls. "A whore's a bankrupt investment," the blond officer derided. "She's a slimy hole and nothing more, and every bitch knows she's just a dog. But with a man, you have to show him the papers of indention before he knows he's dirt." The memory was not precise; it hovered around him like a horde of buzzing flies, only the eidetic ikon of his hate and fear, released in one crimson swipe of the machete. Now he did not know nor care, but scrambled through slimy leaves and vines, seeking to bury himself forever in the fetid jungle. Through twisting plants, surrounded by a steam of hate, the man ran and ran.

Until he could run no more. Fatigue settled like an empty barrel in his chest, lodged like a bloated body in his belly. He had run for three days, through the angry forest, hunted and surveyed by searching eyes he knew were there, but could not see. He felt them peeping at him in his fireless night, turned around bug-eyed to see—nothing—as he crawled along in the unrelenting sun-blast, and heard them cackling to themselves just out of sight in the underbrush . . . or bubbling like sinister molluscs below the surface of the turbid, marshy waters. He stepped lightly and cautiously, at first, then plunged and lumbered ahead with hoarse and coughing desperation as his energy depleted. The man had run, fleeing from imaginary adversaries and the very real baying cats and flitters, but now he could run no longer. He gave up. He surrendered. There was nothing left to do, except lie in the festering swamp and decompose, while things like lice and piranha nibbled at his flesh.

He came out in the open, in a soft meadow, and waited. He was safe now from the jungle; he listened numbly to the trading windsong wheezing through the boughs above. He waited for a while, lying naked in the afternoon sun, not thinking. Soon, towards sundown, satellite spies picked out his aura, and down came clean men in white shirts and shorts, and even pith-helmets. They landed their white silent gravity-craft, and seized the man with routine hands, and took the man away into the sky. The forest shrank to a green plain netted by thick blue varicose veins, the writhing rivers of the jungle heart, then sank beneath the lens of grey haze, distant and flat. Inside the white capsule, the man who had run was silent and inert.

"How do you plead," intoned the vocader voice, plain and uninflected. "Guilty or not guilty?"

The man, like the machine, was numb and cold. He shook his head. "What difference does it make? I did what I did, and you know it. I don't have nothing to say." He was a brown man, speaking with a slurred lower-class accent. He'd been a cutter for the company, working with saws and microwave beams to fell the giant trees. The trees were pulped, processed and distilled, reduced to thick grease in catalytic refineries, and turned into plastic and drugs. The man did not know what for; he only worked in the jungle, not thinking very much. The company fed and housed him and took most of his wages back for rent and board. He did not know his slavery. He took cacao and demerol to allay his nightmares and fatigue.

The machine did not hum or click. It never made a sound, except when it spoke. His captors had handcuffed him out of sheer routine, taken him to the white jungle city, and quietly assigned him a cool, windowless cell where the man had stayed three days, eating food that came out of a slot in the pale yellow wall, watching viditapes, and eliminating with thoughtful grunts in the appropriate recepticals. He never left the room, never saw another person—neither prisoner nor guard—and was never asked a single question by anybody. All the questions and answers were already known; what remained was only to judge and convict him, to pass an almost arbitrary verdict, and decide upon his special fate. He was thus taken to the machine, taken through quiet cool halls, into a bare room with a video camera and display in one corner, to consult the master of his fate. The machine would weigh, deliberate and decide; then he would receive his sentence, whatever that might be. The brown man sat sullenly, not caring what would happen. To him, his life was already over.

"You were an employee of The Company," groaned the machine. "You attacked and killed an officer of The Company. You are Manuel Abdul Jones; you have been tried on a plea of Nolo Contendere, and found guilty of the crime as charged. I shall pass sentence presently. Have you anything else to say?" It waited.

"We are all working for the company store," said the man without apparent sarcasm, without manifest bitterness. He studied his hands, as though talking to his grade-school teacher about some petty sin. He did not know how to deal with authority—even the abstract authority of the mute machine. The man had no authority over himself. "I got nothing else to say, nothing. Get it over with." And he waited.

The man waited. The machine thought. There was much the man did not know. There was *everything* the man, who had run (but would run no more), did not know. He did not know or understand the machine, upon whose function depended his life. He did not know how or why. He waited limply, and did not attempt to think. And he was wise. It would do no good.

The issue was responsibility: The world had reached a state of nearly infinite complexity, which no single person, or group of persons, could hope to comprehend. Nothing had ever happened to sweep away this monster of complexity, so the difficulty of understanding piled up, as the society had piled up. Within this endless maze, men made their daily lives. Sometimes they erred; sometimes, whether meaning to or not, they hurt themselves or other people, or broke one of the endless rules necessary to sustain such utter civilized complexity. Then somebody had to do something to ensure it wouldn't happen again. A person would have to be punished, or treated, or made an example of, or something. The problem was intelligence, sensitivity: nobody was smart or wise enough to settle the disputes or solve the problems. No human being was good enough to judge another. To weigh a human life in the scales of collective justice and individual compassion.

So they built the machine. The Judging Machine. The collective councils of the species voted and decided, argued and convinced, and a judge was built, perfect and true. It could not lie. It could not feel. It had no selfish interests against which to balance its decisions, to intrude upon the cold process of reason. It was a machine, into which the facts were fed, from which an honest and truthful choice was made, based upon the available data.

Such a jury, not of peers, was infallible; it administered equally to all men, basing its actions upon the definitions and insights culled from all the world's shows and literature, which had been programmed into it. It had digested the human mind, as neurological functions and pathways, biochemistry and reason-patterns, the meanings, sub-meanings and root conceptions that lie beneath the syntactical surface of thought. It had charted the human brain—mind, life and energy. It was a bioenergetic device, a psionic robot, a mimicker of conscious-ness. Into it they had fed the equations of the Lord, the dialectical relations of the life-force, and from it spoke the voice of the Lord, ominous and clear. The machine was not man, nor beast nor living prey; it had that *point* around which the mind revolves and around which all minds revolve together, and as such its intelligence was in-finite and pure, its logic perfect and devine.

"Equal justice before the law," the priests and programmers of the machine had called for, and ordered the machine to think the thoughts of real law and order. It uttered the ten commandments; it mewed the code of Hammurabi; it pronounced the eightfold path, and elab-orated upon the four Right Thoughts; it issued a treaty; it beat fifty men at Go, simultaneously. It was a game-player and judge, a strate-gist and conner, mimicking all psychologies at once. It could speak to all men in all languages, regard any problem from any side. Its under-standing was therefore perfect. The machine meditated. The machine weighed, deliberated, and spoke. The machine spoke with a certain tone of voice, authoritative and absolute.

But it was programmed with more than facts, and reasoned with more than mere deduction. It had absorbed the motives, too. The collective guilt and uncertainty of society were invested in the ma-chine. Its reason was guided by an outside source—a cold objective light of truth . . . or so it seemed.

Nobody knew just what to think. No one had ever agreed whether the machine was always right, or right no more often than a human being (for its intelligence was really no greater than an average hu-man's—it merely thought with the logic of an undistracted outside source—a robot, an oracle, a Godhead). But the machine's decisions were always abided. Nobody wanted to take responsibility for another man's life. So they always left it up to the machine.

The people then were too civilized; they knew better than to judge.

"I have thought it over very carefully," moaned the mechanical voice of the machine, "and reached a decision in your case."

"That's good," said the man. "Let's get it over with."

There was a hesitation. "Not so fast," said the machine.

"What do you mean? What're you talking about?" quavered the nervous voice of the man. "We're finished. You said so. It's over, and we're through. I don't have to go through no more of this shit. Tell me my sentence and send me away. I'm tired of playing little games like this."

"I will be the judge of when we are done," said the machine. "And I shall also be the judge of what are games and what are not, and what the game is to be. I am the master of games, and the master of games is the player of none."

The man who had run felt his palms turn cold. "You are playing a game with me. You're playing a game with my life."

"You played a game with another," droned the machine like a methodical wasp. "You played a game and lost. You do not understand the rules."

"There ain't any rules and there ain't any game," the man whined. His cold palms began to sweat. "There is life and death and whatever comes in between."

"I am the judge," said the machine. "I determine what is right and who is wrong. You are not the judge. *You* thought you were the judge, however. You judged. You judged another man, and sentenced him, and executed his thoughtless sentence. You are a murderer, a killer, a worthless taker of life."

The man who had run was furious. "But *he* was judging *me!* He was *judging* me! He was judging me to be dirt."

"Perhaps his judgment was not inaccurate," sneered the cold voice of the machine.

"What do you mean? What're you talking about? They did it—he insulted me! Twenty years . . . a guy gets tired of getting kicked around. One of those times, somebody kicks you and you gotta kick back. So I kicked. Even a dog will fight back if you push him into a corner."

"Are you equating yourself with a dog? Very well, perhaps you are one. If you were in a corner, it was ultimately your decision that put you there. If you are a dog it is because you have decided to become one."

The machine spoke with mathematical precision; it was a creature of logic and facts, speaking a jargon of moral equations, a patois of manipulated certainties and axioms. But it was also a creation of laws of statistics and probability, like a human mind. The machine was a gambler, spinning the wheels of fortune in its own casino—and the laws of chance favor the house. According to the rules of the game which the house has established. If you play the gambler's game, you must abide by the gambler's rules.

And the man (who could no longer run) sat in his chair like a spoiled child and sulked impotently. He was a little man, a short fat man with greasy skin. Thus the vidicamera saw him; the machine took his appearance into consideration along with everything else. The man smelled—the odor of foul pork or dead butter. This also the machine registered. He was barely literate, educated by the Company only to the minimum level his childhood tests showed useful and necessary to the Company. Not the kind of man any sophisticated person would want to know. He wasn't very smart, so he had to work for a living—with his body and his hands. His life was not a pleasant one; his attitudes were negative and dour . . . his face tense and glaring, as though he had something bitter and rancid in his mouth. All these values the machine took into account.

There was nobody to speak for him at this trial; that nonproductive custom had been eliminated long ago, so he spoke alone. There was no witness to see his side. He sat alone. And because he was the only human in that empty room, it was completely silent, except for the echo of his fast and frightened breathing. It was as if he was contaminated, unclean—some kind of vermin to be kept isolated from other human beings. The man suddenly smelled his own sweat and stink, and wished he could go through the locked door and run into the cool streets. Had there been a window, he might have jumped through it—but there was none, so he sat trapped and listened to himself speak in confusion and uncertainty into the microphone, unto the one who judged.

"You have not finished speaking," the machine muttered.

"I am finished."

"No, you are not finished," the machine said, "because I am not finished. The problem is still unresolved. I cannot decide until all the evidence is in, until I have examined the problem from all possible sides, and the evidence is neither in nor fully examined. You must tell me your story again."

"I have no story to tell. I got nothing to say."

"You will speak. You must speak. I must know. Tell me."

The man looked up with tired and empty eyes. "I was mad. I couldn't stand it no more. I took it and took it and then I couldn't take it no more and I had to do something so I killed the bastard. That's all."

"Nevertheless," the machine enunciated (cool and even-tempered as only a machine might be), "nevertheless, you killed, and I have judged, and I must know. I must understand. Tell me—tell me your motive. Everything you think is relevant or important."

The man wiped his lip and shook his head. "For twenty years," the man who'd run replied, "for twenty terrible years I took it. I did not fight back. There was no one to fight back against, and I was aware of the consequences. For twenty years I did nothing–and then I did something. I let the bastards have it." His cold sweaty hands were shaking.

"You let one *man* have it," replied the machine who judged. "You killed a living being. He was as good as you–perhaps better. He lived and labored, and died at your hands. Now he is nothing. And you live on."

"I couldn't stand it no more."

The machine was silent a long time.

"I wish I'd killed them all."

The machine said nothing.

"They was all playing some kind of game with me." The man held up supplicating hands. "They were playing with me and using me."

"Words, empty words," sighed the machine. "Playing games is all you do. You are never tired of playing games."

The man shook his head tiredly. "No, no, they was playing games. *They* was."

"It's all in your head," the machine said patiently. "Everything was all your own fault."

"I don't know."

"That is no defense. It's your karma. The karma always comes back," pronounced the machine, with faint invisible condescension.

"I don't know what you're talking about." He folded his arms and glared petulantly into the camera. "I dunno what you mean."

"You *know* what I mean," the machine remanded. "You know what I mean and do not have to be told. You have no right to demand that I explain. *I* am the judge, and *you* are not the judge, although you judged and thus I judged. Now you shall get what you have bargained for. What you see is what you get."

The machine had studied his position, and concluded that he had no position. It denied the validity of his life. The man sat and said nothing. For fools, he thought, the best speech is cold silence. But silence would not save him. He sneered into the vidicamera, thinking of twenty years in oozing jungles. But the machine was patient, the machine could wait.

Finally, it said, "You have totally abdicated responsibility."

"You a faggot," said the man, with boiling and hidden rage.

The inert machine ignored him. "I have examined and considered the available information," spoke the machine. "I have thought the matter over. You refuse to speak, so I must judge. Judging is not an easy thing to do," pontificated the slow voice of the machine, "but you have left me no choice."

The man's head jerked up as if to protest, but the machine went evenly on.

"I shall cite no precedents, for none exist. There is no precedent for a man's life. I shall restrict myself to the characteristics of the case.

"I shall cite no arguments, for there were none. One does not argue about the truth—one states it, final and confirmed, for others to accept.

"I shall abstain from opinions. Opinions are interpretations of the truth.

"I shall state only the basics of the case." The machine continued unbrokenly. "First, you pleaded Nolo Contendere. Shall I play back the tape? You copped out. You offered nothing substantive in your defense. You had the chance to make your peace, and said instead a wilful nothing. When given the chance to elaborate, to confirm or deny, or modify the evidence in any way, you offered only colored pictures of the event. You told us your motivations, in the vaguest and most general terms, without offering who or how or what or where. It may be of clinical interest to know the reasons why, but 'why' is not a point of law. We are displeased. You killed and ran, man, you slayed another human being, no matter what his sins, and ran away into the twisting jungle. You took into your hands another life, and crumpled it up and threw it away. Such are the facts of this matter."

The voice of the machine went on, distant and severe. "Now I am called upon to judge. Society judges harshly those who break its most sacred trust. Yet no man is all the world. That is why I am judging you, and not a human being: no single man is responsible for another man's life. Or death. The responsibility is up to the collective Whole; herewith I represent the Whole.

"There is a causality here; for every action, there is an equal and an opposite reaction. So it has been written. And there is a relativity here; all actions are judged in relation to all other acts. So it has been deduced. And there is an *objectivity*, also, an entropy, a balancing-out. All matters and events come out even in the final analysis. This is a dialectical matter; I have considered all sides and angles.

"Upon this pedestal, within this graph, all reasoning is based and all decisions ultimately made. This is the ultimate mathematics of human destiny, and I am its final judge, perfect and absolute. I am the jury, without peer. I consider all consequences.

"You ran, man, into the jungle and away from your act—your foul and desperate act. A man who does bad things is not a good man, no; and well enough, a man to whom bad things is done may not be a good man either; and easily may it be, the world into which these two are born that compels them to act in such an evil and desperate way may itself be ugly and a sin. But into thy hands, O sinner, these things are put in trust, and into my hands, wicked little man, your fate has been consigned. So I weighed the evidence and made my choice, and the verdict was that guilt is as plain as your swollen tearful face. The verdict has been made," droned the impassionate voice of the machine, "as is my right and duty—for I am the source of all moral knowledge. The evidence is in, and the process is complete. So if you have any final thing to say, say it now or forever keep your peace."

And the man said nothing.

"Very well, I shall say this. You have the choice of doing what you want. I'll let *you* decide—for it's your life and your responsibility, regardless of what went before. No man may judge another, nor tribe of men, not nation nor world. That's how it was decided. But you have judged—and took action on your judgment. You killed another man. You have coldly and arrogantly destroyed a human life, where all men before could not decide. You took it for your prerogative. And I have judged. And you are free. But who art thou, to judge another?"

5 10:01 A.M.

by Alexander B. Malec

The "wheels of justice" move slowly, we are told, because *fairness,* not *efficiency,* is the major value upon which our criminal justice system is based. But are the values of efficiency and fairness necessarily opposed to each other? Can we conceive of and then design a criminal justice system that is *both* fair and efficient?

The criminal justice system is supported at all levels of government by public funds. Therefore, the public has a right to expect the system to be reasonably efficient and cost-effective. Modern management procedures are utilized in police and court systems to insure efficient operations. But, despite these efforts, complaints are widespread about court delays, police inefficiency, and a rise in the amount of crime in society. Some argue that additional resources are needed to increase efficiency and effectiveness. Others argue that funds currently expended are not used in the most cost-conscious way. Still others argue that no matter how much money is expended on the criminal justice system, the necessity to make it as fair as possible really is the cause of costly delays in such procedures as the gathering of evidence, a criminal trial, and a higher-court appeal.

To deal with the values of fairness and efficiency in the criminal justice process, one must assess the role that *discretion* plays. There is, after all, an element of discretion at every level and in every step of the criminal justice process. Decisions

about whether to arrest a person, to allow bail, to go to trial,
to plea-bargain, to sentence, and to appeal—all these contain
an element of discretion on the part of officials which contain
fundamental issues of fairness and efficiency. To have a
completely efficient system of criminal justice, in which there
is an automatic enforcement of every violation of the criminal
law may sound desirable but on reflection may create additional
problems for society.

"10:01 A.M." is a story by Alexander B. Malec that portrays
such a system. Rapid arrest, trial, conviction, and sentencing
of traffic violators highlight the inexorability of the criminal
justice process. This story should be read in the light of
complaints we make today of the time it takes to bring
criminals to justice.

At 10:01 A.M. the accident occurred, setting off a triple concurrence
of actions, the first which was the following dialogue:

"What was it?" asked Slick when the vehicle pulled over and
stopped.

"I dunno," said the driver as he hopped down, looked at the object
on the mall, and returned, the other vehicles whistling above him.
"Looks just like a rag doll. You know, no frame, no nothin'."

"Did you see it coming?" asked Slick, reclining back with his stogie.

"Naw," said Poxie, who was the driver, as he energized the vehicle
and headed it into the mainstream. "Don't hardly look real or nuthin'.
All covered with catsup it looks like."

"Yeah," said Slick, observing a stream of smoke issuing from his
O-shaped lips, feeling rough and "with it" in his brand-new black
leather boots, his black leather trousers, and his black leather jacket
with the fourteen silver nodes and the five zippered pockets. "These
things happen." He slicked back his bushy mop of black hair with a
comb.

"Yeah," said Poxie, who was so called due to his moon crater-like
complexion, that is, pockmarks. He passed the other vehicles to get
into the top speed lane; passed them vertically, that is.

The second and third concurrence of actions took place also at
10:01 A.M., when that particular section of the roadway, with all its
sensors, noted that something untoward had occurred, and dispatched
onward the time and location of occurrence, the course of involved

machine, and due to the type of signal transmitted, caused to home in on two separate locales, two special and very different from each other vehicles.

At 10:03 A.M. the first vehicle, called simply a "patroller," arrived on the scene, dropped to ground level, found the "rag doll" and carefully placed her within the patroller.

Officer John Cramdon, never really insular from his job, wept slightly taking a retina identification check, while the information automatically traveled via pulsed carrier to a building known only as "Center" some fifty kilometers away.

At 10:07 A.M. the information arrived from Center and stated that her name was Cynthia Marie DeSantis; red hair; blue eyes; weight: 20 kilograms; height: 102 centimeters; age: 8 years old; residence: 10D, 4th quadrant, Lloyd Wright Gardens, Churchill City, Kansas; mother's name: Eva Marie; father's name: Lawrence Joseph; occupation: machinist.

This information appeared on the scope of Sergeant John Cramdon's patroller; the visual display which, before fading out, automatically etched this information onto a blank transparent sheet of Lucite, with the time and code letters to identify same, and dropped into a file.

The same information also appeared on the scope of the second larger vehicle now homing in on its moving target.

Also at 10:07 A.M., at the Traffic Division of Center, Captain Roland Reese, for the nth time, drew his courage together—which was parcel of his job of police captaincy—and pressed the studs on the telephone which would connect him to a residence at 10D, 4th quadrant, Lloyd Wright Gardens, Churchill City, Kansas; which would connect him to Eva Marie, mother of Cynthia Marie DeSantis.

At 10:09 A.M., Officer John Cramdon was already vectoring on a building in Churchill City, near Lloyd Wright Gardens, with his cargo.

Fully twenty-seven kilometers away, where first alerted of the "occurrence," the larger vehicle took fully six minutes to overtake the top-lane carrier of Poxie and Slick, which was hurtling at 200 k.p.h. This was at 10:07 A.M.

Slick noticed it first. "Poxie. You see what's in back of us?" he yelled in dismay.

Poxie looked back and gulped, "Agh! A fetcher!"

"Hit it," hollered Slick.

Poxie jammed the accelerator fully to its limit.

At 10:08 A.M. the "fetcher" enclosed the smaller vehicle of Slick and Poxie, and at that instant the fetcher made a turn unauthorized to ordinary drivers, rerouted and, at top speed, homed in on Center which was now, due to the inline chase, some 133 kilometers distant. The journey would take approximately seventeen minutes.

If being enveloped by a fetcher is a chilling experience, it is not an oft-repeated one; an offshoot doctrine of the civilization that could produce a fetcher and a need for one.

Perhaps if Poxie were to resist incarceration by a fetcher—as some did—by initiating a sudden turn; left, right, up, down, in the hope of at least wrecking the machine that swallowed them in an I'll-take-one-of-them-with-me bravado, he couldn't have done so. For the reason that his reaction was in the realm of the highly probable and therefore implemented against; another way of saying a degaussing network on the inside walls of the fetcher canceled out his control and driving field so that Poxie's machine was as inert and immobile—and about as useful—as a large rock of equal mass.

The sudden switch from sunlight to artificial light alone is enough to induce gooseflesh; the sudden change in noise level and acoustics will again produce the same sensation as the front aperture of the fetcher closed much as a camera lens. Clamps thumped their device securely to the deck, and electromagnetic shoes, as a double precaution, held them fast.

There were no officers in sight; just the white painted, brightly illuminated walls and the *moiré* pattern of the closed aperture ahead.

Suddenly, a public address system sounded, "Leave your vehicle. Enter the doorway to the rear." The PA system then added an emotion-tinged, "Come on, you birds. Move!!"

Poxie and Slick did so. In passing through, Poxie noticed the glowing nodes placed about ten centimeters apart vertically in the doorjamb. He knew it was a frisking mechanism of some kind.

They entered a small, brightly lit room which contained a functional metal desk and stools fastened to the deck, an assortment of "black box" electronic gadgetry, scopes and switches on the bulkheads, and two officers of the law who looked the picture of hard, well-oiled efficiency as if they had been turned out by the same machine. They wore gray uniforms, blue leather boots, triple-ridged white helmets, and to add to their anonymity and authority, they wore translucent masks.

The officer who was standing relieved Poxie of the screwdriver in his right knee pocket.

"For adjustments," said Poxie with a sly grin.

"Shaddap," said the standing officer. At that, the officer who was seated waved at the other to ease off. Poxie knew that the "shaddap" was rare, and unauthorized; he knew these men were fighting to keep a closed lid on their emotions.

"Sit here, please," said the seated officer, indicating two stools which had two optical gadgets about where eye level would be. In the meantime, the other officer consulted a plastic sheet index which was in fine print. Slick noticed the title on the plastic sheet. It read: Accumulator, location of . . . As they sat down, they could hear the other officer stomp out of the small cubicle through the glowing node doorway, in front to where their machine sat captive.

"Look through the eyepieces, keep both eyes open. Focus on the cross you see there."

As Poxie and Slick did so, they knew the officer had depressed some kind of stud, for this was a retina identification check.

"All right," said the officer, and caused the optical gadgets to swivel on their brackets and nestle each in their own niche in the bulkhead.

"Where were you fellows headed?" he asked.

"Albuquerque," said Poxie. The interrogating officer had both hands flat on the desk, writing nothing down, so Poxie knew something, somewhere, was taking a permanent record of this conversation.

"Where were you coming from?"

"Chicago," offered Slick. The officer depressed no stud or toggle to differentiate between the two young men talking. Apparently, then, the recording device had no difficulty in separating and tagging the voices. At that moment, Poxie looked at the wall clock. It said 10:10 A.M.

"At what level?"

"Ah," Poxie stammered, "low level. You know that."

The tone of the officer's voice seemed to contort the inscrutable translucent mask into hardness, if that were possible. "Oh, I know that, all right. But what is low level?" Poxie looked at him blankly. "Come on," said the officer with irritation. "What is low level?" The "come on" prodding of the officer surprised Poxie; very seldom these people showed any emotion.

"Eight meters," said Poxie.

"All right, that's the upper limit," said the hard officer of the Traffic Division. "Now, what's the lower limit . . . of the low level?" he added.

"Four meters," said Poxie. He was beginning to feel very nervous with the line the questioning was taking.

The inflections of the interrogating officer made Poxie think of the old-time prosecuting attorneys as he had seen them on the reconstituted 'loids.* The question he heard now was, "Four meters, huh? You sure you weren't going any lower?"

"How could we?" asked Slick. He was becoming nervous, too. "You can't go lower!"

Poxie wasn't sure the line of questioning was not part of police procedure. But the man asking the questions had a curiosity and an "in" for the two young men before him. He was literally venting off his spleen.

"Why can't you go lower?" asked the lawman. He pointed to Slick. "You."

Slick stammered, "Because the controls are, well, you know, governed, if you go any lower than twelve feet, I mean four meters, well, you might hit somebody."

"A lot of fun, wasn't it?" said the officer. This taunting was really unauthorized, thought Poxie. "Knocking off the tops of trees, scaring the daylights out of people."

"We didn't," said Slick lamely.

"You didn't?" said the officer. "Then how is it you struck a little girl at a cross mall? A little girl who was hardly a meter high."

Slick didn't answer. Poxie gulped and stared at the wall clock. 10:12 A.M.

At this lull in conversation, the other officer returned; the one who had gone to where the enclosed, captured vehicle of Poxie's was. He held in one grimy hand what looked like a battery-operated cutting tool. In the other he held what appeared to be on one side a weathered hexnut, but on the inner side, protected from the weather, looking like something else again; a shiny microelectronic-looking something else.

Slick stared at it bug-eyed. Poxie was somewhat fascinated too.

The seated officer spoke, "Surprise, huh?" Slick, the one who was being addressed, didn't speak. "Thought you had found the accumulator on your vehicle and put a pin through it, didn't you?" The seated officer looked inquiringly at the other officer, who took his cue and spoke.

"The other one had been found—and damaged. But this one is all right," he said, and held up the accumulator.

Slick stared at the untouched, unfound, undamaged accumulator as one hypnotized by a twirling vest pocket watch. He stared at this undamaged but oh so easily reciprocally damaging accumulator.

"How come there were two?" asked Poxie of the standing officer

* Short for Celluloids. Movies.

who held the cutting tool in one hand and that murderous piece of evidence in the other. The addressed officer didn't answer right away but handed the hexnut-disguised accumulator to the seated officer, whereupon that one got up, entered behind a partition that half cut him off from view, and performed some kind of act to the accumulator; an act as yet unknown to the young captives.

"There's no law that says there can't be two," said the officer with the grimy hands and the cutting tool, "or even three." Slick did a take on that "three." "The law only says there must be one." He held up one finger for emphasis, "One." Poxie and Slick followed the officer's soliloquy with no little entrancement. "So many times it happens, the vehicle's accumulator when it leaves the factory—the one in plain sight gets somewhat damaged." He looked at Slick with bland, tongue-in-cheek, saying, "Ordinary, routine damage. Can happen to anybody." Slick turned his eyes down on that one and Poxie looked away to the wall clock. It read 10:15 A.M.

"So you see," said the soliloquying officer (he was obviously the talkative one of the bunch), "why we do what we do. In times of collision between two vehicles and in the ensuing investigation, it is necessary to fix the blame; either driver or both drivers. Or, as happens sometimes, the fact of mechanical failure on the part of the vehicle. In that case the involved driver is not held. We learn all, the data surrounding and contributing to the accident from playing back the accumulator attached to each car. I guess you know that in the event of accident with a vehicle containing a, ah, predamaged accumulator, we would then have to rely on the testimony of drivers, passengers, and other eyewitnesses to the scene. And human testimony" (he said "human" as if it were a dirty word) "is so prejudiced and . . . so inaccurate."

"Oh," said Poxie, wondering if these officers of the law were married; would they have stooped to something as commonly human as marriage.

"So," said the seated officer. "We rely on the accumulator. It gives us a lifetime record of the car's behavior. And, in case of accident of any kind" (he emphasized the "of any kind") "we have an unbiased record of the vehicle's height, lane, speed, attitude at time of impact, and the performance of the driver prior to that impact."

"And," took up the standing officer, arms at his sides, who looked as deadly as a viper, "the performance of the driver . . ." (he looked at Poxie) ". . . after the impact."

Poxie had been reasoning that a man who could stand thus, arms at sides, without any emotional crutches such as a cigarette, must be very sure of himself. When the officer stopped talking, Poxie said, "Oh," coloring in embarrassment and took in the reading on the wall clock. It read 10:17 A.M.

"That's what is happening now," said the standing officer.

"What is?" asked Slick.

"What happens when we put the accumulator in the acceptor mechanism."

"What's that do?" asked Slick.

"It relays the information upon the accumulator," said the seated officer. "Ahead. To Center."

Poxie didn't know why, but he chilled when the man said "Center." The wall clock still read 10:17 A.M.

"Just like happened," asked Slick, "when you had us look into that glass thing? It went on to Center?"

"That is correct," said the standing officer.

At this point Poxie wondered if it wouldn't be wiser to try to overpower the two officers of the law; since these officers appeared to be unworried about such a come about and carried their sidearms outside and accessible, much as officers have always done. Poxie knew they were in deep enough trouble to make such a try worthwhile.

His notions were inadvertently replied to in the next few minutes.

The seated officer arose, and said to the other, "Are there, ah, marks?"

"Yes," said the other.

"I'm going to have a look," he said, and walked through the doorway.

"I'll go with you," said the other, making Poxie's ears perk up almost a rabbit's length. As the officer went through the doorway, his hand flipped something on the right of the doorway and he said, "Sit tight. Don't move." And he was gone. Poxie and Slick were all alone in the interrogating cubicle of a police fetcher vehicle, with the 101 gadgets, meters, toggles, rheostats, and scopes that were fauna of modern-day trafic misdemeanor and felony control. Poxie would have been confused as to what gadget to grab hold of first, except that the decision had been made for him when the officer had flipped that something.

"Look," said Slick, crestfallen.

"Yeah," said Poxie, also crestfallen.

"Laser bars," said Slick.

"Yeah."

All around them in an oval, to encompass them and the two stools they sat on and not much more, was a cage of vertical laser beams.

"These kind give you a shock, I think," said Slick. "An electric shock."

"Some other kinds burn you," said Poxie.

"Yeah. And there's another kind. They use it in mining and in war, I guess. It vaporizes things."

The officers returned. The first one through flicked that toggle something on the right wall of the doorway and the laser cage disappeared. The second officer coming through said, "It's there all right." Poxie reasoned he was speaking for the benefit of the audio pickup device somewhere in the cubicle, for use as further evidence. "Blood" was the officer's follow-through comment. Poxie wondered how many times you can kill a dead ox; how much evidence did they need? He looked at the wall clock. It read 10:22 A.M.

The first officer through, continued through the cubicle and exited through a rearward passageway. "We're getting close," he said before he disappeared.

The second officer sat down behind the desk though the detained young men couldn't know if this one was the original who had been seated or if they had switched.

"He went to bring it in," said Slick.

"Yeah," said Poxie.

"The thing was running by itself," said Slick.

"Yeah."

The second officer had his head down, both hands on the desk, reading, as best as Slick could divine, upside down; An Abstract of Codes and Decrees As Applied to Civilian-Commercial Null-Vehicles Traversing the Alpha Roadway System. This must be, thought Poxie, how they gotta spend their free time; reading law. No novels, no nuthin'. Then Poxie had a question. And the answer, by reflection of what prompted it, pointed out the guilt of the questioner. "What," asked the pockmarked incarcerate not quite into his twenties, "are you going to do with the machine once we get to Center?"

The seated officer looked up, his mask chilling in its inscrutability, and said, "We're going to analyze it." He said this slowly. "No null-vehicle can possibly dip below four meters except . . ." Then he explained, "There are fail-safe circuits and auxiliary servomechanisms that make it possible to alight slowly and safely in case of power failure. But in no case is it possible for a civilian null-vehicle . . ." He paused between the subphrases, "to dip below four meters . . . over a cross mall . . . and still retain power. There are built-in governors. But you know about that, don't you? And there are built-in power cancelers should the factory-sealed governor mechanism be tampered with. As far as we know, there is no way for a layman to tamper with a vehicle in such a manner and still manage to run that vehicle. We are very curious" (he was looking at Slick when he said this) "to see how this was done." The inscrutable impartiality mask of the law paused a few seconds before it spoke again. "It would seem . . . that we have a mechanical genius in our midst." It was a backhanded compliment with a lot of left hand to it. Slick reacted by reddening his ears a little.

While Poxie, sensing his friend's discomfiture, prodded him to give him a cigarette, for Slick's stogie was smoked down. He looked at the wall clock. It read 10:24 A.M. We're almost there, he thought, and sure enough, he sensed a subtle change in the almost inaudible whining tone that is a police "fetcher" vehicle in motion.

At 10:26 A.M., after the awesome whines and clicks outside had ceased, a final sound made itself apparent; that of the vehicle's camera aperture doors opening. It was a whirring sound. The officer who had traced Slick a moment ago for "mechanical genius" remained seated. Except another officer made the scene. He was standing on the platform, in front of the yawning aperture opening. He was dressed in every detail as the mobile officers had been except for the green helmet and the clipboard which he held in front of him, from which he spoke loudly, "Mr. James Smith. Mr. Rodney Cooper." Poxie and Slick respectively responded to their names with a start, for they had not told the two vehicle police their names. "Please follow me." They meekly complied.

They were in a huge auditorium-like building with a lacquered floor and large enough for noises to reverberate. The roof was a dome through which the brilliant late-morning sun shone through some transparent building material; and behind them, the two awestruck young men saw the platform upon which similar police fetcher and patroller vehicles were in a constant state of arrival and departure on a loading platform so long that it dwindled, perspectivewise, into infinity. "Big business," said Slick.

They were escorted across the shining acreage of the Center's interior into a small lounge-like room.

"Wow," said Slick, impressed by the luxurious interior of the room which was done up in hues of green, abstract art, and subdued lighting.

"Make yourself comfortable," said the green-helmeted officer through the translucent mask.

"Sure will," said Slick, and dove on a foam rubber sofa.

"What's all this for?" asked Poxie.

"You are to wait here," said the officer, "for your trial."

"Agh," said Poxie, making a face of distaste. He now decided to sit down.

But the officer didn't leave. He still had some business to attend to. Holding the clipboard stiffly, he said, "Mr. Rodney Cooper." Slick looked up with a "huh?" expression.

"You are to answer one question."

"Go ahead," said Slick.

"I'm not finished," said the officer. "After I ask the question and the answer is in the negative, I must inform you that you will then be subject to a polygraph test. Is that understood?"

"Yeah," said Slick.

"Speak louder."

"Yeah," said Slick, knowing now there was an audio pickup somewhere in this ultracomfortable lounge.

"Here is the question," said the officer with the clipboard. "Did you, Rodney Cooper, knowingly tamper with the controls of your Mark Nine Phaeton null-vehicle so as to enable that same vehicle to traverse below the legal minimum allowable height on the alpha-type roadway when crossing a pedestrian mall?"

"Yes," said Slick. Then he yelled to the hidden pickup, "Yes!"

The officer now turned to Poxie. "Mr. James Smith."

"Yeah."

"After I ask the question and the answer is in the negative, I must inform you that you will then be subject to a polygraph test. Is that understood?"

"Yeah," said Poxie.

"Here is the question," said the officer. "Were you a party to this tampering, either by actual aid, sanction, or knowledge, of this same Mark Nine Phaeton null-vehicle along with the aforementioned Mr. Rodney Cooper?"

"Yes!"

The officer all but clicked his heels when he said, "That is all." As he made to leave, he had one more thing to say. "To your left is a menu selection board. You may eat if you wish. You have a choice of four main courses."

"Specialty of the house," jeered Slick.

The officer made to leave once more, but Poxie ran up to him and asked, "Hey, Mac. Got a cigarette?"

The officer lifted an arm, reached into a pocket, and gave Mr. James (Poxie) Smith a cigarette. He left.

"What'd you do that for?" asked Slick. "You got cigarettes."

"Wanted to see," said Poxie, lighting up, "if that guy was human."

"Smart," said Slick. "Let's go eat." And he rushed to the menu selector. Poxie made to follow him, but not before he noticed the two doors at the far end of the room. Between the doors was a wall chronometer. It read 10:31 A.M.

At 10:33 A.M. the meals came, and the young incarcerates dove on them in gusto.

At 10:36 A.M. the same officer who read the questions to them returned. He had with him two thin plaques.

"What's this?" asked Slick between bites of beef pot roast, as he was handed his plaque.

"An extract of the Criminal Code," said the inscrutable mask of the officer as he handed the other plaque to Poxie. "As it applied to you during the trial." Again, he did an about-face and left.

Said Slick, munching loudly, scanning the plaque given him, "Wow, room service and all. Now they give us reading material with our food." He munched on. "Hey," he said, as if coming upon a gem, "did you know, friend Poxie, it ain't against the law to mess around with the innards of a null-vehicle?"

"No?" said Poxie, tearing at a chicken drumstick, scanning his reading material. "Why not?"

"Because," said Slick. Then he stopped to chew some more. "Nobody ain't ever done it before. So how are you going to make a law about a crime that can't be committed?"

"I dunno. How?"

"Except it's been committed, nit!" said Slick with a grin. "Don't you see? Me, Slick, I'm the first one that ever messed with the innards of a null-vehicle. Me."

Poxie was sugaring his coffee as he said, "Then how is it," he took a sip, "that you're here?"

Slick's face dropped a couple of notches. "Oh, they're getting me on an old, old law, statute they call it." He read ". . . contributing to a felony or being a party to a felony." He looked up. "See, they got ya one way or another. Hey, how about yours? What's yours say?"

Poxie pursed his whole face in reading the thin plaque. "I dunno. Whole bunch of mishmash. Words I never saw, like, ah, well, like eugenics. What's eugenics?"

"I dunno." Poxie read for a few more minutes.

"Well, how about," he perused his plaque hard and sipped his coffee. "Well, how about genetics?"

"Genetics?" asked Slick brightly. He lay full length on the divan, his meal finished.

"Yeah."

"That's your folks, your mother, father, your grandmother, grandfather, all the way down the line."

"Oh," said Poxie, and pushed his plate away; he couldn't finish. He was looking at the wall chronometer which read 10:46 A.M. when the same officer who had visited before entered with the announcement.

"Your trial," he said to both of them, "is over."

When Poxie and Slick had absorbed this news, he continued. "The Tribunal of the State of Kansas . . . finds you guilty!"

Then came the long reading-out by the officer, as per procedure, ample material for this having been brought along.

"You, Mr. James Smith, First Defendant, according to the criminal code of this State, Article 29, are convicted of, due to criminal negligence, the manslaughter of Cynthia Marie DeSantis, a minor of eight years of age, on May the eighth, 10:01 A.M., at Churchill City, Kansas.

"And you, Mr. Rodney Cooper, Second Defendant, are convicted of a lesser count of contributory manslaughter of the same Cynthia Marie DeSantis, in that you, by your own voiced admission, caused, by mechanical manipulation of the drive and control systems of a null-vehicle, Mark Nine Phaeton, License number EV 30899, Chicago, Illinois, owned and operated at the time of the occurrence by Mr. James Smith, First Defendant, caused and enabled this same vehicle to dip below the authorized height for civilian vehicles of this type traversing Alpha Roadways and thereupon bringing about the demise of the said Cynthia Marie DeSantis."

The green-helmeted officer took a couple of breaths and continued. "The accumulation of evidence leading to the conviction of First and Second Defendants, Mr. James Smith and Mr. Rodney Cooper, is as follows:

"An indication of occurrence from triangulation sensors at east-west, Route 103 Roadway, Coordinate B-411, which is at Churchill City, Kansas, and accordingly tracked by these same sensors until apprehension was accomplished. It must be stated now to present defendants, an indication of occurrence by triangulation sensors does not, by itself, constitute evidence. Only a tributary to such evidence.

"The fact of blood found on the seized vehicle of Mr. James Smith did, indeed, match that of the decedent, Cynthia Marie DeSantis.

"A playback from the accumulator of the vehicle of Mr. James Smith showed that indeed there had been a traversing at heights below that authorized, namely one-half a meter from the ground, at point of impact, at a time coinciding with that recorded by the Roadway triangulation sensors, at a time of 10:01 A.M., eighth of May.

"The fact of a brief stop immediately following time of occurrence, as recorded by triangulation sensors.

"The fact of traveling at an excessive rate of speed following this recorded impact and stop by Police Retriever Vehicle 009.

"As further substantiation of the guilt of and a proof of lessened probability that this may have been a freak occurrence, a playback of the accumulator on the vehicle of James Smith shows many such below-authorized height travels, besides other dangerous practices: overspeeding, too rapid level changes, and illegal midroadway stops.

"The hypothesis of whether James Smith and Rodney Cooper, the occupants of involved vehicle when seized, were the same occupants of involved vehicle during time of occurrence, 10:01 A.M., May 8, becomes highly substantiated theory; One: when seen that the post-occurrence speed of involved vehicle was too high to permit disembarkation and changeover of occupants. Two: the fact that involved Police Retriever Vehicle 009 noted no such change on its scope. Three: an unseized upon opportunity to deny involvement in the occurrence by the First and Second Defendants in a playback of conversation from Police Retriever Vehicle 009."

The green-helmeted, translucent-masked officer lowered his clipboard. "That," he said, "sums up all the evidence toward you, Mr. Rodney Cooper." Slick seemed to relax.

"Oh, you mean that's all," said Slick facetiously.

The officer directed this next at Poxie. "However, there's additional evidence against you, Mr. James Smith." He raised the clipboard. "In that James Smith, Personal Identification X-I-X, residence 811 Church Street, Chicago, Illinois, had been operating his vehicle on an Option License, due to a history of the grandfather of James Smith, Beauregard Smith, by name, who was adjudged mentally incompetent and insane, post-occurrence to a driving mishap that took two lives. The case of Beauregard Smith had been relegated to the Authority of the Federal Eugenics Program and an apt notation officially made in regard to the offspring of Beauregard Smith." He lowered the clipboard and asked, "Your father wasn't allowed to drive, right?"

"Right," said Poxie.

"And you were only allowed to drive under an Option?" a question which Poxie did not answer.

"Is that it?" asked Slick, lying back on a divan, chewing on a toothpick. The officer nodded.

"What's next?"

"Sentence," said the green-helmeted officer. Slick sat up in one piece suddenly, and Poxie looked at the chronometer. It read 10:49 A.M.

"Of course you do know," said the officer, "that a complete rundown of all this goes to your immediate relatives. Also, a notification to employers, lodges and associations, debtors and creditors."

"Mostly creditors," said Slick. And Poxie had to grin. Then Slick snapped his fingers impatiently. "Come on, Sentence."

The officer dutifully took to his clipboard and began to read. "Due to the involvement of Rodney Cooper in a fatal accident, his driver's license is hereby revoked . . . forever." Slick didn't seem fazed. "How about him, Poxie here. His license revoked?" The officer presented a blank mask and didn't answer. "Well," admonished Slick, "how about him? His license revoked?"

The officer answered, "Yes, it's revoked." He resumed reading. "It is the contention of the Tribunal that brilliance of any kind be allowed to perpetuate and that Rodney Cooper, showing proof of a high degree of mechanical aptitude, be allowed to serve where he may be most useful; the Lunar Observation Laboratory . . . for a period of one year."

Poxie winced at the "year on the Moon" bit, but Slick went, "Yeow, the Moon! I drew the Moon!" He actually jumped up.

The officer pointed to one of the doors. "Would you leave now, please," he said to Slick. The addressee looked confused. "The left door," said the officer.

Slick dashed out, yelling, "Be good, Poxie. Take care of yourself, Po. See you now," and he was gone.

The chronometer read 10:50 A.M.

"And you, my lad, go through the right doorway," said the inscrutable mask of the green-helmeted officer.

As Poxie made to comply, the officer called after him, "Oh, you will be allowed one phone call."

Poxie didn't answer, just kept right on walking.

"You will also be given counsel."

Poxie stopped, puzzled. "Counsel?" He looked at the officer. "Counsel? Now?" He made a face.

"Just go through the right doorway."

Poxie went through the indicated doorway at 10:51 A.M.

At 10:59 A.M. he kissed the crucifix.

At 11:00 A.M. James (Poxie) Smith was vaporized.

6 Bounty

by T. L. Sherred

Who has the responsibility in society for "enforcing the law"?
Who, in effect, protects society from wrongdoers? The answer
is: it depends! It depends upon the temporal and cultural
contexts in which the answer is sought. For example, in
stateless societies, when the concept of "the state" was
unknown, enforcing the law was a major function of families
and clans. In other words, transgression of the rules of society
was considered a "private" matter, and the method used to
punish wrongdoers was also considered private. Since there
was no state, there could be no crimes against the state—
hence no "public wrong."

But over time, stateless societies evolved into formal states,
and the violations of society's rules became public wrongs
which were to be handled by the state's public machinery of
criminal justice. To be sure, a vestige of the individual's right
to enforce the law still exists in the device of "citizen's arrest";
but even this is an action that is performed by an individual in
his or her *public* capacity as a citizen and thus sanctioned by
the state. However, examples of "private justice" still exist.
In American history, they can be seen as illustrations of vigilante
activity. Indeed, in certain areas of early America, such groups
were the only available criminal justice system. Certainly, the
"lynch mob," so much a part of the early development of the
American West, is an institution whose consequences included
not only the establishment of law and order but also some of
the most tragic stories of miscarriages of justice in our history.

Yet vigilante justice should not be associated solely with the American past and with isolated, sparsely populated areas. Whenever people believe that the public processes of criminal justice are breaking down and that their own safety is thereby jeopardized, the potential for vigilante justice to emerge exists. Several years ago, a movie entitled *Death Wish* caught the imagination of the American public. Everywhere it was shown people flocked to see it. Lectured by politicians about the soaring crime rate and violence in the streets, subject to actual violence in the large urban areas, and fed with a daily diet of evidence of the plausibility of their fears on television news and entertainment programs, individuals must have enjoyed seeing a movie that portrayed a hero who, having lost a daughter and a wife to street hoodlums, suddenly takes the law into his own hands and successfully fights back. The film was recently shown on television over the objections of some citizen groups that its showing would foster a wave of vigilantism in the United States which would undermine the foundation of our society. This question of the conflict between the need for stability and the need for justice is terrifyingly portrayed in the story "Bounty" by T. L. Sherred.

In May, the first week there was one death. The second, there were four, the third, nineteen. The fourth week, 39 people were killed.

Most were shot by pistol, rifle, or shotgun. Four were killed with knives, two by meat cleavers, and one by a dinner fork worked methodically through the spinal cord. It was not the dinner fork that aroused comment but the evident fact that someone had finished his or her meal with its duplicate.

The Mayor said, "This has got to stop."

The Governor said, "This has got to stop."

The President, through his Secretary for Health and Welfare, said somewhat the same thing.

The Police Commissioner and Prosecuting Attorney said there would be no stone left unturned and the FBI said, regretfully, that it was a local matter.

No one ever was quite sure who was on or who was behind the Committee but the advertisement—one issue, double-page spread— had been authentic, had paid off in hard cash; within the city limits, ten thousand dollars cash for the death of anyone caught in the process of armed robbery and one hundred thousand to the estate of anyone killed while attempting to halt armed robbery.

Such an advertisement was definitely not in the public interest and every bristling aspect of the law said so. The suburban booster sheet that had originally printed the ad promised not to do it again.

But this kept on and over the weeks and a few square miles—cities are crowded in their sprawl—over two million dollars had been paid without quibble and sometimes at night secretly, because Internal Revenue considers no income tainted. Things became complex when three policemen in varying parts of the city incautiously let their off-duty holstered guns be spotted by strangers or by fellow customers in a store. Too rapidly for the innocent police to identify themselves, a swirl of action, and three men were dead—all painlessly. Further executions were eliminated by the flaunting of police badges in public, with consequent reduction of vice squad arrests.

By July, pedestrians after dark carried large flashlights and in business districts made no abrupt movements. Vigilante groups at first hired doddering men and women to hobble decoy in certain areas; later, as techniques became perfected, heavily armed and suicidal senior citizens acted as independent Q-ships and frail-looking women waited endlessly at bus stops or lugged expensive-looking packages back and forth across parking lots. Behind grocery store partitions and drycleaner's curtains sat or lazed volunteer part-time, full-time, and nighttime guards.

By September four hundred plus had been killed. Court dockets were clogged with scheduled homicide trials while the incidence of armed and unarmed robberies slid almost to zero. Police are forbidden to accept rewards but cabin cruisers, summer cottages, snowmobiles and trips to Hawaii can be bought and paid for by midnight cash. No one dared to resist arrest.

Then the reward system was extended outstate where rates of crime had been increasing. The 11 by 14 advertising was traced to a small shop on Center Street, but the owner had moved to Winnipeg. The first to die—four men, two of them brothers—tried to hold up an outstate bank. Their dress oxfords clashed with their hunting costumes and the bank manager, one teller, and two customers were waiting.

Armed and unarmed robbery died out together with some three hundred probably guilty persons but the Governor at last appealed for federal aid, pleading his entire legal system was breaking down. Officials of the three bordering states and Canada on the north were equally interested in his plea. Nothing was accomplished at a series of top level conferences.

In sudden succession the three bordering states had their own operating Committees, apparently unconnected with the first. Then other cities some miles away and then other states. A reliable estimate of reward money earned and paid out ran to half a billion dollars before the object was attained, as the reward system spread totally east and totally west of the Mississippi.

In New York City proper, children began to be seen playing in Central Park at dusk and even after.

With all rumors dissected, with duplicate reports discounted, and counting the death-welcoming onslaughts of unarmed applicants for free hundred-thousand-dollar survivor benefits, over the next three years the casualty list was somewhat less than automotive deaths in 1934. The fourth year there was a presidential election.

The winning candidate ran on a Law and Order platform. Two Secret Service men on inauguration day, while mingling with the gay crowd, incautiously let their .44 Magnums be seen and were dismembered quite quickly. After the first session of Congress a Federal ban on portable weapons was passed. This included weapons carried by law enforcement officers. Scotland Yard loaned fourteen quarterstaff specialists to the FBI police school and some seventeen thousand homicide cases were nolle prossed.

Montessori kindergartens expanded curricula to include judo and karate and General Motors phased out its Soapbox Derby and awarded black belts to the most worthy. *Popular Science & Mechanix Illustrated* ran a series on car-spring crossbows. Deer became an everyday sight and somewhat of a nuisance in the streets of Saginaw and Sebewaing.

At present the House Un-American Activities Committee is investigating the sky-rocketing import of Japanese chemical sets for adults.

7 Hawksbill Station

by Robert Silverberg

"Prison" is one of the final steps in the criminal justice system. Clearly, what happens at the beginning of the criminal justice process—arrest—affects what happens at the end of that process. Some argue that if the police were more efficient in the detection, apprehension, and prosecution of criminals, we would have less crime. Whether we would have less crime is a subject of heated debate; but a less ambiguous consequence would be the escalation of the population of our prisons— prisons already overcrowded and generally run-down.

Prisons can be looked at from two basic—but radically different—vantage points: from the "inside" and from the "outside." From the inside, a prison is much more than a place where one "spends time"; it is a culture. For it has its own rites, symbols, values, rules, language, communications system, and reward system. In addition, it has its own political structure: political leaders, "legislators," "judges," law enforcers, public opinion makers, and, alas, even executioners. Oftentimes, an individual who enters a prison becomes less concerned with being rehabilitated in order to return to society as a "good citizen" and more concerned with adjusting to this new culture, without which his chances for being returned safely to society will be somewhat lessened.

A study of a prison is really a study of the process of law and order. For the purpose of law and order is to *routinize* human behavior so as to achieve the stability without which no society can exist. No matter how benign, captivity—a word that perhaps better than any other captures the essence of prison life—routinizes human life and is by definition antihuman. This is ironic, because one of the most important purposes of sending people to prison is to deprogram them from the life of criminality and to reprogram them for entrance into society as an essentially "born-again" individual. The existence of high rates of recidivism is a measurement of the failure of prisons to achieve this fundamental objective.

In Robert Silverberg's story "Hawksbill Station," the prison system as a culture is portrayed. The author deftly analyzes the condition of captivity. As one reads this story, the question of what criteria should be used in making decisions about which individuals have to be removed from society for the sake of the general welfare needs to be kept in mind.

Barrett was the uncrowned king of Hawksbill Station. He had been there the longest; he had suffered the most; he had the deepest inner resources of strength.

Before his accident, he had been able to whip any man in the place. Now he was a cripple, but he still had that aura of power that gave him command. When there were problems at the Station, they were brought to Barrett. That was axiomatic. He was the king.

He ruled over quite a kingdom, too. In effect it was the whole world, pole to pole, meridian to meridian. For what it was worth. It wasn't worth very much.

Now it was raining again. Barrett shrugged himself to his feet in the quick, easy gesture that cost him an infinite amount of carefully concealed agony and shuffled to the door of his hut. Rain made him impatient; the pounding of those great greasy drops against the corrugated tin roof was enough even to drive a Jim Barrett loony. He nudged the door open. Standing in the doorway, Barrett looked out over his kingdom.

Barren rock, nearly to the horizon. A shield of raw dolomite going on and on. Raindrops danced and bounced on that continental slab of rock. No trees. No grass. Behind Barrett's hut lay the sea, gray and vast. The sky was gray, too, even when it wasn't raining.

He hobbled out into the rain. Manipulating his crutch was getting to be a simple matter for him now. He leaned comfortably, letting his crushed left foot dangle. A rockslide had pinned him last year during a trip to the edge of the Inland Sea. Back home, Barrett would have been fitted with prosthetics, and that would have been the end of it: a new ankle, a new instep, refurbished ligaments and tendons. But home was a billion years away; and home, there's no returning.

The rain hit him hard. Barrett was a big man, six and a half feet tall, with hooded dark eyes, a jutting nose, a chin that was a monarch among chins. He had weighed two hundred fifty pounds in his prime, in the good old agitating days when he had carried banners and pounded out manifestos. But now he was past sixty and beginning to shrink a little, the skin getting loose around the places where the mighty muscles used to be. It was hard to keep your weight in Hawksbill Station. The food was nutritious, but it lacked intensity. A man got to miss steak. Eating brachiopod stew and trilobite hash wasn't the same thing at all. Barrett was past all bitterness, though. That was another reason why the men regarded him as the leader. He didn't scowl. He didn't rant. He was resigned to his fate, tolerant of eternal exile, and so he could help the others get over that difficult heart-clawing period of transition.

A figure arrived, jogging through the rain: Norton. The doctrinaire Khrushchevist with the Trotskyite leanings. A small, excitable man who frequently appointed himself messenger whenever there was news at the Station. He sprinted toward Barrett's hut, slipping and sliding over the naked rocks.

Barrett held up a meaty hand.

"Whoa, Charley. Take it easy or you'll break your neck!"

Norton halted in front of the hut. The rain had pasted the widely spaced strands of his brown hair to his skull. His eyes had the fixed, glossy look of fanaticism—or perhaps just astigmatism. He gasped for breath and staggered into the hut, shaking himself like a wet puppy. He obviously had run all the way from the main building of the Station, three hundred yards away—a long dash over rock that slippery.

"Why are you standing around in the rain?" Norton asked.

"To get wet," said Barrett, following him. "What's the news?"

"The Hammer's glowing. We're getting company."

"How do you know it's a live shipment?"

"It's been glowing for half an hour. That means they're taking precautions. They're sending a new prisoner. Anyway, no supply shipment is due."

Barrett nodded. "Okay. I'll come over. If it's a new man, we'll bunk him in with Latimer."

Norton managed a rasping laugh. "Maybe he's a materialist. Latimer will drive him crazy with all that mystic nonsense. We could put him with Altman."

"And he'll be raped in half an hour."

"Altman's off that kick now," said Norton. "He's trying to create a real woman, not looking for second-rate substitutes."

"Maybe our new man doesn't have any spare ribs."

"Very funny, Jim." Norton did not look amused. "You know what I want the new man to be? A conservative, that's what. A black-souled reactionary straight out of Adam Smith. God, that's what I want."

"Wouldn't you be happy with a fellow Bolshevik?"

"This place is full of Bolsheviks," said Norton. "Of all shades from pale pink to flagrant scarlet. Don't you think I'm sick of them? Sitting around fishing for trilobites and discussing the relative merits of Kerensky and Malenkov? I need somebody to *talk* to, Jim. Somebody I can fight with."

"All right," Barrett said, slipping into his rain gear. "I'll see what I can do about hocusing a debating partner out of the Hammer for you. A rip-roaring objectivist, okay?" He laughed. "You know something, maybe there's been a revolution Up Front since we got our last man. Maybe the left is in and the right is out, and they'll start shipping us nothing *but* reactionaries. How would you like that? Fifty or a hundred storm troopers, Charley? Plenty of material to debate economics with. And the place will fill up with more and more of them, until we're outnumbered, and then maybe they'll have a *putsch* and get rid of all the stinking leftists sent here by the old regime, and—"

Barrett stopped. Norton was staring at him in amazement, his faded eyes wide, his hand compulsively smoothing his thinning hair to hide his embarrassment.

Barrett realized that he had just committed one of the most heinous crimes possible at Hawksbill Station: he had started to run off at the mouth. There hadn't been any call for his little outburst. What made it more troublesome was the fact that *he* was the one who had permitted himself such a luxury. He was supposed to be the strong one of this place, the stabilizer, the man of absolute integrity and principle and sanity on whom the others could lean. And suddenly he had lost control. It was a bad sign. His dead foot was throbbing again; possibly that was the reason.

In a tight voice he said, "Let's go. Maybe the new man is here already."

They stepped outside. The rain was beginning to let up; the storm was moving out to sea. In the east over what would one day be the Atlantic, the sky was still clotted with gray mist, but to the west a different grayness was emerging, the shade of normal gray that meant dry weather. Before he had come out here, Barrett had expected to find the sky practically black, because there'd be fewer dust particles to bounce the light around and turn things blue. But the sky seemed to be weary beige. So much for advance theories.

Through the thinning rain they walked toward the main building. Norton accommodated himself to Barrett's limping pace, and Barrett, wielding his crutch furiously, did his damndest not to let his infirmity slow them up. He nearly lost his footing twice and fought hard not to let Norton see.

Hawksbill Station spread out before them.

It covered about five hundred acres. In the center of everything was the main building, an ample dome that contained most of their equipment and supplies. At widely spaced intervals, rising from the rock shield like grotesque giant green mushrooms, were the plastic blisters of the individual dwellings. Some, like Barrett's, were shielded by tin sheeting salvaged from shipments from Up Front. Others stood unprotected, just as they had come from the mouth of the extruder.

The huts numbered about eighty. At the moment, there were a hundred forty inmates in Hawksbill Station, pretty close to the all-time high. Up Front hadn't sent back any hut-building materials for a long time, and so all the newer arrivals had to double up with bunkmates. Barrett and all those whose exile had begun before 2014 had the privilege of private dwellings if they wanted them. (Some did not wish to live alone; Barrett, to preserve his own authority, felt that he was required to.) As new exiles arrived, they bunked in with those who currently lived alone, in reverse order of seniority. Most of the 2015 exiles had been forced to take roommates now. Another dozen deportees and the 2014 group would be doubling up. Of course, there were deaths all up and down the line, and there were plenty who were eager to have company in their huts.

Barrett felt, though, that a man who has been sentenced to life imprisonment ought to have the privilege of privacy, if he desires it. One of his biggest problems here was keeping people from cracking up because there was too little privacy. Propinquity could be intolerable in a place like this.

Norton pointed toward the big, shiny-skinned, green dome of the main building. "There's Altman going in now. And Rudiger. And Hutchett. Something's happening!"

Barrett stepped up his pace. Some of the men entering the building saw his bulky figure coming over the rise in the rock and waved to him. Barrett lifted a massive hand in reply. He felt mounting excitement. It was a big event at the Station whenever a new man arrived. Nobody had come for six months, now. That was the longest gap he could remember. It had started to seem as though no one would ever come again.

That would be a catastrophe.

New men were all that stood between the older inmates and insanity. New men brought news from the future, news from the world that was eternally left behind. They contributed new personalities to a group that always was in danger of going stale.

And, Barrett knew, some men—he was not one—lived in the deluded hope that the next arrival might just turn out to be a woman.

That was why they flocked to the main building when the Hammer began to glow. Barrett hobbled down the path. The rain died away just as he reached the entrance.

Within, sixty or seventy Station residents crowded the chamber of the Hammer—just about every man in the place who was able in body and mind and still alert enough to show curiosity about a newcomer. They shouted greetings to Barrett. He nodded, smiled, deflected their questions with amiable gestures.

"Who's it going to be this time, Jim?"

"Maybe a girl, huh? Around nineteen years old, blonde, and built like—"

"I hope he can play stochastic chess, anyway."

"Look at the glow! It's deepening!"

Barrett, like the others, stared at the Hammer. The complex, involuted collection of unfathomable instruments burned a bright cherry red, betokening the surge of who knew how many kilowatts being pumped in at the far end of the line.

The glow was beginning to spread to the Anvil now, that broad aluminum bedplate on which all shipments from the future were dropped. In another moment—

"Condition Crimson!" somebody suddenly yelled. "Here he comes!"

II

One billion years up the time-line, power was flooding into the real Hammer of which this was only the partial replica. A man—or something else, perhaps a shipment of supplies—stood in the center of the real Anvil, waiting for the Hawksbill Field to enfold him and kick him back to the early Paleozoic. The effect of time-travel was very much like being hit with a gigantic hammer and driven clear through the walls of the continuum: hence the governing metaphors for the parts of the machine.

Setting up Hawksbill Station had been a long, slow job. The Hammer had knocked a pathway and had sent back the nucleus of the receiving station, first. Since there was no receiving station on hand to receive the receiving station, a certain amount of waste had occurred. It wasn't necessary to have a Hammer and Anvil on the receiving end, except as a fine control to prevent temporal spread; without the equipment, the field wandered a little, and it was possible to scatter consecutive shipments over a span of twenty or thirty years. There was plenty of such temporal garbage all around Hawksbill Station, stuff that had been intended for original installation, but which because of tuning imprecisions in the pre-Hammer days had landed a couple of decades (and a couple of hundred miles) away from the intended site.

Despite such difficulties, they had finally sent through enough components to the master temporal site to allow for the construction of a receiving station. Then the first prisoners had gone through; they were technicians who knew how to put the Hammer and Anvil together. Of course, it was their privilege to refuse to cooperate. But it was to their own advantage to assemble the receiving station, thus making it possible for them to be sure of getting further supplies from Up Front. They had done the job. After that, outfitting Hawksbill Station had been easy.

Now the Hammer glowed, meaning that they had activated the Hawksbill Field on the sending end, somewhere up around 2028 or 2030 A.D. All the sending was done there. All the receiving was done here. It didn't work the other way. Nobody really knew why, although there was a lot of superficially profound talk about the rules of entropy.

There was a whining, hissing sound as the edges of the Hawksbill Field began to ionize the atmosphere in the room. Then came the expected thunderclap of implosion, caused by an imperfect overlapping of the quantity of air that was subtracted from this era and the quantity that was being thrust into it. And then, abruptly, a man dropped out of the Hammer and lay, stunned and limp, on the gleaming Anvil.

He looked young, which surprised Barrett considerably. He seemed to be well under thirty. Generally, only middle-aged men were sent to Hawksbill Station. Incorrigibles, who had to be separated from humanity for the general good. The youngest man in the place now had been close to forty when he arrived. The sight of this lean, clean-cut boy drew a hiss of anguish from a couple of the men in the room, and Barrett understood the constellation of emotions that pained them.

The new man sat up. He stirred like a child coming out of a long, deep sleep. He looked around.

His face was very pale. His thin lips seemed bloodless. His blue eyes blinked rapidly. His jaws worked as though he wanted to say something, but could not find the words.

There were no harmful physiological effects to time-travel, but it could be a jolt to the consciousness. The last moments before the Hammer descended were very much like the final moments beneath the guillotine, since exile to Hawksbill Station was tantamount to a sentence of death. The departing prisoner took his last look at the world of rocket transport and artificial organs, at the world in which he had lived and loved and agitated for a political cause, and then he was rammed into the inconceivably remote past on a one-way journey. It was a gloomy business, and it was not very surprising that the newcomers arrived in a state of emotional shock.

Barrett elbowed his way through the crowd. Automatically, the others made way for him. He reached the lip of the Anvil and leaned over it, extending a hand to the new man. His broad smile was met by a look of blank bewilderment.

"I'm Jim Barrett. Welcome to Hawksbill Station. Here—get off that thing before a load of groceries lands on top of you." Wincing a little as he shifted his weight, Barrett pulled the new man down from the Anvil. It was altogether likely for the idiots Up Front to shoot another shipment along a minute after sending a man.

Barrett beckoned to Mel Rudiger, and the plump anarchist handed the new man an alcohol capsule. He took it and pressed it to his arm without a word. Charley Norton offered him a candy bar. The man shook it off. He looked groggy. A real case of temporal shock, Barrett thought, possibly the worst he had ever seen. The newcomer hadn't even spoken yet. Could the effect really be that extreme?

Barrett said, "We'll go to the infirmary and check you out. Then I'll assign you your quarters. There's time for you to find your way around and meet everybody later on. What's your name?"

"Hahn. Lew Hahn."

"I can't hear you."

"Hahn," the man repeated, still only barely audible.

"When are you from, Lew?"

"2029."

"You feel pretty sick?"

"I feel awful. I don't even believe this is happening to me. There's no such place as Hawksbill Station, is there?"

"I'm afraid there is," Barrett said. "At least, for most of us. A few of the boys think it's all an illusion induced by drugs. But I have my doubts of that. If it's an illusion, it's a damned good one. Look."

He put one arm around Hahn's shoulders and guided him through the press of prisoners, out of the Hammer chamber and toward the nearby infirmary. Although Hahn looked thin, even fragile, Barrett was surprised to feel the rippling muscles in those shoulders. He suspected that this man was a lot less helpless and ineffectual than he seemed to be right now. He *had* to be, in order to merit banishment to Hawksbill Station.

They passed the door of the building. "Look out there," Barrett commanded.

Hahn looked. He passed a hand across his eyes as though to clear away unseen cobwebs and looked again.

"A late Cambrian landscape," said Barrett quietly. "This would be a geologist's dream, except that geologists don't tend to become political prisoners, it seems. Out in front is the Appalachian Geosyncline. It's a strip of rock a few hundred miles wide and a few thousand miles long, from the Gulf of Mexico to Newfoundland. To the east we've got the Atlantic. A little way to the west we've got the Inland Sea. Somewhere two thousand miles to the west there's the Cordilleran Geosyncline, that's going to be California and Washington and Oregon someday. Don't hold your breath. I hope you like seafood."

Hahn stared, and Barrett standing beside him at the doorway, stared also. You never got used to the alienness of this place, not even after you lived here twenty years, as Barrett had. It was Earth, and yet it was not really Earth at all, because it was somber and empty and unreal. The gray oceans swarmed with life, of course. But there was nothing on land except occasional patches of moss in the occasional patches of soil that had formed on the bare rock. Even a few cockroaches would be welcome; but insects, it seemed, were still a couple of geological periods in the future. To land-dwellers, this was a dead world, a world unborn.

Shaking his head, Hahn moved away from the door. Barrett led him down the corridor and into the small, brightly lit room that served as the infirmary. Doc Quesada was waiting. Quesada wasn't really a doctor, but he had been a medical technician once, and that was good enough. He was a compact, swarthy man with a look of complete self-assurance. He hadn't lost too many patients, all things considered. Barrett had watched him removing appendices with total aplomb. In his white smock, Quesada looked sufficiently medical to fit his role.

Barrett said, "Doc, this is Lew Hahn. He's in temporal shock. Fix him up."

Quesada nudged the newcomer onto a webfoam cradle and unzipped his blue jersey. Then he reached for his medical kit. Hawksbill Station was well equipped for most medical emergencies, now. The people Up Front had no wish to be inhumane, and they sent back all sorts of useful things, like anesthetics and surgical clamps and medicines and dermal probes. Barrett could remember a time at the beginning when there had been nothing much here but the empty huts; and a man who hurt himself was in real trouble.

"He's had a drink already," said Barrett.

"I see that," Quesada murmured. He scratched at his short-cropped, bristly mustache. The little diagnostat in the cradle had gone rapidly to work, flashing information about Hahn's blood pressure, potassium count, dilation index, and much else. Quesada seemed to comprehend the barrage of facts. After a moment he said to Hahn, "You aren't really sick, are you? Just shaken up a little. I don't blame you. Here— I'll give you a quick jolt to calm your nerves, and you'll be all right. As all right as any of us ever are."

He put a tube to Hahn's carotid and thumbed the snout. The subsonic whirred, and a tranquilizing compound slid into the man's bloodstream. Hahn shivered.

Quesada said, "Let him rest for five minutes. Then he'll be over the hump."

They left Hahn in his cradle and went out of the infirmary. In the hall, Barrett looked down at the little medic and said, "What's the report on Valdosto?"

Valdosto had gone into psychotic collapse several weeks before. Quesada was keeping him drugged and trying to bring him slowly back to the reality of Hawksbill Station. Shrugging, he replied, "The status is quo. I let him out from under the dream-juice this morning, and he was the same as he's been."

"You don't think he'll come out of it?"

"I doubt it. He's cracked for keeps. They could paste him together Up Front, but—"

"Yeah," Barrett said. "If he could get Up Front at all, Valdosto wouldn't have cracked. Keep him happy, then. If he can't be sane, he can at least be comfortable. What about Altman? Still got the shakes?"

"He's building a woman."

"That's what Charley Norton told me. What's he using? A rag, a bone—"

"I gave him surplus chemicals. Chosen for their color, mainly. He's got some foul green copper compounds and a little bit of ethyl alcohol and six or seven other things, and he collected some soil and threw in a lot of dead shellfish, and he's sculpting it all into what he claims is female shape and waiting for lightning to strike it."

"In other words, he's gone crazy," Barrett said.

"I think that's a safe assumption. But he's not molesting his friends any more, anyway. You didn't think his homosexual phase would last much longer, as I recall."

"No, but I didn't think he'd go off the deep end. If a man needs sex and he can find some consenting playmates here, that's quite all right with me. But when he starts putting a woman together out of some dirt and rotten brachiopod meat it means we've lost him. It's really just too bad."

Quesada's dark eyes flickered. "We're all going to go that way sooner or later, Jim."

"I haven't. You haven't."

"Give us time. I've only been here eleven years."

"Altman's been here only eight. Valdosto even less."

"Some shells crack faster than others," said Quesada. "Here's our new friend."

Hahn had come out of the infirmary to join them. He still looked pale, but the fright was gone from his eyes. He was beginning to adjust to the unthinkable.

He said, "I couldn't help overhearing your conversation. Is there a lot of mental illness here?"

"Some of the men haven't been able to find anything meaningful to do here," Barrett said. "It eats them away. Quesada here has his medical work. I've got administrative duties. A couple of the fellows are studying the sea life. We've got a newspaper to keep some busy. But there are always those who just let themselves slide into despair, and they crack up. I'd say we have thirty or forty certifiable maniacs here at the moment, out of a hundred forty residents."

"That's not so bad," Hahn said. "Considering the inherent instability of the men who get sent here and the unusual conditions of life here."

Barrett laughed. "Hey, you're suddenly pretty articulate, aren't you? What was in the stuff Doc Quesada jolted you with?"

"I didn't mean to sound superior," Hahn said quickly. "Maybe that came out a little too smug. I mean—"

"Forget it. What did you do Up Front, anyway?"

"I was sort of an economist."

"Just what we need," said Quesada. "He can help us solve our balance-of-payments problem."

Barrett said, "If you were an economist, you'll have plenty to discuss here. This place is full of economic theorists who'll want to bounce their ideas off you. Some of them are almost sane, too. Come with me and I'll show you where you're going to stay."

III

The path from the main building to the hut of Donald Latimer was mainly downhill, for which Barrett was grateful even though he knew that he'd have to negotiate the uphill return in a little while. Latimer's hut was on the eastern side of the Station, looking out over the ocean. They walked slowly toward it. Hahn was solicitous of Barrett's game leg, and Barrett was irritated by the exaggerated care the younger man took to keep pace with him.

He was puzzled by this Hahn. The man was full of seeming contradictions—showing up here with the worst case of arrival shock Barrett had ever seen, then snapping out of it with remarkable quickness; looking frail and shy, but hiding solid muscles inside his jersey; giving an outer appearance of incompetence, but speaking with calm control. Barrett wondered what this young man had done to earn him the trip to Hawksbill Station, but there was time for such inquiries later. All the time in the world.

Hahn said, "Is everything like this? Just rock and ocean?"

"That's all. Land life hasn't evolved yet. Everything's wonderfully simple, isn't it? No clutter. No urban sprawl. There's some moss moving onto land, but not much."

"And in the sea? Swimming dinosaurs?"

Barrett shook his head. "There won't be any vertebrates for half a million years. We don't even have fish yet, let alone reptiles out there. All we can offer is that which creepeth. Some shellfish, some big fellows that look like squids and trilobites. Seven hundred billion different species of trilobites. We've got a man named Rudiger—he's the one who gave you the drink—who's making a collection of them. He's writing the world's definitive text on trilobites."

"But nobody will ever read it in—in the future."

"Up Front, we say."

"Up Front."

"That's the pity of it," said Barrett. "We told Rudiger to inscribe his book on imperishable plates of gold and hope that it's found by paleontologists. But he says the odds are against it. A billion years of geology will chew his plates to hell before they can be found."

Hahn sniffed. "Why does the air smell so strange?"

"It's a different mix," Barrett said. "We've analyzed it. More nitrogen, a little less oxygen, hardly any CO_2 at all. But that isn't really why it smells odd to you. The thing is, it's pure air, unpolluted by the exhalations of life. Nobody's been respiring into it but us lads, and there aren't enough of us to matter."

Smiling, Hahn said, "I feel a little cheated that it's so empty. I expected lush jungles of weird plants and pterodactyls swooping through the air and maybe a tyrannosaur crashing into a fence around the Station."

"No jungles. No pterodactyls. No tyrannosaurs. No fences. You didn't do your homework."

"Sorry."

"This is the late Cambrian. Sea life exclusively."

"It was very kind of them to pick such a peaceful era as the dumping ground for political prisoners," Hahn said. "I was afraid it would be all teeth and claws."

"Kind, hell! They were looking for an era where we couldn't do any harm. That meant tossing us back before the evolution of mammals, just in case we'd accidentally get hold of the ancestor of all humanity and snuff him out. And while they were at it, they decided to stash us so far in the past that we'd be beyond all land life, on the theory that maybe even if we slaughtered a baby dinosaur it might affect the entire course of the future."

"They don't mind if we catch a few trilobites?"

"Evidently they think it's safe," Barrett said. "It looks as though they were right. Hawksbill Station has been here for twenty-five years, and it doesn't seem as though we've tampered with future history in any measurable way. Of course, they're careful not to send us any women."

"Why is that?"

"So we don't start reproducing and perpetuating ourselves. Wouldn't that mess up the time-lines? A successful human outpost in one billion B.C., that's had all that time to evolve and mutate and grow? By the time the twenty-first century came around, our descendants would be in charge, and the other kind of human being would probably be in penal servitude, and there'd be more paradoxes created than you could shake a trilobite at. So they don't send women here. There's a prison camp for women, too, but it's a few hundred million years up the time-line in the late Silurian, and never the twain shall meet. That's why Ned Altman's trying to build a woman out of dust and garbage."

"God made Adam out of less."

"Altman isn't God," Barrett said. "That's the root of his whole problem. Look, here's the hut where you're going to stay. I'm rooming you with Don Latimer. He's a very sensitive, interesting, pleasant person. He used to be a physicist before he got into politics, and he's been here about a dozen years, and I might as well warn you that he's developed a strong and somewhat cockeyed mystic streak lately. The fellow he was rooming with killed himself last year, and since then he's been trying to find some way out of here through extrasensory powers."

"Is he serious?"

"I'm afraid he is. And we try to take him seriously. We all humor each other at Hawksbill Station; it's the only way we avoid a mass psychosis. Latimer will probably try to get you to collaborate with him on his project. If you don't like living with him, I can arrange a transfer for you. But I want to see how he reacts to someone new at the Station. I'd like you to give him a chance."

"Maybe I'll even help him find his psionic gateway."

"If you do, take me along," said Barrett. They both laughed. Then he rapped at Latimer's door. There was no answer, and after a moment Barrett pushed the door open. Hawksbill Station had no locks.

Latimer sat in the middle of the bare rock floor, cross-legged, meditating. He was a slender, gentle-faced man just beginning to look old. Right now he seemed a million miles away, ignoring them completely. Hahn shrugged. Barrett put a finger to his lips. They waited in silence for a few minutes, and then Latimer showed signs of coming up from his trance.

He got to his feet in a single flowing motion, without using his hands. In a low, courteous voice he said to Hahn, "Have you just arrived?"

"Within the last hour. I'm Lew Hahn."

"Donald Latimer. I regret that I have to make your acquaintance in these surroundings. But maybe we won't have to tolerate this illegal imprisonment much longer."

Barrett said, "Don, Lew is going to bunk with you. I think you'll get along well. He was an economist in 2029 until they gave him the Hammer."

"Where do you live?" Latimer asked, animation coming into his eyes.

"San Francisco."

The glow faded. Latimer said, "Were you ever in Toronto? I'm from there. I had a daughter—she'd be twenty-three now, Nella Latimer. I wondered if you knew her."

"No. I'm sorry."

"It wasn't very likely. But I'd love to know what kind of a woman she became. She was a little girl when I last saw her. Now I guess she's married. Or perhaps they've sent her to the other Station. Nella Latimer—you're sure you didn't know her?"

Barrett left them together. It looked as though they'd get along. He told Latimer to bring Hahn up to the main building at dinner for introductions and went out. A chilly drizzle had begun again. Barrett made his way slowly, painfully up the hill. It had been sad to see the light flicker from Latimer's eyes when Hahn said he didn't know his daughter. Most of the time, men at Hawksbill Station tried not to speak about their families, preferring to keep those tormenting memories well repressed. But the arrival of newcomers generally stirred old ties. There was never any news of relatives and no way to obtain any, because it was impossible for the Station to communicate with anyone Up Front. No way to ask for the photo of a loved one, no way to request specific medicines, no way to obtain a certain book or a coveted tape. In a mindless, impersonal way, Up Front sent periodic shipments to the Station of things thought useful—reading matter, medical supplies, technical equipment, food. Occasionally they were startling in their generosity, as when they sent a case of Burgundy, or a box of sensory spools, or a recharger for the power pack. Such gifts usually meant a brief thaw in the world situation, which customarily produced a short-lived desire to be kind to the boys in Hawksbill Station. But they had a policy about sending information about relatives. Or about contemporary newspapers. Fine wine, yes; a tridim of a daughter who would never be seen again, no.

For all Up Front knew, there was no one alive in Hawksbill Station. A plague could have killed everyone off ten years ago, but there was no way of telling. That was why the shipments still came back.

The government whirred and clicked with predictable continuity. The government, whatever else it might be, was not malicious. There were other kinds of totalitarianism besides bloody repressive tyranny.

Pausing at the top of the hill, Barrett caught his breath. Naturally, the alien air no longer smelled strange to him. He filled his lungs with it. Once again the rain ceased. Through the grayness came the sunshine, making the naked rocks sparkle. Barrett closed his eyes a moment and leaned on his crutch and saw, as though on an inner screen, the creatures with many legs climbing up out of the sea, and the mossy carpets spreading, and the flowerless plants uncoiling and spreading their scaly branches, and the dull hides of eerie amphibians glistening on the shores and the tropic heat of the coal-forming epoch descending like a glove over the world.

All that lay far in the future. Dinosaurs. Little chittering mammals. Pithecanthropus in the forests of Java. Sargon and Hannibal and Attila and Orville Wright and Thomas Edison and Edmond Hawksbill. And finally a benign government that would find the thoughts of some men so intolerable that the only safe place to which they could be banished was a rock at the beginning of time. The government was too civilized to put men to death for subversive activities and too cowardly to let them remain alive. The compromise was the living death of Hawksbill Station. One billion years of impassable time was suitable insulation even for the most nihilistic idea.

Grimacing a little, Barrett struggled the rest of the way back toward his hut. He had long since come to accept his exile, but accepting his ruined foot was another matter entirely. The idle wish to find a way to regain the freedom of his own time no longer possessed him; but he wished with all his soul that the blank-faced administrators Up Front would send back a kit that would allow him to rebuild his foot.

He entered his hut and flung his crutch aside, sinking down instantly on his cot. There had been no cots when he had come to Hawksbill Station. He had come here in the fourth year of the Station, when there were only a dozen buildings and little in the way of creature comforts. It had been a miserable place, then, but the steady accretion of shipments from Up Front had made it relatively tolerable. Of the fifty or so prisoners who had preceded Barrett to Hawksbill, none remained alive. He had held the highest seniority for almost ten years. Time moved here at one-to-one correlation with time Up Front; the Hammer was locked on this point of time, so that Hahn, arriving here today more than twenty years after Barrett, had departed from a year Up Front more than twenty years after the time of Barret's expulsion.

Barrett had not had the heart to begin pumping Hahn for news of 2029 so soon. He would learn all he needed to know, and small cheer it would be, anyway.

Barrett reached for a book. But the fatigue of hobbling around the station had taken more out of him than he realized. He looked at the page for a moment. Then he put it away and closed his eyes and dozed.

IV

That evening, as every evening, the men of Hawksbill Station gathered in the main building for dinner and recreation. It was not mandatory, and some men chose to eat alone. But tonight nearly everyone who was in full possession of his faculties was there, because this was one of the infrequent occasions when a newcomer had arrived to be questioned about the world of men.

Hahn looked uneasy about his sudden notoriety. He seemed to be basically shy, unwilling to accept all the attention now being thrust upon him. There he sat in the middle of the group while men twenty and thirty years his senior crowded in on him with their questions, and it was obvious that he wasn't enjoying the session.

Sitting to one side, Barrett took little part in the discussion. His curiosity about Up Front's ideological shifts had ebbed a long time ago. It was hard for him to realize that he had once been so passionately concerned about concepts like syndicalism and the dictatorship of the proletariat and the guaranteed annual wage that he had been willing to risk imprisonment over them. His concern for humanity had not waned, merely the degree of his involvement in the twenty-first century's political problems. After twenty years at Hawksbill Station, Up Front had become unreal to Jim Barrett, and his energies centered around the crises and challenges of what he had come to think of as "his own" time—the late Cambrian.

So he listened, but more with an ear for what the talk revealed about Lew Hahn than for what it revealed about current events Up Front. And what it revealed about Lew Hahn was mainly a matter of what was not revealed.

Hahn didn't say much. He seemed to be feinting and evading.

Charley Norton wanted to know, "Is there any sign of a weakening of the phony conservatism yet? I mean, they've been promising the end of big government for thirty years, and it gets bigger all the time."

Hahn moved restlessly in his chair. "They still promise. As soon as conditions become stabilized—"

"Which is when?"

"I don't know. I suppose they're making words."

"What about the Martian Commune?" demanded Sid Hutchett. "Have they been infiltrating agents onto Earth?"

"I couldn't really say."

"How about the Gross Global Product?" Mel Rudiger wanted to know. "What's its curve? Still holding level, or has it started to drop?"

Hahn tugged at his ear. "I think it's slowly edging down."

"Where does the index stand?" Rudiger asked. "The last figures we had, for '25, it was at 909. But in four years—"

"It might be something like 875 now," said Hahn.

It struck Barrett as a little odd that an economist would be so hazy about the basic economic statistic. Of course, he didn't know how long Hahn had been imprisoned before getting the Hammer. Maybe he simply wasn't up on the recent figures. Barrett held his peace.

Charley Norton wanted to find out some things about the legal rights of citizens. Hahn couldn't tell him. Rudiger asked about the impact of weather control—whether the supposedly conservative government of liberators was still ramming programmed weather down the mouths of the citizens—and Hahn wasn't sure. Hahn couldn't rightly say much about the functions of the judiciary, whether it had recovered any of the power stripped from it by the Enabling Act of '18. He didn't have any comments to offer on the tricky subject of population control. In fact, his performance was striking for its lack of hard information.

"He isn't saying much at all," Charley Norton grumbled to the silent Barrett. "He's putting up a smokescreen. But either he's not telling what he knows, or he doesn't know."

"Maybe he's not very bright," Barrett suggested.

"What did he do to get here? He must have had some kind of deep commitment. But it doesn't show, Jim! He's an intelligent kid, but he doesn't seem plugged in to anything that ever mattered to any of us."

Doc Quesada offered a thought. "Suppose he isn't a political at all. Suppose they're sending a different kind of prisoner back now. Axe murderers, or something. A quiet kid who quietly chopped up sixteen people one Sunday morning. Naturally he isn't interested in politics."

Barrett shook his head. "I doubt that. I think he's just clamming up because he's shy or ill at ease. It's his first night here, remember. He's just been kicked out of his own world and there's no going back. He may have left a wife and baby behind, you know. He may simply not give a damn tonight about sitting up there and spouting the latest word on abstract philosophical theory, when all he wants to do is go off and cry his eyes out. I say we ought to leave him alone."

Quesada and Norton looked convinced. They shook their heads in agreement; but Barrett didn't voice his opinion to the room in general. He let the quizzing of Hahn continue until it petered out of its own accord. The men began to drift away. A couple cf them went in back to convert Hahn's vague generalities into the lead story for the next handwritten edition of the Hawksbill Station *Times*. Rudiger stood on a table and shouted out that he was going night fishing, and four men asked to join him. Charley Norton sought out his usual debating partner, the nihilist Ken Belardi, and reopened, like a festering wound, their discussion of planning versus chaos, which bored them both to the point of screaming. The nightly games of stochastic chess began. The loners who had made rare visits to the main building simply went back to their huts to do whatever they did in them alone each night.

Hahn stood apart, fidgeting and uncertain.

Barrett went up to him. "I guess you didn't really want to be quizzed tonight," he said.

"I'm sorry I couldn't have been more informative. I've been out of circulation a while, you see."

"But you were politically active, weren't you?"

"Oh, yes," Hahn said. "Of course." He flicked his tongue over his lips. "What's supposed to happen now?"

"Nothing in particular. We don't have organized activities here. Doc and I are going out on sick call. Care to join us?"

"What does it involve?" Hahn asked.

"Visiting some of the worst cases. It can be grim, but you'll get a panoramic view of Hawksbill Station in a hurry."

"I'd like to go."

Barrett gestured to Quesada, and the three of them left the building. This was a nightly ritual for Barrett, difficult as it was since he had hurt his foot. Before turning in, he visited the goofy ones and the psycho ones and the catatonic ones, tucked them in, wished them a good night and a healed mind in the morning. Someone had to show them that he cared. Barrett did.

Outside, Hahn peered up at the moon. It was nearly full tonight, shining like a burnished coin, its face a pale salmon color and hardly pockmarked at all.

"It looks so different here," Hahn said. "The craters—where are the craters?"

"Most of them haven't been formed yet," said Barrett. "A billion years is a long time even for the moon. Most of its upheavals are still ahead. We think it may still have an atmosphere, too. That's why it looks pink to us. Of course, Up Front hasn't bothered to send us much in the way of astronomical equipment. We can only guess."

Hahn started to say something. He cut himself off after one blurted syllable.

Quesada said, "Don't hold back. What were you about to suggest?"

Hahn laughed in self-mockery. "That you ought to fly up there and take a look. It struck me as odd that you'd spend all these years here theorizing about whether the moon's got an atmosphere and wouldn't ever once go up to look. But I forgot."

"It would be useful to have a commut ship from Up Front," Barrett said. "But it hasn't occurred to them. All we can do is look. The moon's a popular place in '29, is it?"

"The biggest resort in the system," Hahn said. "I was there on my honeymoon. Leah and I—"

He stopped again.

Barrett said hurriedly, "This is Bruce Valdosto's hut. He cracked up a few weeks ago. When we go in, stand behind us so he doesn't see you. He might be violent with a stranger. He's unpredictable."

Valdosto was a husky man in his late forties, with swarthy skin, coarse curling black hair, and the broadest shoulders any man had ever had. Sitting down, he looked even burlier than Jim Barrett, which was saying a great deal. But Valdosto had short, stumpy legs, the legs of a man of ordinary stature tacked to the trunk of a giant, which spoiled the effect completely. In his years Up Front he had totally refused any prosthesis. He believed in living with deformities.

Right now he was strapped into a webfoam cradle. His domed forehead was flecked with beads of sweat, his eyes were glittering beadily in the darkness. He was a very sick man. Once he had been clearminded enough to throw a sleet bomb into a meeting of the Council of Syndics, giving a dozen of them a bad case of gamma poisoning, but now he scarcely knew up from down, right from left.

Barrett leaned over him and said, "How are you, Bruce?"

"Who's that?"

"Jim. It's a beautiful night, Bruce. How'd you like to come outside and get some fresh air? The moon's almost full."

"I've got to rest. The committee meeting tomorrow—"

"It's been postponed."

"But how can it? The Revolution—"

"That's been postponed too. Indefinitely."

"Are they disbanding the cells?" Valdosto asked harshly.

"We don't know yet. We're waiting for orders. Come outside, Bruce. The air will do you good."

Muttering, Valdosto let himself be unlaced. Quesada and Barrett pulled him to his feet and propelled him through the door of the hut. Barrett caught sight of Hahn in the shadows, his face somber with shock.

They stood together outside the hut. Barrett pointed to the moon. "It's got such a lovely color here. Not like the dead thing Up Front. And look, look down there, Bruce. The sea breaking on the rocky shore. Rudiger's out fishing. I can see his boat by moonlight."

"Striped bass," said Valdosto. "Sunnies. Maybe he'll catch some sunnies."

"There aren't any sunnies here. They haven't evolved yet." Barrett fished in his pocket and drew out something ridged and glossy, about two inches long. It was the exoskeleton of a small trilobite. He offered it to Valdosto, who shook his head.

"Don't give me that cockeyed crab."

"It's a trilobite, Bruce. It's extinct, but so are we. We're a billion years in our own past."

"You must be crazy," Valdosto said in a calm, low voice that belied his wild-eyed appearance. He took the trilobite from Barrett and hurled it against the rocks. "Cockeyed crab," he muttered.

Quesada shook his head sadly. He and Barrett led the sick man into the hut again. Valdosto did not protest as the medic gave him the sedative. His weary mind, rebelling entirely against the monstrous concept that he had been exiled to the inconceivably remote past, welcomed sleep.

When they went out Barrett saw Hahn holding the trilobite on his palm, and staring at it in wonder. Hahn offered it to him, but Barrett brushed it away. "Keep it if you like," he said. "There are more."

They went on. They found Ned Altman beside his hut, crouching on his knees and patting his hands over the crude, lopsided form of what, from its exaggerated breasts and hips, appeared to be the image of a woman. He stood up when they appeared. Altman was a neat little man with yellow hair and nearly invisible white eyebrows. Unlike anyone else in the Station, he had actually been a government man once, fifteen years ago, before seeing through the myth of syndicalist capitalism and joining one of the underground factions. Eight years at Hawksbill Station had done things to him.

Altman pointed to his golem and said, "I hoped there'd be lightning

in the rain today. That'll do it, you know. But there isn't much lightning this time of year. She'll get up alive, and then I'll need you, Doc,
to give her her shots and trim away some of the rough places."

Quesada forced a smile. "I'll be glad to do it, Ned. But you know the
terms."

"Sure. When I'm through with her, you get her. You think I'm a
goddam monopolist? I'll share her. There'll be a waiting list. Just so
you don't forget who made her, though. She'll remain mine, whenever
I need her." He noticed Hahn. "Who are you?"

"He's new," Barrett said. "Lew Hahn. He came this afternoon."

"Ned Altman," said Altman with a courtly bow. "Formerly in
government service. You're pretty young, aren't you? How's your sex
orientation? Hetero?"

Hahn winced. "I'm afraid so."

"It's okay. I wouldn't touch you. I've got a project going, here. But
I just want you to know, I'll put you on my list. You're young and
you've probably got stronger needs than some of us. I won't forget
about you, even though you're new here."

Quesada coughed. "You ought to get some rest now, Ned. Maybe
there'll be lightning tomorrow."

Altman did not resist. The doctor took him inside and put him to
bed, while Hahn and Barrett surveyed the man's handiwork. Hahn
pointed toward the figure's middle.

"He's left out something essential," he said. "If he's planning to
make love to this girl after he's finished creating her, he'd better—"

"It was there yesterday," said Barrett. "He must be changing orientation again." Quesada emerged from the hut. They went on, down
the rocky path.

Barrett did not make the complete circuit that night. Ordinarily, he
would have gone all the way down to Latimer's hut overlooking the
sea, for Latimer was on his list of sick ones. But Barrett had visited
Latimer once that day, and he didn't think his aching good leg was up
to another hike that far. So after he and Quesada and Hahn had
been to all of the easily accessible huts and had visited the man who
prayed for alien beings to rescue him and the man who was trying
to break into a parallel universe where everything was as it ought to be
in the world and the man who lay on his cot sobbing for all his wakeful
hours, Barrett said goodnight to his companions and allowed Quesada
to escort Hahn back to his hut without him.

After observing Hahn for half a day, Barrett realized he did not known much more about him than when he had first dropped onto the Anvil. That was odd. But maybe Hahn would open up a little more, after he'd been here a while. Barrett stared up at the salmon moon and reached into his pocket to finger the little trilobite before he remembered that he had given it to Hahn. He shuffled into his hut. He wondered how long ago Hahn had taken that lunar honeymoon trip.

V

Rudiger's catch was spread out in front of the main building the next morning when Barrett came up for breakfast. He had had a good night's fishing, obviously. He usually did. Rudiger went out three or four nights a week, in a little dinghy that he had cobbled together a few years ago from salvaged materials, and he took with him a team of friends whom he had trained in the deft use of the trawling nets.

It was an irony that Rudiger, the anarchist, the man who believed in individualism and the abolition of all political institutions, should be so good at leading a team of fishermen. Rudiger didn't care for teamwork in the abstract. But it was hard to manipulate the nets alone, he had discovered. Hawksbill Station had many little ironies of that sort. Political theorists tend to swallow their theories when forced back on pragmatic measures of survival.

The prize of the catch was a cephalopod about a dozen feet long—a rigid conical tube out of which some limp squid-like tentacles dangled. Plenty of meat on that one, Barrett thought. Dozens of trilobites were arrayed around it, ranging in size from the inch-long kind to the three-footers with their baroquely involuted exoskeletons. Rudiger fished both for food and for science; evidently these trilobites were discards, species that he already had studied, or he wouldn't have left them here to go into the food hoppers. His hut was stacked ceiling-high with trilobites. It kept him sane to collect and analyze them, and no one begrudged him his hobby.

Near the heap of trilobites were some clusters of hinged brachiopods, looking like scallops that had gone awry, and a pile of snails. The warm, shallow waters just off the coastal shelf teemed with life, in striking contrast to the barren land. Rudiger had also brought in a mound of shiny black seaweed. Barrett hoped someone would gather all this stuff up and get it into their heat-sink cooler before it spoiled. The bacteria of decay worked a lot slower here than they did Up Front, but a few hours in the mild air would do Rudiger's haul no good.

Today Barrett planned to recruit some men for the annual Inland Sea expedition. Traditionally, he led the trek himself, but his injury made it impossible for him even to consider going any more. Each year, a dozen or so able-bodied men went out on a wide-ranging reconnaissance that took them in a big circle, looping northwestward until they reached the sea, then coming around to the south and back to the Station. One purpose of the trip was to gather any temporal garbage that might have materialized in the vicinity of the Station during the past year. There was no way of knowing how wide a margin of error had been allowed during the early attempts to set up the Station, and the scattershot technique of hurling material into the past had been pretty unreliable. New stuff was turning up all the time that had been aimed for Minus One Billion, Two Thousand Oh Five A.D., but which didn't get there until a few decades later. Hawksbill Station needed all the spare equipment it could get, and Barrett didn't miss a chance to round up any of the debris.

There was another reason for the Inland Sea expeditions, though. They served as a focus for the year, an annual ritual, something to peg a custom to. It was a rite of spring here.

The dozen strongest men, going on foot to the distant rock-rimmed shore of the tepid sea that drowned the middle of North America, were performing the closest thing Hawksbill Station had to a religious function, although they did nothing more mystical when they reached the Inland Sea than to net a few trilobites and eat them. The trip meant more to Barrett himself than he had ever suspected, also. He realized that now, when he was unable to go. He had led every such expedition for twenty years.

But last year he had gone scrabbling over boulders loosened by the tireless action of the waves, venturing into risky territory for no rational reason that he could name, and his aging muscles had betrayed him. Often at night he woke sweating to escape from the dream in which he relived that ugly moment: slipping and sliding, clawing at the rocks, a mass of stone dislodged from somewhere and came crashing down with an agonizing impact on his foot, pinning him, crushing him. He could not forget the sound of grinding bones. Nor was he likely to lose the memory of the homeward march, across hundreds of miles of bare rock, his bulky body slung between the bowed forms of his companions.

He thought he would lose the foot, but Quesada had spared him from the amputation. He simply could not touch the foot to the ground and put weight on it now, or ever again. It might have been simpler to have the dead appendage sliced off. Quesada vetoed that, though. "Who knows," he said, "some day they might send us a transplant kit. I can't rebuild a leg that's been amputated." So Barrett had kept his crushed foot. But he had never been quite the same since, and now someone else would have to lead the march.

Who would it be? he asked himself.

Quesada was the likeliest. Next to Barrett, he was the strongest man here, in all the ways that it was important to be strong. But Quesada couldn't be spared at the Station. It might be handy to have a medic along on the trip, but it was vital to have one here. After some reflection Barrett put down Charley Norton as the leader. He added Ken Belardi—someone for Norton to talk to. Rudiger? A tower of strength last year after Barrett had been injured; Barrett didn't particularly want to let Rudiger leave the Station so long though. He needed able men for the expedition, true, but he didn't want to strip the home base down to invalids, crackpots, and psychotics. Rudiger stayed. Two of his fellow fishermen went on the list. So did Sid Hutchett and Arny Jean-Claude.

Barrett thought about putting Don Latimer in the group. Latimer was coming to be something of a borderline mental case, but he was rational enough except when he lapsed into his psionic meditations, and he'd pull his own weight on the expedition. On the other hand, Latimer was Lew Hahn's roommate and Barrett wanted Latimer around to observe Hahn at close range. He toyed with the idea of sending both of them out, but nixed it. Hahn was still an unknown quantity. It was too risky to let him go with the Inland Sea party this year. Probably he'd be in next spring's group, though.

Finally Barrett had his dozen men chosen. He chalked their names on the slate in front of the mess hall and found Charley Norton at breakfast to tell him he was in charge.

It felt strange to know that he'd have to stay home while the others went. It was an admission that he was beginning to abdicate after running this place so long. A crippled old man was what he was, whether he liked to admit it to himself or not, and that was something he'd have to come to terms with soon.

In the afternoon, the men of the Inland Sea expedition gathered to select their gear and plan their route. Barrett kept away from the meeting. This was Charley Norton's show, now. He'd made eight or ten trips, and he knew what to do. Barrett didn't want to interfere.

But some masochistic compulsion in him drove him to take a trek of his own. If he couldn't see the western waters this year, the least he could do was pay a visit to the Atlantic, in his own backyard. Barrett stopped off in the infirmary and, finding Quesada elsewhere, helped himself to a tube of neural depressant. He scrambled along the eastern trail until he was a few hundred yards from the main building, dropped his trousers and quickly gave each thigh a jolt of the drug, first the good leg, then the gimpy one. That would numb the muscles just enough so that he'd be able to take an extended hike without feeling the fire of the fatigue in his protesting joints. He'd pay for it, he knew, eight hours from now, when the depressant wore off and the full impact of his exertion hit him like a million daggers. But he was willing to accept that price.

The road to the sea was a long, lonely one. Hawksbill Station was perched on the eastern rim of the geosyncline, more than eight hundred feet above sea level. During the first half dozen years, the men of the Station had reached the ocean by a suicidal route across sheer rock faces, but Barrett had incited a ten-year project to carve a path. Now wide steps descended to the sea. Chopping them out of the rock had kept a lot of men busy for a long time, too busy to worry or to slip into insanity. Barrett regretted that he couldn't conceive some comparable works project to occupy them nowadays.

The steps formed a succession of shallow platforms that switch-backed to the edge of the water. Even for a healthy man it was still a strenuous walk. For Barrett in his present condition it was an ordeal. It took him two hours to descend a distance that normally could be traversed in a quarter of that time. When he reached the bottom, he sank down exhaustedly on a flat rock, licked by the waves, and dropped his crutch. The fingers of his left hand were cramped and gnarled from gripping the crutch, and his entire body was bathed in sweat.

The water looked gray and somehow oily. Barrett could not explain the prevailing colorlessness of the late Cambrian world, with its somber sky and somber land and somber sea, but his heart quietly ached for a glimpse of green vegetation again. He missed chlorophyll. The dark wavelets lapped against his rock, pushing a mass of floating black seaweed back and forth. The sea stretched to infinity. He didn't have the faintest idea how much of Europe, if any, was above water in this epoch.

At the best of times most of the planet was submerged; here, only a few hundred million years after the white-hot rocks of the land had pushed into view, it was likely that all that was above water on Earth was a strip of territory here and there. Had the Himalayas been born yet? The Rockies? The Andes? He knew the approximate outlines of late Cambrian North America, but the rest was a mystery. Blanks in knowledge were not easy to fill when the only link with Up Front was by one-way transport; Hawksbill Station had to rely on the random assortment of reading matter that came back in time, and it was furiously frustrating to lack information that any college geology text could supply.

As he watched, a big trilobite unexpectedly came scuttering up out of the water. It was the spike-tailed kind, about a yard long, with an eggplant-purple shell and a bristling arrangement of slender spines along the margins. There seemed to be a lot of legs underneath. The trilobite crawled up on the shore—no sand, no beach, just a shelf of rock—and advanced until it was eight or ten feet from the waves.

Good for you, Barrett thought. *Maybe you're the first one who ever came out on land to see what it was like. The pioneer. The trailblazer.*

It occurred to him that this adventurous trilobite might well be the ancestor of all the land-dwelling creatures of the eons to come. It was biological nonsense, but Barrett's weary mind conjured a picture of an evolutionary procession, with fish and amphibians and reptiles and mammals and man all stemming in unbroken sequence from this grotesque armored thing that moved in uncertain circles near his feet.

And if I were to step on you? he thought.

A quick motion—the sound of crunching chitin—the wild scrabbling of a host of little legs—

And the whole chain of life snapped in its first link. Evolution undone. No land creatures ever developed. With the descent of that heavy foot all the future would change, and there would never have been any Hawksbill Station, no human race, no James Edward Barrett. In an instant he would have both revenge on those who had condemned him to live out his days in this place and release from his sentence.

He did nothing. The trilobite completed its slow perambulation of the shoreline rocks and scuttled back into the sea unharmed.

The soft voice of Don Latimer said, "I saw you sitting down here, Jim. Do you mind if I join you?"

Barrett swung around, momentarily surprised. Latimer had come down from his hilltop hut so quietly that Barrett hadn't heard a thing. He recovered and grinned and beckoned Latimer to an adjoining rock.

"You fishing?" Latimer asked.

"Just sitting. An old man sunning himself."

"You took a hike like that just to sun yourself?" Latimer laughed. "Come off it. You're trying to get away from it all, and you probably wish I hadn't disturbed you."

"That's not so. Stay here. How's your new roommate getting along?"

"It's been strange," said Latimer. "That's one reason I came down here to talk to you." He leaned forward and peered searchingly into Barrett's eyes. "Jim, tell me: do you think I'm a madman?"

"Why should I?"

"The esping business. My attempt to break through to another realm of consciousness. I know you're tough-minded and skeptical. You probably think it's all a lot of nonsense."

Barrett shrugged and said, "If you want the blunt truth, I do. I don't have the remotest belief that you're going to get us anywhere, Don. I think it's a complete waste of time and energy for you to sit there for hours harnessing your psionic powers, or whatever it is you do. But no, I don't think you're crazy. I think you're entitled to your obsession and that you're going about a basically futile thing in a reasonably level-headed way. Fair enough?"

"More than fair. I don't ask you to put any credence in my research, but I don't want you to think I'm a total lunatic for trying it. It's important that you regard me as sane, or else what I want to tell you about Hahn won't be valid to you."

"I don't see the connection."

"It's this," said Latimer. "On the basis of one evening's acquaintance, I've formed an opinion about Hahn. It's the kind of an opinion that might be formed by a garden variety paranoid, and if you think I'm nuts you're likely to discount my idea."

"I don't think you're nuts. What's your idea?"

"That he's been spying on us."

Barrett had to work hard to keep from emitting the guffaw that would shatter Latimer's fragile self-esteem. "Spying?" he said casually. "You can't mean that. How can anyone spy here? I mean, how can he report his findings?"

"I don't know," Latimer said. "But he asked me a million questions last night. About you, about Quesada, about some of the sick men. He wanted to know everything."

"The normal curiosity of a new man."

"Jim, he was taking notes. I saw him after he thought I was asleep. He sat up for two hours writing it all down in a little book."

Barrett frowned. "Maybe he's going to write a novel about us."

"I'm serious," Latimer said. "Questions—notes. And he's shifty. Try to get him to talk about himself!"

"I did. I didn't learn much."

"Do you know why he's been sent here?"

"No."

"Neither do I," said Latimer. "Political crimes, he said, but he was vague as hell. He hardly seemed to know what the present government was up to, let alone what his own opinions were toward it. I don't detect any passionate philosophical convictions in Mr. Hahn. And you know as well as I do that Hawksbill Station is the refuse heap for revolutionaries and agitators and subversives and all sorts of similar trash, but that we've never had any other kind of prisoner here."

Barrett said coolly, "I agree that Hahn's a puzzle. But who could he be spying for? He's got no way to file a report, if he's a government agent. He's stranded here for keeps, like us."

"Maybe he was sent to keep an eye on us—to make sure we aren't cooking up some way to escape. Maybe he's a volunteer who willingly gave up his twenty-first-century life so he could come among us and thwart anything we might be hatching. Perhaps they're afraid we've invented forward time-travel. Or that we've become a threat to the sequence of the time-lines. Anything. So Hahn comes among us to snoop around and block any dangers before they arrive."

Barrett felt a twinge of alarm. He saw how close to paranoia Latimer was hewing, now. In half a dozen sentences he had journeyed from the rational expression of some justifiable suspicions to the fretful fear that the men from Up Front were going to take steps to choke off the escape route that he was so close to perfecting.

He kept his voice level as he told Latimer, "I don't think you need to worry, Don. Hahn's an odd one, but he's not here to make trouble for us. The fellows Up Front have already made all the trouble for us they ever will."

"Would you keep an eye on him anyway?"

"You know I will. And don't hesitate to let me know if Hahn does anything else out of the ordinary. You're in a better spot to notice than anyone else."

"I'll be watching," Latimer said. "We can't tolerate any spies from Up Front among us." He got to his feet and gave Barrett a pleasant smile. "I'll let you get back to your sunning now, Jim."

Latimer went up the path. Barrett eyed him until he was close to the top, only a faint dot against the stony backdrop. After a long while Barrett seized his crutch and levered himself to his feet. He stood staring down at the surf, dipping the tip of his crutch into the water to send a couple of little crawling things scurrying away. At length he turned and began the long, slow climb back to the Station.

VI

A couple of days passed before Barrett had the chance to draw Lew Hahn aside for a spot of political discussion. The Inland Sea party had set out, and in a way that was too bad, for Barrett could have used Charley Norton's services in penetrating Hahn's armor. Norton was the most gifted theorist around, a man who could weave a tissue of dialectic from the least promising material. If anyone could find out the depth of Hahn's Marxist commitment, if any, it was Norton.

But Norton was leading the expedition, so Barrett had to do the interrogating himself. His Marxism was a trifle rusty, and he couldn't thread his path through the Leninist, Stalinist, Trotskyite, Khrushchevist, Maoist, Berenkovskyite and Mgumbweist schools with Charley Norton's skills. Yet he knew what questions to ask.

He picked a rainy evening when Hahn seemed to be in a fairly outgoing mood. There had been an hour's entertainment that night, an ingenious computer-composed film that Sid Hutchett had programmed last week. Up Front had been kind enough to ship back a modest computer, and Hutchett had rigged it to do animations by specifying line widths and lengths, shades of gray and progression of raster units. It was a simple but remarkably clever business, and it brightened a dull night.

Afterward, sensing that Hahn was relaxed enough to lower his guard a bit, Barrett said, "Hutchett's a rare one. Did you meet him before he went on the trip?"

"Tall fellow with a sharp nose and no chin?"

"That's the one. A clever boy. He was the top computer man for the Continental Liberation Front until they caught him in '19. He programmed that fake broadcast in which Chancellor Dantell denounced his own regime. Remember?"

"I'm not sure I do." Hahn frowned. "How long ago was this?"

"The broadcast was in 2018. Would that be before your time? Only eleven years ago—"

"I was nineteen then," said Hahn. "I guess I wasn't very politically sophisticated."

"Too busy studying economics, I guess."

Hahn grinned. "That's right. Deep in dismal science."

"And you never heard that broadcast? Or even heard *of* it?"

"I must have forgotten."

"The biggest hoax of the century," Barrett said, "and you forgot it. You know the Continental Liberation Front, of course."

"Of course." Hahn looked uneasy.

"Which group did you say you were with?"

"The People's Crusade for Liberty."

"I don't know it. One of the newer groups?"

"Less than five years old. It started in California."

"What's its program?"

"Oh, the usual," Hahn said. "Free elections, representative government, an opening of the security files, restoration of civil liberties."

"And the economic orientation? Pure Marxist or one of the offshoots?"

"Not really any, I guess. We believed in a kind of—well, capitalism with some government restraints."

"A little to the right of state socialism, and a little to the left of *laissez-faire?*" Barrett suggested.

"Something like that."

"But that system was tried and failed, wasn't it? It had its day. It led inevitably to total socialism, which produced the compensating backlash of syndicalist capitalism, and then we got a government that pretended to be libertarian while actually stifling all individual liberties in the name of freedom. So if your group simply wanted to turn the clock back to 1955, say, there couldn't be much to its ideas."

Hahn looked bored. "You've got to understand I wasn't in the top ideological councils."

"Just an economist?"

"That's it. I drew up plans for the conversion to our system."

"Basing your work on the modified liberalism of Ricardo?"

"Well, in a sense."

"And avoiding the tendency to fascism that was found in the thinking of Keynes?"

"You could say so," Hahn said. He stood up, flashing a quick, vague smile. "Look, Jim, I'd love to argue this further with you some other time, but I've really got to go now. Ned Altman talked me into coming around and helping him do a lightning-dance to bring that pile of dirt to life. So if you don't mind—"

Hahn beat a hasty retreat, without looking back.

Barrett was more perplexed than ever. Hahn hadn't been "arguing" anything. He had been carrying on a lame and feeble conversation, letting himself be pushed hither and thither by Barrett's questions. And he had spouted a lot of nonsense. He didn't seem to know Keynes from Ricardo, nor to care about it, which was odd for a self-professed economist. He didn't have a shred of an idea what his own political party stood for. He had so little revolutionary background that he was unaware even of Hutchett's astonishing hoax of eleven years back.

He seemed phony from top to bottom.

How was it possible that this kid had been deemed worthy of exile to Hawksbill Station, anyhow? Only the top firebrands went there. Sentencing a man to Hawksbill was like sentencing him to death, and it wasn't done lightly. Barrett couldn't imagine why Hahn was here. He seemed genuinely distressed at being exiled, and evidently he had left a beloved wife behind, but nothing else rang true about the man.

Was he—as Latimer suggested—some kind of spy?

Barrett rejected the idea out of hand. He didn't want Latimer's paranoia infecting him. The government wasn't likely to send anyone on a one-way trip to the Late Cambrian just to spy on a bunch of aging revolutionaries who could never make trouble again. But what *was* Hahn doing here, then?

He would bear further watching, Barrett thought.

Barrett took care of some of the watching himself. But he had plenty of assistance. Latimer. Altman. Six or seven others. Latimer had recruited most of the ambulatory psycho cases, the ones who were superficially functional but full of all kinds of fears and credulities.

They were keeping an eye on the new man.

On the fifth day after his arrival, Hahn went out fishing in Rudiger's crew. Barrett stood for a long time on the edge of the geosyncline, watching the little boat bobbing in the surging Atlantic. Rudiger never went far from shore—eight hundred, a thousand yards out—but the water was rough even there. The waves came rolling in with X thousand miles of gathered impact behind them. A continental shelf sloped off at a wide angle, so that even at a substantial distance off shore the water wasn't very deep. Rudiger had taken soundings up to a mile out, and had reported depths no greater than a hundred sixty feet. Nobody had gone past a mile.

It wasn't that they were afraid of falling off the side of the world if they went too far east. It was simply that a mile was a long distance to row in an open boat, using stubby oars made from old packing cases. Up Front hadn't thought to spare an outboard motor for them.

Looking toward the horizon, Barrett had an odd thought. He had been told that the women's equivalent of Hawksbill Station was safely segregated out of reach, a couple of hundred million years up the timeline. But how did he know that? There could be another Station somewhere else in this very year, and they'd never know about it. A camp of women, say, living on the far side of the ocean, or even across the Inland Sea.

It wasn't very likely, he knew. With the entire past to pick from, the edgy men Up Front wouldn't take any chance that the two groups of exiles might get together and spawn a tribe of little subversives. They'd take every precaution to put an impenetrable barrier of epochs between them. Yet Barrett thought he could make it sound convincing to the other men. With a little effort he could get them to believe in the existence of several simultaneous Hawksbill Stations scattered on this level of time.

Which could be our salvation, he thought.

The instances of degenerative psychosis were beginning to snowball, now. Too many men had been here too long, and one crackup was starting to feed the next, in this blank lifeless world where humans were never meant to live. The men needed projects to keep them going. They were starting to slip off into harebrained projects, like Altman's Frankenstein girlfriend and Latimer's psi pursuit.

Suppose, Barrett thought, *I could get them steamed up about reaching the other continents?*

A round-the-world expedition. Maybe they could build some kind of big ship. That would keep a lot of men busy for a long time. And they'd need navigational equipment—compasses, sextants, chronometers, whatnot. Somebody would have to design an improvised radio, too. It was the kind of project that might take thirty or forty years. *A focus for our energies,* Barrett thought. *Of course, I won't live to see the ship set sail. But even so, it's a way of staving off collapse. We've built our staircase to the sea. Now we need something bigger to do. Idle hands make for idle minds . . . sick minds . . .*

He liked the idea he had hatched. For several weeks now Barrett had been worrying about the deteriorating state of affairs in the Station, and looking for some way to cope with it. Now he thought he had his way.

Turning, he saw Latimer and Altman standing behind him.

"How long have you been there?" he asked.

"Two minutes," said Latimer. "We brought you something to look at."

Altman nodded vigorously. "You ought to read it. We brought it for you to read."

"What is it?"

Latimer handed over a folded sheaf of papers. "I found this tucked away in Hahn's bunk after he went with Rudiger. I know I'm not supposed to be invading his privacy, but I had to have a look at what he's been writing. There it is. He's a spy, all right."

Barrett glanced at the papers in his hand. "I'll read it a little later. What is it about?"

"It's a description of the Station, and profile of most of the men in it," said Latimer. He smiled frostily. "Hahn's private opinion of me is that I've gone mad. His private opinion of you is a little more flattering, but not much."

Altman said, "He's also been hanging around the Hammer."

"What?"

"I saw him going there late last night. He went into the building. I followed him. He was looking at the Hammer."

"Why didn't you tell me that right away?" Barrett snapped.

"I wasn't sure it was important," Altman said. "I had to talk it over with Don first. And I couldn't do that until Hahn had gone out fishing."

Sweat burst out on Barrett's face. "Listen, Ned, if you ever catch Hahn going near the time-travel equipment again, you let me know in a hurry. Without consulting Don or anyone else. Clear?"

"Clear," said Altman. He giggled. "You know what I think? They've decided to exterminate us Up Front. Hahn's been sent here to check us out as a suicide volunteer. Then they're going to send a bomb through the Hammer and blow the Station up. We ought to wreck the Hammer and Anvil before they get a chance."

"But why would they send a suicide volunteer?" Latimer asked. "Unless they've got some way to rescue their spy—"

"In any case we shouldn't take any chance," Altman argued. "Wreck the Hammer. Make it impossible for them to bomb us from Up Front."

"That might be a good idea. But—"

"Shut up, both of you," Barrett growled. "Let me look at these papers."

He walked a few steps away from them and sat down on a shelf of rock. He began to read.

VII

Hahn had a cramped, crabbed handwriting that packed a maximum of information into a minimum of space, as though he regarded it as a mortal sin to waste paper. Fair enough. Paper was a scarce commodity here, and evidently Hahn had brought these sheets with him from Up Front. His script was clear, though. So were his opinions. Painfully so.

He had written an analysis of conditions at Hawksbill Station, setting forth in about five thousand words everything that Barrett knew was going sour here. He had neatly ticked off the men as aging revolutionaries in whom the old fervor had turned rancid. He listed the ones who were certifiably psycho, and the ones who were on the edge, and the ones who were hanging on, like Quesada and Norton and Rudiger. Barrett was interested to see that Hahn rated even those three as suffering from severe strain and likely to fly apart at any moment. To him, Quesada and Norton and Rudiger seemed just about as stable as when they had first dropped onto the Anvil of Hawksbill Station, but that was possibly the distorting effect of his own blurred perceptions. To an outsider like Hahn, the view was different and perhaps more accurate.

Barrett forced himself not to skip ahead of Hahn's evaluation of him.

He wasn't pleased when he came to it. "Barrett," Hahn had written, "is like a mighty beam that's been gnawed from within by termites. He looks solid, but one good push would break him apart. A recent injury to his foot has evidently had a bad effect on him. The other men say he used to be physically vigorous and derived much of his authority from his size and strength. Now he can hardly walk. But I feel the trouble with him is inherent in the life of Hawksbill Station and doesn't have much to do with his lameness. He's been cut off from normal human drives for too long. The exercise of power here has provided the illusion of stability for him, but it's power in a vacuum, and things have happened within Barrett of which he's totally unaware. He's in bad need of therapy. He may be beyond help."

Barrett read that several times. *Gnawed from within by termites . . . one good push . . . things have happened within him . . . bad need of therapy . . . beyond help . . .*

He was less angered than he thought he should have been. Hahn was entitled to his views. Barrett finally stopped rereading his profile and pushed his way to the last page of Hahn's essay. It ended with the words, "Therefore I recommend prompt termination of the Hawksbill Station penal colony and, where possible, the therapeutic rehabilitation of its inmates."

What the hell was this?

It sounded like the report of a parole commissioner! But there was no parole from Hawksbill Station. That final sentence let all the viability of what had gone before bleed away. Hahn was pretending to be composing a report to the government Up Front, obviously. But a wall a billion years thick made filing of that report impossible. So Hahn was suffering from delusions, just like Altman and Valdosto and the others. In his fevered mind he believed he could send messages Up Front, pompous documents delineating the flaws and foibles of his fellow prisoners.

That raised a chilling prospect. Hahn might be crazy, but he hadn't been in the Station long enough to have gone crazy here. He must have brought his insanity with him.

What if they had stopped using Hawksbill Station as a camp for political prisoners, Barrett asked himself, and were starting to use it as an insane asylum?

A cascade of psychos descending on them. Men who had gone honorably buggy under the stress of confinement would have to make room for ordinary Bedlamites. Barrett shivered. He folded up Hahn's papers and handed them to Latimer, who was sitting a few yards away, watching him intently.

"What did you think of that?" Latimer asked.

"I think it's hard to evaluate. But possibly friend Hahn is emotionally disturbed. Put this stuff back exactly where you got it, Don. And don't give Hahn the faintest inkling that you've read or removed it."

"Right."

"And come to me whenever you think there's something I ought to know about him," Barrett said. "He may be a very sick boy. He may need all the help we can give."

The fishing expedition returned in early afternoon. Barrett saw that the dinghy was overflowing with the haul, and Hahn, coming into the camp with his arms full of gaffed trilobites, looked sunburned and pleased with his outing. Barrett came over to inspect the catch. Rudiger was in an effusive mood and held up a bright red crustacean that might have been the great-great-grandfather of all boiled lobsters, except that it had no front claws and a wicked-looking triple spike where a tail should have been. It was about two feet long, and ugly.

"A new species!" Rudiger crowed. "There's nothing like this in any museum. I wish I could put it where it would be found. Some mountaintop, maybe."

"If it could be found, it *would* have been found," Barrett reminded him. "Some paleontologist of the twentieth century would have dug it out. So forget it, Mel."

Hahn said, "I've been wondering about that point. How is it no-body Up Front ever dug up the fossil remains of Hawksbill Station? Aren't they worried that one of the early fossil-hunters will find it in the Cambrian strata and raise a fuss?"

Barrett shook his head. "For one thing, no paleontologist from the beginning of science to the founding of the Station in 2005 ever *did* dig up Hawksbill. That's a matter of record, so there was nothing to worry about. If it came to light after 2005, why, everyone would know what it was. No paradox there."

"Besides," said Rudiger sadly, "in another billion years this whole strip of rock will be on the floor of the Atlantic, with a couple of miles of sediment over it. There's not a chance we'll be found. Or that anyone Up Front will ever see this guy I caught today. Not that I give a damn. I've seen him. I'll dissect him. Their loss."

"But you regret the fact that science will never know of this species," Hahn said.

"Sure I do. But is it my fault? Science does know of this species. Me. I'm science. I'm the leading paleontologist of this epoch. Can I help it if I can't publish my discoveries in the professional journals?" He scowled and walked away, carrying the big red crustacean.

Hahn and Barrett looked at each other. They smiled, in a natural mutual response to Rudiger's grumbled outburst. Then Barrett's smile faded.

. . . *termites* . . . *one good push* . . . *therapy* . . .

"Something wrong?" Hahn asked.

"Why?"

"You looked so bleak all of a sudden."

"My foot gave me a twinge," Barrett said. "It does that, you know. Here. I'll give you a hand carrying those things. We'll have fresh trilobite cocktail tonight."

VIII

A little before midnight, Barrett was awakened by footsteps outside his hut. As he sat up, groping for the luminescence switch, Ned Altman came blundering through the door. Barrett blinked at him.

"What's the matter?"

"Hahn!" Altman rasped. "He's fooling around with the Hammer again. We just saw him go into the building."

Barrett shed his sleepiness like a seal bursting out of water. Ignoring the insistent throb in his leg, he pulled himself from his bed and grabbed some clothing. He was more apprehensive than he wanted Altman to see. If Hahn, fooling around with the temporal mechanisms, accidentally smashed the Hammer, they might never get replacement equipment from Up Front. Which would mean that all future shipments of supplies—if there were any—would come as random shoots that might land in any old year. What business did Hahn have with the machine, anyway?

Altman said, "Latimer's up there keeping an eye on him. He got suspicious when Hahn didn't come back to the hut, and he got me, and we went looking for him. And there he was, sniffing around the Hammer."

"Doing what?"

"I don't know. As soon as we saw him go in, I came down here to get you. Don's watching."

Barrett stumped his way out of the hut and did his best to run toward the main building. Pain shot like trails of hot acid up the lower half of his body. The crutch dug mercilessly into his left armpit as he leaned all his weight into it. His crippled foot, swinging freely, burned with a cold glow. His right leg, which was carrying most of the burden, creaked and popped. Altman ran breathlessly alongside him. The Station was silent at this hour.

As they passed Quesada's hut, Barrett considered waking the medic and taking him along. He decided against it. Whatever trouble Hahn might be up to, Barrett felt he could handle it himself. There was some strength left in the old gnawed beam.

Latimer stood at the entrance to the main dome. He was right on the edge of panic, or perhaps over the edge. He seemed to be gibbering with fear and shock. Barrett had never seen a man gibber before.

He clamped a big paw on Latimer's thin shoulder and said harshly, "Where is he? Where's Hahn?"

"He—disappeared."

"What do you mean? Where did he go?"

Latimer moaned. His face was fishbelly white. "He got onto the Anvil," Latimer blurted. "The light came on—the glow. And then Hahn disappeared!"

"No," Barrett said. "It isn't possible. You must be mistaken."

"I saw him go!"

"He's hiding somewhere in the building," Barrett insisted. "Close that door! Search for him!"

Altman said, "He probably did disappear, Jim. If Don says he disappeared—"

"He climbed right on the Anvil. Then everything turned red, and he was gone."

Barrett clenched his fists. There was a white-hot blaze just behind his forehead that almost made him forget about his foot. He saw his mistake now. He had depended for his espionage on two men who were patently and unmistakably insane, and that had been itself a not very sane thing to do. A man is known by his choice of lieutenants. Well, he had relied on Altman and Latimer, and now they were giving him the sort of information that such spies could be counted on to supply.

"You're hallucinating," he told Latimer curtly. "Ned, go wake Quesada and get him here right away. You, Don, you stand here by the entrance, and if Hahn shows up I want you to scream at the top of your lungs. I'm going to search the building for him."

"Wait," Latimer said. He seemed to be in control of himself again. "Jim, do you remember when I asked you if you thought I was crazy? You said you didn't. You trusted me. I tell you I'm not hallucinating. I saw Hahn disappear. I can't explain it, but I'm rational enough to know what I saw."

In a milder tone Barrett said, "All right. Maybe so. Stay by the door, anyway. I'll run a quick check."

He started to make the circuit of the dome, beginning with the room where the Hammer was located. Everything seemed to be in order there. No Hawksbill Field glow was in evidence, and nothing had been disturbed. The room had no closets or cupboards in which Hahn could be hiding. When he had inspected it thoroughly, Barrett moved on, looking into the infirmary, the mess hall, the kitchen, the recreation room. He looked high and low. No Hahn. Of course, there were plenty of places in those rooms where Hahn might have secreted himself, but Barrett doubted that he was there. So it had all been some feverish fantasy of Latimer's, then. He completed the route and found himself back at the main entrance. Latimer still stood guard there. He had been joined by a sleepy Quesada. Altman, pale and shaky-looking, was just outside the door.

"What's happening?" Quesada asked.

"I'm not sure," said Barrett. "Don and Ned had the idea they saw Lew Hahn fooling around with the time equipment. I've checked the building, and he's not here, so maybe they made a little mistake. I suggest you take them both into the infirmary and give them a shot of something to settle their nerves, and we'll all try to get back to sleep."

Latimer said, "I tell you, I saw—"

"Shut up!" Altman broke in. "Listen! What's that noise?"

Barrett listened. The sound was clear and loud: the hissing whine of ionization. It was the sound produced by a functioning Hawksbill Field. Suddenly there were goosepimples on his flesh. In a low voice he said, "The field's on. We're probably getting some supplies."

"At this hour?" said Latimer.

"We don't know what time it is Up Front. All of you stay here. I'll check the Hammer."

"Perhaps I ought to go with you," Quesada suggested mildly.

"Stay here!" Barrett thundered. He paused, embarrassed at his own explosive show of wrath. "It only takes one of us. I'll be right back."

Without waiting for further dissent, he pivoted and limped down the hall to the Hammer room. He shouldered the door open and looked in. There was no need for him to switch on the light. The red glow of the Hawksbill Field illuminated everything.

Barrett stationed himself just within the door. Hardly daring to breathe, he stared fixedly at the Hammer, watching as the glow deepened through various shades of pink toward crimson, and then spread until it enfolded the waiting Anvil beneath it.

Then came the implosive thunderclap, and Lew Hahn dropped out of nowhere and lay for a moment in temporal shock on the broad plate of the Anvil.

IX

In the darkness, Hahn did not notice Barrett at first. He sat up slowly, shaking off the stunning effects of a trip through time. After a few seconds he pushed himself toward the tip of the Anvil and let his legs dangle over it. He swung them to get the circulation going. He took a series of deep breaths. Finally he slipped to the floor. The glow of the field had gone out in the moment of his arrival, and so he moved warily, as though not wanting to bump into anything.

Abruptly Barrett switched on the light and said, "What have you been up to, Hahn?"

The younger man recoiled as though he had been jabbed in the gut. He gasped, hopped backward a few steps, and flung up both hands in a defensive gesture.

"Answer me," Barrett said.

Hahn regained his equilibrium. He shot a quick glance past Barrett's bulky form toward the hallway and said, "Let me go, will you? I can't explain now."

"You'd better explain now."

"It's easier for everyone if I don't," said Hahn. "Let me pass."

Barrett continued to block the door. "I want to know where you've been. What have you been doing with the Hammer?"

"Nothing. Just studying it."

"You weren't in this room a minute ago. Then you appeared. Where'd you come from, Hahn?"

"You're mistaken. I was standing right behind the Hammer. I didn't—"

"I saw you drop down on the Anvil. You took a time trip, didn't you?"

"No."

"Don't lie to me! You've got some way of going forward in time, isn't that so? You've been spying on us, and you just went somewhere to file your report—somewhen—and now you're back."

Hahn's forehead was glistening. He said, "I warn you, don't ask too many questions. You'll know everything in due time. This isn't the time. Please, now. Let me pass."

"I want answers first," Barrett said. He realized that he was trembling. He already knew the answers, and they were answers that shook him to the core of his soul. He knew where Hahn had been.

Hahn said nothing. He took a few hesitant steps toward Barrett, who did not move. He seemed to be gathering momentum for a rush at the doorway.

Barrett said, "You aren't getting out of here until you tell me what I want to know."

Hahn charged.

Barrett planted himself squarely, crutch braced against the doorframe, his good leg flat on the floor, and waited for the younger man to reach him. He figured he outweighed Hahn by eighty pounds. That might be enough to balance the fact that he was spotting Hahn thirty years and one leg. They came together, and Barrett drove his hands down onto Hahn's shoulders, trying to hold him, to force him back into the room.

Hahn gave an inch or two. He looked up at Barrett without speaking and pushed forward again.

"Don't—don't—" Barrett grunted. "I won't let you—"

"I don't want to do this," Hahn said.

He pushed again. Barrett felt himself buckling under the impact. He dug his hands as hard as he could into Hahn's shoulders and tried to shove the other man backward into the room, but Hahn held firm, and all of Barrett's energy was converted into a thrust rebounding on himself. He lost control of his crutch, and it slithered out from under his arm. For one agonizing moment Barrett's full weight rested on the crushed uselessness of his left foot, and then, as though his limbs were melting away beneath him, he began to sink toward the floor. He landed with a reverberating crash.

Quesada, Altman and Latimer came rushing in. Barrett writhed in pain on the floor. Hahn stood over him, looking unhappy, his hands locked together.

"I'm sorry," he said. "You shouldn't have tried to muscle me like that."

Barrett glowered at him. "You were traveling in time, weren't you? You can answer me now!"

"Yes," Hahn said at last. "I went Up Front."

An hour later, after Quesada had pumped him with enough neural depressants to keep him from jumping out of his skin, Barrett got the full story. Hahn hadn't wanted to reveal it so soon, but he had changed his mind after his little scuffle.

It was all very simple. Time travel now worked in both directions. The glib, impressive noises about the flow of entropy had turned out to be just noises.

"How long has this been known?" Barrett asked.

"At least five years. We aren't sure yet exactly when the breakthrough came. After we're finished going through all the suppressed records of the former government—"

"The former government?"

Hahn nodded. "The revolution came in January. Not really a violent one, either. The syndicalists just mildewed from within, and when they got the first push they fell over."

"Was it mildew?" Barrett asked, coloring. "Or termites? Keep your metaphors straight."

Hahn glanced away. "Anyway, the government fell. We're got a provisional liberal regime in office now. Don't ask me much about it. I'm not a political theorist. I'm not even an economist. You guessed as much."

"What are you, then?"

"A policeman," Hahn said. "Part of the commission that's investigating the prison system of the former government. Including this prison."

Barrett looked at Quesada, then at Hahn. Thoughts were streaming turbulently through him, and he could not remember when he had last been so overwhelmed by events. He had to work hard to keep from breaking into the shakes again. His voice quavered a little as he said, "You came back to observe Hawksbill Station, right? And you went Up Front tonight to tell them what you saw here. You think we're a pretty sad bunch, eh?"

"You've all been under heavy stress here," Hahn said. "Considering the circumstances of your imprisonment—"

Quesada broke in. "If there's a liberal government in power now and it's possible to travel both ways in time, then am I right in assuming that the Hawksbill prisoners are going to be sent Up Front?"

"Of course," said Hahn. "It'll be done as soon as possible. That's been the whole purpose of my reconnaissance mission. To find out if you people were still alive, first, and then to see what shape you're in, how badly in need of treatment you are. You'll be given every available benefit of modern therapy, naturally. No expense spared—"

Barrett scarcely paid attention to Hahn's words. He had been fearing something like this all night, ever since Altman had told him Hahn was monkeying with the Hammer, but he had never fully allowed himself to believe that it could really be possible.

He saw his kingdom crumbling.

He saw himself returned to a world he could not begin to comprehend—a lame Rip Van Winkle, coming back after twenty years.

He saw himself leaving a place that had become his home.

Barrett said tiredly, "You know, some of the men aren't going to be able to adapt to the shock of freedom. It might just kill them to be dumped into the real world again. I mean the advanced psychos—Valdosto, and such."

"Yes," Hahn said. "I've mentioned them in my report."

"It'll be necessary to get them ready for a return in gradual stages. It might take several years to condition them to the idea. It might even take longer than that."

"I'm no therapist," said Hahn. "Whatever the doctors think is right for them is what'll be done. Maybe it will be necessary to keep them here. I can see where it would be pretty potent to send them back, after they've spent all these years believing there's no return."

"More than that," said Barrett. "There's a lot of work that can be done here. Scientific work. Exploration. I don't think Hawksbill Station ought to be closed down."

"No one said it would be. We have every intention of keeping it going, but not as a prison."

"Good," Barrett said. He fumbled for his crutch, found it and got heavily to his feet. Quesada moved toward him as though to steady him but Barrett shook him off. "Let's go outside," he said.

They left the building. A gray mist had come in over the Station, and a fine drizzle had begun to fall. Barrett looked around at the scattering of huts. At the ocean, dimly visible to the east in the faint moonlight. He thought of Charley Norton and the party that had gone on the annual expedition to the Inland Sea. That bunch was going to be in for a real surprise, when they got back here in a few weeks and discovered that everybody was free to go home.

Very strangely, Barrett felt a sudden pressure forming around his eyelids, as of tears trying to force their way out into the open.

He turned to Hahn and Quesada. In a low voice he said, "Have you followed what I've been trying to tell you? Someone's got to stay here and ease the transition for the sick men who won't be able to stand the shock of return. Someone's got to keep the base running. Someone's got to explain to the new men who'll be coming back here, the scientists."

"Naturally," Hahn said.

"The one who does that—the one who stays behind—I think it ought to be someone who knows the Station well, someone who's fit to return Up Front, but who's willing to make the sacrifice and stay. Do you follow me? A volunteer." They were smiling at him now. Barrett wondered if there might not be something patronizing about those smiles. He wondered if he might not be a little too transparent. To hell with both of them, he thought. He sucked the Cambrian air into his lungs until his chest swelled grandly.

"I'm offering to stay," Barrett said in a loud tone. He glared at them to keep them from objecting. But they wouldn't dare object, he knew. In Hawksbill Station, he was the king. And he meant to keep it that way. "I'll be the volunteer," he said. "I'll be the one who stays."

He looked out over his kingdom from the top of the hill.

Part III

CRIMINAL JUSTICE OUTCOMES

8 The Cage

by Bertram Chandler

How does one define a "rational"—or intelligent—being? This story—about people who are captured by a superior alien species and must prove their rationality in order to free themselves—is a brilliant commentary on one way of defining a species as rational. For the superior aliens conclude that "only rational beings . . . put other beings in cages."

Punishment for crimes committed is clearly one of the major outcomes of the criminal justice system. One major form of punishment is incarceration. Municipal, county, state, and national governments spend a sizable portion of their budgets for the construction and maintenance of prison systems. They have become a major focus for public debate. Some citizens argue that we are building prisons like fancy motels, with air-conditioning, television, and similar amenities, and that somehow this is wrong, especially when there are other, legitimate services that need resources and that serve people who are not criminals. Other people argue that our prison systems constitute one of America's greatest tragedies, where broken men and women waste their lives, learn how to be better criminals, and are anything but rehabilitated when they are released from them.

What is imprisonment in our criminal justice system a measurement of? Rationality? Fear? Bertram Chandler's story "The Cage" forces us to come to grips with this question.

Imprisonment is always a humiliating experience, no matter how philosophical the prisoner. Imprisonment by one's own kind is bad

131

enough—but one can, at least, talk to one's captors, one can make one's wants understood; one can, on occasion, appeal to them man to man.

Imprisonment is doubly humiliating when one's captors, in all honesty, treat one as a lower animal.

The party from the survey ship could perhaps, be excused for failing to recognize the survivors from the interstellar liner *Lode Star* as rational beings. At least two hundred days had passed since their landing on the planet without a name—an unintentional landing made when *Lode Star's* Ehrenhaft generators, driven far in excess of their normal capacity by a breakdown of the electronic regulator, had flung her far from the regular shipping lanes to an unexplored region of Space. *Lode Star* had landed safely enough; but shortly thereafter (troubles never come singly) her Pile had got out of control and her captain had ordered his First Mate to evacuate the passengers and such crew members not needed to cope with the emergency, and to get them as far from the ship as possible.

Hawkins and his charges were well clear when there was a flare of released energy, a not very violent explosion. The survivors wanted to turn to watch, but Hawkins drove them on with curses and at times, blows. Luckily they were up wind from the ship and so escaped the fall-out.

When the fireworks seemed to be over Hawkins, accompanied by Dr. Boyle, the ship's surgeon, returned to the scene of the disaster. The two men, wary of radioactivity were cautious and stayed a safe distance from the shallow, still smoking crater that marked where the ship had been. It was all too obvious to them that the Captain, together with his officers and technicians, was now no more than an infinitesimal part of the incandescent cloud that had mushroomed up into the low overcast.

Thereafter the fifty-odd men and women, the survivors of *Lode Star,* had degenerated. It hadn't been a fast process—Hawkins and Boyle, aided by a committee of the more responsible passengers, had fought a stout rearguard action. But it had been a hopeless sort of fight. The climate was against them, for a start. Hot it was, always in the neighborhood of 85° Fahrenheit. And it was wet—a thin, warm drizzle falling all the time. The air seemed to abound with the spores of fungi—luckily these did not attack living skin but throve on dead organic matter, on clothing. They throve to an only slightly lesser degree on metals and on the synthetic fabrics that many of the castaways wore.

Danger, outside danger, would have helped to maintain morale.

But there were no dangerous animals. There were only little smooth-skinned things, not unlike frogs, that hopped through the sodden undergrowth, and, in the numerous rivers, fishlike creatures ranging in size from the shark to the tadpole, and all of them possessing the bellicosity of the latter.

Food had been no problem after the first few hungry hours. Volunteers had tried a large, succulent fungus growing on the boles of the huge fern-like trees. They had pronounced it good. After a lapse of five hours they had neither died nor even complained of abdominal pains. That fungus was to become the staple diet of the castaways. In the weeks that followed other fungi had been found, and berries, and roots—all of them edible. They provided a welcome variety.

Fire—in spite of the all-pervading heat—was the blessing most missed by the castaways. With it they could have supplemented their diet by catching and cooking the little frogthings of the rain forest, the fishes of the streams. Some of the hardier spirits did eat these animals raw, but they were frowned upon by most of the other members of the community. Too, fire would have helped to drive back the darkness of the long nights, would, by its real warmth and light, have dispelled the illusion of cold produced by the ceaseless dripping of water from every leaf and frond.

When they fled from the ship most of the survivors had possessed pocket lighters—but the lighters had been lost when the pockets, together with the clothing surrounding them, had disintegrated. In any case, all attempts to start a fire in the days when there were still pocket lighters had failed—there was not, Hawkins swore, a single dry spot on the whole accursed planet. Now the making of fire was quite impossible: even if there had been present an expert on the rubbing together of two dry sticks he could have found no material with which to work.

They made their permanent settlement on the crest of a low hill. (There were, so far as they could discover, no mountains.) It was less thickly wooded there than the surrounding plains, and the ground was less marshy underfoot. They succeeded in wrenching fronds from the fern-like trees and built for themselves crude shelters—more for the sake of privacy than for any comfort that they afforded. They clung, with a certain desperation, to the governmental forms of the worlds that they had left, and elected themselves a council. Boyle, the ship's surgeon, was their chief. Hawkins, rather to his surprise, was returned as a council member by a majority of only two votes—on thinking it over he realized that many of the passengers must still bear a grudge against the ship's executive staff for their present predicament.

The first council meeting was held in a hut—if so it could be called

—especially constructed for the purpose. The council members squatted in a rough circle. Boyle, the president, got slowly to his feet. Hawkins grinned wryly as he compared the surgeon's nudity with the pomposity that he seemed to have assumed with his elected rank, as he compared the man's dignity with the unkempt appearance presented by his uncut, uncombed gray hair, his uncombed and straggling gray beard.

"Ladies and gentlemen," began Boyle.

Hawkins looked around him at the naked, pallid bodies, at the stringy, lusterless hair, the long, dirty fingernails of the men and the unpainted lips of the women. He thought, I don't suppose I look much like an officer and a gentleman myself.

"Ladies and gentlemen," said Boyle, "we have been, as you know, elected to represent the human community upon this planet. I suggest that at this, our first meeting, we discuss our chances of survival—not as individuals, but as a race—"

"I'd like to ask Mr. Hawkins what our chances are of being picked up," shouted one of the two women members, a dried-up, spinsterish creature with prominent ribs and vertebrae.

"Slim," said Hawkins. "As you know, no communication is possible with other ships, or with planet stations when the Interstellar Drive is operating. When we snapped out of the Drive and came in for our landing we sent out a distress call—but we couldn't say where we were. Furthermore, we don't know that the call was received—"

"Miss Taylor," said Boyle huffily, "Mr. Hawkins, I would remind you that I am the duly elected president of this council. There will be time for a general discussion later.

"As most of you may already have assumed, the age of this planet, biologically speaking, corresponds roughly with that of Earth during the Carboniferous Era. As we already know, no species yet exists to challenge our supremacy. By the time such a species does emerge—something analogous to the giant lizards of Earth's Triassic Era—we should be well established—"

"*We* shall be dead!" called one of the men.

"We should be dead," agreed the doctor, "but our descendants will be very much alive. We have to decide how to give them as good a start as possible. Language we shall bequeath to them—"

"Never mind the language, Doc," called the other woman member. She was a small blonde, slim, with a hard face. "It's just this question of descendants that I'm here to look after. I represent the women of childbearing age—there are, as you must know, fifteen of us here. So far the girls have been very, very careful. We have reason to be. Can you, as a medical man, guarantee—bearing in mind that you have no drugs, no instruments—safe deliveries? Can you guarantee that our children will have a good chance of survival?"

Boyle dropped his pomposity like a worn-out garment.

"I'll be frank," he said. "I have not, as you, Miss Hart, have pointed out, either drugs or instruments. But I can assure you, Miss Hart, that your chances of a safe delivery are far better than they would have been on Earth during, say, the Eighteenth Century. And I'll tell you why. On this planet, so far as we know (and we have been here long enough now to find out the hard way), there exist no micro-organisms harmful to Man. Did such organisms exist, the bodies of those of us still surviving would be, by this time, mere masses of sup-puration. Most of us, of course, would have died of septicemia long ago. And that, I think, answers *both* your questions."

"I haven't finished yet," she said. "Here's another point. There are fifty-three of us here, men and women. There are ten married couples —so we'll count them out. That leaves thirty-three people, of whom twenty are men. Twenty men to thirteen (aren't we girls always un-lucky?) women. All of us aren't young—but we're all of us women. What sort of marriage set-up do we have? Monogamy? Polyandry?"

"Monogamy, of course," said a tall, thin man sharply. He was the only one of those present who wore clothing—if so it could be called. The disintegrating fronds lashed around his waist with a strand of vine did little to serve any useful purpose.

"All right, then," said the girl. "Monogamy. I'd rather prefer it that way myself. But I warn you that if that's the way we play it there's going to be trouble. And in any murder involving passion and jealousy the woman is as liable to be a victim as either of the men—and I don't want *that.*"

"What do you propose, then, Miss Hart?" asked Boyle.

"Just this, Doc. When it comes to our matings we leave love out of it. If two men want to marry the same woman, then let them fight it out. The best man gets the girl—and keeps her."

"Natural selection . . ." murmured the surgeon. "I'm in favor—but we must put it to the vote."

At the crest of the low hill was a shallow depression, a natural arena. Round the rim sat the castaways—all but four of them. One of the four was Dr. Boyle—he had discovered that his duties as president embraced those of a referee; it had been held that he was best competent to judge when one of the contestants was liable to suffer permanent damage. Another of the four was the girl Mary Hart. She had found a serrated twig with which to comb her long hair, she had contrived a wreath of yellow flowers with which to crown the victor. Was it, wondered Hawkins as he sat with the other council members, a hankering after an Earthly wedding ceremony, or was it a harking back to something older and darker?

"A pity that these blasted molds got our watches," said the fat man on Hawkins' right. "If we had any means of telling the time we could have rounds, make a proper prizefight of it."

Hawkins nodded. He looked at the four in the center of the arena —at the strutting, barbaric woman, at the pompous old man, at the two dark-bearded young men with their glistening white bodies. He knew them both—Fennet had been a Senior Cadet of the ill-fated *Lode Star;* Clemens, at least seven years Fennet's senior, was a passenger, had been a prospector on the frontier worlds.

"If we had anything to bet with," said the fat man happily, "I'd lay it on Clemens. That cadet of yours hasn't a snowball's chance in hell. He's been brought up to fight clean—Clemens has been brought up to fight dirty."

"Fennet's in better condition," said Hawkins. "He's been taking exercise, while Clemens has just been lying around sleeping and eating. Look at the paunch on him!"

"There's nothing wrong with good healthy flesh and muscle," said the fat man, patting his own paunch.

"No gouging, no biting!" called the doctor. "And may the best man win!"

He stepped back smartly away from the contestants, stood with the Hart woman.

There was an air of embarrassment about the pair of them as they stood there, each with his fists hanging at his sides. Each seemed to be regretting that matters had come to such a pass.

"Go *on!*" screamed Mary Hart at last. "Don't you want me? You'll live to a ripe old age here—and it'll be lonely with no woman!"

"They can always wait around until your daughters grow up, Mary!" shouted one of her friends.

"If I ever have any daughters!" she called. "I shan't at this rate!"

"Go on!" shouted the crowd. "Go on!"

Fennet made a start. He stepped forward almost diffidently, dabbed with his right fist at Clemens' unprotected face. It wasn't a hard blow, but it must have been painful. Clemens put his hand up to his nose, brought it away and stared at the bright blood staining it. He growled, lumbered forward with arms open to hug and crush. The cadet danced back, scoring twice more with his right.

"Why doesn't he *hit* him?" demanded the fat man.

"And break every bone in his fist? They aren't wearing gloves, you know," said Hawkins.

Fennet decided to make a stand. He stood firm, his feet slightly apart, and brought his right into play once more. This time he left his opponent's face alone, went for his belly instead. Hawkins was surprised to see that the prospector was taking the blows with apparent equanimity—he must be, he decided, much tougher in actuality than in appearance.

The cadet sidestepped smartly . . . and slipped on the wet grass. Clemens fell heavily onto his opponent; Hawkins could hear the *whoosh* as the air was forced from the lad's lungs. The prospector's thick arms encircled Fennet's body—and Fennet's knee came up viciously to Clemens' groin. The prospector squealed, but hung on grimly. One of his hands was around Fennet's throat now, and the other one, its fingers viciously hooked, was clawing for the cadet's eyes.

"No gouging!" Boyle was screaming. "No gouging!"

He dropped down to his knees, caught Clemens' thick wrist with both his hands.

Something made Hawkins look up then. It may have been a sound, although this is doubtful; the spectators were behaving like boxing fans at a prizefight. They could hardly be blamed—this was the first piece of real excitement that had come their way since the loss of the ship. It may have been a sound that made Hawkins look up, it may have been the sixth sense possessed by all good spacemen. What he saw made him cry out.

Hovering about the arena was a helicopter. There was something about the design of it, a subtle oddness, that told Hawkins that this was no Earthly machine. Suddenly, from its smooth, shining belly, dropped a net, seemingly of dull metal. It enveloped the struggling figures on the ground, trapped the doctor and Mary Hart.

Hawkins shouted again—a wordless cry. He jumped to his feet, ran to the assistance of his ensnared companions. The net seemed to be alive. It twisted itself around his wrists, bound his ankles. Others of the castaways rushed to aid Hawkins.

"Keep away!" he shouted. "Scatter!"

The low drone of the helicopter's rotors rose in pitch. The machine lifted. In an incredibly short space of time the arena was to the First Mate's eyes no more than a pale green saucer in which little white ants scurried aimlessly. Then the flying machine was above and through the base of the low clouds, and there was nothing to be seen but drifting whiteness.

When, at last, it made its descent Hawkins was not surprised to see the silvery tower of a great spaceship standing among the low trees on a level plateau.

The world to which they were taken would have been a marked improvement on the world they had left had it not been for the mistaken kindness of their captors. The cage in which the three men were housed duplicated, with remarkable fidelity, the climatic conditions of the planet upon which *Lode Star* had been lost. It was glassed in, and from sprinklers in its roof fell a steady drizzle of warm water. A couple of dispirited tree ferns provided little shelter from the depressing precipitation. Twice a day a hatch at the back of the cage, which was made of a sort of concrete, opened, and slabs of a fungus remarkably similar to that on which they had been subsisting were thrown in. There was a hole in the floor of the cage; this the prisoners rightly assumed was for sanitary purposes.

On either side of them were other cages. In one of them was Mary Hart—alone. She could gesture to them, wave to them, and that was all. The cage on the other side held a beast built on the same general lines as a lobster, but with a strong hint of squid. Across the broad roadway they could see other cages, but could not see what they housed.

Hawkins, Boyle and Fennet sat on the damp floor and stared through the thick glass and the bars at the beings outside who stared at them.

"If only they were humanoid," sighed the doctor. "If only they were the same shape as we are we might make a start towards convincing them that we, too, are intelligent beings."

"They aren't the same shape," said Hawkins. "And we, were the situations reversed, would take some convincing that three six-legged beer barrels were men and brothers. . . . Try Pythagoras' Theorem again," he said to the cadet.

Without enthusiasm the youth broke fronds from the nearest tree fern. He broke them into smaller pieces, then on the mossy floor laid them out in the design of a right-angled triangle with squares constructed on all three sides. The natives—a large one, one slightly smaller and a little one—regarded him incuriously with their flat, dull eyes. The large one put the tip of a tentacle into a pocket—the things wore clothing—and pulled out a brightly colored packet, handed it to the little one. The little one tore off the wrapping, started stuffing pieces of some bright blue confection into the slot on its upper side that, obviously, served it as a mouth.

"I wish they were allowed to feed the animals," sighed Hawkins. "I'm sick of that damned fungus."

"Let's recapitulate," said the doctor. "After all, we've nothing else to do. We were taken from our camp by the helicopter—six of us. We were taken to the survey ship—a vessel that seemed in no way superior to our own interstellar ships. You assure us, Hawkins, that the ship used the Ehrenhaft Drive or something so near to it as to be its twin brother. . . ."

"Correct," agreed Hawkins.

"On the ship we're kept in separate cages. There's no ill treatment, we're fed and watered at frequent intervals. We land on this strange planet, but we see nothing of it. We're hustled out of cages like so many cattle into a covered van. We know that we're being driven *somewhere*, that's all. The van stops, the door opens and a couple of these animated beer barrels poke in poles with smaller editions of those fancy nets on the end of them. They catch Clemens and Miss Taylor, drag them out. We never see them again. The rest of us spend the night and the following day and night in individual cages. The next day we're taken to this . . . zoo . . ."

"Do you think they were vivisected?" asked Fennet. "I never liked Clemens, but . . ."

"I'm afraid they were," said Boyle. "Our captors must have learned of the difference between the sexes by it. Unluckily there's no way of determining intelligence by vivisection—"

"The filthy brutes!" shouted the cadet.

"Easy, son," counseled Hawkins. "You can't blame them, you know. We've vivisected animals a lot more like us than we are to these things."

"The problem," the doctor went on, "is to convince these things —as you call them, Hawkins—that we are rational beings like themselves. How would they define a rational being? How would *we* define a rational being?"

"Somebody who knows Pythagoras' Theorem," said the cadet sulkily.

"I read somewhere," said Hawkins, "that the history of Man is the history of the fire-making, tool-using animal . . ."

"Then make fire," suggested the doctor. "Make us some tools, and use them."

"Don't be silly. You know that there's not an artifact among the bunch of us. No false teeth even—not even a metal filling. Even so . . ." He paused. "When I was a youngster there was, among the cadets in the interstellar ships, a revival of the old arts and crafts. We considered ourselves in a direct line of descent from the old windjammer sailormen, so we learned how to splice rope and wire, how to make sennit and fancy knots and all the rest of it. Then one of us hit on the idea of basketmaking. We were in a passenger ship, and we used to make our baskets secretly, daub them with violent colors and then sell them to passengers as genuine souvenirs from the Lost Planet of Arcturus VI. There was a most distressing scene when the Old Man and the Mate found out. . . ."

"What are you driving at?" asked the doctor.

"Just this. We will demonstrate our manual dexterity by the weaving of baskets—I'll teach you how."

"It might work. . . ." said Boyle slowly. "It might just work. . . . On the other hand, don't forget that certain birds and animals do the same sort of thing. On Earth there's the beaver, who builds quite cunning dams. There's the bower bird, who makes a bower for his mate as part of the courtship ritual . . ."

The Head Keeper must have known of creatures whose courting habits resembled those of the Terran bower bird. After three days of feverish basketmaking, which consumed all the bedding and stripped the tree ferns, Mary Hart was taken from her cage and put in with the three men. After she had got over her hysterical pleasure at having somebody to talk to again she was rather indignant.

It was good, thought Hawkins drowsily, to have Mary with them. A few more days of solitary confinement must surely have driven the girl crazy. Even so, having Mary in the same cage had its drawbacks. He had to keep a watchful eye on young Fennet. He even had to keep a watchful eye on Boyle—the old goat!

Mary screamed.

Hawkins jerked into complete wakefulness. He could see the pale form of Mary—on this world it was never completely dark at night— and, on the other side of the cage, the forms of Fennet and Boyle. He got hastily to his feet, stumbled to the girl's side.

"What is it?" he asked.

"I . . . I don't know. . . . Something small, with sharp claws . . . It ran over me. . . ."

"Oh," said Hawkins, "that was only Joe."

"*Joe?*" she demanded.

"I don't know exactly what he—or she—is," said the man.

"I think he's definitely *he*," said the doctor.

"What is Joe?" she asked again.

"He must be the local equivalent to a mouse," said the doctor, "although he looks nothing like one. He comes up through the floor somewhere to look for scraps of food. We're trying to tame him—"

"You encourage the brute?" she screamed. "I demand that you do something about him—at once! Poison him, or trap him. Now!"

"Tomorrow," said Hawkins.

"Now!" she screamed.

"Tomorrow," said Hawkins firmly.

The capture of Joe proved to be easy. Two flat baskets, hinged like the valves of an oyster shell, made the trap. There was bait inside —a large piece of the fungus. There was a cunningly arranged upright that would fall at the least tug at the bait. Hawkins, lying sleepless on his damp bed, heard the tiny click and thud that told him that the trap had been sprung. He heard Joe's indignant chitterings, heard the tiny claws scrabbling at the stout basket-work.

Mary Hart was asleep. He shook her.

"We've caught him," he said.

"Then kill him," she answered drowsily.

But Joe was not killed. The three men were rather attached to him. With the coming of daylight they transferred him to a cage that Hawkins had fashioned. Even the girl relented when she saw the harmless ball of multi-colored fur bouncing indignantly up and down in its prison. She insisted on feeding the little animal, exclaimed gleefully when the thin tentacles reached out and took the fragment of fungus from her fingers.

For three days they made much of their pet. On the fourth day beings whom they took to be keepers entered the cage with their nets, immobilized the occupants, and carried off Joe and Hawkins.

"I'm afraid it's hopeless," Boyle said. "He's gone the same way . . ."

"They'll have him stuffed and mounted in some museum," said Fennet glumly.

"No," said the girl. "They couldn't!'"

"They could," said the doctor.

Abruptly the hatch at the back of the cage opened.

Before the three humans could retreat to the scant protection supplied by a corner a voice called, "It's all right, come on out!"

Hawkins walked into the cage. He was shaved, and the beginnings of a healthy tan had darkened the pallor of his skin. He was wearing a pair of trunks fashioned from some bright red material.

"Come on out," he said again. "Our hosts have apologized very sincerely, and they have more suitable accommodation prepared for us. Then, as soon as they have a ship ready, we're to go to pick up the other survivors."

"Not so fast," said Boyle. "Put us in the picture, will you? What made them realize that we were rational beings?"

Hawkins' face darkened.

"Only rational beings," he said, "put other beings in cages."

9 December 28th

by Theodore L. Thomas

Count the ways that I punish you: torturing, garroting, impaling, dissecting, quartering, crucifying, gassing, asphyxiating, hanging, cutting, gouging, electrocuting, stomping, shooting, and poisoning. How many ways are there? How to punish and make people suffer has preoccupied much of our energy as human beings. We not only consider the effectiveness of punishment but also its aesthetics. Some methods are "beautiful"; others, merely "neat." Even the costs of punishment have occupied a great deal of our time. Is an electrocution "cheaper" than a firing squad? Is gas "more efficient" than hanging? These are not pretty questions, yet they are serious public policy issues.

Much can be said about a culture in terms of the methods it chooses to punish the transgressors of its laws. In our own society, we are faced with a constitutional proscription against "cruel and unusual" punishment. The definition and application of criteria that constitute "cruel and unusual" punishment are the subject of much legal action as well as political debate. The concept is not restricted only to physical punishment; it has also been expanded to include mental and psychological conditions.

What does the future hold in store for the evolution of new methods for punishing human beings? As our scientific and technological knowledge advances, we can expect changes in the techniques of punishment. Our knowledge of chemical and biological processes, in conjunction with our state of biophysics, certainly implies a number of ways to kill human beings effectively, efficiently, and relatively painlessly.

But will these advances in science and technology actually be translated into more "humane" forms of punishment? Most of the fifty states use rather antiquated methods to punish felons convicted of capital offenses, hanging, electrocution, and gas being among the most "popular."

"December 28th" is a story about a future form of punishment. Scientific advances are used but in an unbelievably horrible context. The method is perhaps not as "cruel and unusual" as is the context.

Why must they do it on December 28th? John Stapleton considered the question. That was the worst part of it, the date. December 28th, tucked neatly between the brightest holidays of the year.

Stapleton spun from the small window in a characteristic rush of motion. Hands locked behind him, he stared at the door. In the back of his mind he knew there was a good reason for the date. They had picked the anniversary of the day he and Ardelle had married, a day of special gladness, in the heart of the holiday season. Yes, December 28th was a time for many things, but it was not a time for a hanging.

In three steps Stapleton was at the door; he took the bars into his two great hands. Understanding the reason for the date did nothing to sap his anger at it. Most of the world celebrated, and it seemed to Stapleton that this universal jubilee was at his expense. The world danced at his hanging.

Stapleton somberly began his exercises. The guards saw, and looked at each other uncomfortably. Stapleton took the pencil-thin bars into his two hands and methodically tried to pull them apart. First, the right hand directly in front of the massive chest, the left hand off to one side. The tendons stretched audibly. Then the hands were reversed, and again the tightening of great muscles. Then both hands on a single bar, and both feet on another. The soft grunts and the low rumbles deep in the throat echoed in the chamber as Stapleton worked on the bars, worked until his body was covered with a fine sweat. Stapleton knew, and the guards knew, that the thin shafts were of an alloy capable of withstanding the best efforts of ten men such as Stapleton. Yet the slow and careful straining, the deliberate and intense attack on the bars by the massive man created the illusion that he was able to rip them out of their moorings. Twice a day Stapleton took his exercises on the bars, and twice a day the guards watched with a fear that knowledge could not dispel.

Stapleton finished. He stood at the door breathing deeply, his hands clenching and unclenching, the fingers making a scraping sound as he forced the tips across the callused and furrowed palms. The guards visibly relaxed and turned away. Stapleton looked at the clock and grunted. It was almost time. In a few moments now they would come for him.

He grunted louder. Let them come. Ardelle was dead, Ardelle and that other. And no matter what they said or did, it was right it should be that way. There are things a man knows who has been one with a woman like Ardelle. Between such a man and such a woman there could be nothing concealed, not for long. How strange that she should have tried.

But the time came when he looked at her with a mild question in his eyes. The response—the incredible, soul-shaking response—was a flicker of the panic of discovery. Just a brief flash in her eyes, but he read it well; it was enough.

Ardelle was silent throughout all that followed. She understood this man of iron and fire, and so through it all she made no sound, no moan. With the other it was different. The other had been playing a kind of game, and he was not at all prepared to pay the price of losing. He died badly.

And Stapleton? There was an enigma. Here and now, when men need no longer die for their crimes, was a man who refused to admit that a crime had been committed. So little was needed to save him, but that little he refused to give. Here and now, a man need only cry out, "Forgive me, I was wrong. Forgive me," and he was saved.

Stapleton turned to watch as the outer door opened to admit a tall gray-haired man. With measured strides the man came close to the bars and looked through at Stapleton. The pain was as strong in his face as ever, the sorrow and pleading as eloquent. His words when he spoke were husky with suffering. "John Stapleton, how say you? Have you erred?"

Stapleton looked at him and said, "I have not erred. I did what had to be done, nothing more."

The man with the gray hair turned away. The walk back to the door was solemn, for his head was bent and his shoulders trembled. Then he was gone.

There was a stirring and a shuffling of many feet outside the outer door. Stapleton knew they were coming for him, and he stepped back to the center of the cell. He knew how this would be. They would come into his cell fearful that he would unleash his physical might, yet they would be unable to look at him. He would wait a moment, then laugh, then lead the procession to the gallows chamber. He would stand with his head in the enfolding blackness, feeling the snug rope around his throat and the knot behind his left ear. When the moment came there would be no sensation of falling; there would be a mere lightening of pressure against his feet. And the thudding shock and the searing flash of light. Then blackness.

These things he knew well, but there were other things. There was the doctor who stood by to pronounce him dead at the earliest possible moment; the oxygen-carrying blood must not be kept from the brain longer than 4.3 minutes. Once dead the intravenous needles were inserted and the pumps took over where the heart had failed.

The surgeons came on next. With high dexterity they repaired the broken cervical vertebra, the torn muscles, the crushed veins and arteries. When they were finished they placed the head and neck in a cast, and turned their attention to the restoration of the heartbeat. This was soon accomplished and, unconscious, Stapleton was wheeled to his cell.

Usually he recovered consciousness during the middle of January. By March he was out of bed, still wearing his cast. In June he started his exercises, for he insisted on being strong. In August he put aside his cast. All during the fall he grew strong in order that the cycle might begin again on December 28th. How many times had it been since that first time back in 1997? Fourteen? Eighteen? One loses count, but no matter. If this is what they must do, let them.

But why must they always do it on December 28th?

Because it's one more year of
the path ~~that~~ that has to be done.
Or it's one year closer to death
as you do the path.

10 Two-Handed Engine

by Henry Kuttner

Deterrence is supposed to be one of the major outcomes of the criminal justice system. How we can stop people from committing crimes is a perennial question about which there is much legal, political, and scholarly debate. The answer to this question comes easily: punishment—and the more serious the crime, the more severe the punishment. Most societies have made this single hypothesis the foundation of their criminal justice policy.

In the story "Two-Handed Engine," the law is enforced—and punishment is meted out—by incorruptible machines, analog computers called "Furies." The idea behind them is that swift, inexorable punishment, publicly performed, will not cure the criminal and will not prevent crime in that sense; rather, such punishment is intended to instill fear in others who witness it and therefore deter them from committing crime.

But in the Middle Ages, when public executions were accompanied by festivals, they drew many people who usually became victims to pickpockets who worked the crowds watching the public execution. This was at a time when pickpocketing itself was considered a major crime for which hanging was the appropriate punishment! Although this is an interesting and somewhat telling commentary on the inadequacy of punishment as a deterrent to crime, one gets the feeling that punishment by the "Furies" is not subject to the same weakness.

Danner leaned back comfortably in his contoured restaurant chair and rolled expensive wine across his tongue, closing his eyes to enjoy the taste of it better. He felt perfectly safe. Oh, perfectly protected. For nearly an hour now he had been sitting here, ordering the most expensive food, enjoying the music breathing softly through the air, the murmurous, well-bred hush of his fellow diners. It was a good place to be. It was very good, having so much money—now.

True, he had had to kill to get the money. But no guilt troubled him. There was no guilt if you aren't found out, and Danner had protection. Protection straight from the source, which was something new in the world. Danner knew the consequences of killing. If Hartz hadn't satisfied him that he was perfectly safe, Danner would never have pulled the trigger . . .

The memory of an archaic word flickered through his mind briefly. *Sin.* It evoked nothing. Once it had something to do with guilt, in an incomprehensible way. Not any more. Mankind had been through too much. Sin was meaningless now.

He dismissed the thought and tried the heart-of-palms salad. He found he didn't like it. Oh well, you had to expect things like that. Nothing was perfect. He sipped the wine again, liking the way the glass seemed to vibrate like something faintly alive in his hand. It was good wine. He thought of ordering more, but then he thought no, save it, next time. There was so much before him, waiting to be enjoyed. Any risk was worth it. And of course, in this there had been no risk.

Danner was a man born at the wrong time. He was old enough to remember the last days of utopia, young enough to be trapped in the new scarcity economy the machines had clamped down on their makers. In his early youth he'd had access to free luxuries, like everybody else. He could remember the old days when he was an adolescent and the last of the Escape Machines were still operating, the glamorous, bright, impossible, vicarious visions that didn't really exist and never could have. But then the scarcity economy swallowed up pleasure. Now you got necessities but no more. Now you had to work. Danner hated every minute of it.

When the swift change came, he'd been too young and unskilled to compete in the scramble. The rich men today were the men who had built fortunes on cornering the few luxuries the machines still produced. All Danner had left were bright memories and a dull, resentful feeling of having been cheated. All he wanted were the bright days back, and he didn't care how he got them.

Well, now he had them. He touched the rim of the wine glass with his finger, feeling it sing silently against the touch. Blown glass? he wondered. He was too ignorant of luxury items to understand. But he'd learn. He had the rest of his life to learn in, and be happy.

He looked up across the restaurant and saw through the transparent dome of the roof the melting towers of the city. They made a stone forest as far as he could see. And this was only one city. When he was tired of it, there were more. Across the country, across the planet the network lay that linked city with city in a webwork like a vast, intricate, half-alive monster. Call it society.

He felt it tremble a little beneath him.

He reached for the wine and drank quickly. The faint uneasiness that seemed to shiver the foundations of the city was something new. It was because—yes, certainly it was because of a new fear.

It was because he had not been found out.

That made no sense. Of course the city was complex. Of course it operated on a basis of incorruptible machines. They, and only they, kept man from becoming very quickly another extinct animal. And of these the analog computers, the electronic calculators, were the gyroscope of all living. They made and enforced the laws that were necessary now to keep mankind alive. Danner didn't understand much of the vast changes that had swept over society in his lifetime, but this much even he knew.

So perhaps it made sense that he felt society shiver because he sat here luxurious on foam-rubber, sipping wine, hearing soft music, and no Fury standing behind his chair to prove that the calculators were still guardians for mankind . . .

If not even the Furies are incorruptible, what can a man believe in?

It was at that exact moment that the Fury arrived.

Danner heard every sound suddenly die out around him. His fork was halfway to his lips, but he paused, frozen, and looked up across the table and the restaurant towards the door.

The Fury was taller than a man. It stood there for a moment, the afternoon sun striking a blinding spot of brightness from its shoulder. It had no face, but it seemed to scan the restaurant leisurely, table by table. Then it stepped in under the doorframe and the sun-spot slid away and it was like a tall man encased in steel, walking slowly between the tables.

Danner said to himself, laying down his untasted food, "Not for me. Everyone else here is wondering. I *know*."

And like a memory in a drowning man's mind, clear, sharp and condensed into a moment, yet every detail clear, he remembered what Hartz had told him. As a drop of water can pull into its reflection a wide panorama condensed into a tiny focus, so time seemed to focus down to a pinpoint the half-hour Danner and Hartz had spent together, in Hartz's office with the walls that could go transparent at the push of a button.

He saw Hartz again, plump and blond, with the sad eyebrows. A man who looked relaxed until he began to talk, and then you felt the burning quality about him, the air of driven tension that made even the air around him seem to be restlessly trembling. Danner stood before Hartz's desk again in memory, feeling the floor hum faintly against his soles with the heartbeat of the computers. You could see them through the glass, smooth, shiny things with winking lights in banks like candles burning in colored glass cups. You could hear their faraway chattering as they ingested facts, meditated them, and then spoke in numbers like cryptic oracles. It took men like Hartz to understand what the oracles meant.

"I have a job for you," Hartz said. "I want a man killed."

"Oh no," Danner said. "What kind of a fool do you think I am?"

"Now wait a minute. You can use money, can't you?"

"What for?" Danner asked bitterly. "A fancy funeral?"

"A life of luxury. I know you're not a fool. I know damned well you wouldn't do what I ask unless you got money *and* protection. That's what I can offer. Protection."

Danner looked through the transparent wall at the computers.

"Sure," he said.

"No, I mean it. I—" Hartz hesitated, glancing around the room a little uneasily, as if he hardly trusted his own precautions for making sure of privacy. "This is something new," he said. "I can redirect any Fury I want to."

"Oh, sure," Danner said again.

"It's true. I'll show you. I can pull a Fury off any victim I choose."

"How?"

"That's my secret. Naturally. In effect, though, I've found a way to feed in false data, so the machines come out with the wrong verdict before conviction, or the wrong orders after conviction."

"But that's—dangerous, isn't it?"

"Dangerous?" Hartz looked at Danner under his sad eyebrows. "Well, yes. I think so. That's why I don't do it often. I've done it only once, as a matter of fact. Theoretically, I'd worked out the method. I tested it, just once. It worked. I'll do it again, to prove to you I'm telling the truth. After that I'll do it once again, to protect you. And that will be it. I don't want to upset the calculators any more than I have to. Once your job's done, I won't have to."

"Who do you want killed?"

Involuntarily Hartz glanced upward, towards the heights of the building where the top-rank executive offices were. "O'Reilly," he said.

Danner glanced upward too, as if he could see through the floor and observe the exalted shoe-soles of O'Reilly, Controller of the Calculators, pacing an expensive carpet overhead.

"It's very simple," Hartz said. "I want his job."

"Why not do your own killing, then, if you're so sure you can stop the Furies?"

"Because that would give the whole thing away," Hartz said impatiently. "Use your head. I've got an obvious motive. It wouldn't take a calculator to figure out who profits most if O'Reilly dies. If I saved myself from a Fury, people would start wondering how I did it. But you've got no motive for killing O'Reilly. Nobody but the calculators would know, and I'll take care of them."

"How do I know you can do it?"

"Simple. Watch."

Hartz got up and walked quickly across the resilient carpet that gave his steps a falsely youthful bounce. There was a waist-high counter on the far side of the room, with a slanting glass screen on it. Nervously Hartz punched a button, and a map of a section of the city sprang out in bold lines on its surface.

"I've got to find a sector where a Fury's in operation now," he explained. The map flickered and he pressed the button again. The unstable outlines of the city streets wavered and brightened and then went out as he scanned the sections fast and nervously. Then a map flashed on which had three wavering streaks of colored light criss-crossing it, intersecting at one point near the center. The point moved very slowly across the map, at just about the speed of a walking man reduced to miniature in scale with the street he walked on. Around him the colored lines wheeled slowly, keeping their focus always steady on the single point.

"There," Hartz said, leaning forward to read the printed name of the street. A drop of sweat fell from his forehead on to the glass, and he wiped it uneasily away with his fingertip. "There's a man with a Fury assigned to him. All right, now. I'll show you. Look here."

Above the desk was a news screen. Hartz clicked it on and watched impatiently while a street scene swam into focus. Crowds, traffic noises, people hurrying, people loitering. And in the middle of the crowd a little oasis of isolation, an island in the sea of humanity. Upon that moving island two occupants dwelt, like a Crusoe and a Friday, alone. One of the two was a haggard man who watched the ground as he walked. The other islander in this deserted spot was a tall, shining man-formed shape that followed at his heels.

As if invisible walls surrounded them, pressing back the crowds they walked through, the two moved in an empty space that closed in behind them, opened up before them. Some of the passers-by stared, some looked away in embarrassment or uneasiness. Some watched with a frank anticipation, wondering perhaps at just what moment the Friday would lift his steel arm and strike the Crusoe dead.

"Watch, now," Hartz said nervously. "Just a minute. I'm going to pull the Fury off this man. Wait." He crossed to his desk, opened a drawer, bent secretively over it. Danner heard a series of clicks from inside, and then the brief chatter of tapped keys. "Now," Hartz said, closing the drawer. He moved the back of his hand across his forehead. "Warm in here, isn't it? Let's get a closer look. You'll see something happen in a minute."

Back to the news screen. He flicked the focus switch and the street scene expanded, the man and his pacing jailer swooped upward into close focus. The man's face seemed to partake subtly of the impassive quality of the robot's. You would have thought they had lived a long time together, and perhaps they had. Time is a flexible element, infinitely long sometimes in a very short space.

"Wait until they get out of the crowd," Hartz said. "This mustn't be conspicuous. There, he's turning now." The man, seeming to move at random, wheeled at an alley corner and went down the narrow, dark passage away from the thoroughfare. The eye of the news screen followed him as closely as the robot.

"So you do have cameras that can do that," Danner said with interest. "I always thought so. How's it done? Are they spotted at every corner, or is it a beam trans—"

"Never mind," Hartz said. "Trade secret. Just watch. We'll have to wait until—no, no! Look, he's going to try it now!"

The man glanced furtively behind him. The robot was just turning the corner in his wake. Hartz darted back to his desk and pulled the drawer open. His hand poised over it, his eyes watched the screen anxiously. It was curious how the man in the alley, though he could have no inkling that other eyes watched, looked up and scanned the sky, gazing directly for a moment into the attentive, hidden camera and the eyes of Hartz and Danner. They saw him take a sudden, deep breath, and break into a run.

From Hartz's drawer sounded a metallic click. The robot, which had moved smoothly into a run the moment the man did, checked itself awkwardly and seemed to totter on its steel for an instant. It slowed. It stopped like an engine grinding to a halt. It stood motionless.

At the edge of the camera's range you could see the man's face, looking backward, mouth open with shock as he saw the impossible happen. The robot stood there in the alley, making indecisive motions as if the new orders Hartz pumped into its mechanisms were grating against inbuilt orders in whatever receptor it had. Then it turned its steel back upon the man in the alley and went smoothly, almost sedately, away down the street, walking as precisely as if it were obeying valid orders, not stripping the very gears of society in its aberrant behavior.

You got one last glimpse of the man's face, looking strangely stricken, as if his last friend in the world had left him.

Hartz switched off the screen. He wiped his forehead again. He went to the glass wall and looked out and down as if he were half afraid the calculators might know what he had done. Looking very small against the background of the metal giants, he said over his shoulder, "Well, Danner?"

Was it well? There had been more talk, of course, more persuasion, a raising of the bribe. But Danner knew his mind had been made up from that moment. A calculated risk, and worth it. Well worth it. Except—

In the deathly silence of the restaurant all motion had stopped. The Fury walked calmly between the tables, threading its shining way, touching no one. Every face blanched, turned towards it. Every mind thought, "Can it be for me?" Even the entirely innocent thought, "This is the first mistake they've ever made, and it's come for me. The first mistake, but there's no appeal and I could never prove a thing." For while guilt had no meaning in this world, punishment did have meaning, and punishment could be blind, striking like the lightning.

Danner between set teeth told himself over and over, "Not for me. I'm safe. I'm protected. It hasn't come for me." And yet he thought how strange it was, what a coincidence, wasn't it, that there should be two murderers here under this expensive glass roof today? Himself, and the one the Fury had come for.

He released his fork and heard it clink on the plate. He looked down at it and the food, and suddenly his mind rejected everything around him and went diving off on a fugitive tangent like an ostrich into sand. He thought about food. How did asparagus grow? What did raw food look like? He had never seen any. Food came ready-cooked out of restaurant kitchens or automatic slots. Potatoes, now. What did they look like? A moist white mash? No, for sometimes they were oval slices, so the thing itself must be oval. But not round. Sometimes you got them in long strips, squared off at the ends. Something quite long and oval, then chopped into even lengths. And white, of course. And they grew underground, he was almost sure. Long, thin roots twining white arms among the pipes and conduits he had seen laid bare when the streets were under repair. How strange that he should be eating something like thin, ineffectual human arms that embraced the sewers of the city and writhed pallidly where the worms had their being. And where he himself, when the Fury found him, might . . .

He pushed the plate away.

An indescribable rustling and murmuring in the room lifted his eyes for him as if he were an automaton. The Fury was halfway across the room now, and it was almost funny to see the relief of those whom it had passed by. Two or three of the women had buried their faces in their hands, and one man had slipped quietly from his chair in a dead faint as the Fury's passing released their private dreads back into their hidden wells.

The thing was quite close now. It looked to be about seven feet tall, and its motion was very smooth, which was unexpected when you thought about it. Smoother than human motions. Its feet fell with a heavy, measured tread upon the carpet. Thud, thud, thud. Danner tried impersonally to calculate what it weighed. You always heard that they made no sound except for that terrible tread, but this one creaked very slightly somewhere. It had no features, but the human mind couldn't help sketching in lightly a sort of airy face upon that blank steel surface, with eyes that seemed to search the room.

It was coming closer. Now all eyes were converging towards Danner. And the Fury came straight on. It almost looked as if—

"No!" Danner said to himself. "Oh, no, this can't be!" He felt like a man in a nightmare, on the verge of waking. "Let me wake soon," he thought. "Let me wake *now*, before it gets here!"

But he did not wake. And now the thing stood over him, and the thudding footsteps stopped. There was the faintest possible creaking as it towered over his table, motionless, waiting, its featureless face turned towards his.

Danner felt an intolerable tide of heat surge up into his face—rage, shame, disbelief. His heart pounded so hard the room swam and a sudden pain like jagged lightning shot through his head from temple to temple.

He was on his feet, shouting.

"No, no!" he yelled at the impassive steel. "You're wrong! You've made a mistake! Go away, you damned fool! You're wrong, you're wrong!" He groped on the table without looking down, found his plate and hurled it straight at the armored chest before him. China shattered. Spilled food smeared a white and green and brown stain over the steel.

Danner floundered out of his chair, around the table, past the tall metal figure towards the door.

All he could think of now was Hartz.

Seas of faces swam by him on both sides as he stumbled out of the restaurant. Some watched with avid curiosity, their eyes seeking him. Some did not look at all, but gazed at their plates rigidly or covered their faces with their hands. Behind him the measured tread came on, and the rhythmic faint creak from somewhere inside the armor.

The faces fell away on both sides and he went through a door without any awareness of opening it. He was in the street. Sweat bathed him and the air struck icy, though it was not a cold day. He looked blindly left and right, and then plunged for a bank of phone booths half a block away, the image of Hartz swimming before his eyes so clearly he blundered into people without seeing them. Dimly he heard indignant voices begin to speak and then die into awestruck silence. The way cleared magically before him. He walked in the newly created island of his isolation up to the nearest booth.

After he had closed the glass door the thunder of his own blood in his ears made the little sound-proofed booth reverberate. Through the door he saw the robot stand passionlessly waiting, the smear of spilled food still streaking its chest like some robotic ribbon of honor across a steel shirt front.

Danner tried to dial a number. His fingers were like rubber. He breathed deep and hard, trying to pull himself together. An irrelevant thought floated across the surface of his mind. I forgot to pay for my dinner. And then: A lot of good the money will do me now. Oh, damn Hartz, damn him, damn him!

He got the number.

A girl's face flashed into sharp, clear colors on the screen before him. Good, expensive screens in the public booths in this part of town, his mind noted impersonally.

"This is Controller Hartz's office. May I help you?"

Danner tried twice before he could give his name. He wondered if the girl could see him, and behind him, dimly through the glass, the tall waiting figure. He couldn't tell, because she dropped her eyes immediately to what must have been a list on the unseen table before her.

"I'm sorry. Mr. Hartz is out. He won't be back today."

The screen drained of light and color.

Danner folded back the door and stood up. His knees were unsteady. The robot stood just far enough back to clear the hinge of the door. For a moment they faced each other. Danner heard himself suddenly in the midst of an uncontrollable giggling which even he realized verged on hysteria. The robot with the smear of food like a ribbon of honor looked so ridiculous. Danner to his dim surprise found that all this while he had been clutching the restaurant napkin in his left hand.

"Stand back," he said to the robot. "Let me out. Oh, you fool, don't you know this is a mistake?" His voice quavered. The robot creaked faintly and stepped back.

"It's bad enough to have you follow me," Danner said. "At least, you might be clean. A dirty robot is too much—too much—" The thought was idiotically unbearable, and he heard tears in his voice. Half-laughing, half-weeping, he wiped the steel chest clean and threw the napkin to the floor.

And it was at that very instant, with the feel of the hard chest still vivid in his memory, that realization finally broke through the protective screen of hysteria, and he remembered the truth. He would never in life be alone again. Never while he drew breath. And when he died, it would be at these steel hands, perhaps upon this steel chest, with the passionless face bent to his, the last thing in life he would ever see. No human companion, but the black steel skull of the Fury.

It took him nearly a week to reach Hartz. During the week, he changed his mind about how long it might take a man followed by a Fury to go mad. The last thing he saw at night was the street light shining through the curtains of his expensive hotel suite upon the metal shoulder of his jailer. All night long, waking from uneasy slumber, he could hear the faint creaking of some inward mechanism functioning under the armor. And each time he woke it was to wonder whether he would ever wake again. Would the blow fall while he slept? And what kind of blow? How did the Furies execute? It was always a faint relief to see the bleak light of early morning shine upon the watcher by his bed. At least he had lived through the night. But was this living? And was it worth the burden?

He kept his hotel suite. Perhaps the management would have liked him to go, but nothing was said. Possibly they didn't dare. Life took on a strange, transparent quality, like something seen through an invisible wall. Outside of trying to reach Hartz, there was nothing Danner wanted to do. The old desires for luxuries, entertainment, travel, had melted away. He wouldn't have traveled alone.

He did spend hours in the public library, reading all that was available about the Furies. It was here that he first encountered the two haunting and frightening lines Milton wrote when the world was small and simple—mystifying lines that made no certain sense to anybody until man created a Fury out of steel, in his own image.

> *But that two-handed engine at the door*
> *Stands ready to smite once, and smite no more....*

Danner glanced up at his own two-handed engine, motionless at his shoulder, and thought of Milton and the long-ago times when life was simple and easy. He tried to picture the past. The twentieth century, when all civilizations together crashed over the brink in one majestic downfall to chaos. And the time before that, when people were . . . different, somehow. But how? It was too far and too strange. He could not imagine the time before the machines.

But he learned for the first time what had really happened, back there in his early years, when the bright world finally blinked out entirely and gray drudgery began. And the Furies were first forged in the likeness of man.

Before the really big wars began, technology advanced to the point where machines bred upon machines like living things, and there might have been an Eden on earth, with everybody's wants fully supplied, except that the social sciences fell too far behind the physical sciences. When the decimating wars came on, machines and people fought side by side, steel against steel and man against man, but man was the more perishable. The wars ended when there were no longer two societies left to fight against each other. Societies splintered apart into smaller and smaller groups until a state very close to anarchy set in.

The machines licked their metal wounds meanwhile and healed each other as they had been built to do. They had no need for the social sciences. They went on calmly reproducing themselves and handing out to mankind the luxuries which the age of Eden had designed them to hand out. Imperfectly of course. Incompletely, because some of their species were wiped out entirely and left no machines to breed and reproduce their kind. But most of them mined their raw materials, refined them, poured and cast the needed parts, made their own fuel, repaired their own injuries and maintained their breed upon the face of the earth with an efficiency man never even approached.

Meanwhile mankind splintered and splintered away. There were no longer any real groups, not even families. Men didn't need each other much. Emotional attachments dwindled. Men had been conditioned to accept vicarious surrogates and escapism was fatally easy.

Men reoriented their emotions to the Escape Machines that fed them joyous, impossible adventure and made the waking world seem too dull to bother with. And the birth rate fell and fell. It was a very strange period. Luxury and chaos went hand in hand, anarchy and inertia were the same thing. And still the birth rate dropped . . .

Eventually a few people recognized what was happening. Man as a species was on the way out. And man was helpless to do anything about it. But he had a powerful servant. So the time came when some unsung genius saw what would have to be done. Someone saw the situation clearly and set a new pattern in the biggest of the surviving electronic calculators. This was the goal he set: "Mankind must be made self-responsible again. You will make this your only goal until you achieve the end."

It was simple, but the changes it produced were worldwide and all human life on the planet altered drastically because of it. The machines were an integrated society, if man was not. And now they had a single set of orders which all of them reorganized to obey.

So the days of the free luxuries ended. The Escape Machines shut up shop. Men were forced back into groups for the sake of survival. They had to undertake now the work the machines withheld, and slowly, slowly, common needs and common interests began to spawn the almost lost feeling of human unity again.

But it was so slow. And no machine could put back into man what he had lost—the internalized conscience. Individualism had reached its ultimate stage and there had been no deterrent to crime for a long while. Without family or clan relations, not even feud retaliation occurred. Conscience failed, since no man identified with any other.

The real job of the machines now was to rebuild in man a realistic superego to save him from extinction. A self-responsible society would be a genuinely interdependent one, the leader identifying with the group, and a realistically internalized conscience which would forbid and punish "sin"—the sin of injuring the group with which you identify.

And here the Furies came in.

The machines defined murder, under any circumstances, as the only human crime. This was accurate enough, since it is the only act which can irreplaceably destroy a unit of society.

The Furies couldn't prevent crime. Punishment never cures the criminal. But it can prevent others from committing crime through simple fear, when they see punishment administered to others. The Furies were the symbol of punishment. They overtly stalked the streets on the heels of their condemned victims, the outward and visible sign that murder is always punished, and punished most publicly and terribly. They were very efficient. They were never wrong. Or at least, in theory they were never wrong, and considering the enormous quantities of information stored by now in the analog computers, it seemed likely that the justice of the machines was far more efficient than that of humans could be.

Some day man would rediscover sin. Without it he had come near to perishing entirely. With it, he might resume his authority over himself and the race of mechanized servants who were helping him to restore his species. But until that day, the Furies would have to stalk the streets, man's conscience in metal guise, imposed by the machines man created a long time ago.

What Danner did during this time he scarcely knew. He thought a great deal of the old days when the Escape Machines still worked, before the machines rationed luxuries. He thought of this sullenly and with resentment, for he could see no point at all in the experiment mankind was embarked on. He had liked it better in the old days. And there were no Furies then, either.

He drank a good deal. Once he emptied his pockets into the hat of a legless beggar, because the man like himself was set apart from society by something new and terrible. For Danner it was the Fury. For the beggar it was life itself. Thirty years ago he would have lived or died unheeded, tended only by machines. That a beggar could survive at all, by begging, must be a sign that society was beginning to feel twinges of awakened fellow feeling with its members, but to Danner that meant nothing. He wouldn't be around long enough to know how the story came out.

He wanted to talk to the beggar, though the man tried to wheel himself away on his little platform.

"Listen," Danner said urgently, following, searching his pockets. "I want to tell you. It doesn't feel the way you think it would. It feels—"

He was quite drunk that night, and he followed the beggar until the man threw the money back at him and thrust himself away rapidly on his wheeled platform, while Danner leaned against a building and tried to believe in its solidity. But only the shadow of the Fury, falling across him from the street lamp, was real.

Later that night, somewhere in the dark, he attacked the Fury. He seemed to remember finding a length of pipe somewhere, and he struck showers of sparks from the great, impervious shoulders above him. Then he ran, doubling and twisting up alleys, and in the end he hid in a dark doorway, waiting, until the steady footsteps resounded through the night.

He fell asleep, exhausted.

It was the next day that he finally reached Hartz.

"What went wrong?" Danner asked. In the past week he had changed a good deal. His face was taking on, in its impassivity, an odd resemblance to the metal mask of the robot.

Hartz struck the desk edge a nervous blow, grimacing when he hurt his hand. The room seemed to be vibrating not with the pulse of the machines below but with his own tense energy.

"*Something* went wrong," he said. "I don't know yet. I–"

"You don't know!" Danner lost part of his impassivity.

"Now wait." Hartz made soothing motions with his hands. "Just hang on a little longer. It'll be all right. You can–"

"How much longer have I got?" Danner asked. He looked over his shoulder at the tall Fury standing behind him, as if he were really asking the question of it, not Hartz. There was a feeling, somehow, about the way he said it that made you think he must have asked that question many times, looking up into the blank steel face, and would go on asking hopelessly until the answer came at last. But not in words . . .

"I can't even find that out," Hartz said. "Damn it, Danner, this was a risk. You knew that."

"You said you could control the computer. I saw you do it. I want to know why you didn't do what you promised."

"Something went wrong, I tell you. It should have worked. The minute this–business–came up I fed in the data that should have protected you."

"But what happened?"

Hartz got up and began to pace the resilient flooring. "I just don't know. We don't understand the potentiality of the machines, that's all. I thought I could do it. But–"

"You *thought!*"

"I know I can do it. I'm still trying. I'm trying everything. After all, this is important to me, too. I'm working as fast as I can. That's why I couldn't see you before. I'm certain I can do it, if I can work this out my own way. Damn it, Danner, it's complex. And it's not like juggling a comptometer. Look at those things out there."

Danner didn't bother to look.

"You'd better do it," he said. "That's all."

Hartz said furiously, "Don't threaten me! Let me alone and I'll work it out. But don't threaten me."

"You're in this too," Danner said.

Hartz went back to his desk and sat down on the edge of it.

"How?" he asked.

"O'Reilly's dead. You paid me to kill him."

Hartz shrugged. "The Fury knows that," he said. "The computers know it. And it doesn't matter a damn bit. Your hand pulled the trigger, not mine."

"We're both guilty. If I suffer for it, you—"

"Now wait a minute. Get this straight. I thought you knew it. It's a basis of law enforcement, and always has been. Nobody's punished for intention. Only for actions. I'm no more responsible for O'Reilly's death than the gun you used on him."

"But you lied to me! You tricked me! I'll—"

"You'll do as I say, if you want to save yourself. I didn't trick you, I just made a mistake. Give me time and I'll retrieve it."

"How long?"

This time both men looked at the Fury. It stood impassive.

"I don't know how long," Danner answered his own question. "You say you don't. Nobody even knows how he'll kill me, when the time comes. I've been reading everything that's available to the public about this. Is it true that the method varies, just to keep people like me on tenterhooks? And the time allowed—doesn't that vary too?"

"Yes, it's true. But there's a minimum time—I'm almost sure. You must still be within it. Believe me, Danner, I can still call off the Fury. You saw me do it. You know it worked once. All I've got to find out is what went wrong this time. But the more you bother me the more I'll be delayed. I'll get in touch with you. Don't try to see me again."

Danner was on his feet. He took a few quick steps towards Hartz, fury and frustration breaking up the impassive mask which despair had been forming over his face. But the solemn footsteps of the Fury sounded behind him. He stopped.

The two men looked at each other.

"Give me time," Hartz said. "Trust me, Danner."

In a way it was worse, having hope. There must until now have been a kind of numbness of despair that had kept him from feeling too much. But now there was a chance that after all he might escape into the bright and new life he had risked so much for—if Hartz could save him in time.

Now, for a period, he began to savor experience again. He bought new clothes. He traveled, though never, of course, alone. He even sought human companionship again and found it—after a fashion. But the kind of people willing to associate with a man under this sort of death sentence was not a very appealing type. He found, for instance, that some women felt strongly attracted to him, not because of himself or his money, but for the sake of his companion. They seemed enthralled by the opportunity for a close, safe brush with the very instrument of destiny. Over his very shoulder, sometimes, he would realize they watched the Fury in an ecstasy of fascinated anticipation. In a strange reaction of jealousy, he dropped such people as soon as he recognized the first coldly flirtatious glance one of them cast at the robot behind him.

He tried farther travel. He took the rocket to Africa, and came back by way of the rain-forests of South America, but neither the night clubs nor the exotic newness of strange places seemed to touch him in any way that mattered. The sunlight looked much the same, reflecting from the curved steel surfaces of his follower, whether it shone over lion-colored savannahs or filtered through the hanging gardens of the jungles. All novelty grew dull quickly because of the dreadfully familiar thing that stood for ever at his shoulder. He could enjoy nothing at all.

And the rhythmic beat of footfalls behind him began to grow unendurable. He used earplugs, but the heavy vibration throbbed through his skull in a constant measure like an eternal headache. Even when the Fury stood still, he could hear in his head the imaginary beating of its steps.

He bought weapons and tried to destroy the robot. Of course he failed. And even if he succeeded he knew another would be assigned to him. Liquor and drugs were no good. Suicide came more and more often into his mind, but he postponed that thought, because Hartz had said there was still hope.

In the end, he came back to the city to be near Hartz—and hope. Again he found himself spending most of his time in the library, walking no more than he had to because of the footsteps that thudded behind him. And it was here, one morning, that he found the answer . . .

He had gone through all available factual material about the Furies. He had gone through all the literary references collated under that heading, astonished to find how many there were and how apt some of them had become—like Milton's two-handed engine—after the lapse of all these centuries. *"Those strong feet that followed, followed after,"* he read. ". . . *with unhurrying chase, And unperturbed pace, Deliberate speed, majestic instancy. . . .*" He turned the page and saw himself and his plight more literally than any allegory:

> *I shook the pillaring hours*
> *And pulled my life upon me; grimed with smears,*
> *I stand amid the dust of the mounded years—*
> *My mangled youth lies dead beneath the heap.*

He let several tears of self-pity fall upon the page that pictured him so clearly.

But then he passed on from literary references to the library's store of filmed plays, because some of them were cross-indexed under the heading he sought. He watched Orestes hounded in modern dress from Argos to Athens with a single seven-foot robot Fury at his heels instead of the three snake-haired Erinyes of legend. There had been an outburst of plays on the theme when the Furies first came into usage. Sunk in a half-dream of his own boyhood memories when the Escape Machines still operated, Danner lost himself in the action of the films.

He lost himself so completely that when the familiar scene first flashed by him in the viewing booth he hardly questioned it. The whole experience was part of a familiar boyhood pattern and he was not at first surprised to find one scene more vividly familiar than the rest. But then memory rang a bell in his mind and he sat up sharply and brought his fist down with a bang on the stop-action button. He spun the film back and ran the scene over again.

It showed a man walking with his Fury through city traffic, the two of them moving in a little desert island of their own making, like a Crusoe with a Friday at his heels . . . It showed the man turn into an alley, glance up at the camera anxiously, take a deep breath and break into a sudden run. It showed the Fury hesitate, make indecisive motions and then turn and walk quietly and calmly away in the other direction, its feet ringing on the pavement hollowly . . .

Danner spun the film back again and ran the scene once more, just to make doubly sure. He was shaking so hard he could scarcely manipulate the viewer.

"How do you like that?" he muttered to the Fury behind him in the dim booth. He had by now formed a habit of talking to the Fury a good deal, in a rapid, mumbling undertone, not really aware he did it. "What do you make of that, you? Seen it before, haven't you? Familiar, isn't it? Isn't it! *Isn't it!* Answer me, you damned dumb hulk!" And reaching backward, he struck the robot across the chest as he would have struck Hartz if he could. The blow made a hollow sound in the booth, but the robot made no other response, though when Danner looked back inquiringly at it, he saw the reflections of the over-familiar scene, running a third time on the screen, running in tiny reflection across the robot's chest and faceless head, as if it too remembered.

So now he knew the answer. And Hartz had never possessed the power he claimed. Or if he did, had no intention of using it to help Danner. Why should he? His risk was over now. No wonder Hartz had been so nervous, running that film-strip off on a news-screen in his office. But the anxiety sprang not from the dangerous thing he was tampering with, but from sheer strain in matching his activities to the action in the play. How he must have rehearsed it, timing every move! And how he must have laughed, afterwards.

"How long have I got?" Danner demanded fiercely, striking a hollow reverberation from the robot's chest. "How long? Answer me! Long enough?"

Release from hope was an ecstasy, now. He need not wait any longer. He need not try any more. All he had to do was get to Hartz and get there fast, before his own time ran out. He thought with revulsion of all the days he had wasted already, in travel and time-killing, when for all he knew his own last minutes might be draining away now. Before Hartz's did.

"Come along," he said needlessly to the Fury. "Hurry!"

It came, matching its speed to his, the enigmatic timer inside it ticking the moments away towards that instant when the two-handed engine would smite once, and smite no more.

Hartz sat in the Controller's office behind a brand-new desk, looking down from the very top of the pyramid now over the banks of computers that kept society running and cracked the whip over mankind. He sighed with deep content.

The only thing was, he found himself thinking a good deal about Danner. Dreaming of him, even. Not with guilt, because guilt implies conscience, and the long schooling in anarchic individualism was still deep in the roots of every man's mind. But with uneasiness, perhaps.

Thinking of Danner, he leaned back and unlocked a small drawer which he had transferred from his old desk to the new. He slid his hand in and let his fingers touch the controls lightly, idly. Quite idly.

Two movements, and he could save Danner's life. For, of course, he had lied to Danner straight through. He could control the Furies very easily. He could save Danner, but he had never intended to. There was no need. And the thing was dangerous. You tamper once with a mechanism as complex as that which controlled society, and there would be no telling where the maladjustment might end. Chain-reaction, maybe, throwing the whole organization out of kilter. No.

He might some day have to use the device in the drawer. He hoped not. He pushed the drawer shut quickly, and heard the soft click of the lock.

He was Controller now. Guardian, in a sense, of the machines which were faithful in a way no man could ever be. *Quis custodiet*, Hartz thought. The old problem. And the answer was: Nobody. Nobody, today. He himself had no superiors and his power was absolute. Because of this little mechanism in the drawer, nobody controlled the Controller. Not an internal conscience, and not an external one. Nothing could touch him . . .

Hearing the footsteps on the stairs, he thought for a moment he must be dreaming. He had sometimes dreamed that he was Danner, with those relentless footfalls thudding after him. But he was awake now.

It was strange that he caught the almost subsonic beat of the approaching metal feet before he heard the storming steps of Danner rushing up his private stairs. The whole thing happened so fast that time seemed to have no connection with it. First he heard the heavy, subsonic beat, then the sudden tumult of shouts and banging doors downstairs, and then last of all the thump, thump of Danner charging up the stairs, his steps so perfectly matched by the heavier thud of the robot's that the metal trampling drowned out the tramp of flesh and bone and leather.

Then Danner flung the door open with a crash, and the shouts and tramplings from below funnelled upward into the quiet office like a cyclone rushing towards the hearer. But a cyclone in a nightmare, because it would never get any nearer. Time had stopped.

Time had stopped with Danner in the doorway, his face convulsed, both hands holding the revolver because he shook so badly he could not brace it with one.

Hartz acted without any more thought than a robot. He had dreamed of this moment too often, in one form or another. If he could have tempered with the Fury to the extent of hurrying Danner's death, he would have done it. But he didn't know how. He could only wait it out, as anxiously as Danner himself, hoping against hope that the blow would fall and the executioner strike before Danner guessed the truth. Or gave up hope.

So Hartz was ready when trouble came. He found his own gun in his hand without the least recollection of having opened the drawer.

The trouble was that time had stopped. He knew, in the back of his mind, that the Fury must stop Danner from injuring anybody. But Danner stood in the doorway alone, the revolver in both shaking hands. And farther back, behind the knowledge of the Fury's duty, Hartz's mind held the knowledge that the machines could be stopped. The Furies could fail. He dared not trust his life to their incorruptibility, because he himself was the source of a corruption that could stop them in their tracks.

The gun was in his hand without his knowledge. The trigger pressed his finger and the revolver kicked back against his palm, and the spurt of the explosion made the air hiss between him and Danner.

He heard his bullet clang on metal.

Time started again, running double-pace to catch up. The Fury had been no more than a single pace behind Danner after all, because its steel arm encircled him and its steel hand was deflecting Danner's gun. Danner had fired, yes, but not soon enough. Not before the Fury reached him. Hartz's bullet struck first.

It struck Danner in the chest, exploding through him, and rang upon the steel chest of the Fury behind him. Danner's face smoothed out into a blankness as complete as the blankness of the mask above his head. He slumped backwards, not falling because of the robot's embrace, but slowly slipping to the floor between the Fury's arm and its impervious metal body. His revolver thumped softly to the carpet. Blood welled from his chest and back.

The robot stood there impassive, a streak of Danner's blood slanting across its metal chest like a robotic ribbon of honor.

The Fury and the Controller of the Furies stood staring at each other. And the Fury could not, of course, speak, but in Hartz's mind it seemed to.

"Self-defense is no excuse," the Fury seemed to be saying. "We never punish intent, but we always punish action. Any act of murder. Any act of murder."

Hartz barely had time to drop his revolver in his desk drawer before the first of the clamorous crowd from downstairs came bursting through the door. He barely had the presence of mind to do it, either. He had not really thought the thing through this far.

It was, on the surface, a clear case of suicide. In a slightly unsteady voice he heard himself explaining. Everybody had seen the madman rushing through the office, his Fury at his heels. This wouldn't be the first time a killer and his Fury had tried to get at the Controller, begging him to call off the jailer and forestall the executioner. What had happened, Hartz told his underlings calmly enough, was that the Fury had naturally stopped the man from shooting Hartz. And the victim had then turned his gun upon himself. Powder-burns on his clothing showed it. (The desk was very near the door.) Back-blast in the skin of Danner's hands would show he had really fired a gun.

Suicide. It would satisfy any human. But it would not satisfy the computers.

They carried the dead man out. They left Hartz and the Fury alone, still facing each other across the desk. If anyone thought this was strange, nobody showed it.

Hartz himself didn't know if it was strange or not. Nothing like this had ever happened before. Nobody had ever been fool enough to commit murder in the very presence of a Fury. Even the Controller did not know exactly how the computers assessed evidence and fixed guilt. Should this Fury have been recalled, normally? If Danner's death were really suicide, would Hartz stand here alone now?

He knew the machines were already processing the evidence of what had really happened here. What he couldn't be sure of was whether this Fury had already received its orders and would follow him wherever he went from now on until the hour of his death. Or whether it simply stood motionless, waiting recall.

Well, it didn't matter. This Fury or another was already, in the present moment, in the process of receiving instructions about him. There was only one thing to do. Thank God there was something he *could* do.

So Hartz unlocked the desk drawer and slid it open, touched the clicking keys he had never expected to use. Very carefully he fed the coded information, digit by digit, into the computers. As he did, he looked out through the glass wall and imagined he could see down there in the hidden tapes the units of data fading into blankness and the new, false information flashing into existence.

He looked up at the robot. He smiled a little.

"Now you'll forget," he said. "You and the computers. You can go now. I won't be seeing you again."

Either the computers worked incredibly fast—as of course they did —or pure coincidence took over, because in only a moment or two the Fury moved as if in response to Hartz's dismissal. It had stood quite motionless since Danner slid through its arms. Now new orders animated it, and briefly its motion was almost jerky as it changed from one set of instructions to another. It almost seemed to bow, a stiff little bending motion that brought its head down to a level with Hartz's.

He saw his own face reflected in the blank face of the Fury. You could very nearly read an ironic note in that stiff bow, with the diplomat's ribbon of honor across the chest of the creature, symbol of duty discharged honorably. But there was nothing honorable about this withdrawal. The incorruptible metal was putting on corruption and looking back at Hartz with the reflection of his own face.

He watched it stalk towards the door. He heard it go thudding evenly down the stairs. He could feel the thuds vibrate in the floor, and there was a sudden sick dizziness in him when he thought the whole fabric of society was shaking under his feet.

The machines were corruptible.

Mankind's survival still depended on the computers, and the computers could not be trusted. Hartz looked down and saw that his hands were shaking. He shut the drawer and heard the lock click softly. He gazed at his hands. He felt their shaking echoed in an inner shaking, a terrifying sense of the instability of the world.

A sudden, appalling loneliness swept over him like a cold wind. He had never felt before so urgent a need for the companionship of his own kind. No one person, but people. Just people. The sense of human beings all around him, a very primitive need.

He got his hat and coat and went downstairs rapidly, hands deep in his pockets because of some inner chill no coat could guard against. Halfway down the stairs he stopped dead still.

There were footsteps behind him.

He dared not look back at first. He knew those footsteps. But he had two fears and he didn't know which was worse. The fear that a Fury was after him—and the fear that it was not. There would be a sort of insane relief if it really was, because then he could trust the machines after all, and this terrible loneliness might pass over him and go.

He took another downward step, not looking back. He heard the ominous footfall behind him, echoing his own. He sighed one deep sigh and looked back.

There was nothing on the stairs.

He went on down after a timeless pause, watching over his shoulder. He could hear the relentless feet thudding behind him, but no visible Fury followed. No visible Fury.

The Erinyes had struck inward again, and an invisible Fury of the mind followed Hartz down the stairs.

It was as if sin had come anew into the world, and the first man felt again the first inward guilt. So the computers had not failed, after all.

Hartz went slowly down the steps and out into the street, still hearing as he would always hear the relentless, incorruptible footsteps behind him that no longer rang like metal.

11 And Keep Us From Our Castles

by Cynthia Bunn

What if, having committed and been convicted of a crime, you
could have your own prison? Suppose you could choose your
own individual and private prison, where congested and run-
down prison conditions did not exist? "And Keep Us From
Our Castles" by Cynthia Bunn is a powerful drama about the
effects of a peculiar form of incarceration that fits these
conditions. A "telemachine"—a halo with three walls—is a
moving prison that follows a convicted criminal relentlessly.
The relationship between the prisoner and this highly
individualized prison highlights the alienation and suffering
associated with incarceration.

In an interesting way, the story forces us to think about our
moral responsibilities to prisoners. Religious beliefs often
mandate followers to help the poor, the infirm, and the
imprisoned. Should we be bothered by accounts of poor living
conditions, congestion, and other factors associated with the
quality of life in a prison? Prison reform is a major issue of
contemporary criminal justice in the United States. What is
the role of basic morality in such reform?

He found the farmhouse the seventeenth day out from the city.

It almost went unnoticed, faded to gray-brown among those hills
where all—seared grass, trees, ruins of fences and fallen telephone
poles—was equally colorless. The collapsing walls were huddled against

a ragged hillside, waiting only for one of the frequent tornadoes to
bring the final implosion.

Almost missed, but betrayed by the sharp late afternoon shadows of
man-made edges. The man who otherwise would have kept walking,
along the rim of that hill and others, stumbled down the slope through
dry prairie grass, stopping on the stones that had been a porch.

He peered into the dusk of the interior, seeing stray dimmed light-
beams that had somehow passed through the dust-caked windows. Low,
broken shapes of furniture. Opened, empty, rusting cans scattered
across the floor. There were no sounds but grass rustled by the flight
of grasshoppers.

Moving with cautious grace, he stepped inside, left hand already
gripping the hilt of his hunting knife. This late in the summer it was
unlikely that he would encounter any of the fair-weather backpackers,
who always returned to the cities by September. But a few renegades
stayed out permanently, dispersed, one or two for every few hundred
square kilometers. Cut off from their urban umbilical cord, they ob-
tained their supplies in any way possible, often from a dead man's
backpack. And a small fraction of the permanent wanderers were
exiled criminals, like himself. Not to be trusted.

There was no one in the room.

It had been inhabited recently, more recently than the layer of rust
on the cans indicated. Ashes lay in a rough circle a centimeter deep
where someone had been careless or stupid enough to risk a fire inside
this shell of rotting wood. The ashes were cold but not yet scattered by
the eddies of wind that came through the open door. A week old, if
that.

He began to check the rest of the house. The kitchen with its battered, squat stove and refrigerator, mid-Twentieth Century style. Left
when the last residents moved away or died. The house was a few
decades older than the furniture, probably built more than a century
and a half before his uninvited arrival.

He glanced briefly into the mold-covered bathroom, and the dining
room where a few pieces remained of the table that had been chopped
for kindling. No signs of habitation recent enough to make him wary.

The narrow stairway was sharply canted, and at the top of the landing had half-collapsed, breaking away from the surrounding floor. He
kept to the relative security of the top step, which trembled under his
feet as he looked around the single large dormitory-style room. Rem-
nants of beds were left, frames held together by rusted springs, tot-
tering above dusty fragments of cloth that had been mattresses until
they rotted and fell to the floor.

The house was totally deserted. Safe.

Returning to the downstairs floor, he emptied his backpack, the food, cooking utensils, air mattress. These he set in a corner of the living room behind the ruin of a chair. No one looking in would spot them immediately.

This done, he left, with only knife, gun, and the empty backpack to carry whatever he killed for dinner. There was still an hour of daylight left, time to hunt, time to walk the half-kilometer he had to cover to insure his freedom that night.

It was dark before he returned, the still-bleeding carcass of a rabbit wrapped in a plastic bag in his backpack. It was hard to spot game, camouflaged grays and browns in the high, rough grass. This animal had been frightened into bolting and running as he approached. A sure sign that men had left for the cities: the wariness of the small animals was disappearing.

He stared at the ashes on the floor for a few moments, debating the danger of an inside fire versus the possibility of attracting unwelcome company. The door decided his inner argument. Empty, yawning, he could not block it, and even an inside fire would be visible to anyone nearby.

Back outside, with a stack of table legs laced by the dry grass, he roasted the small rabbit. By the time he had finished eating and extinguished the fire the halo was back, shutting off his view of all the stars but those near the horizon, hovering over him, its translucent dark blue now appearing black. Fifteen minutes already, as he'd timed it. It would be good to sleep inside tonight, stealing the remaining hours of peace from the telemachines that constantly pushed him onward, driving him with the halo and three walls, the threat of the final death-bringing fourth wall and floor.

He paused for a moment in the doorway and looked out at the sky again. The halo, which always floated at three meters above ground level, vanished when he stood beneath a lower ceiling. Had he been naive, he would have tried the sanctuary of caves or tunnels, but he knew—as the dead men learned—that the walls, unlike the ceiling, would materialize even if their presence pre-empted stone or earth. He was not the type of man to refuse to benefit from another's mistakes.

Finally he went in, needing sleep more than the unobstructed view of the heavens. He set his watch to let him sleep for seven hours, giving him more than an hour to elude the walls for another twelve-hour period. As he set the alarm his mouth twisted into a mockery of a smile. If it failed, he would die. Even a hundred kilometers from the nearest city his life was forfeit to a machine.

He spent more than a week at the farmhouse, leaving the area in the early morning and again each late afternoon, walking until the halo and walls disappeared from around him. The region was peaceful, far enough from the cities that he saw no one, far enough from the jet routes that he was not disturbed by the noise. He'd planned to stay there through the autumn, perhaps even through winter.

His plans ended one afternoon, his tenth day on the northeast Kansas farm, when he returned to the house to see a man sitting outside on the porch. A boy, rather, eighteen or so. With a young and frightened face. But there was nothing of fear in the way the youth held his rifle as he watched the expected returning figure scramble down the hill, finally stopping five meters from the door.

"Are those your things inside?"

He nodded cautiously, forcing his hands to hang loosely at his sides. Another face appeared in the doorway, small, also timid, and after a moment a girl of about sixteen stepped out onto the flagstone porch.

"Get back inside!"

"If this is the man, we have to return his belongings to him. We're sorry, but this was the only shelter within kilometers, and we had to rest."

Yes, she would need rest, he thought, noticing the bulging waistline that even her loose shirt didn't hide. It could be fat—but her arms and face were thin. Pregnant, and with the population controls of the last decade that pregnancy was probably illegal. Especially since she'd chosen to leave the cities at a time when other women were confined to hospitals.

She flushed, aware of his survey of her bulky figure.

"Who are you?" the boy demanded. The gun was beginning to shake.

If he'd wanted, he could have tried to kill the youth. The odds were in his favor. Other criminals would do such a thing, killing the boy and taking the young girl, and the same thought must have occurred to the youth. The gun continued to shake.

"Just a backpacker." A lie that worked at times like this, when he'd just finished a long walk, while he still had more than an hour until the halo materialized.

"You're out here awfully late in the year."

"So are you."

Impasse, broken by the girl saying, "Don't question him. Give him his food and equipment and let him leave."

"Yeah, and let him come back some night."

"I was going to move on soon, anyway."

"Sure."

He shook his head. "Then don't believe me. You can either kill me or let me leave. Which?"

The girl bolted back inside, emerging seconds later with an armload of his remaining supplies and the mattress. She ran a few steps past the boy, dropped the objects, and rushed back.

"OK," she said. "Take your things and leave."

He looked questioningly at the boy, still aiming the rifle in the general direction of his chest. "Well?"

"Take them."

He replaced the objects in the backpack as quickly as possible, worrying that the time required to deflate the air mattress might keep him there until the halo reappeared. Anything might happen then. After a sweaty twenty minutes he was finished. He pointed at the plastic sack on the ground, containing a freshly-killed pheasant.

"Do you want that?"

"Maybe." The boy removed one hand from the gun, letting the barrel drop, and wiped his palm against his jeans. "Don't you want it?"

"No. I don't need it, anyway." True enough—the area was thick with small game birds and mammals, and he was learning how to hunt them expertly.

"All right." The rifle was pointed at him again. "You want to leave, you said."

He backed away until he reached the foot of the hill, then turned to climb, knowing he wouldn't be shot unless he did something to frighten the youth. He moved carefully, checking each foothold so he would not slip. At the top he kept going, down the other side, not looking back. The crackling of grass and twigs behind him let him know the boy was following.

He continued to move on that autumn, west, north, south, east, walking in any direction, guided only by terrain, the safety of the crumbling roads, and fear of the phantom cell. Whichever way he turned he took a path to keep himself unsheltered by the halo. Occasionally finding himself entering regions he knew to be unsafe, he would turn back, taking a parallel path, but one more than half a kilometer from his earlier steps.

He did not halt now. There were other abandoned houses, shells of buildings scattered across the Midwest, but as the weather cooled even the most ramshackle of these were inhabited by renegades and other criminals. And he had to keep moving if he was to avoid the identifying panel floating above his head, a beacon for predators, betraying him as a man driven to exhaustion, easy prey.

The rivers slowed him. Months at a fast walk took him across hundreds of kilometers, and he crossed the Mississippi once and returned, crossed and recrossed the Missouri often. There was a trick to getting across, even after he knew where the ferries were located. He had to time his arrival perfectly, coming to the boat just after a long walk, and hope the ferryman would take him over the river before the cell began to materialize. Ferrymen didn't like criminals, even though their predecessors had violated the law to destroy the bridges, below whose shattered frames they monopolized river traffic. He had to pay, of course: dead game, food for the ferryman's often numerous family, the offspring of illegal fertility, the brats and worn women living in shacks at the river's edge.

The winter's freeze formed ice thick enough to walk across on the smaller streams and lakes, but on the swiftly moving large rivers it was treacherously thin. Worse, the owners of the ferryboats were unwilling to cross during the winter. He was caught on the west side of the Missouri, the empty snow-blanketed plains of the Dakotas and Nebraska and Kansas, which had always been sparsely populated, where the houses were fewer and farther apart than in the more fertile areas of the Midwest. Bleakness where he found no haven from snow or wind.

He learned during the first months of winter to risk his life for a few hours' shelter, staying in one place until the ceiling and three walls formed around him. It was especially effective if he faced the south; the first wall appeared at his back, intended by the government's psychologists to keep him watching nervously over his shoulder. Not planned as a windbreak for a winter backpacker on the plains, but it served. It served.

He kept moving. Once he waited too long, letting the fourth wall join itself to the others, its addition drawing the floating cell down into the drifts, as the originators had planned. He walked blindly for an hour, snow blind as well as caught behind the crystals forming on the wall before him. Walking sightless, timing himself, the ever-louder hum of the watch remining him that the floor was due very soon. He would be sealed inside a cube of impenetrable plastic and his walk would end. Eternally.

Somehow he made it safely through. He stumbled forward through the remains of drifts broken by the passage of the preceding wall, a blue, cubical, human-powered snowplow on an otherwise empty plain. Just fifteen minutes were left when he passed that unmarked boundary, the walls vanishing to return to their storage rooms, leaving him unprotected in the snow storm. Whipped and frozen by wind. More grateful than ever before in his life.

December left him emaciated but alive.

January brought hallucinations:

A village, plucked from history or fiction, with no resemblance to the multileveled cities. A small town of narrow streets, low buildings, smiling citizens. He plunged into the village, among the people and through their insubstantial forms, staggering and falling through deep drifts. Colors flickered before his eyes: dead white/brightly painted small homes of turquoise, rose, gold/blinding white/ruddy faces above patchwork costumes/snow. He stumbled past the last side street of the dream town, past the last picket fence, fought the urge to look back, turned and saw swirling drifts. Then tried to hold back the tears, knowing they would only freeze on his eyelashes and cheeks. They did.

He saw his family that winter, his son, his wife as she was while alive. Envisioned welcoming arms and fell against icy wetness and black tree branches that hadn't been there a moment before. And once, only once, he viewed her corpse, red-stained before the undertaker treated it, burying wounds in cosmetics, head held in place by wires, not the thin remaining strip of flesh.

Not stopping, never stopping. He lost track of time and place, forgetting which direction he had traveled the previous week, remembering only the direction of that day and the day before. East/west/north/south, reversed, transversed, bound by the Missouri on one side, the Rockies on the other.

Sand dunes welcomed him along a beach as he blundered through the last of January. Beckoning hot sand invited him to shed his clothes, bask in the sun, wade through the shallow warm water near the shore. He ignored it, walked without pausing, knowing the illusory warmth in his feet for the danger it was. That afternoon he found a cattle shed, three tenuous wooden walls and a crumbling roof that no one else had wanted, and he decimated the walls to build a warming fire.

The next day, shadowed by his halo, he moved on. More kilometers, more snow in the harshest of recorded winters, and more mirages.

Crocodiles, once. He saw them watching him, waiting for the tender flesh of his unwary toes. He dodged the bulking long shapes, breaking a wide semicircular path around the fallen telephone poles.

More extreme, improbable hallucinations with the beginning of February. Castles where there were trees. He learned the folly of climbing staircases to tumble off a shattered limb.

Lakes, then. Watery shelters of gleaming Atlantises, tempting him to bury his head in a drift, ending the hopeless flight.

A girl, a very pretty girl, sitting on a tree branch that sagged under her weight, her small booted feet hanging centimeters above the snow . . .

"Hi," the apparition said. "I thought you'd never get here. I've been waiting half an hour."

The first talking mirage he'd encountered. He stared at her blankly, frozen until her laughter shocked him into speech. "What?"

"Sit down," she told him, "before you collapse. You're reacting exactly like every other person I've met out here. Right now you're probably thinking I'm a figment of your imagination."

"No." *Yes,* a fraction of his psyche was screaming, the voice that had led him around crocodiles and up nonexistent staircases.

"You're unusual, then. Good. I can always use an exception to the norm. It makes my findings more realistic. Not that they're faked, but they need just those few flaws in behavioral patterns as the polishing touch."

The puckish subself that had convinced him of the reality of other mirages was shrieking again: *Mad, totally mad, you've found a lost maniac, get away!* He took a step, another, away from the girl, now studying him with the same suspicion he had of her.

"What's wrong?"

The words halted him.

"Are you leaving?" Her voice had suddenly gone ragged with fear. *Madwoman.* Trapped between his fracturing mental *Doppelgänger* and a girl who acted too strange, in a place and time when even the most commonplace could be dangerous.

"I don't know—"

"Don't. Please. It's been almost a week since I talked to anyone, except myself." A nervous little laugh. "Six days."

Try it for three weeks, he thought. *Nearly a month without seeing anyone, and find out that solitude is better than the company of someone else who's been affected by loneliness.*

"You don't look like an exile," he said. Outcasts might be healthy and well-dressed during the summer; by midwinter all were worn, wrinkled, grubby. Too clean, this girl.

"I came out here voluntarily."

He laughed.

"No. Really. Please, just let me walk with you, whatever direction you're going, I don't care. I'll explain as we walk. I'm frozen. Thought you'd never get here."

He resumed his trek, a straight continuation of the line formed by his earlier footprints.

"East?"

"Does it matter? You said it didn't."

"No, I guess not."

"There's no destination you want to reach?"

She shook her head emphatically. Her long hair—clean hair, in the middle of the plains in the middle of winter—had spilled out of the hood of her jumpsuit, and it clung to the beads of sweat and melted snow on her face, masking her.

"You're just going to follow me?"

"Yes, for a while, if you'll let me. I want to ask you some questions. I need answers only prisoners can give."

His stride broke for a second, a hesitation before he placed the boot firmly on bright snow, unshadowed by the halo he'd eluded an hour earlier.

"How long did you say you'd been waiting for me?"

"Half an hour, maybe, waiting. I spotted you a few hours ago. You were at the bottom of a hill, not much of a hill, though. Lots of trees at the top."

He nodded, remembering the stand of pine blackening a summit a few hundred meters from his path.

"I was standing in the shelter of the trees. Two days there, waiting for someone to pass within visual range. I was beginning to think it was hopeless, worse than wandering in a haphazard search. I'd almost given up when you walked by."

Good for me. Cheer the man who brought this nut down from her hilltop.

"You had the halo already. You were hurrying. I was going to follow you, run and try to catch up, but I wasn't sure how you'd have reacted."

He had to grin at that possibility. Pursued across the fields by a wild figure in a black jumpsuit. "I'd have run," he admitted. The mildest of understatements.

"That's what I thought. So I ran parallel to you, where I thought you were going, and when I thought I'd be ahead of you, in your path, I stopped."

"On a tree branch."

"Did it really look so odd? It was better than sitting in the snow, and my legs were giving away. I never considered that I might seem even more unreal perched in a tree."

"Like a dryad," he assured her. "North American variety."

"Oh, you're educated! Well-educated! Most people know absolutely nothing about classical mythology these days."

"Most people could care less," he said. *Like me.* "So you waited for me—what would you have done if I hadn't shown up, if I'd turned and taken another path somewhere?"

She shrugged. "I'd have looked for someone else to interview, I guess. That's all I want from you anyway."

As he stared at her, not understanding, she laughed. "No, I'm not after your backpack. Your body, either. Forget that."

"All right." The uneasiness was back, slipping sideways into nausea. He was tired. "Look for some shelter, OK? I need to rest for a few hours."

"Of course."

They found an improbable shelter, a round structure with a pointed roof and walls that were more gaping windows and doors than wall, designed to shield storm-caught picnickers in what had been a park. Its floor was covered with drifted snow, shallowest at the north end where the solid wall had been extended, and there they unrolled the air mattresses and sat down.

Cold. The temperature was only a few degrees below freezing but the winds were strong. Here they were protected from the wind, but shaded, and it seemed even colder than in the gale-torn brightness outside.

After a few moments the girl began to rummage through her backpack, finally removing a crumpled package of metal rods which she unfolded into a spindly tripod. Then a mobile of two shallow metal pans, one above the other, separated and suspended from the top of the tripod by fire-blackened chains.

"If we had some wood," she said, "we could heat food." She made no move to stand and he realized she'd been hinting, not very subtly, that he was to do the foraging.

"There's food in my backpack, a rabbit I shot yesterday. I'll carve it up for frying while you gather wood."

She looked at him in disbelief. *Protected,* he thought. *Spoiled. While she's alone she can take care of herself, but now she thinks I'll protect her, hunt for her.*

She was silent for a moment, then struggled to her feet, untangling the long legs she'd folded in a lotus position, and left the building. He watched as she stumbled toward the nearest, scraggly trees, then opened his backpack.

By the time she returned with an armload of branches he had sliced the carcass into thin strips, filling the upper tray of the tripod.

"They're green," she said as she arranged the branches in the bottom pan. "There'll be a lot of smoke, but maybe the wind will blow most of it away from us."

"We can always move."

"Yes." She held her lighter to the stack of twigs, patiently waiting until a few wilted leaves caught fire, then resumed the lotus position on her mattress.

He had a lot of questions he wanted to ask: who she was, what she was doing out on the plains—voluntarily, for Christ's sake. But he held back, waiting for her to offer the answers to unspoken inquiries, more complete answers than could be pried from her.

She was quiet as the meat cooked, sometimes leaning over to add more branches to the fire, coughing occasionally. Most of the smoke rolled past them and up, vanishing past the edge of the roof, but once in a while a gust would blow the smoke toward them. Below the tripod the snow had melted away, revealing a littered concrete floor.

They ate in silence, too. While he gulped the food, she held her portions gingerly, letting it cool before she'd try eating it. *She hasn't been out here very long,* he decided, then, aloud:

"How long have you been out here?"

"Two years, on and off. Does that surprise you? I usually stay out for only a week or two and then go back to the city for a few days' rest and fresh supplies."

"How long this time?"

"A week." She'd finished eating and was rubbing snow on her hands to remove the grease. "My copter broke down. I was planning to go further north, to the badlands, but I had to land it here: I couldn't call for help because I never take a radio—the only ones I can buy are two-way, traceable, and I prefer to work without being watched or followed. I always take enough supplies to keep me alive for weeks, in case something goes wrong."

"You must be doing something illegal, if you'd risk being without a radio."

"No. That is, not exactly. Not-approved, I suppose you'd call it. I have a few sympathizers, like the charities that bring you fresh supplies. You must have run into them. That looks like the type of insulated jumpsuit they distribute."

He nodded, remembering . . .

A wildly descending helicopter, following him as it searched for a landing place. He tried to elude it, suspecting at first that it held the sort of sadists who'd chased him once in October, making mad, suicidal dives that kept him pinned against the ground while the halo and three walls surrounded his prone form. They'd left with the appearance of the third wall, allowing him the chance to run and live, perhaps to be pursued another day. So when the black-and-white striped copter found him, that foggy November morning, he ran until exhaustion stopped him.

Two people climbed out, masked by smoky face shields, formless in bulky jumpsuits. He watched their approach with cornered, deadened weariness, holding his small handgun. Waiting for them to get within a range where he could shoot them accurately.

They stopped fifty meters from him, just as he raised his right arm and aimed the gun. A third figure emerged from the copter, dragging large boxes across the field to where his/her two companions had halted. They conferred for a moment, or he guessed they were talking as they looked at each other, though he could neither hear them nor see their faces. Then they returned to the copter, without coming closer or calling to him, although he couldn't be sure of that either. The gusting wind would have blown away even the loudest shout.

After their copter was gone he approached the packages cautiously, aware of the possibility of concealed bombs, but when he risked opening the boxes he found supplies. Food. Four winter jumpsuits, one of which fit him. A recent newsmagazine, published in Denver, as though they thought he wanted news of the world that had evicted him permanently. Another air mattress. Many items of camping equipment, light enough for a backpack. Items he didn't need spares of, since he couldn't carry the extra weight. He left all but the food and jumpsuit . . .

"At the time I left the cities, the charities that helped prisoners were being uncovered and publicized. It was very unfavorable publicity. I didn't think they'd last much longer."

"Most of the members have had to give it up under social pressure. All that's left of the Denver organization, I've heard, is the staff, and even that's been reduced."

"That's where you're from?"

"Yes."

He told her about the people who'd brought supplies to him; the Denver magazine.

"Were you one of them?" he asked.

"No. I don't know who they were, either. I contributed money to the charities, but I never found out where their headquarters were located. No one did. And if any of my friends worked actively to help the exiled criminals, they kept it a secret."

"If you're not working with them, why are you out here?"

"I'm a psychologist. Don't look at me that way! I don't work for the government. And I'm not affiliated with an institute, either. I'm freelancing, researching independently, trying to gather information to prove the inhumanity and stupidity of this particular type of punishment. I won't be able to publish my findings for a while, but I plan to stay in the cities after another year, work for an institute, and maybe after I've established a reputation I can publish unorthodox theses."

"That would be years from now."

"Five or six years, at the least."

"You won't be helping those who are out here now. Do you expect them to live until your thesis is finished?"

"No. They'll be dead by then. As you will be, long before that time. I'm not certain I'll be able to speak out, and even if I can it's doubtful that public opinion can be altered. The odds are against any reform coming. But I'm trying anyway, because there's still a small chance that ten years from now the sentenced criminals exiled from the cities will be allowed to wander freely. Without that halo you'll be under in a few minutes."

He glanced down at his watch. They'd been in the shelter an hour and a half. "Five minutes left, I estimate. If you're not one of those people who are frightened by the sight of cells, I'll stay here until the third wall arrives."

"No, I don't mind. The first time I saw a man walking with that cell hanging over him, it upset me. I've adjusted."

"Not everybody can. There are more than a few psychotics out here, men who still scream and panic every time the ceiling appears. They don't last very long."

"How many weeks have you been out?"

"Six months."

"Oh, no. No prisoner I've ever heard of lasts that long."

"Good. That makes me even more of an exception for your survey, doesn't it?"

She flushed at his sarcasm. "You're just like all the others with your resentment of me."

"Why shouldn't I resent you? You want to use me as a statistic, reduce me to a number or a letter or a percentage—I prefer a letter. Exile D thought such-and-such of his sentence. That would be better than appearing as a percentage, say one man out of sixty-six, if you can locate that many to help you with your madness. Then I'd be the anonymous one-point-five percent that believe—"

"Shut up!"

"Why does that bother you? Haven't you found that many exiles yet? That would make me even more significant. Five percent? Ten?"

"More like one tenth of one percent."

"That many? What a shame. In that case I hope I'm exceptional enough to qualify as a letter."

"Stop mocking me!"

"All right. Go on with this important interview. First question?"

She glared at him, started to speak, but clamped her mouth shut. Again she searched through her backpack, this time pulling out a notebook and pen.

"Primitive. Don't you have a recorder?"

"I left it in the copter. There's too much chance of it breaking down, and I'd have to walk all the way back to the city to get it repaired. This is slower but more practical."

"Practicality is the one characteristic I'd never expect of you."

"Did anyone ever tell you how sarcastic you are?"

"My wife, sometimes."

"I'll bet she was glad to see you go."

"She's dead."

"Oh. Is that—no, I'll get to that question later. First, I need your name. Don't worry, it won't be in my paper to embarrass any living relatives."

"Hedrick. Raymond Hedrick."

"Age?"

"Thirty-four."

"Marital—never mind. Family?"

The interview—which she'd said was only preliminary, background questioning—took more than an hour. He answered questions about his childhood and parents, his wife and son. Religion: agnostic. Education: MA in computer science.

"Typical," she'd said.

"Why? Typical for a criminal, you mean?"

She'd smiled and shrugged. "Income per year?"

He was irritated. She was showing the all-too-common snobbery of social scientists who believed their professions superior to physical science. He didn't voice his anger because too many physical scientists were equally aloof and condescending.

There were more questions about his pre-crime background, and then he began to relive the near past for her, describing how he learned of his wife's death.

"The police?"

"Yes. I got their message that afternoon at work. Her body had already been prepared for burial, but they had pictures of her, taken when they found her on the bedroom floor. I was held for two hours while they tested my physiological reactions to the photographs and their questions."

"Guilty until proven innocent. Happens all the time. You're not that much of an exception. So they let you go overnight, ran you through a trial the next morning, sent you to the clinic for the implant operation, and then released you outside the city."

"Not quite. I killed a man first."

Her fingers slipped on the pen, dropping it but catching it before it could roll off the notebook. In the seconds before she looked up again, she managed to freeze her face into a calm mask. *Admirable self-control,* he admitted inwardly.

"I thought you said you weren't a murderer."

"I don't consider killing that man a crime. Revenge, maybe. I knew who'd killed my wife, one of my neighbors, due to undergo treatment as a child-molester. My wife had seen him with our son one afternoon and reported him. That must have pushed him the final step into psychosis."

She was writing rapidly, making the small neat symbols of short-hand. Frowning. "I'm sorry about what I said earlier. You're not at all typical. So you killed the man, and the police caught you . . ."

"I turned myself in."

She scratched through a line. "Did they drop the charge of murdering your wife?"

"No."

"Any idea why not?"

He shrugged.

"All right. Tried and convicted on two counts of murder. How long did it take the jury to decide?"

"A few minutes."

She stared at him, then said, "No offense, but are you lying to me? This sounds more unusual with every answer."

"I can't help that, though I have to admit that I was surprised, too. I had a good attorney, and I thought he gave a brilliant defense. The emphasis was on my 'emotional disturbance', as he called it. He was trying to obtain psychiatric treatment for me, rather than exile."

"Do you realize how few cases like that fail? Less than five percent, since the psychiatric program has proven so successful."

"I know."

"Tell me about the jury."

"They were like all other jurors. Most of them were in their thirties, I suppose. A few more men than women."

"Hmm. Typical jurors . . . You know, there is one theory that might explain your sentence, about how average people, the type that pride themselves on their normality, react most righteously to any trespasses by others of the same mold . . ."

"Go on."

"Never mind. It's not very well substantiated, anyway. OK, the operation."

He reached up self-consciously to touch the scar tissue, now hidden by long hair. Just the barest discernible lump. The tiny implant nicknamed "Telltale," the wandering companion of the telemachines. "What about the operation?"

"The time."

"That afternoon, three hours after the trial."

She closed the notebook after a few more scribbled lines, replaced it in her backpack. "Enough interviewing for today."

But not the end of interviewing for that week. Or the next.

Her curiosity was insatiable. She carried five thick notebooks in her backpack, and by the end of the second week all but one were filled with cramped symbols. She asked ever more general questions and requested ever more elaborate answers, delineating with her hieroglyphs the skeleton of his view of society and self, fleshing the bones as he talked for hours. Monologues on his work, his opinion of life in the city, the people who'd surrounded him. Most often, his punishment.

"You've already told me that you paid little attention to the introduction of the mobile cells four years ago," she said one day after several frowning moments spent perusing her notes. "Yet you've never referred to seeing a demonstration of the cells, and statistics indicate that all but an insignificant fraction of one percent of adults viewed such demonstrations, either broadcasts or live. Didn't you?"

"I attended one of the demonstrations in an auditorium on my level."

His wife had gone with him. They could have watched the broadcast exhibitions, but were bored and preferred to go out.

Other couples and singles must have thought along the same lines. The auditorium was crowded, and they were routed to the balcony. It had just been opened for the overflow but was filling rapidly. They managed to get seats in the front row, along the railing, looking down on the small, square, empty temporary platform.

Half an hour later no more seats were left and the doors of the auditorium were locked. A man clutching a microphone climbed onto the platform and stood in its center. His straight-cut gray tunic and pants identified him as a government representative; his face was pale and cold. Obviously his natural habitat was the world of gray metal desks, filing cabinets, and squat office machines. He was nervously out of place in a citizen's auditorium.

He began to speak, explaining that he had willingly undergone the implantation of a Telltale, the miniaturized broadcaster which always betrayed his location to the computers of the telemachine complex. If the data received indicated he had stayed in one area for too long a time—a half-kilometer diameter/two-hour limit for criminals, fifty meters/three minutes for him—the six cell walls would be automatically transported at equal intervals. The panels, three-by-three-meter squares, could be cut only by diamond-edged tools or lasers, neither of which criminals were likely to find outside the cities. (He paused for a moment as several in the audience laughed.)

In the few remaining seconds before the cell began to materialize, the official explained that this particular castle would disappear within a minute after it had completely formed. Hedrick through he could detect a trace of fear in the man's voice, but before he was certain the ceiling appeared—halo, as it had been nicknamed, because it identified criminals as surely as the mythical golden circlets hovered above saints. The man had stopped speaking and stood motionless with only a few upward glances. His face looked even paler, but Hedrick had to concede that the light filtering through the halo could produce that effect.

Minutes slipped past, and throughout the auditorium people shifted restlessly. Three walls, then the fourth, and through the blue plastic surrounding him the government representative was a dim, barely visible figure. Still standing straight. His features could no longer be distinguished.

Then the floor panel, displacing the platform surface for an instant before it rose and lifted the trapped man. Sealed to the walls, a barely visible seam above its two centimeters of thickness. For a moment the man inside kept his composure, then his legs folded and he crumpled to the floor. When the cell vanished—in less than a minute, as promised—he was helped off the platform and out the back exit.

The doors of the auditorium were unlocked and the audience filed out, all talking at once about the strangeness of the official's behavior.

He finished his description of the demonstration, looked away from the snowdrift he'd fixed his gaze on, and saw that the girl was shaking her head. "I wasn't very impressed," he said. "Perhaps I should have been. Lind, you act as though you don't approve of my reaction."

"Poor man. The official you saw was claustrophobic, a screaming neurotic. Perfectly ordinary except for that one flaw. He offended his superiors in some way, and to punish him they had him demonstrate the castles, thinking that would be an effective way of frightening potential criminals. They were mistaken. The public interpreted his overreaction as a poor job of acting, and the demonstrations had little effect."

"The cells never have appeared very threatening to anyone outside them, and since they're only used on exiles, people in the cities can forget about them. Having the press label them 'castles' didn't help either."

"What did you think of the use of the word 'castle' when it originated?"

"I didn't think about it. Some of my friends considered it a clever play on words, though."

She was shaking her head again. "That's what the government discovered was the general attitude. So last year—after you left the city—they gave up trying to intimidate the public and started using a few spare castles to frighten juvenile criminals."

"What?"

"Really. Psychologists objected, petitions were circulated, but some bureaucrat with a long title thought it would be good to let the kids in juvenile homes spend a night or two in the castles. Sort of a modern bogeyman. The way it turned out—"

"I can guess that it backfired."

"Completely. The children rioted, parents filed law suits, citizen committees were formed, et cetera. The genius who'd planned the program lost his position. But now they have a study group trying to think up uses for the cells that aren't needed for sentenced criminals. The telemachines are too expensive to be left lying idle."

"Wasn't thriftiness one of the party's campaign platforms?"

"Yes, but so was intelligent leadership."

After two weeks in the wilderness that had been a park they had to move on. His constant hunting had thinned the animal population, the tracks he left warning off the more cautious creatures.

Lind didn't want to stay with him.

"I have all the information I can incorporate into a thesis. Too much material, in fact. Most of what I've transcribed will be superfluous data."

"Then why the hell did you ask so many questions?"

She looked uncomfortable and pretended to be absorbed in repacking her backpack. Finally: "You're the most intelligent prisoner I've met so far. Communicative. What you've given me is a very personal insight into how a condemned man feels."

He snorted.

"I mean it. What I have now is a record of your life, your trial and out-city wandering. It will be very valuable, even though there won't be room in any thesis for all the details. But you've given me a better perspective, something I couldn't get with the standard brief interview. I feel an empathy with your life."

"What about my death?"

The question startled her for a moment, then came the usual swift recovery. "I feel sympathy. I know that sounds cold, but I am sorry that your death is inevitably close. I hope you have some months left."

"You should stay with me. Yes. *Really,* as you say so often. Unless you witness my death, that empathy you value will be incomplete."

"Don't be ridiculous! There's no way to judge how long you'll be out here, unless you plan to commit suicide by waiting for the castle just so I can witness—"

"No. No way."

"All right, then. I have to use my time to interview other men."

"What did you say that first day? That you've already interviewed hundreds of exiles. You know as well as I that you have enough of a sample. Eight hundred or a thousand, it will make little difference to the people who'll read your thesis. What will matter is how you view the data."

She laughed weakly. "Are you certain you never studied psychology? Or maybe law. This is turning into an interrogation."

"Well?"

"I'll run out of supplies if I stay out here."

"I finished the last of my packaged food months ago, but I've managed to get by on meat and whatever I can gather from orchards and fields. You can do the same."

"This jumpsuit will be too heavy to wear this spring and summer."

"The inner layer can be ripped out."

"I have friends! They'll worry."

He stared at her skeptically until she said, "OK, so they won't panic. They're used to my not contacting them for months at a time."

"Any more excuses?"

"One. I have just one notebook left."

"How much paper do you need to record empathy?"

She didn't answer. They finished packing and left the park, slipping in the mud and slush of the first spring thaw.

By mid-March they had established an easy relationship. Not sexual —he had propositioned her once and she'd refused, saying she didn't want that final involvement with a man who carried his death sentence over his head. He never asked again, partly because he respected her decision, but also because the months alone on the plains had accustomed him to celibacy.

They stopped infrequently now, only for a few hours at a time to let him rest. Despite the easiness of hunting, he was losing weight and the jumpsuit that had fitted in November was loose and awkward. She assured him that the suits were cheaply made and often stretched, but he saw the expression in her eyes and knew she didn't believe her own lie. He was weakening and the halo was often above them. She shivered beneath it but did not leave his side. Sometimes he would spend an hour jogging, escaping the ceiling, but the exertion demanded that he rest later while even the walls materialized. At those times, seeing him partially enclosed by the castle, she would move away, and the fear would not leave her face until he'd walked so far that the cell disappeared.

Southeast, that month. She'd never been that far east, confining her survey to the plains west of the Missouri, so he took her across that river, through Iowa and northern Missouri. With state governments abolished the names no longer signified anything, but she took an intense interest in the ruins and border signs. *History-oriented,* he thought. *Common in a society that prefers to keep attention away from the present.*

Across the Mississippi and back, over and back again because the flowing water fascinated this girl who'd known only still indoor pools. Each time she attracted the stares of ferrymen. Hedrick suspected that, even without recognizing him as an exile, they'd have liked to push him into the river and keep Lind. He watched them carefully.

By April they were wandering west again. He'd suggested going south, through the former states of Arkansas and Texas, but she'd objected. Too many people had rejected the cities in that region, she'd said. So they returned to the plains.

The first three weeks of April were unusually dry, even for that area of the country. The land was hard, easy to walk across, no hampering mud—yet he began to falter. Tripping and stumbling frequently, barely a stick figure inside the suit. His digestion was no longer good and some days he refused food to avoid the sickness that followed.

West. Farther west. With each kilometer they were closer to Denver and the medicine she'd promised to bring him, keeping him alive as long as possible.

He collapsed repeatedly as they walked across the flatness of eastern Colorado. The hallucinations were back, and in his most delirious moments he tried to attack her, seeing her as a spirit of death trailing him. And he was not ready to die yet. When he was rational he walked calmly, saying nothing, and she did not interrupt his silence.

Above them floated his ever-present, waiting halo.

They rested for a few hours when they were still kilometers from the walls of Denver. She used the time to mark their maps, his worn old one, hers that was barely less crumpled and stained. Red circles. She drew tiny red circles, seven of them, equally far apart, equidistant from the city.

"This," she said, pointing, "is our location now." The number one and the current date were scribbled on each map beside the correct circle.

"Tomorrow, between eight and nine a.m." She marked a second circle. April twenty-third.

And continued marking, each circle numbered to indicate to him where she would meet him and when. And, in case his weakness made him lose count of the passing days, each circle with a date. His watch had miraculously kept running. If nothing else, it would let him know which location he should arrive at each morning.

"Before you go—"

"Yes?" She had taken off for the city at a lope, and he was already forty meters behind her. They had to shout.

"Get some pills."

"What?"

"Pills."

She ran back to him. "Pills? I thought you'd given up on that."

"Not those. Sleeping pills."

"No, Ray. Don't ask that of me."

"Just in case I need them."

"Or in case you want to give up and die?"

"That's my decision."

"Then get your own pills."

"Lind—"

"Damn you! I thought you wanted to live."

"I do. But when I reach the point where I can't run any more, I want to die decently, not of anoxia. Not in madness."

She stared at him, wild and unhappy, then turned to run toward Denver.

He got to his feet slowly. It was a warm spring, too warm, despite the shade provided by the halo. The next circle, less than a centimeter away on the map, was fifteen kilometers distant. As fast as possible, he walked toward it.

She was not there the next morning. He waited the full hour, another half hour, fifteen minutes more. Sipped from the canteen, rested, and waited. At nine-fifty he left.

April twenty-fourth. The third circle. She did not come.

Neither did he see her on the twenty-fifth or twenty-sixth. The fifteen kilometers between meeting points were getting longer. He did not eat during those days, his stomach could not tolerate food. It was psychosomatic, he repeated to himself, the result of the square death-shadow hounding him. But the mental assurances did no good, and the acid pain in his belly continued.

The evening of April twenty-sixth caught him far from shelter in one of the sudden hailstorms of the plains. He sat through it, head bent forward as he stared at the ground while hailstones pummeled and bruised his back. Later he found it difficult to stand and straighten his spine, but he kept going across the land, arriving only twenty minutes late at the sixth meeting point. And waited, knowing Lind was not the type of person to arrive on time and leave in anger or desperation because he wasn't there promptly.

Optimism supported that waiting. It near-died as he consulted the map again, checking the location of the one remaining circle. "If I don't come out within a week," she'd told him, "don't wait for me. Assume something happened to keep me in the city."

After six days he was certain something had happened: her own decision to stay. She hadn't wanted to remain with him two months earlier. She didn't want to watch him die. Now she had returned to a normal life, studies, research, writing, probably trying to wipe out memories of him. He hoped—sincerely hoped—she would succeed.

Eternal optimist. He had disdained the common escape of suicide, chosen by so many sentenced criminals within hours of the trial. He'd lived longer than the others, walked farther, clung to life as though he didn't know he'd already lost it, forfeited to six plastic walls. He continued his circular path around Denver.

The last day of the allotted week. He no longer expected to see her, had already planned to leave exactly at nine, walking and running until he fell permanently and the cell enclosed him. He waited impatiently, wishing the hour at an end.

At ten minutes of nine he saw her running toward him. Stumbling but never falling, not slowing until she reached him. Arms flung around him.

"I didn't think you'd be here," she gasped, pulling away to stare at his burned face.

"Why not?"

"I didn't think you'd wait for me. I wasn't even sure you'd still be alive." She slipped her pack from her shoulders—a different pack, he noticed, than the one she'd carried into the city. Different clothes: a short summer tunic instead of the tattered, grimy jumpsuit she'd worn for two months.

"I have some medicine. Enzymes, so you can eat again. Tranquilizers and stimulants in case you ever want them. Vitamins and protein supplements a doctor said might help you." Food and supplies were tumbled onto the grass as she searched.

"Wait." She looked up at him. "Did you get any barbiturates?"

"You don't need those." She went back to her search.

"Lind, I don't have time to see if your vitamins and protein work. I won't make it that far. The halo's here already, and the first wall will arrive soon."

"You'll have a few hours to recuperate before we leave."

"No. I won't be able to move that fast. I couldn't even stop to sleep last night. I needed every hour to get here in time. And I was afraid I might not wake up, even with the alarm. Lind, I want those sleeping pills."

"No!"

She stepped away, but he had grabbed one shoulder strap of the backpack. Weak as he was, his strength still matched hers.

"Didn't you get them?"

She let go abruptly. He was sitting Indian-fashion, and the release of tension sent him rolling back on the grass. "Yes, I got them," she said bitterly. "They're at the very bottom of the pack."

He turned the backpack upside down and checked the labels on two other bottles before he found them. "Were they difficult to get?"

She shrugged, looking away, back at the city that was only a hazy shadow on the horizon.

"All right, don't answer me." He opened the bottle, poured several of the pills into his left palm, then back into the bottle. "How long do these need to take effect?"

"A quarter of an hour."

"That long . . . well, I don't need to take them yet. Maybe an hour after the third wall arrives. Are you crying?"

"No. The sunlight hurts my eyes after a week inside."

"I'm not surprised." More gently: "How was the city?"

"The same." She stared west, at its high walls. "Nothing important has changed, except for the fact that *The Atheist Weekly* is no longer published."

"What happened? It was doing very well." Better than the other newsmagazines, he knew. Atheists outnumbered the supporters of any single religion, and most atheists and many agnostics subscribed.

"They printed something that was just a bit too political."

"They've always been politically oriented."

"They've always published satire of the established churches, too, but they combined the two interests and found they'd annoyed quite a few influential people. One of their editors wrote a parody of the Lord's Prayer—you know, Christian?" He nodded. His parents had been Reformed Buddhists and he was a professed skeptic, but he'd studied the more important religions. "Anyway, they converted it into a protest of the use of castles to punish criminals. It seems their humanistic creed demands that men be treated better than caged animals. So—"

" 'Our leaders, who art in Washington'?"

"Close. Very close." She frowned, concentrating.

> " 'Our father, who art in Washington,
> Hallowed be thy mandate.
> Thy electorate come, thy will be done
> Here as well as abroad.
> Give us this day our daily welfare,
> And keep us from our castles.
> As we keep those who commit crimes against us.' "

"Isn't there supposed to be an 'amen' tagged onto the end of those prayers?"

"I don't know. I'm not Christian."

"So the government simply rescinded their publishing license."

"And fined them into bankruptcy. And the editors were exiled. The other magazines are very dull reading now."

"I'm surprised there were any sleeping pills left. They'd be very popular."

"You'd be more surprised to see how many citizens have forgotten that *The Atheist Weekly* ever existed. No one mentions it."

"How'd you find out what happened?"

"Psychologists—my colleagues in particular—have longer memories and more stringent consciences than other people."

"Not to mention more vanity. I'd like to hear about the rest of your visit."

She checked her watch and stood up. "Not now. I'm going for a walk."

"You'll miss out on a lot of empathy if you don't watch me die." The attempt to keep his voice light failed.

"You have six hours before the last wall arrives. I'll be back by then." And she left, walking steadily, with occasional glances over her shoulder to confirm that he was watching her. Finally out of sight, she began to run.

Flight. Mad running: purging, cleansing, seeking forgetfulness in exhaustion. Amnesia in pain of falling and bruising. Catharsis in staggering on while her lungs burned, one wooden leg after the other, remembrances of past journeys.

Farthest point, and return. Just as far to go, the same amount of time, and less energy. Much less. Finding new limits of endurance. Five hours past and more kilometers to go. Eyes watering, tears and pain of wind striking the face, running with the last reserve of energy.

Six hours.

"Christ, you actually came back."

Collapse on hands and knees on warm afternoon earth.

"I didn't think you'd get back in time."

Exhausted nods, answered by a smile from the sunburned scarecrow now sheltered by three walls and the ceiling, his skin purple in the light filtering through the incomplete castle.

"I was lonely without you. That's not a lie. I know why you left. It's cruel of me to ask you to say here while I die, but I'm a social animal." A shrug behind that statement. "I need company."

"Perhaps," she gasped, "I should have brought others, many others, mourners of your death."

He smiled again, a beatific smile, balancing the bottle of sleeping pills on the upturned palm of his right hand. His earthly salvation and heavenly resurrection. "You're sufficient, Lind. One honest mourner is better than fifty insincere. I only wish we'd been lovers."

She shook her head.

"No, I'm not asking you now. But it would have been a good relationship." He opened the bottle, poured out a palmful of barbiturates, swallowed them with a few sips from his canteen. "Fifteen minutes. If it was thirty I might attack you. I've wanted you all this time."

"You know why I refused."

"Yes. I only regret my morality, which let me respect you. Fourteen and one half . . . did you have a nice walk?"

"No."

"I see you're bleeding. You should return to Denver after I die and have those cuts treated. Meanwhile you may as well use my medikit." He tossed it so that it landed near her. "There's no point in letting those cuts get infected."

She opened the kit and daubed antiseptic on her wounds. "What did you do while I was gone?"

"Thirteen . . . I reviewed my conscience and tried to repent past sins. Just in case whatever god might exist favors the religious. I still feel no regret for killing the psychotic who murdered my wife."

"You don't think you should have let the courts punish him?" Idiotic conversation, but what else could she say: Why don't we discuss your final dying opinion of the world?

"No," he said flatly. "They might have just sent him in for psychiatric treatment earlier. He didn't deserve to live, even with an altered mind."

She shook her head, silent, concentrating on the pain of antiseptic against raw flesh.

"Eleven minutes. I almost decided not to wait for you before taking the pills. I didn't think you would return."

"I didn't want to," she mumbled.

"What?"

She repeated, and he looked smug and said, "I was right after all. I'm feeling high. You didn't mention that effect. I expected only drowsiness." He looked at his watch again, his left wrist wavering as he tried to hold it steady. "Damn. Nine and a half minutes. Is that what you have? Good. I don't trust this watch after so long, and I can hardly read it. How long until the fourth wall arrives? I'm in no shape to calculate the remaining time."

"Thirty-seven minutes," she answered. He was looking in her general direction, but his eyes weren't focusing on her. Or on anything.

"I won't be awake then. Thirty-seven minutes, then two hours until the floor arrives. Forty-eight hours until the pick-up crew comes to get my decomposing body. Why do you suppose they leave these ugly cubes of plastic out here so long?"

She shrugged helplessly.

"God, you're quiet." He swallowed more pills, emptying the bottle to the half-full mark.

"That's all you need." She stepped toward him, reaching out to take the bottle, but he pulled it away, clasping it against his shallow chest. She stopped where the shadow of the castle touched the ground.

"Why?"

"The doctor said that just half would kill you. That's all you have to take."

"You mean you asked him how many pills were required to commit suicide?"

She shook her head. "No. He told me what quantity constituted a fatal overdose."

"So?"

"You don't need the rest."

He grinned wildly, continuing to empty the bottle and gulp pills. Between mouthfuls he said, "So I'll take an over-overdose. Overkill on an individual scale. That's fashionable, isn't it?"

Three-fourths of the bottle gone.

"I guess so," she said.

"I just want to be certain," he told her. "I don't want to wake up again, shut inside the castle, halfway between life and death. Five minutes. No, four. I have trouble focusing." He chuckled. "Christ, I can't see. Four minutes. Is that right?"

"Yes." The bottle was empty.

"You could at least give it more emotion. Empathy, woman. I'm dying. Me, the only man with this genetic pattern, anywhere, any-when. The end of an individual . . .

"Where's the chorus? I need only one official mourner—you're appointed—but no music? No recognition of my passing? Am I going to die as anonymously as I was tried? You've read the court records, Lind. An accused eight-digit number sentenced to a three-digit punishment . . . three minutes.

"No tragedy now, just numbers. Stop crying, damn it, you're disturbing my thoughts. Cry later. No *Weltangst* anymore. Private, unnoticed pain, anonymous misery. You can't construct tragedies from anonymous suffering . . . two minutes.

"This is not a world for Hamlets and Macbeths, Lind. Or even Butch Cassidys—no, that was long before your time, a story told by my grandfather. No ultimates. No perfect fulfillment. No Tristan and Isolde . . . you were not my lover, yet ideally you should lie . . ."

His voice died in sleep.

She watched the prone figure, open-mouthed, emaciated, undignified.

The fourth wall came as a separation. Blue and glassy, and behind it the figure of a man lying in stillness and the inertia of death. She looked wistfully at the emptied bottle of sleeping pills.

The floor arrived finally, waited for in light and shadow, appearing as the bare two centimeters. She knew that with its materialization went the signal to the pick-up squad. There was no longer any need for her to wait.

She left, with only one short glance at the blue translucence of the halo over her head, courtesy of a government that did not like to underuse its telemachines. The same government that disliked public sympathy for exiled criminals.

If she hurried, she would be out of the area before the first wall could appear.

12 The Public Hating

by Steve Allen

Science fiction is noted for its depiction of rapid change in highly advanced scientific and technological societies. Everything is subject to change: social, political, and economic institutions, values, knowledge, and science and technology themselves. Indeed, science fiction is frequently characterized as the "literature of change." Fantasy literature, on the other hand, usually portrays a set of basic values as unchanging. Fairy tales, for example, clearly outline structures of good and evil, in which easily identifiable good people and bad people engage in conflict and struggle, with the "good people" usually winning at the end.

In some ways, a society's criminal justice system is like a fantasy world, with good people defined as those who do not break the law and bad people as those who do. A violation of a criminal law is generally construed to be a crime "against society." One of the major functions of the criminal justice system, besides trying to deter others from committing crime, is to obtain *expiation* from the criminal on behalf of society. In this sense, crime becomes less a violation of a criminal law and more a "sin" against society itself. It is as though the moral code has been put out of balance by the committing of a crime and somehow the rebalancing is considered something without which society's stability could not exist.

In "The Public Hating" by Steve Allen, the function of expiation for sins against society is graphically demonstrated by an execution in a future setting. Not only is the execution functional to society as a whole in terms of expiation; it is also therapeutically beneficial to each individual. Are criminal justice punishment systems simply modern counterparts of more "primitive" sacrificial rites? What are the benefits and costs of such rites?

The weather was a little cloudy on that September 9, 1978, and here and there in the crowds that surged up the ramps into the stadium people were looking at the sky and then at their neighbors and squinting and saying, "Hope she doesn't rain."

On television the weatherman had forecast slight cloudiness but no showers. It was not cold. All over the neighborhood surrounding the stadium, people poured out of street-cars and buses and subways. In ant-like lines they crawled across streets, through turnstiles, up stairways, along ramps, through gates, down aisles.

Laughing and shoving restlessly, damp-palmed with excitement, they came shuffling into the great concrete bowl, some stopping to go to the restrooms, some buying popcorn, some taking free pamphlets from the uniformed attendants.

Everything was free this particular day. No tickets had been sold for the event. The public proclamations had simply been made in the newspapers and on TV, and over 65,000 people had responded.

For weeks, of course, the papers had been suggesting that the event would take place. All during the trial, even as early as the selection of the jury, the columnists had slyly hinted at the inevitability of the outcome. But it had only been official since yesterday. The television networks had actually gotten a slight jump on the papers. At six o'clock the government had taken over all network facilities for a brief five-minute period during which the announcement was made.

"We have all followed with great interest," the Premier had said, looking calm and handsome in a gray double-breasted suit, "the course of the trial of Professor Ketteridge. Early this afternoon the jury returned a verdict of guilty. This verdict having been confirmed within the hour by the Supreme Court, in the interests of time-saving, the White House has decided to make the usual prompt official announcement. There will be a public hating tomorrow. The time: 2:30 P.M. The place: Yankee Stadium in New York City. Your assistance is earnestly requested. Those of you in the New York area will find . . ."

The voice had gone on, filling in other details, and in the morning, the early editions of the newspapers included pictures captioned, "Bronx couple first in line," and "Students wait all night to view hating" and "Early birds."

By one-thirty in the afternoon there was not an empty seat in the stadium and people were beginning to fill up a few of the aisles. Special police began to block off the exits and word was sent down to the street that no more people could be admitted. Hawkers slipped through the crowd selling cold beer and hot-dogs.

Sitting just back of what would have been first base had the Yankees not been playing in Cleveland, Frederic Traub stared curiously at the platform in the middle of the field. It was about twice the size of a prize-fighting ring. In the middle of it there was a small raised section on which was placed a plain wooden kitchen chair.

To the left of the chair there were seating accommodations for a small group of dignitaries. Downstage, so to speak, there was a speaker's lectern and a battery of microphones. The platform was hung with bunting and pennants.

The crowd was beginning to hum ominously.

At two minutes after two o'clock a small group of men filed out onto the field from a point just back of home plate. The crowd buzzed more loudly for a moment and then burst into applause. The men carefully climbed a few wooden steps, walked in single file across the platform, and seated themselves in the chairs set out for them. Traub turned around and was interested to observe high in the press box, the winking red lights of television cameras.

"Remarkable," said Traub softly to his companion.

"I suppose," said the man. "But effective."

"I guess that's right," said Traub. "Still, it all seems a little strange to me. We do things rather differently."

"That's what makes horse-racing," said his companion.

Traub listened for a moment to the voices around him. Surprisingly, no one seemed to be discussing the business at hand. Baseball, movies, the weather, gossip, personal small-talk, a thousand-and-one subjects were introduced. It was almost as if they were trying not to mention the hating.

His friend's voice broke in on Traub's reverie.

"Think you'll be okay when we get down to business? I've seen 'em keel over."

"I'll be all right," said Traub. Then he shook his head. "But I still can't believe it."

"What do you mean?"

"Oh, you know, the whole thing. How it started. How you found you could do it."

"Beats the hell out of me," said the other man. "I think it was that guy at Duke University first came up with the idea. The mind over matter thing has been around for a long time, of course. But this guy, he was the first one to prove scientifically that mind can control matter."

"Did it with dice, I believe," Traub said.

"Yeah, that's it. First he found some guys who could drop a dozen or so dice down a chute of some kind and actually control the direction they'd take. Then they discovered the secret—it was simple. The guys who could control the dice were simply the guys who *thought* they could.

"Then one time they got the idea of taking the dice into an auditorium and having about 2,000 people concentrate on forcing the dice one way or the other. That did it. It was the most natural thing in the world when you think of it. If one horse can pull a heavy load so far and so fast it figures that 10 horses can pull it a lot farther and a lot faster. They had those dice fallin' where they wanted 'em 80 percent of the time."

"When did they first substitute a living organism for the dice?" Traub asked.

"Damned if I know," said the man. "It was quite a few years ago and at first the government sort of clamped down on the thing. There was a little last-ditch fight from the churches, I think. But they finally realized you couldn't stop it."

"Is this an unusually large crowd?"

"Not for a political prisoner. You take a rapist or a murderer now, some of them don't pull more than maybe twenty, thirty thousand. The people just don't get stirred up enough."

The sun had come out from behind a cloud now and Traub watched silently as large map-shaped shadows moved majestically across the grass.

"She's warming up," someone said.

"That's right," a voice agreed. "Gonna be real nice."

Traub leaned forward and lowered his head as he retied the laces on his right shoe and in the next instant he was shocked to attention by a gutteral roar from the crowd that vibrated the floor.

In distant right center-field, three men were walking toward the platform. Two were walking together, the third was slouched in front of them, head down, his gait unsteady.

Traub had thought he was going to be all right but now, looking at the tired figure being prodded toward second base, looking at the bare, bald head, he began to feel slightly sick.

It seemed to take forever before the two guards jostled the prisoner up the stairs and toward the small kitchen chair.

When he reached it and seated himself the crowd roared again. A tall, distinguished man stepped to the speaker's lectern and cleared his throat, raising his right hand in an appeal for quiet. "All right," he said, "all right."

The mob slowly fell silent. Traub clasped his hands tightly together. He felt a little ashamed.

"All right," said the speaker. "Good afternoon, ladies and gentlemen. On behalf of the President of the United States I welcome you to another Public Hating. This particular affair," he said, "as you know is directed against the man who was yesterday judged guilty in United States District Court here in New York City—Professor Arthur Ketteridge."

At the mention of Ketteridge's name the crowd made a noise like an earthquake-rumble. Several pop-bottles were thrown, futilely, from the center-field bleachers.

"We will begin in just a moment," said the speaker, "but first I should like to introduce the Reverend Charles Fuller, of the Park Avenue Reborn Church, who will make the invocation."

A small man with glasses stepped forward, replaced the first speaker at the microphone, closed his eyes. and threw back his head.

"Our Heavenly Father," he said, "to whom we are indebted for all the blessings of this life, grant, we beseech Thee, that we act today in justice and in the spirit of truth. Grant, O Lord, we pray Thee, that what we are about to do here today will render us the humble servants of Thy divine will. For it is written *the wages of sin is death.* Search deep into this man's heart for the seed of repentance if there be such, and if there be not, plant it therein, O Lord, in Thy goodness and mercy."

There was a slight pause. The Reverend Fuller coughed and then said, "Amen."

The crowd, which had stood quietly during the prayer, now sat down and began to buzz again.

The first speaker rose. "All right," he said. "You know we all have a job to do. And you know why we have to do it."

"Yes!" screamed thousands of voices.

"Then let us get to the business at hand. At this time I would like to introduce to you a very great American who, to use the old phrase, needs no introduction. Former president of Harvard University, current adviser to the Secretary of State, ladies and gentlemen, Dr. Howard S. Weltmer!"

A wave of applause vibrated the air.

Dr. Weltmer stepped forward, shook hands with the speaker, and adjusted the microphone. "Thank you," he said. "Now, we won't waste any more time here since what we are about to do will take every bit of our energy and concentration if it is to be successfully accomplished. I ask you all," he said, "to direct your unwavering attention toward the man seated in the chair to my left here, a man who in my opinion is the most despicable criminal of our time—Professor Arthur Ketteridge!"

The mob shrieked.

"I ask you," said Weltmer, "to rise. That's it, everybody stand up. Now, I want every one of you . . . I understand we have upwards of seventy thousand people here today . . . I want every single one of you to stare directly at this fiend in human form, Ketteridge. I want you to let him know by the wondrous power that lies in the strength of your emotional reservoirs, I want you to let him know that he is a criminal, that he is worse than a murderer, that he has committed treason, that he is not loved by anyone, anywhere in the universe, and that he is, rather, despised with a vigor equal in heat to the power of the sun itself!"

People around Traub were shaking their fists now. Their eyes were narrowed, their mouths turned down at the corners. A woman fainted.

"Come on," shouted Weltmer. "Let's feel it!"

Under the spell of the speaker Traub was suddenly horrified to find that his blood was racing, his heart pounding. He felt anger surging up in him. He could not believe he hated Ketteridge. But he could not deny he hated something.

"On the souls of your mothers," Weltmer was saying, "on the future of your children, out of your love for your country, I demand of you that you unleash your power to despise. I want you to become ferocious. I want you to become as the beasts of the jungle, as furious as they in the defense of their homes. Do you hate this man?"

"Yes!" roared the crowd.

"Fiend!" cried Weltmer, "Enemy of the people— Do you hear, Ketteridge?"

Traub watched in dry-mouthed fascination as the slumped figure in the chair straightened up convulsively and jerked at his collar. At this first indication that their power was reaching home the crowd roared to a new peak of excitement.

"We plead," said Weltmer, "with you people watching today on your television sets, to join with us in hating this wretch. All over America stand up, if you will, in your living rooms. Face the East. Face New York City, and let anger flood your hearts. Speak it out, let it flow!"

A man beside Traub sat down, turned aside, and vomited softly into a handkerchief. Traub picked up the binoculars the man had discarded for the moment and fastened them on Ketteridge's figure, twirling the focus-knob furiously. In a moment the man leaped into the foreground. Traub saw that his eyes were full of tears, that his body was wracked with sobs, that he was in obvious pain.

"He is not fit to live," Weltmer was shouting. "Turn your anger upon him. Channel it. Make it productive. Be not angry with your family, your friends, your fellow citizens, but let your anger pour out in a violent torrent on the head of this human devil," screamed Weltmer. "Come on! Let's do it! Let's get it over with!"

At that moment Traub was at last convinced of the enormity of Ketteridge's crime, and Weltmer said, "All right, that's it. Now let's get down to brass tacks. Let's concentrate on his right arm. Hate it, do you hear. Burn the flesh from the bone! You can do it! Come on! Burn him alive!"

Traub stared unblinking through the binoculars at Ketteridge's right arm as the prisoner leaped to his feet and ripped off his jacket, howling. With his left hand he gripped his right forearm and then Traub saw the flesh turning dark. First a deep red and then a livid purple. The fingers contracted and Ketteridge whirled on his small platform like a dervish, slapping his arm against his side.

"That's it," Weltmer called. "You're doing it. You're doing it. Mind over matter! That's it. Burn this offending flesh. Be as the avenging angels of the Lord. Smite this devil! That's it!"

The flesh was turning darker now, across the shoulders, as Ketteridge tore his shirt off. Screaming, he broke away from his chair and leaped off the platform, landing on his knees on the grass.

"Oh, the power is wonderful," cried Weltmer. "You've got him. Now let's really turn it on. Come on!"

Ketteridge writhed on the grass and then rose and began running back and forth, directionless, like a bug on a griddle.

Traub could watch no longer. He put down the binoculars and staggered back up the aisle.

Outside the stadium he walked for 12 blocks before he hailed a cab.

13 The Modern Penitentiary

by Hayden Howard

Another major outcome of the criminal justice system is rehabilitation—the attempt, through a variety of incarceration structures and experiences, to transform an individual from criminal status to a person who is worthy to return to society and to make a contribution. Usually, rehabilitation is thought to be a form of reeducation. In "The Modern Penitentiary" by Hayden Howard, a futuristic prison system is described where prisoners are referred to as students, not inmates; and release from prison is referred to as "graduation." Education, love, and understanding are emphasized as the major conditions for the success of rehabilitation. The reader should compare this prison system with that of today, where violence, inhumanity, and recidivism are the major features.

Is there such a thing as "prison technology"? Put in other words, what is the state of our knowledge of the technology of prison systems and of rehabilitation? What are the major concepts in this technology? What are the costs and benefits of this technology to society and to individuals in a prison? And is there a gap between what we know and what we do with our prison system?

I

Alone in the comfortable apartment which was his cell, Dr. Joe West chewed the inside of his cheek in self-torment. Quivering, his scalpel exposed the tiny pituitary gland of the Arctic Ground Squirrel.

"Blind fools!" His real guilt was so much worse than the angry orators in the United Nations General Assembly had shouted.

Racial murder? Unpredictably, twenty-two Canadian Eskimos had died. The Ottawa court convicted him of murder.

"I'm guilty of worse." His face twisted. Less than 30% of the Esk women had developed the planned uterine infection. Not a single Esk died. Their resistance to human pathogens was so much stronger than he expected. The Esks continued happily eating and breeding and breeding and breeding—

"Damn me! Instead of me controlling their birth-rate, I'm their Santa Claus!"

It was his murder trial which attracted world-wide attention and aid to the hungry Esks. Ironically, it was his trial which awakened humanitarians and politicians to the plight of the overcrowding Esks. Rapidly multiplying Esks were starving.

Both the outraged Chinese and the embarrassed United States were air-delivering food, baby clothing, portable barracks.

"Blind fools! Like providing food and shelter for lemmings." Dr. West's youthful face winced, gaunt as a pensioner's.

The last rumor Dr. West had overheard as he was led to his bullet-proof glass booth in the Ottawa courtroom for sentencing: a Chinese VTOL aircraft had "evacuated" more than one hundred starving "Eskimos," surely Esks, from Canada's Boothia Peninsula. Like an infectious boil, the population pressure of the Esks had burst.

"God! What's happening out there?" Trapped in the New Ottawa Reformation Center, Dr. West knew he should make a second attempt to escape—at once.

His cell was frighteningly comfortable. Safe as a womb. Already the friendly Staff were changing him.

Outside the Esks would change the world.

The hiss of increasing air pressure alerted Dr. West that the outer door to his suite was being opened. Ignoring the Ceiling Lens, Dr. West hastily wrapped the dissected squirrel in metallic-green Christmas paper; he was not allowed newspapers. Dropping to his knees, he hid the squirrel under the compressor.

As he lurched to the sofa, his abdominal incision tugged. His heart thudded more quickly than the compressor pumping coolant through frosty copper tubes past his work counter to the huge insulated cage.

It was an ingenious but scary means of escape.

Peering out through the double glass window of the cage, a single chilled Arctic Ground Squirrel (*Citellus undulatus*) still resisted hibernation. The other squirrels slept under the sawdust. This lonely squirrel shrank back as the inner door to Dr. West's suite moved open and Nona walked in with a therapeutic smile.

His pulse racing, Dr. West couldn't remember whether he'd shaved. Every day for a week, at 10:00 a.m. she had entered his suite, made his bed, done his dishes and tried cheerful conversation.

Her blue uniform no longer reminded Dr. West of a guard or airline stewardess. Through his insane glass wall, he was staring at her eyes.

"Merry Christmas, Student," Nona laughed, but her self-assurance visibly fell away. "This is supposed to be a present to you from the Staff. But I don't know what's in this package." She wasn't smiling now. "I didn't have anything to do with it."

Dr. West reached for the package, which was wrapped in grinning Santa Claus paper. He felt as if he could almost reach Nona through his imaginary glass wall. His fingers closing around the bottle-shaped package touched her hand. His muscles tightened. After a year alone in Territorial Prison, and then in the bullet-proof glass booth while on trial, and then in Classification Prison, always alone and cut off, Dr. West could not quite break through the illusion there was a glass wall—

"Gurgles like a fifth of rye," he remarked with a weak smile, cautiously shaking the package.

"I doubt that." Nona sat herself down on the coffee table, still breathing hard as if she had been hurrying to her hour-a-day appointment with him. Always she seemed to be perched on the coffee table, her knees pressed together, her hand tugging down her blue uniform skirt.

"That's Christmas on your head," Dr. West stammered, not sure what he meant to say.

Her silvery flower-shaped hair decoration of foil, tinsel and yellow-green mistletoe rustled as she raised her face with dimpled pleasure. "Thank you," she said.

After a moment she said, "There's still a package in your hand."

Dr. West's fingers stripped down the red and white Santa Claus paper, exposing the clear glass neck; he laughed with confusion. "A fifth of gin?" He stared at something worm-shaped and pink drifting back and forth in the alcohol. "I'll be damned! It's my appendix."

"I'm sorry!" Nona blurted. "What a horrid thing for the Medical Officer to send."

At her upturned face, Dr. West blinked, more surprised by her shocked reaction than by the fact that the Medical Officer would send him back his appendix for Christmas. Dr. West's smile hardened as he silently read the note: *Mr. West, our pathologist reports—*

II

That first night in his suite, Dr. West had lain waiting for his fever to rise. The dull pain spread. His abdominal muscles became rigid. He vomited, crawling toward the bathroom. As he had hoped, the Ceiling Lens was transmitting, and thirty floors below in the basement where 240 tally screens were banked, the Night Observer noticed and telephoned the Medical Officer.

Dr. West had expected to be rushed out of his solitary cell into the elevator, and down, then out through the icy Canadian night to the hospital building. Apparently that was someone's plan. Perhaps an orderly had been bribed. The rectangular hospital seemed to have more escape possibilities than these tall cylindrical towers of the New Ottawa Reformation Center.

From a distance the towers had resembled concrete grain elevators. His first glimpse, as the armored car delivered him toward the penitentiary, had shifted from the towers to the Canadians massing in the sleet. PRESERVE OUR ESKIMOS, a placard read.

Flailing their signs, the screaming mob broke through the police line and halted the armored car with their bodies. SAVE OUR ESKIMOS. A sign hammered against the bullet-proof window. HUMAN LIFE IS SACRED. A contorted face pressed against the glass, recognized Dr. West. "Kill the bastard!"

Dr. West had closed his eyes. They were right.

Shivering inside warm Tower #3 that first night, finally alone in his solitary suite, still shivering Dr. West had hung up his gray denim trousers, and the capsule fell out of his cuff. He had blinked at it. On the pink gelatin was scratched HOSPAPP. At first he did not realize what the APP stood for. With irony he thought the capsule might contain cyanide from his billions of telly admirers who had witnessed his trial and conviction for genocide and were outraged there no longer was a death penalty in Canada. Their dead Eskimos were lovable people, easily idealized. "Tool of capitalist genocide!" "Communist fiend!" the confused Canadians had shouted after him.

Swiftly, willing to accept whatever it contained, Dr. West had gulped the capsule and lain down. His actual crime, his ineffectiveness, was more terrible than the billions knew.

The numbing of death did not come. As his temperature rose and his symptoms proliferated, Dr. West had realized that APP stood for appendix. Someone was trying to get him out. Someone must believe him.

Fever engulfed him in delirium.

A potent capsule! He imagined he saw Eskimos entering his suite, and he shouted with terror.

The Medical Officer's fingers were pressing his rigid abdomen. "Nurse, best take a thermometer reading from this chap."

The massive whiteness of a polar bear loomed over the Medical Officer's shoulder, and Joe West had yelled.

To his dismay, instead of carrying him out to the hospital, gauze-masked monsters wheeled a portable operating table into his suite. "Best give the patient a spinal."

Mirrored in the reflector of the portable overhead light they were turning his body. Their yellowish rubber hands gleamed. A grease pencil marked a line from his navel to his hip. He felt the numb tugging of the scapel.

When the appendectomy was complete, a masked face had bent over him. "I say, West, your appendix appears remarkably healthy. In retrospect, your symptoms all seem rather odd. You've made me feel the fool. Was this another one of those unnecessary operations?" The Medical Officer had turned away. "Best deliver his appendix to the pathologist."

Now, for a Christmas present, or a warning, the Medical Officer had returned his appendix in a bottle with a note.

Mr. West, our pathologist reports that a foreign substance, probably ingested, raised your white blood count and induced other symptoms typical of peritonitis. As a former medical man, you may have a more specific explanation?

Why not feign a brain tumor next time? We would welcome the exercise. Merry Christmas from the Staff, New Ottawa Reformation Center.

P.S. Looking forward to your continued presence during the New Year.

Dr. West's bitter grin sagged while he turned his head from side to side as if searching for a window to the Outside. Windowless concrete. He stared past Nona at the concave wall and violently stiffened, his fist crushing the note.

Her voice intruded: "Did he write one of his funny notes?"

"Funny? My sense of humor's dead. I'm dead. Don't waste your hour in here with me. Don't waste the taxpayers' money. Get out, dammit!"

Instantly he was sorry—and terribly lonely.

She looked up at him. To his surprise, she moved toward him, smiling.

He stiffened. "Get out. While you can, go!" he shouted. "Get out. I can't stand your—is it sympathy?"

She edged toward the door but turned around, her face solemn. "If you want, you can apply for someone else, a different social Therapist."

"No! What choice has a rat in a trap?" He looked her up and down. "Bait, is that what you are? Get out."

"After you've been here a while," she answered softly, "you'll realize this is like your home. You'll feel differently. Please, if you want to— you can apply for a different—"

"No, dammit, I want to get out of here! At least you—get out!"

After he had caught his breath, he realized she was still standing there. Trying to hold his voice from trembling, he said: "You don't scare very easily, do you?"

"Sometimes. But not of you."

"I'm sorry. But I've got to get out of here. I forget you have problems, too. Here you are a woman alone all day with us murderers and maniacs."

"I'm not alone."

"Do you mean that physically or spiritually? Outside, they'd lynch me," Dr. West said finally. "In here you people try to make me feel comfortable but won't even tell me the news."

Wryly he smiled. "There was a prophetess named Cassandra. Now I know why she wailed. A man, a prophet, would have battered his head against a marble pillar. Cassandra could fortell what was going to destroy Troy, but no one would listen. She warned them not to drag the wooden horse into Troy. No wonder she wailed. Helplessly knowing what is going to happen, but not being able to do anything is so much more painful than not knowing!"

"Aren't you being rather dramatic," she remarked. "That wooden horse, isn't it in a school book about Greece?" Turning away from his tormented face, she walked into the kitchenette and opened the sliding door which concealed his sink and electric stove. She boiled water. "Instant coffee?"

"So you're the unshakable type," he laughed bitterly. "Must help in a madhouse like this."

"I believe in living along from day to day." She sat down on the other end of the sofa and smiled at him over her steaming cup. "Now that you've had your tantrum for this day, I'm going to tell you something which may give you a second one."

"No, I'm through," he said, smiling faintly. "Your child psychology has overpowered me."

"The Pharmacist asked me to ask you—" she put down her coffee cup—"if a hypodermic was, shall we say, overlooked and left in your cell. During the first three nights after your appendix operation the nurse gave you sleeping injections. In a government institution like this everything has to be accounted for—even if it's all used up like a one-shot disposable hypo. Anyway, the nurse must have become confused in her equipment count. A used hypo is missing. Of course she had other patients to visit, but you're the newest in this tower; and this has never happened before, so the Pharmacist wonders, if you still have the hypo, would you return it?"

"I haven't any hypo."

"Good. I'll ask the Recreation Officer if he'll start the search in someone else's suite. The Administratrix has told him to search, so he has to search."

"That's all right," Dr. West leaned back on the sofa. "The Recreation Officer can start here. I won't feel persecuted. He's my buddy," Dr. West bluffed and nodded at the insulated cage, the compressor, the centrifuge, the gleaming glass equipment, all of which the Recreation Officer cheerfully and ingeniously had acquired for him—with Dr. West's own impounded funds.

Dr. West's heart palpitated as he remembered the dissected squirrel concealed under the compressor. But he went on talking. "The Recreation Officer showed the Administratrix my hibernation-study proposal. I may be repeating old metabolic and glandular research, but it's more therapeutic for me than weaving baskets. He says he got her approval by suggesting Tower #3 surely must be more enlightened than Alcatraz—some prison where they once let an old lifer raise canaries. So the Recreation Officer's my buddy, and I raise squirrels. He's welcome to search. When is he likely to?"

"He'll probably start someplace else." She put down her coffee. "At least two students who've been sick and visited by the nurse are former drug addicts and might steal hypos, I suppose." She looked solemnly at him, and he was surprised how small she really was. Her hand on the couch was fragile compared with his. "The truth is," she laughed, "some men in this tower are—rather scary. That's why in your suite I feel so much better—with you."

Dr. West recognized the pitch, the helpless bit, and he almost smiled with pleasure. He not only felt protective, he felt almost possessive. From the sofa, she looked up at him, smiling with her eyes as if she knew that he knew, and he felt his imaginary glass wall dissolving.

III

"What are you smiling about?" she said.

"I was just thinking that we—"

The outer door hissed. Dr. West's muscle contracted like a criminal's caught in the act. The inner door shoved open.

"May I come in?" said the Recreation Officer, already in and sniffing his toothbrush mustache in his most characteristic gesture. He had an old face, but his mustache and hair were black with dye. "I can come back later." His unreadable gaze bounced off Nona's face, and he stared at Dr. West. "I've been asked, shall we say ordered, to search for a small useless, uh, item in your suite."

Dr. West grinned. "Nona told me it was a hypo. Feel free to search away. I'll help any way I can, but I haven't got a hypo for you. I wish there was a prison grapevine so I could tell you who's got the hypo."

The Recreation Officer failed to smile. To Dr. West's surprise the Recreation Officer's usually sly sense of humor was gone, blank.

"Would it be possible to start with another suite?" Dr. West asked apologetically. "This is my therapeutic hour. You said you could come back later."

"No, I'm already here, so I'll start here," the Recreation Officer replied. "She can vacuum this dirty floor whether I'm here or not."

Dr. West tried again. "Sir, if you could come back later, after Nona's gone—I need to talk with you alone."

Dr. West was careful not to glance toward the compressor. Beneath it the dissected squirrel was hidden, and Dr. West was afraid Nona's reaction would be revulsion when it was found. He thought the Recreation Officer's reaction would have been no more than mild interest if the dissected squirrel had been in plain sight on the work counter.

Unfortunately, Dr. West had concealed the dead squirrel, as if guilty of something. Now the Recreation Officer's reaction when he found the bloody package might be suspicion. Dr. West knew the Recreation Officer lacked the medical background to put two and two together. But if the squirrel were shown to the Medical Officer, that intelligent man would recognize this was not merely a squirrel autopsy. The squirrel had been cut open for another purpose. The Medical Officer would ponder this problem, and knowing Dr. West's controlling motivation was escape—

"—in the kitchenette," the Recreation Officer was saying, opening and closing drawers. "You haven't even done his dishes yet, Nona." He opened a cupboard. "A more logical hiding place for a hypo would be—the bathroom."

Dr. West began to perspire. He knew he needed to maneuver both of them out of the suite in order to dispose of that dissected squirrel. If the Recreation Officer continued searching, eventually he would discover the body of the squirrel.

The Recreation Officer spent a surprisingly long time banging around in the bathroom. All it contained was a medicine cabinet, toilet, basin and tub. The bathroom was located in the narrow inner end of the suite.

Whenever he had sat in the tub Dr. West could hear the eight elevators humming up and down the central shaft of the cylindrical tower. His thirtieth floor suite was shaped like an eighth of a pie. The center of the pie was occupied by the huge open shaft, which contained the elevators and the air-conditioning ducts. The elevators were code-controlled. To escape without an elevator would be a long fall.

The Recreation Officer emerged from the bathroom, smiling beneath his toothbrush mustache. "I took the liberty of searching your medicine cabinet." His smile widened. "I deduce from the bottles and tubes that you suffer from piles." His smile spread so wide it almost appeared malicious. "Not a very romantic ailment for a world famous Arctic adventurer. Or for a convicted mass murderer."

Dr. West blinked with surprise. Until now, the Recreation Officer always had treated him with human respect, never mentioned his crime.

"You've murdered more people," the Recreation Officer remarked, "than the rest of the Students in this tower combined, and you top it off by stealing a worthless one-shot hypo."

"I haven't got your hypo."

"You're a disgusting example of futility. Do you know, if you'd simply applied for a hypo, if you needed a hypo, I would have purchased you a dozen. But during your second or third night in the tower you didn't know that yet, did you? So you stole one."

Dr. West did not reply. He was wondering if the Recreation Officer had just planted a hypo in the bathroom. From a friend, the Recreation Officer inexplicably had turned into tormentor.

"I brought you scalpels, didn't I," the Recreation Officer persisted. "Enough scalpels to butcher a dozen women."

"Please, sir," Nona protested.

"Don't you approve of humor?" the Recreation Officer asked. "You and I are both on the Staff—to assist in therapy, to make the Students happy. Isn't that right?"

The Recreation Officer strode across the room toward the entry and kicked Dr. West's bed. "What do they expect me to do, split the mattress to find your hypo?"

"I haven't got the hypo." Dr. West stepped forward, his sweating face twisted in an answering smile. "From what I've been told, the policy of this prison, excuse me, educational institution, toward the so-called Student is—"

"—to treat the disturbed student with respect," the Recreation Officer interrupted in a sing-song voice. "Make him feel this is home. Rebuild his feeling of inner worth. Nona, have you been reciting your book to this filthy murderer?"

"No, she hasn't, Dad," Dr. West retorted, smiling harder, losing control. "You did, remember? Where's your warm Father-Image today? The student is to be drawn into a warm familylike relationship and, I quote, encouraged to lower his defensive barriers. In the Ottawa Reformation Center he is considered reborn. It is the purpose of the Staff to offer the Student so warm and reassuring an emotional environment that he will find the inner support he failed to feel in his childhood. Strengthened, basically changed, he can return to society. Isn't that right, Dad?"

"Back off!" The Recreation Officer spoke like an angrily barking dog. "Because you're younger, stronger, more sarcastic doesn't mean you can't be spanked! Figuratively spanked—no. Literally spanked!" He walked away from Dr. West, lifted the top of the insulated hibernation cage and plunged his arm into it.

The one conscious squirrel jumped aside and squealed with fright.

For the last minute, Dr. West had been considering goading the Recreation Officer to such anger he would stop the search and rush out of the suite. But now Dr. West's heart was hammering, his fists clenched, and he realized his own self-control was so uncertain that the Recreation Officer might be successfully goading him. Perhaps the Recreation Officer's strange behavior was intended to goad him to violence. Then would he be transferred? Was that the Recreation Officer's intent?

Nona, her face pale, her lips narrow, was shaking her head in warning at Dr. West. Silently they watched while the Recreation Officer distastefully lifted out a handful of sawdust.

"What a stench! I noticed it as soon as I entered your suite. Are you sure they're not decaying instead of hibernating?" The Recreation Officer reached deeper into the cage. "This stench, is it to discourage us from looking for the hypo? Is it dead?"

By the tail, the Recreation Officer raised a hibernating ground squirrel. "Since you formerly were an expert on Arctic ecology, among other things, I would have expected you to play with something more typically Arctic. Such as those beastly little lemmings which you reputedly compared to Eskimos."

"To Esks. I explained to you the differences between Eskimos and Esks. I talked for hours when you listened so sympathetically, Dad," Dr. West added savagely. "You ought to be intelligent enough to differentiate between Eskimos and Esks. As for lemmings, they don't hibernate."

The Recreation Officer shrugged, dropped the limp squirrel back into the cage. "Dear me, you're right. You told me no Arctic animal truly hibernates—except these putrid ground squirrels. I'm not going to search through this stinking mess for the hypo. I'm going to recommend that the contents of this cage be emptied down the incinerator."

"I haven't got the hypo," Dr. West repeated, watching the Recreation Officer step to the wider end of the suite where the compressor chugged erratically.

Concealed under the compressor was the dissected squirrel. The compressor unit vibrated against the white concrete wall.

The wall was smooth concrete, slightly concave because it also was the outer wall of the tower. Like a cylindrical concrete grain elevator, the tower had no windows, and its exterior construction was both economical and escape-proof, and functional in other ways.

The Recreation Officer glanced from the compressor to the concave wall spread out behind it like a wide-angle screen. "This noisy compressor must intrude into the corner of the picture. Or do you never turn on the projector any more? For emotionally disturbed students like you I recommend a minimum of two hours per day." The Recreation Officer smiled infuriatingly at him.

IV

Dr. West stepped violently toward the compressor, the Recreation Officer and the blank wall. At first, while recovering from his appendectomy, he had lain for hours watching the moving scenery on that wall, his only window. Trying to ignore the subliminal cartoons pressing him back against childhood, his favorite escape had been following movies of the surf flashing white along the Northern California coastline on the wall. At first he'd stared helplessly. The artificial window had been his only release from claustrophobia.

"Nona, don't leave," Dr. West said, without looking back, knowing she was still sitting on the coffee table. This caused the Recreation Officer to glance back at her.

Dr. West's hand darted into the compressor case.

The compressor unit consisted of an electric motor humming at high R.P.M.'s and revolving a series of larger and larger gears, the largest turning least rapidly and most powerfully, forcing the piston of the air compressor in and out no faster than a frightened heart. Last week, when Dr. West had assembled this jerry-built contraption, he had set an oiling can to drip at five minute intervals on the moving elbow of the compressor, and now, in this instant, his hand reset the nozzle of the can to dribble rapidly.

As the Recreation Officer turned back to the compressor, a fine mist of oil rose against his blue uniform. Dr. West already was walking away.

There was a moment of silence as if the Recreation Officer had not yet realized what had happened. "Your damned machine is leaking! There's little droplets all over my coat."

At this, Dr. West turned back. "Either oil or coolant. If it's coolant —the coolant is strongly alkaline, irritating to the lungs." He wrapped his handkerchief protectively around his hand and rushed at the compressor, turning his head aside, as if from poison gas, holding his breath while he readjusted the oiler to its former rate of one drop of oil every five minutes. "The coolant will decompose cloth. It should be soaped off the skin as soon as possible."

The Recreation Officer sniffed the back of his hand and glared from Dr. West to Nona. "The least you could do is help me search," he accused her. "Damn, my hand is burning!"

Seated on the low coffee table, Nona stared down at her own hands, cupped on her lap. "Sir, my job's to maintain a close relationship with my Students. The Administratrix never asks us to involve ourselves in searches."

"You have the soul of a—They let anybody into Civil Service these days!" The Recreation Officer dashed out of the suite, scrubbing his hand with his handkerchief, and the elevator hummed.

"I'm sorry," Nona murmured.

"He's never acted before as if making a search was—beneath his dignity. Normally he's a nice man. Maybe he's having problems out-side—"

"Oh, sure. Nice man." Dr. West sat down on the sofa in order to stop shaking. "The Staff has to stick together."

"I'm telling you the truth. I've never seen him like this." Suddenly she smiled. "On duty, we're supposed to be saints and let you Students have all the tantrums."

Perched on the low coffee table, she pressed her legs together and tugged down at her skirt. She was peering toward the compressor. "Is that a Christmas present underneath? Sort of green shiny paper."

"You'll have to wait till Christmas to find out," Dr. West said and reached forward, seizing her hand before she could stand all the way up and escape to look under the compressor.

Pulled forward off balance, she raised her eyebrows as she smiled at him, and plumped down beside him on the sofa. "You didn't need to let go of my hand."

Dr. West grinned with embarrassment, knowing he should try to get her to leave the suite as quickly as possible, so he could dispose of the squirrel. "Do you think my ex-buddy, the Recreation Officer, is likely to pop back in here unannounced?"

She shrugged, jiggling her shirt waist. "He might." She smiled, glancing at him from the corners of her eyes. "I don't think he will, though. He probably went down to the basement to wash and gulp coffee and brood. This was supposed to be his free hour. That's why he was assigned to help search. Next hour he has to be smiling again and sympathetic because he must face his next appointment with another of you exasperating Students."

"Exasperated is the word. I feel like I'm in a fishbowl." Dr. West jerked his head at the Ceiling Lens.

Nona looked up, then down as if she was staring through thirty floors to the basement. "Privacy is mostly in your head. There are 240 screens down there, but only one observer on duty since the budget cut. Mainly the observer keeps his attention on the red-tagged screens, the new admissions. After all, they're the men most apt to set their suites on fire or slash their wrists or—uh, develop appendicitis."

Dr. West almost smiled at that. Then he asked a leading question. "When the clock says it's night, and the luminous panels dim, and finally I turn out my reading light, there's still a dim red glow in the dark. I deduce I'm also spied on by infrared transmission?"

"You are a bashful one! The night observer has only one set of eyes. He's worked here for years, and he's seen everything. He's so bored, he's slyly wired one telly to watch outside hockey games." She giggled. "It takes my own inside alarm system to get any protection from him."

Dr. West laughed in surprise. "Inside alarm? Don't tell me, if a buxom member of the Staff is grabbed by a Student and squeezed, does that set off her built-in electronic alarm button, gongs clanging, red lights flashing—"

"You tease! That depends on the member of the Staff." Nona stood up unexpectedly.

As if in pain, Dr. West leaped to his feet, reaching for her elbow. But her other hand pressed lightly against his chest, and her gaze shifted from his eyes to someplace over his shoulder.

"The clock says your time's up."

"Listen, Nona, seriously, I need you now." He was startled that he was begging.

"I wish I could stay, but I'm hired to look after my students equally. I wish I could stay, but my 11:00-till-12:00 man is expecting me. It's his hour. He's a terribly nervous, disturbed old man. He has no inner resources at all. He's sitting there expecting me—"

"But what about *my* hour? That damned Recreation Officer used up my whole hour bumbling around in here. Listen, you wouldn't understand that I've been hung up in—hell. I've been dead until today, and now I need you."

She stepped close to him. "I'll be back tomorrow. Since you're described in the Files as a cerebral type, you can get along," she teased, then added seriously: "I'm so happy you came out of your withdrawal." She smiled again. "Some silly-billies on the Staff were making bets you would turn into a vegetable."

"A vegetable? Listen, tell your 11:00-till-12:00 man I'll trade my whole hour tomorrow for thirty of his minutes today, now."

"I'm flattered—I think. But he's unadaptable. I'll dicker with him for you, but don't hold your breath. I won't be back for at least a half hour, if at all—lover."

"Dammit, Nona," Dr. West almost grabbed for her, then laughed wryly, trying to hide himself behind a sense of humor. "You're playing with dynamite. Nona, is that what you love—playing with human dynamite?"

"That's my job. I'm supposed to civilize you." She winked and went out through the hissing door.

V

Alone, but perhaps not unseen, Dr. West was careful not to glance at the Ceiling Lens. To conceal what he wanted to do, he knew that turning off the lights in the suite during waking hours would be the wrong move. That simply would attract the attention of the observer. Innocently he ambled toward the compressor, knelt and removed the gleaming green package, and walked to the sink. He went through the motions of washing the dishes Nona had neglected to wash, and in the sink he cut the ground squirrel into quarters and ground it down the disposal, all the while bending over the sink, obscuring his actions from the observer, who might be watching, but more likely not.

Dr. West did not glance at the hiding place of the steel needle he had removed from the hypo. The needle was sticking in the fiberboard partition between the kitchenette and the bathroom. He had extracted the nail which originally supported the lightly framed print of a voyageur portaging a canoe. The screw-in base of the hypodermic needle now served the same purpose as had the head of the nail. Thus the needle was concealed in plain sight.

Two weeks ago, Dr. West had smashed the relatively large plastic plunger of the hypo for which they now were searching and flushed it down the toilet.

While in bed after his appendectomy, he had confused the nurse in her hypo count. Like the old shell game. Having stolen a full hypo rather than the empty they thought was missing, he had injected its content into his empty nose-drops bottle, which stood on a shelf in the medicine cabinet next to his eye-drops bottle, which he had filled with a second sedative injection the following night while the nurse's attention was distracted by a white wad of paper he had ricocheted off the concave wall—after telling the nurse he had seen a white mouse in his cell.

Now Dr. West visualized the Ceiling Lens above his head without looking at it. If he stacked the kitchen chair on top of the coffee table and climbed up and taped a paper towel over the Ceiling Lens, the blank-out probably would attract the attention of the observer, who might send someone to investigate which would be most embarrassing.

A shy and difficult man, Dr. West wanted privacy. He needed privacy.

Even the bathroom lacked privacy. There was a separate Ceiling Lens in there. Dr. West blinked in realization. The Staff all had said there were 240 telly screens in the basement. The tower was 30 stories high with 8 pie-shaped suites to a floor, so that there must be 240 suites. But there were *two* Ceiling Lenses per suite, one in the main room, one in the bathroom, so why weren't there 480 screens in the basement?

Wrong! He had forgotten the *third* Ceiling Lens in the entrance passageway between the inner and outer doors. It was to reveal attempted escapes or ambushes by Students who had gained the code for opening the inner door. Why weren't there 720 screens in the basement?

As his hypothesis germinated, Dr. West smiled. One Ceiling Lens was in the main room of the studio apartment, the second in the bathroom and the third in the entry hall next to the bathroom in the narrow end of the semi-pie-shaped suite, a total of three Ceiling Lenses per suite. Therefore, there should be 3 times 240 telly screens in the basement, a total of 720 screens. But there were only 240 screens. Dr. West squinted, trying to visualize how the designers of the remote T.V. system managed to project 720 pictures to only 240 receiving sets. He nodded. From each suite 3 pictures were transmitted onto one screen.

In televising baseball games, it was customary to show the pitcher winding up and at the same time in the corner of the screen show a separate picture from a separate camera of the runner taking his lead off of first base.

Dr. West assumed that the pictures from his bathroom and from the entry hall were projected as overlaps in two corners of the main picture from his suite. Thus, very likely there were two privacy spots within the main room of his suite. But which two corners of the four corners of the screen, which two corners of the main room would contain this privacy overlap?

Unfortunately, the shape of the main room was not square and could not fill a square telly screen. From the concave, white outside wall of the suite, the two side walls tapered inward. The slice of pie narrowed where the bathroom and the entry hall stood side-by-side, both abutting the central elevator shaft.

If, on the telly screen, the bathroom and entry hall were moved down and out to the corners of the screen, there would be only a partial overlap because the main room was narrowest at the top of the screen. But there still would be some overlap—some place to hide from the Observer.

Dr. West walked into the bathroom. It was about eight feet long. At its wider end, it was five feet wide. He glanced out at the kitchenette in the main room. On the T.V. screen, if the bathroom were moved down into the unfilled corner of the screen, it would overlap with the china cabinet, the dumbwaiter pipe which delivered frozen foods and his refrigerator.

Since the private actions Dr. West had in mind couldn't be conducted in such a small refrigerator, he walked to the other side of the main room, near the inner entry door.

The entry hall also appeared to be five feet wide, and he supposed it was the same length as the bathroom, eight feet. He looked back. The coffee table, sofa, easy chair and standing lamp were grouped near the center of the main room. Beside him, his bed already stood against the side wall, but exposed because it was too far down on the T.V. screen. It was too near the wide, white projection wall to be in the telly overlap.

Standing with his back to the bed and his calves pressed against the foot of the bed, imperceptibly Dr. West pushed the bed along the side wall until the head of the bed was near the entry door. If he moved the bed any closer, Nona wouldn't be able to squeeze through the partially blocked door. Nevertheless, virtually the entire bed should be concealed by the overlapping picture transmitted from the entry hall. In the upper left hand corner of the telly screen in the basement, the bed would be hidden . . . he hoped.

Because he was by training a conscientious man, he began to cross-check. He stared at the entry door. Perhaps, the Ceiling Lens in the entry hall only operated when someone was entering? Not likely. More threatening was the probability that the suite could be scanned. By throwing a switch, the Observer could shift the overlapping pictures from the upper corners of the screen to the lower corners. With so many unknowns and variables, there might be even more embarrassing possibilities. "Dammit, there's more than one way to skin a cat."

Dr. West smiled with excitement, hurried across the suite to his work counter and collected a ball of twine, a scalpel and some safety pins. On his trip back to the bed he dragged his wooden work chair. Listening for the hiss of the outer door, he pushed down the pillow and set up the chair on top of the bed. He tied two chair legs to the tubular iron head of the bedstead.

Hastily, he stretched a string from the high back of the anchored chair down over the bed to its tubular iron foot. Fumbling with knots, spreading blankets over the string, pinning blankets together, pinning edges of blankets to the mattress, he worked as rapidly as a camper when the raindrops begin to fall.

His face contracted with uncertainty. That two-faced, unpredictable Recreation Officer might return—

The outer door hissed, and Dr. West jumped like a man awakened by an alarm clock. Across the suite he carried the scalpel he had used to cut string to the work counter and turned, breathing hard, as the inner door opened.

"Surprise," she laughed. "My 11:00-till-12:00 man was so grumpy when I asked him why he hadn't shaved he said I was a worse nagger than his daughter. My heavens, he would have *given* you the rest of his hour. But he'll feel differently tomorrow, so I traded him your hour tomorrow for his 45 minutes left. You're looking at me like my eyeshadow's on upside-down." She giggled. "I talk too much. I don't know why I should be in a tizzy, but whenever—well, we don't really know each other. We're friends, but we're still sort of—strangers."

As Dr. West walked toward her, she stepped sideways, and the back of her leg came in contact with the bed. She whirled, startled.

"My heavens! A tent!" She pealed with laughter. "A tent," she giggled. "I'm going to have to explain a few things to you. You're so new here you don't know the rules." Then her laughter stopped. "I'm sorry. I'm not laughing at you. I'm laughing at the tent. I think it's cute."

Dr. West took hold of her upper arm.

"You don't need to look so serious and earth-shaking," she breathed. "Life should be fun. It is fun, a tent! You are the most ingenious man I ever did see. Safety pins! A tent flap. Wasn't Omar Khayyam a tentmaker, too?"

She put her head inside the tent. "Oops, am I psychic? I never did make your bed. I talk too much, don't I?" Head first she vanished into the tent, as Dr. West's hand guided her.

Forgetting even a sidewise glance at the door, Dr. West followed, the tent shaking as he disappeared under the blanket room. From the Ceiling Lens only the tent was visible.

"My heavens," her voice emerged from the tent, "a chair for a tent pole! Not so fast! It's crowded in here. You have lots of ingenuity, but . . . Oh."

"I'm sorry, such a hurry," Dr. West's voice gasped. "More than a year I've been alone, Nona, trapped in jails alone."

"That's all right, lover. Let me rub your neck, your back and in a little while—"

"A year is so long for a live man. No, a dead man."

"Well, now, I wouldn't say you were quite dead," she giggled.

"But a whole year! A year passes. What's a year." He laughed wryly, "I shouldn't feel sorry for myself. Those Mars expeditions were gone far more than a year, and married men at that. Listen, I feel better. I can take anything."

"Now you're cheering up. Already you're changing for the better. I may not accomplish much in life," she said, "but at least I'm accomplishing something when you smile, student. Squeeze me. This is your chance to change, and you'll change, really change and return to the world. We Canadians do like to think we're somewhat enlightened. After you graduate, lover—remember me."

"Graduate, hell!" Dr. West's voice blurted. "Sentenced to life!"

"No, you're not. You can't be. All Ottawa sentences are indeterminate."

"I'm not a fool! I know I'll never be freed."

"You have the same right," her voice exclaimed unsurely, "to graduate as any other student. I'm sure you must. Why else would the staff go to all the trouble and expense of getting you all that equipment, the cage, the compressor? It's occupational therapy. The Recreation Officer—"

"That two-faced psycho? Not only did he try to humiliate me in front of you, he showed a vicious attitude toward you."

"Please," she protested, "you already have enough adjustment problems without developing a persecution complex. The Recreation Officer just had a bad day. Even Recreation Officers are human."

"He's not your husband, is he?"

"What? What a stupid and unexpected question! Certainly he's not my husband. Just because I have a ring on my finger doesn't mean— well, why don't you simply try to enjoy life here in your suite."

"And don't ask personal questions," Dr. West's voice filled in.

"No, I'm happy to answer personal questions. We're in an awfully personal position right now, and you can get as personal with me as you want—if you'll promise me you'll let the Recreation Officer start out again tomorrow with a clean slate. All is forgiven?"

"Could it be that he's jealous of me?"

"Uh-uh. I'm also Den Mother to five other students. He's never acted this way before. I'm sure he's not jealous. I only know the man in a professional way, and he's rather old and quite professional."

"Not today he wasn't professional," Dr. West's voice insisted. "He didn't even finish searching my suite. What has he got, a triple personality? At first, after my appendix operation, he showed no real interest in me. He wanted me to take up microscopy as a hobby merely because Tower #3 happened to have an unused microscope."

"Yes, my microscope boy graduated. He has a technical job in Saskatchewan Oil Fields," she said proudly. "Oil core drilling samples are full of the tiny shells of—He wrote me a beautiful letter."

"I told the Recreation Officer, for my occupational therapy I didn't want to weave baskets," Dr. West's voice swept on. "I wanted to review a line of research begun when I was Director of Oriental Population Problems Research at the University of California."

VI

"My heavens, what has population problems got to do with hibernation?"

"Nothing, except that birth and growth and hibernation all are dependent on glandular activity. My original medical specialty was endocrinology. Glands. But as I was saying—all of a sudden the Recreation Officer took a personal interest in me, went to great trouble to acquire equipment for me, told me how he cut through red tape. We had long talks. He was interested in the squirrels. I thought he was my buddy."

"He just got up on the wrong side of his bed this morning. His bunk, perhaps," she laughed. "He's a retired naval officer. Your navy, by the way. But he's Canadian born."

"Born in hell," Dr. West's voice muffled.

"Mmm, that's better. Don't nibble too hard. Forget, mm, everything. Think about me. Has all that isolation made you too sensitive? See—you're ticklish. Lover, that big white square, that scar on your leg—?"

"You're warm and smooth, the end of the world."

"What do you mean by that?"

"I don't know," Dr. West's voice breathed.

"My heavens, you're certainly trying to find out," her voice squealed in delighted alarm.

Dr. West's voice hoarsened. "Listen, I feel, Nona, Nona—"

"Yes, that's it, wonderful—"

From the tent for a little while there was no coherent conversation and finally quietness.

"Darling, so nice—" her voice sighed. "So relaxed."

"Nona, I feel wonderful," Dr. West's voice laughed. "Let's you and me break out of this prison."

"Now that you've regained your self-confidence," her voice teased him. "Don't get so overconfident. I still work here. I like it here. You are my student, my job."

"To charm us cons away from reality?" his voice laughed.

"Would you rather be in one of those gigantic penitentiaries in the States—with 5,000 criminal types, all supposedly male? March, march! No privacy. Fellow prisoners to teach you better ways to stick up filling stations. Guards who shave and aren't as—ahem—sympathetic as I am. Now would you trade places?"

"You do have nice smooth skin," his voice exhaled. "But here I've never seen another prisoner. When I tapped on the walls, nobody answered."

"Which would you rather have?" her voice insisted.

"We're really all in solitary, the 240 men in this tower, and in how many other towers."

"Ten towers," she said. "It's not solitary unless you think of it as solitary."

"2,400 men. How many women? Divide by 6?"

"You always try to be too precise," her voice laughed. "Our men are changing and graduating all the time. The average stay is less than a year. Thousands and thousands." Her voice grew serious. "I think of a stream of men being reborn."

"I think of thieves and murderers, criminals, myself, crouched in their cells waiting for you." His voice rose. "Listen, I'll never get out of here. For political reasons, I'll never make it."

"Oh shut up. Don't act so egotistical. If you want to act like a pessimistic, guilt-tortured little boy, go ahead and roll in your own mess." In the blanket tent rose the bulge of a head. "Until you take a more positive attitude, you jolly well won't roll on the sheets with me."

"You mean it, don't you?" His voice softened, then exclaimed with wry laughter, "I understand too well! So simple but I don't know how effective. Solitary confinement is the stick, and you're the carrot. I've been given donkey ears."

"You stubborn donk," her voice laughed, "don't you see any further than your big nose? You men in here can't be deeply changed by rewards and punishments. Outside, carrots and sticks certainly failed to civilize you or you wouldn't be in here. All your life you've been rewarded and punished but you wouldn't conform and you ended in here."

"I need to get out. There is a great need for me to get out. Outside, the Esks are—"

"Sweet, harmless, law-abiding people. There's no use talking about Eskimos in here. Listen, we want you to like it in here. Lover, when you adjust—We love you."

"My God, Nona, are you going to give me the Family bit? The Recreation Officer already shoveled it on me—during his friendly period." Dr. West's voice rose with anger. "The Staff is my family. I am provided with a new childhood, loving and secure, so that I can grow up to the world again. Strengthened by my secure second childhood, or is that the wrong terminology? With new inner security we criminals graduate from our prison families into the world to be law-abiding and patient and sympathetic with our fellow man. Bugles, please!"

"It works. The family-group produces the—"

"Yes, Mom. But Dad was nasty today. Was he cranky because he thought I wanted to get in bed with you?"

"You don't need to be that sarcastic," her voice said.

"I'm sorry. But my eloquence gets—poisonous. How can you bring yourself to lie beside a maniac like me? The Civil Service ought to give you a medal. If you're supposed to feel motherly toward me, you don't have to. Just leave me, please."

"I love you."

"I should accept that as it is, now. You also love five other men in five other suites."

"Yes, I love men. I love women. I love my children. I try to love everybody."

"Next you'll tell me you also have a husband to love. I was hoping —and I wasn't so jealous of my five invisible cellmates," Dr. West's voice stammered, "but I was hoping that ring on your third finger left hand was just for show."

"Every evening after work I take the monorail back to the apartment district. Did you get much of a look at Ottawa?"

"I saw those angry people waving signs at me."

"I have three children, three little girls. The oldest, she puts the T.V. dinners in the oven before I get home. After supper I help them with their homework. On the rug even the second grader mutters at her homework. The older two have begun to giggle about boys, and the oldest is only in sixth grade, my heavens. Then we watch T.V., and no one wants to go take the first bath. When my angels are asleep, I think

—they're another day older and stronger and wiser, I hope. I sit watching T.V. Me, I'm another day older. I crawl into bed."

"I wish I were there with you."

"You are. Squeeze me hard. You're in bed with me now."

"That wasn't all that I meant," Dr. West's voice replied. "At the moment I feel more protective than amorous."

"You needn't be. I can get along very well, thank you," she said. "Except when my children were helpless babies, I always worked, worked as an I.B.M. operator, even when my husband was working." Her voice for the first time rose in anger.

Her voice tried again more softly. "My husband was a nice guy, he really was. I didn't just love him because he was the father of my children. He was a sweet guy, not scheming, not adjustable the way we have to be. Everything's changing faster and faster, and he got quieter every time they automated away his job. What did I do? Did I give him inner strength? No. I began to earn more money than he did. He said less and less. When I brought my—our kids home from my father's into the kitchen, I ran to turn off the gas."

Her voice sank. "I tried to give him artificial respiration.

"It wasn't until then, after then," her voice laughed unhappily, "I learned what brief animals we are. You're all schemers. If you and I were Outside, don't expect a dinner date downtown and a cinerama will make me—owe you anything just because I haven't got a husband. You understand me?"

"So you got the perfect job here. No, I'm oversimplifying you."

"Yes, I'm simple. I'm just a simple bundle of mother love. Always cheery. Pardon me for sounding cynical with you, but my other students happen to be such uneducated children. They wouldn't understand."

"Or notice you're not perfect, I hope," Dr. West laughed. "I hope not. You're our only hope. Don't hurt us. You are too powerful. Without your personal love this would be solitary confinement, and we convicts would go insane. Right now you are miraculously changing me and five other men."

Dr. West's voice suddenly probed. "If any of your prisoners fail, I mean, are released and then hold up a liquor store, do you have such a masochistic and guilty view of yourself that you believe you are responsible for the failure of this man?"

"I don't understand you."

"As with the failure of your husband."

"What are you saying?"

"Nona, do you think you are so godawful powerful that if we cons fail it is because of something you did or didn't do?"

"I don't understand. Not one of my students has become a recidivist. I've worked here four years. Twenty-two of my students have graduated. None have had any trouble with the law."

"You misunderstood my question."

"Of course, I'm holding my breath about a few of my boys," she said. "They all get pretty fair jobs because we've retrained them, and the government subsidizes, pays their employers during the first year."

"So they get along without you?" Dr. West's voice laughed suddenly. "Marry girls just like you?"

"You *are* a flatterer. My students write to me, some of them, and I save the letters and photos. One boy is going with a woman a little bit older than he is, but very pretty. I shouldn't have said that. What I meant to say was she looks enough like me to be my sister."

"No doubt the government wishes you could be divided more than six ways."

"Silly. The whole purpose of the government's reformation policy is to help them—you—stand on their own feet when they go Outside. Someday, you'll—now you stop that," her voice sighed languidly.

"Nona, you're so warm, so smooth—"

"I think you just want me to stop preaching at you."

"Nona, what I want—"

"Lover, turn your wrist the other way. My heavens! If your wristwatch is correct, and I'm sure it is, your borrowed time is up."

"You aren't going to leave me like this?"

"Sort of let me up, lover. Where's my bra? You're lying on it."

"But I was just beginning."

"But you've no more time today," she laughed. "Be here tomorrow? On second thought, I won't be back till Wednesday. You traded away tomorrow. Oh, there's a run in my stocking. Now stop that! You can wait till Wednesday, lover."

The blanket tent shook, and Nona's legs swung out. She fumbled for her shoes. "Where's my comb?" Zipping up the hip of her blue skirt, she clicked on high heels to the door. There was a departing hiss as the inner door opened and closed. Dr. West was alone.

VII

Dr. West emerged from the blanket tent. He stared blankly at the huge cage where the Arctic ground squirrels slept in artificially induced hibernation. Then he smiled and squinted up at the artificial afternoon in his suite.

The luminous ceiling panels were synchronized to a clock and rheostat. There also was an OFF switch, but if he left the panels alone the evening would come gradually, and then night. Then Tuesday. On Wednesday morning at 10:00—

He smiled down at the coffee table where she had sat looking up at him. He hurried to dismantle the tent, folding the blankets, his pulse racing, his face hot with suppressed memory. For an instant he pictured her inside the tent, moving. The view was too powerful, and he laughed and shook his head and blinked his eyes. "Wednesday, Wednesday, hurry up, Wednesday."

He vaulted over the couch, grinning. Tomorrow was only Tuesday but—"When Tuesday's here, can Wednesday be far behind?"

He reached for a glass tube on his work counter and grinned at the bunsen burner in his lab set up. He felt young. If he softened the glass tubing, bending, twisting the glass, he could make something for her. "A glass giraffe to make her laugh?"

Behind him, the inner door hissed open. With a surge of warmth, wanting to believe she had returned already, Dr. West whirled.

"Surprise," the Recreation Officer said. "I'm off-duty now—Doctor. Before you get too well adjusted in here I'm to deliver this."

Beneath his toothbrush mustache, the Recreation Officer forced a smile as he flapped down a manila folder on the coffee table. "You wanted news of the world, didn't you?"

"Get out." Dr. West stared at the folder with its projecting newspaper clippings as if he was looking at a snake. Obviously it did not come from the Staff. It was from Outside.

"I'm sorry," the Recreation Officer's voice said. "I apologize for my eccentric performance this morning. Nothing personal, really."

"Get out, and take it with you." Dr. West felt no desire to open the folder.

"I'm not trying to frame you, Doctor. I'm the one who should be disciplined—for bringing these clippings into your suite."

"You tried to trigger me to violence during your so-called search. You tried to wash me out. I assume you're trying again. Get out!"

"It's a pity no one will leave you alone," the Recreation Officer remarked. "Look, we can be frank. I've done two things at great personal risk. One, during my search this morning I disconnected the audio bug to your suite. Two, this noon in the basement I damn near electrocuted myself. Your Ceiling Lens no longer is transmitting. Instead,

I've spliced a projector to your transmission line in the basement. If the observer should happen to inspect your telly screen, he'll see what you were doing two days ago. Your screen is showing a replay of your old micro-video tape, 48 hours long. I hope you weren't doing anything suspicious during the last 48 hours since I started my video tape recorder. I hadn't time to review 48 hours of tape."

The Recreation Officer pointed at the manila folder. "In any case, *now* you don't need to try to earn brownie points in here by claiming you don't want to break the rules. No one is watching you. Sit down and read a year's clippings. What has really happened during this year you've been isolated in a series of jails? Weren't you the doctor who was so concerned about the Esks increasing?"

"Right now, I don't give a damn what's happening Outside. Get out."

"She's all heart, Nona really is," the Recreation Officer said slyly. "She's the best woman in Tower #3. I don't blame you for forgetting your purpose in life."

"What are you trying to do? Goad me to break out of here?"

"I don't know. I'm not paid to think. I'm sure this tower is escape-proof. You should be intelligent enough to get yourself moved." The Recreation Officer began spreading clippings from the *New York Times, MacLean's Magazine, Life, Time, American Medical Journal, Arctic Review*, completely covering the coffee table. "I'm supposed to say to you: hospital or the Cold Room. You're the one with brains!"

The Recreation Officer spread more clippings on the work counter and more clippings on top of the insulated cage. "I didn't realize so much had been written in the last year about the Esks," the Recreation Officer's voice went on. "I suppose all of these are from a clipping service. Here's a tear sheet from the Bulletin of Population Scientists. Someone let slip—you used to be editor."

"Get out!"

"They didn't tell me exactly why you were discharged from your position at the University of California or why you returned to the Arctic. But I'm beginning to understand why you tried to infect the Esks. The newspaper accounts at the time of your trial simplified you for the simple minds of their simple readers as simply a murderous maniac. But now the *New York Times* seems to be having second thoughts on the matter."

"Get out!" Dr. West's voice rose with alarm as the Recreation Officer actually did walk out of the suite, leaving Dr. West alone with hundreds of clippings and articles staring whitely at him from the terrifying world Outside.

Dr. West chewed his cheek in self-torment. Until today with Nona he had been preparing for the future with almost suicidal calm. Now he didn't want to take any risks. All he wanted was Wednesday, when Nona would return.

Swaying, Dr. West imagined himself gathering up the clippings, eyes averted. Without reading, he would soak the clippings in the bath-tub, tearing and squeezing the paper into dying lumps. He would not read what other men were thinking about the Esks, the research that must be going on, perhaps the frightened admissions in scientific circles that he might be right, that the terrible thing he had attempted was justified. "I won't read! I'm a prisoner and safe. Tear them up and flush them down the toilet without reading—"

"That heartless son-of- . . ." Dr. West was under such stress he was speaking out loud. "Mysterious, lousy wretches who're paying him. I won't read. What do you want me to do? I can't hoist the world on my shoulders. I already dropped it. Very funny." Dr. West stared down at the clippings on the coffee table.

His flashing arm swept clippings fluttering onto the floor. "I refuse to destroy myself. I will not read."

Dr. West dropped to his knees and hands on the floor, his head throbbing as he read of the multiplying Esks.

An agnostic, he began to pray for guidance.

VIII

No one entered Dr. West's suite the next day, which was Tuesday. Not by happenstance, the Recreation Officer had telephoned to the Tower from outside saying he had the flu and would not be reporting for duty for a day or two.

Nona did not enter Dr. West's suite because of the exchange of his Tuesday hour to her 11:00-till-12:00 man. She paused outside Dr. West's suite and did not enter and went on to the adjoining cell.

In the basement the Observer, monitoring the red-tagged screens, yawned and glanced at a hockey magazine.

At 5:00 p.m. when Nona went off-duty she hurried to the monorail because the hair-dresser's would close at 6:00. In the high-speed car suspended above the city, as Nona found a seat she recognized the Man, the back of his head, the Man.

A week before, this short-haircut Man had sat down beside her. At first she hadn't realized his conversation about Ottawa Reformation Center was more than casual. Then she had become quite abrupt, because her first loyalty, her life was tied up in the Reformation Center, and she was afraid the Man might be someone preparing to bribe her. She had left the car so she would not have to hear where his conversation was leading.

Now, the same Man, short-haircut, was sitting in front of her. When she got off and rode the escalator down to ground level, she hoped he wasn't following.

In the evening, after supper, Nona played jacks with her smallest daughter on the floor, while the Tuesday T.V. news blared half-heard everyday topics: the Maoists, unemployment, the Third Mars Expedition, hockey fights, the underprivileged Esks who were being resettled in Tibet.

"Mommy, your new hair-do is so pretty."

At this, Nona laughed with pleasure. "Now go to bed." And soon she slept herself.

Wednesday morning at 10:00, Nona entered Dr. West's suite with her hair up and gleaming and her heart beating unexpectedly. She stopped.

Stripped to the waist, Dr. West was lying on his back on top of his bed, his jaw sagging like a dead man's, his eyes closed as if he were sleeping.

"My God, he isn't breathing! His heart—?"

She rushed to telephone the Medical Officer. She ran back. Her frantic hands shook Dr. West's body. The push of her hand against his terribly cool chest stimulated a shallow gasping breath, then nothing.

"Please, please." She flung herself upon him, mouth to mouth, trying to breathe for him, endlessly.

With exhaustion, her own heart was fluttering. Her fingernails were fastened to his cold flesh.

"Keep going," hissed the Medical Officer's voice. "First I'm going to give him a shot of adrenalin." After awhile the Medical Officer said: "Get off. I'm going to attempt external heart massage."

A half hour later, sweating, the Medical Officer stood back. "This is the man who feigned appendicitis." He stared at the thermometer. "72.6 degrees, and only one or two shallow breaths per minute. If the room temperature sank to 60 degrees, I suppose his body temperature would follow it down. The crazy fool induced this somehow. For a reason."

"Do something for him!" Nona protested. "I'm going to telephone the hospital."

"No, first telephone the Tower Administratrix. She's in command here." For the first time, the Medical Officer looked around the suite and noticed the shambles. "Bloody butcher shop!"

On the work counter lay the opened squirrels. Beside them stood centrifuge and red-brown, stained glass tubing. "He was a murderous maniac," the Medical Officer's voice croaked.

"No, he wasn't. They were hibernating. They didn't feel anything," Nona gasped. "I don't believe he cut them open. I mean, he cut them open with a purpose."

"He bloody well did," the Medical Officer muttered, stooping to pick up a hypodermic needle from the floor. "No plunger. Used rubber bulb from this nose drops bottle. This is the needle from that missing hypo. May have injected a sedative to start the downward metabolic slide."

The Medical Officer's fingers turned the rubber bulb inside-out. "A goo, an extract. Of course he would have been aware that massive injection of any foreign concentration from glandular protein, such as a hibernating squirrel's, will produce a lethal fever reaction. Foreign protein in a human being should be fever. Quite odd. No fever, just the opposite."

"Do something!" Nona's voice protested. "For all you know, he may die any minute."

"This involves legal as well as medical decisions." The Medical Officer appeared relieved when the Tower Administratrix arrived.

The Medical Officer laughed nervously. "Quite diabolically, this man has trapped us between killing him or doing something he wishes." He tried to explain. "Human life is sacred, we say, so we have to save him."

"We have no right to increase his chances of escape. It would be unwise to take him to the hospital building," the Administratrix replied. "I was so long in arriving here because I received a telephone call from the police at the border of the States. They searched the luggage of what turned out to be our Recreation Officer from this Tower—with his mustache shaved off. They found $10,000.00 in small bills."

"I believe the medical problem the former Dr. West has prepared for us is this," the Medical Officer muttered. "If we leave him as he is, he will die. Alternately, if we attempt to bring him out of his hypothermal coma he will die."

"My God," Nona breathed. "You already shot him with adrenalin to bring him out of it."

"A natural mistake. I'm hoping—it already appears that he has not reacted to it—I hope. Perhaps he has buffered his system against such an eventuality—I hope. As I was saying, if we try to bring him out of it, his metabolic activity will increase. His system will begin to react in a typical defensive manner to the foreign protein, and his temperature will rise. This will increase the violence of his reaction to the protein, further raising his temperature. A self-destroying reaction. Violently, his body will attempt to defend itself against the foreign protein, raising his temperature higher and higher until he dies."

"No doubt he planned this in order to be taken to the hospital building." The Tower Administratrix asked, "Could we simply leave him here? Assign a nurse."

The Medical Officer smiled at this. "Much more than a nurse is needed if we really believe in saving human life regardless of cost. His life processes should be monitored. I suspect his body now is in a delicate equilibrium. His metabolism is too sluggish to react to the foreign protein. No reaction, no disease. What is needed is speedy consultation with experts in human hibernation research, who may know how, who may have the equipment to bring him out of this condition alive. In the States, hibernation research is being conducted in connection with the Space Program, I believe at the University of California."

"Strange coincidence," the Tower Administratrix said. "Not a coincidence. According to his files this man formerly was director of a medical research program at the University of California. Population control. Do you think, interlocking medical staffs with their hibernation space transit program? . . . An attorney in California may be waiting to file habeas corpus, legal trickery, bail."

"I wasn't suggesting that," the Medical Officer said. "I simply was suggesting we make a reasonably humane effort to keep this man alive. Surely he can be adequately guarded in our own hospital building. I want to telephone the University of California. Perhaps a complete change of blood—"

The Tower Administratrix shook her head. "Look for a note," she said sharply to Nona. "Suicide. A note."

On the coffee table lay a manila folder. Nona opened it. Empty. Swiftly she looked around the suite.

Something white showed under the huge insulated cage and Nona knelt down, reaching under. A newspaper clipping had fallen behind the cage, and her cold hand drew it out. FURTHER ESKIMO INCREASE NOTED.

"You didn't smuggle this in, did you?" the Administratrix asked Nona. "The Recreation Officer!" The Administratrix turned toward the Medical Officer. "If people outside could bribe the Recreation Officer so easily, how much easier to bribe underpaid orderlies in the hospital!

You yourself determined that this student's so-called appendicitis attack was feigned in order to get him out of my Tower and into the hospital."

The Medical Officer shrugged. "He'll die here."

Nona's hand clamped on the Administratrix's arm. "You're not going to let him die."

"Is that a question? I'm sure it's not intended as an order," the Administratrix replied. "Nona, this is my responsibility. I know you. I know you're thinking, somehow you failed him. You didn't. This man's urge to escape was too strong. He has taken too big a gamble. He can't escape."

"You can't let him die," Nona repeated.

IX

"The best guarded building outside of the Tower," the Administratrix murmured, "is the Cold Room. There, no decision would be irrevocable. It starts a new problem but—"

"That would be the place for him, the safest place." The Medical Officer stared down at Dr. West. "He ignored my warning when I sent him back his appendix in a bottle. Such powerful motivation is driving him. Alive, conscious, he would try again to escape. I think we are agreed this student has shown himself not amenable to therapeutic reformation. The Cold Room—"

"But he's not an incorrigible," Nona protested. "He hasn't attacked the staff." She turned from the Administratrix to confront the Medical Officer. "You both want to evade—"

"I'm wholly in agreement with the Administratrix," the Medical Officer continued. "The man has shown himself to be dangerous, suicidal. No regard for his own life. How much regard would you expect him to show for yours?"

"I believe he is essentially a good man. Better than you!" Nona retorted, but they weren't listening.

"To preserve his life in the Cold Room," the Administratrix addressed the Medical Officer, "I assume he should be cryofiled as quickly as possible. The legal steps can be justified post-facto."

"Yes, before irreversible physical deterioration takes place," the Medical Officer apologized in Nona's direction. "In five or ten years when we learn how to thaw them out—"

"You can't do this without a court hearing," Nona cried. "The two of you standing there can't convict, sentence and execute him."

"Execute is an unfair word." Instead of growing angry, the Administratrix put her arm around Nona. "It's not your fault. I'm sorry you're emotionally involved with this man, but then you're emotionally involved with so many of them. That's why you are so good."

"Please!" Nona stepped back.

"Nona, there's nothing you can do," the Medical Officer said. "Nona, you still have five. Do your best for them."

"You damn weak bootlicker!" Nona cried at him. "Would you tell that to a mother whose baby has died? Would you say, so what, you still have five?"

"If you need to shout, Nona, do so at me," the Administratrix said, lowering her head. "Forget that I am your superior. If you want to accuse me, do so. It is I who must bear the responsibility.

"You did your best for him. You only had him—was it two weeks?" The Administratrix's hand closed around Nona's wrist. "Now go home, take the rest of the day off, tomorrow off, all week off. You are our best. All I can hire is an untrained substitute to take care of your students until you return. But don't feel guilty about your absence."

Without looking at Dr. West's body, Nona walked out of the suite. She went to her 11:00-to-12:00 man as if nothing had happened. The day, the night—

That night on T.V. a politician stated that the anticipated increase of Eskimos would be a blessing. They could be trained as government nurses and guards. Eskimos needed less pay from the taxpayers. Increase would be good for Canada, which still had plenty of room. Nona could not sleep remembering Dr. West.

In the morning when she entered the Tower, Nona went to the office of the Administratrix.

"Nona, you're looking unwell." The Administratrix stood up behind her desk.

"I couldn't sleep, thinking he may have tricked us." Nona said slowly, "How do you know the body in the drawer in the Cold Room is his? Perhaps his real plan was a switch of bodies."

"Well, surely—" the Administratrix blurted.

"The Cold Room is guarded," Nona pressed on, "the drawers are locked. But last night who worked in the cryogenic preparation room? Who prepared the body?"

"I don't know. One of the orderlies!" The Administratrix grabbed the phone.

"I want to go with you to identify the body," Nona said.

The Cold Room consisted of tiers of numbered drawers. As the Guard unlocked the drawer, Nona memorized the number. When she looked down at Dr. West's wax-pale face, Nona shivered. "Yes, that is the man."

Now she could tell exactly where he was.

That night in the monorail car, to her alarm the Man with the short haircut was not there. The night before, still numb from the terrible scene beside Dr. West's body, she had sat down beside the short-haircut Man—deliberately. He had seemed perceptibly disturbed, trapped, hiding behind his newspaper while she told him she didn't want money, she wanted Dr. West to be removed from the Cold Room. "There are thousands of drawers in there," he had murmured. "Find out the drawer number." And he had left the car at the next stop.

Tonight he was not in the monorail car, nor waiting at her stop. As she walked past the magazine rack and the soda fountain, a dark young man tried to pick her up. She kept walking. "What is the number?" he was murmuring.

She paused in the crowd by the bus stand. "I won't tell you the number of his cryo-drawer until you show proof," she said slowly, "that there is someone qualified to bring him out of the Cold Room and then out of his—hibernation."

The dark young man seemed startled. "I'll find out," he said and walked away.

Nona watched him thread his way through the crowd into the icy night. Her face felt old with determination. Dr. West or whoever he was—the man who built the tent with chair and blanket—he was hers, still in her care.

Her jaw hardened. Her teeth felt as if they were about to crack. It was even possible that these two men, short haircut and dark young man, were maneuvering to kill Dr. West. They might be some of those emotional Canadians who waved SAVE OUR ESKIMOS signs and wanted to lynch Dr. West. Or might be rescuers. She knew she must deal with them with great caution.

As Nona stepped out into the razor-sharp Canadian night, the stars were glittering like ice. She tipped her head high. Invisible up there she knew U.S. astronauts were supposed to be coasting on the long voyage to Mars, in their hibernation capsules.

"It truly is possible to rescue a man from hibernation." In the cold she hugged her body feeling hope as when she had carried each of her unborn children.

Breathing hard, Nona stared in the direction of the New Ottawa Reformation Center.

"You'll get out," she whispered. "I'll get you out."

Reading Suggestions

Alexander, Franz, and Staub, Hugo. *The Criminal, the Judge, and the Public*. New York: Free Press, 1956.

Allen, Francis A. "Criminal Justice, Legal Values, and the Rehabilitative Ideal." *Journal of Criminal Law, Criminology and Police Science* L, no. 3 (September–October 1959): 226–32.

Baker, Newman F. "The Prosecutor-Initiation of Prosecution." *Journal of Criminal Law, Criminology and Police Science* XXIII (January–February 1933): 770–96.

Banfield, Edward C. *The Unheavenly City: The Nature and Future of Our Urban Crisis*. Boston: Little, Brown, 1970.

Bittner, Egon. "The Police on Skid-Row: A Study of Peace Keeping." *American Sociological Review* XXXII, no. 5 (October 1967): 699–715.

Blumberg, Abraham S. *Criminal Justice*. Chicago: Quadrangle Books, 1967.

Campbell, James S., Sahid, Joseph R., and Stang, David P. *Law and Order Reconsidered: Report of the Task Force on Law and Law Enforcement to the National Commission on the Causes and Prevention of Violence*. Washington, D.C.: U.S. Government Printing Office, 1969.

Clinard, Marshall B., and Quinney, Richard. *Criminal Behavior Systems*. New York: Holt, Rinehart and Winston, 1967.

Cloward, Richard A. et al. *Theoretical Studies in Social Organization of the Prison*. New York: Social Science Research Council, 1960.

Cohen, Albert K. *Delinquent Boys: The Culture of the Gang.* Glencoe, Ill.: Free Press, 1955.

———. *Deviance and Control.* Englewood Cliffs, N.J.: Prentice-Hall, 1966.

Conklin, John E. *The Crime Establishment.* Englewood Cliffs, N.J.: Prentice-Hall, 1973.

Cressey, Donald R. *Crime and Criminal Justice.* Chicago: Quadrangle Books, 1971.

———. *The Prison: Studies in Institutional Organization and Change.* New York: Holt, Rinehart and Winston, 1961.

Diana, Lewis. "The Rights of Juvenile Delinquents: An Appraisal of Juvenile Court Procedures." *Journal of Criminal Law, Criminology and Police Science* XLVII, no. 5 (January–February 1957): 561–69.

Donnelly, Richard C. "Police Authority and Practices." *Annals* CCCXXXIX (January 1962): 90–110.

Dowling, Donald C. "Escobedo and Beyond: The Need for a Fourteenth Amendment Code of Criminal Procedure." *Journal of Criminal Law, Criminology and Police Science* LVI, no. 2 (June 1965): 143–57.

Edwards, George. *The Police on the Urban Frontier.* New York: Institute of Human Relations Press, 1968.

Forkosch, Morris D. "American Democracy and Procedural Due Process." *Brooklyn Law Review* XXIV (1958): 176–95.

Gans, Herbert. *The Urban Villagers.* New York: Free Press of Glencoe, 1962.

Glueck, Sheldon, and Glueck, Eleanor T. *Five Hundred Criminal Careers.* New York: Commonwealth Fund, 1950.

Goldstein, Herman. "Police Discretion: The Ideal versus the Real." *Public Administration Review* XXIII (September 1963): 140–48.

Goldstein, Joseph. "Police Discretion Not to Invoke the Criminal Process: Low Visibility Decisions in the Administration of Justice." *Yale Law Journal* LXIX (March 1960): 543–94.

Graham, Hugh Davis, and Gurr, Ted Robert. *Violence in America: Historical and Comparative Perspectives.* Washington, D.C.: U.S. Government Printing Office, 1969.

Hakeem, Michael. "A Critique of the Psychiatric Approach to Crime and Correction." *Law and Contemporary Problems* XXIII (Autumn 1958): 650–82.

Hartung, Frank E. *Crime, Law, and Society.* Detroit: Wayne State University Press, 1965.

Kephart, William M. *Racial Factors and Urban Law Enforcement.* Philadelphia: University of Pennsylvania Press, 1957.

Kirkham, James F., Levy, Sheldon G., and Crotty, William J. *Assassination and Political Violence: A Report of the National Commission on the Causes and Prevention of Violence.* Washington, D.C.: U.S. Government Printing Office, 1969.

LaFave, Wayne R. *Arrest: The Decision to Take a Suspect into Custody.* Boston: Little, Brown, 1965.

Letkemann, Peter. *Crime as Work.* Englewood Cliffs, N.J.: Prentice-Hall, 1973.

Malinowski, Bronislaw. *Crime and Custom in Savage Society.* Paterson, N.J.: Littlefield, 1959.

Matza, David. *Becoming Deviant.* Englewood Cliffs, N.J.: Prentice-Hall, 1969.

Mayers, Lewis. *The American Legal System.* New York: Harper & Row, 1964.

Morris, Norval and Hawkins, Gordon. *The Honest Politician's Guide to Crime Control.* Chicago: University of Chicago Press, 1970.

————. "Politics and Pragmatism in Crime Control." *Federal Probation,* June 1968, pp. 9–16.

Newman, Charles L. "Trial by Jury: An Outmoded Relic?" *Journal of Criminal Law, Criminology and Police Science* XLVI, no. 4 (November–December 1955): 512–18.

Newman, Donald J. *Conviction: Determination of Guilt or Innocence Without Trial.* Boston: Little, Brown, 1966.

Packer, Herbert L. "Two Models of the Criminal Process." *University of Pennsylvania Law Review* CXIII, no. 1 (November 1964): 1–68.

————. *The Limits of the Criminal Sanction.* Stanford, Calif.: Stanford University Press, 1968.

Platt, Anthony M. *The Child Savers: The Invention of Delinquency.* Chicago: University of Chicago Press, 1969.

President's Commission on Law Enforcement and Administration. *Task Force Report: Juvenile Delinquency and Youth Crime.* Washington, D.C.: U.S. Government Printing Office, 1967.

Quinney, Richard. *The Social Reality of Crime.* Boston: Little, Brown, 1970.

————. *Crime and Justice in Society.* Boston: Little, Brown, 1969.

Reiss, Albert J., Jr., and Black, Donald J. "Interrogation and the Criminal Process." *Annals* CCCLXXIV (November 1967).

————. "Police Brutality—Answers to Key Questions." *Trans-action* V, no. 8 (July–August 1968): 10–19.

Scheff, Thomas J. "The Societal Reaction to Deviance." *Social Problems* II (Spring 1964): 401–13.

Schlesinger, Joseph A. "Lawyers and American Politics: A Clarified View." *Midwest Journal of Political Science* I (May 1957): 26–29.

Schuessler, Karl F., and Cressey, Donald R. "Personality Characteristics of Criminals." *American Journal of Sociology* LV (March 1950): 476–84.

Schur, Edwin M. *Crimes Without Victims.* Englewood Cliffs, N.J.: Prentice-Hall, 1965.

Scurlock, John. "Procedural Protection of the Individual Against the State." *University of Kansas City Law Review* XXX (Summer 1962): 111–48.

Sellin, Thorsten, and Wolfgang, Marvin E. *The Measurement of Delinquency.* New York: Wiley, 1964.

Short, James F., Jr., and Strodtbeck, Fred L. *Group Process and Gang Delinquency.* Chicago: University of Chicago Press, 1965.

Silver, Isidore. *The Crime-Control Establishment.* Englewood Cliffs, N.J.: Prentice-Hall, 1974.

Skolnick, Jerome H. *Justice Without Trial.* New York: Wiley, 1966.

————. *The Politics of Protest.* New York: Simon and Schuster, 1969.

Spergel, Irving. *Street Gang Work: Theory and Practice.* Reading, Mass.: Addison-Wesley, 1966.

Stone, Harlan F. "The Public Influence of the Bar." *Harvard Law Review* XLVIII, no. 1 (November 1934): 1–14.

Sutherland, Edwin H. *White Collar Crime.* New York: Holt, Rinehart and Winston, 1949.

————, and Cressey, Donald R. *Criminology.* Philadelphia: J. B. Lippincott, 1970.

Sykes, Gresham M. *Crime and Society.* New York: Random House, 1967.

Tappan, Paul W. "Who Is the Criminal?" *American Sociological Review* XII (February 1947): 96–102.

Turk, Austin T. *Criminality and Legal Order.* Chicago: Rand McNally, 1969.

Tyler, Gus. *Organized Crime in America.* Ann Arbor: University of Michigan Press, 1962.

Vetri, Dominick R. "Guilty Plea Bargaining: Compromises by Prosecutors to Secure Guilty Pleas." *University of Pennsylvania Law Review* CXII (April 1964): 865–95.

Vold, George B. *Theoretical Criminology.* New York: Oxford University Press, 1958.

Westley, William A. "Violence and the Police." *American Journal of Sociology* LIX (July 1953): 34–41.

Wilson, James Q. *Varieties of Police Behavior.* Cambridge, Mass.: Harvard University Press, 1968.

Winick, Charles. "The Psychology of Juries." In *Legal and Criminal Psychology,* edited by Hans Toch, pp. 96–120. New York: Holt, Rinehart and Winston, 1961.

Wolfgang, Marvin. *Patterns in Criminal Homicide.* New York: Wiley, 1966.

About the Editors

Joseph D. Olander is Special Assistant to the Florida Commissioner of Education. Martin Harry Greenberg is Professor of Modernization Processes and Director of the Office of Graduate Studies at the University of Wisconsin, Green Bay. They are coeditors of a number of science fiction anthologies, including *Run to Starlight,* which was selected by *The New York Times* as an "Outstanding Book of the Year."